The Glass Throne

J.W. Webb

Acknowledgement for:
Susan Bentley, for editing
Roger Garland, for the illustrations
Ravven, for cover design www.ravven.com
Debbi Stocco, for book design MyBookDesigner.com
Julia Gibbs, for proofreading @ProofreadJulia

ISBN 13: 978-0-9863507-9-5 (Paperback)
ISBN 13: 978-0-9863507-8-8 (Digital)

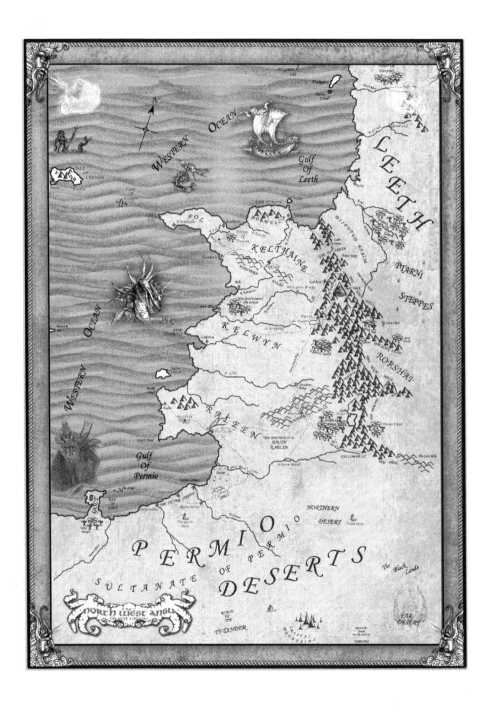

For Captain John Gold Borden, dearest friend and fellow New South Wales Beer Drinking Champion.

'May the wind fill your sails and your course run true...'

Table of Contents

Part One

The High Wall

Chapter 1

The Rider

The Ptarni Plains surrounded both rider and horse, a vast expanse of featureless grey. No solitary tree or hillock broke the monotony, just mile upon mile of tall grasses, swaying and sighing, as the bitter wind carried with it the fresh promise of snow. A desolate landscape, its only occupants were wild birds and prowling beasts, and the odd thin river struggling through. Men said the Ptarni Plains were endless, or that nothing but void lay at the other side.

Olen knew better. He alone of the Rorshai people had seen the other side. A journey of many days - during which he nearly starved - had revealed dark mountains, and high amongst them an alien city high in the clouds. Olen had told no one of his journey or the arduous task he had set upon himself after taking advice from the Seeress of Silent Mountain. She had warned so long of the coming war.

Four weeks ago, he'd ridden to Silent Mountain, climbed the long-winding, wind-freezing stairs, and then entered the horse-skull adorned cave that led to her silent chamber. Once there, he had lain with her, as was expected, paying her price for counsel and warning.

No one knew her age, though they said she was around in his grand-sire's day. The Seeress appeared a woman in her forties, wild-haired and dark of eye, her body sharp and lean. Her voice was husky with the potions she took to aid her inner vision.

"What brings you here, Kaanson?" she had asked Olen, knowing well the answer, her smile teasing him and long fingernails tracing a thin line of blood down his cheek. "Are the dreams taking shape inside your head?" She smiled as she loosened the drawstrings of his breeches.

"The dreams are stronger, wise one," Olen had replied, and after they were done, he told her of his nightly visions. Dreams of war and dreams of blood. Nightmares where dark silent creatures stirred in empty tombs. And the stranger, the image in the water. The harbinger of war. A warrior, scarred of face, across his back a huge sword and in his eyes intense purpose.

"The fulcrum, yes, I've seen him too." The Seeress crouched by the fire. She'd thrown a cloak over her nakedness to shield herself from the chill. She held something in her left hand. Olen couldn't see what it was. He gasped as she tossed it into the fire and the flames roared and crackled with sudden urgent life.

"He is coming soon," the Seeress told Olen. "He and another, arriving from the south. They bring with them the first snows of winter. They also bring death."

"What must I do?"

"You must ride south, Olen of the Yellow Clan. But before that you must ride east."

"East? I don't understand. That way lies only grasses and wind and the edge of the world."

"Not so." The Seeress tossed another tiny object into the fire, and again the flames surged and fizzed. "Beyond the plains are mountains and past those, wide fertile lands where men and women dwell, and fight and screw and starve and hunt, much like any other land. The closest of these lands is called Ptarni, the furthermost Shen. There are others, but they don't concern us. Ptarni does. Those ruling that land have long had their eyes on the Four Kingdoms."

"I have heard of Ptarni of course, but I thought it myth. A place of whimsical fancies, a city in the clouds lost to dream and mystery." The Seeress smiled her secret smile. Her teeth were perfect, though her eyes were shadowed with darker purpose. She turned toward him, her nakedness revealed again. Despite who she was, Olen felt his loins stir anew.

"You've seen the riders out on the plains? Where do you think they come from, fool?" The Seeress's laugh was cold and brittle, like breaking ice on a thawing lake. Her eyes were charcoal daggers, sardonic and knowing.

"There are many lands both north and south; perhaps those riders are from these." Olen struggled to make his point. "We Rorshai watch over the grasslands in constant vigilance. I myself have seen strange horsemen watching from afar. I deemed them merchants, or else maybe scouts from Permio, or Raleen across the mountains."

"Raleen across the mountains?" The Seeress cackled and rounded on him, pulling Olen toward her and kissing his lips hungrily. The need was upon her again, but Olen wanted answers. He pulled away and wiped her spittle from his mouth. She glared at him in frosty silence.

"I have been out on the steppes, as far as any of our people. I once rode east for three long days, seeing nothing but wind, eagle, and sky. An empty land I deemed it."

"You need to travel for thirty days. Then you'll see the mountains, Olen of the Yellow Clan. Then you'll see the city in the clouds." She reached forward smiling again. "Come fill me again with your urgent seed, then shall I tell all I know of the threat in the east." And so Olen had loved her again, hard and fast until she yelled out his name in sated rapture. As he stood above her, donning his garments in watchful silence, the Seeress had crouched close to the fire, whispering words and tossing rune charms into its hissing midst.

At last she had stopped, and as Olen stood waiting at her cave's entrance, the Seeress had stood before him naked and bleeding. It was then that she told him what he must do.

That had been a month ago.

And he'd done her bidding. Ridden mile upon wind-tossed mile, over grasslands, low hills, and craggy slopes. Passing wind-torn trees and fording icy creeks that hurried to the gods only knew where. On the thirtieth day, Olen had reined in, gasping at the mountains revealed by winter dawn. Tall and stark they stood, and in their midst a golden city.

Ptarni—the fabled realm. Olen had ridden closer throughout that day. He'd stopped at the west bank of a huge brown river, its mile-wide waters sluggish, the banks rimed with ice. In the distance, that golden city glimmered some twenty miles ahead, appearing to float in the mist surrounding the mountains.

Olen gazed north along the river. A mile or so that way, a great bend stole the river from his gaze, its midst lost to willow and grasses. He turned south. Here the river flowed more or less straight. Olen shielded his eyes and stared harder along its banks. He saw shingle banks and eyots, where lone cranes stood as patient sentinels. Beyond the islands and birds, Olen could just make out the square shapes of what looked to be buildings on his side of the river.

Intrigued, Olen guided Loroshai - his black stallion—southward along the banks until the buildings revealed themselves alongside a road, a road leading west away from the river and vanishing into the vastness of the plains.

Olen urged Loroshai forward until he reached the road. To his right the building loomed high. A great storehouse it appeared. There was no one around, so Olen slid from Loroshai's saddle and tied the beast to a stunted tree. Silent—as only his people can be - Olen stole close to the building. A single door waited ajar.

He ventured within, only now realising just how huge this building was. Huge and empty. But Olen could see where wains and carts had been stowed, as there were wheel tracks strewn all across the cobbled floor of the building. He wandered through, seeing stables and rooms with hooks and racks where tools or weapons must have been stowed.

For what purpose? Olen guessed he already knew the answer to that. Grim-faced he left the building behind, and remounting Loroshai, he urged the horse to follow the road into the sighing maze of grasses ahead.

For five days Olen followed that track. It was pitted and churned by wheel and hoof, evidence that a large force company had passed this way recently. As night fell, the track faded into the gloom of a steep ravine. Olen chose that moment to take shelter and rest beneath a quiet cluster of trees a half-mile ahead of the ravine.

He woke to the distant grumble and grind of metal on stone. Olen rolled free of his blanket and reached up to Loroshai's saddle, where he retrieved his horn bow and a half dozen arrows; his golden-hilted scimitar was already strapped to his waist. Rorshai riders seldom parted with their swords.

He spoke a few cool words to Loroshai and then silently, and painstakingly slow, crept and crawled closer to the ravine. Behind him the sun rose glorious and bright. The creaking grew louder, announcing wagons on the move, and Olen could hear voices too. Guttural accents speaking a tongue he didn't understand. Ptarnians no doubt.

Olen reached the point where the track channeled into the ridge. Here he left it and took to scaling the sharp rise on the left. Half an hour later, he crested that shale slope and gazed down in astonishment at the sight greeting him below.

An army was camped in the wedge between the hills. Down there a stream glittered in the morning sun; on either side were scattered bushes and clumps of stunted trees. Amongst these and as far as his eyes could see along the ravine, Olen saw men, horses, and carts and wagons of all sizes and construction.

He tried to count the wagons but there were too many. They filled the deep cut of the ravine, spanning its fifty-feet-wide basin for at least a mile until a shoulder of rock thrust across his vision and

Olen could see it no longer. Instead he focussed on the men, antlike and scurrying to and fro below.

They were strange to behold. To his Rorshai eyes they appeared clumsy and awkward, weighed down by heavy plate armour of various colour and style. Their faces were mostly hidden behind chained masks hanging from the pointed helms they wore. Occasionally a man would doff his helm to wash his face in the stream, or else wipe sweat from his forehead, revealing hard faces, scarred and swarthy. Despite their apparent awkwardness, these were professional warriors.

For almost two hours Olen crouched in discomfort, watching and listening as the strange men shouted and yelled at each other and the army broke camp and made ready to move. In the distance he could see the wagons already rolling out of view. There must have been over a thousand. A thousand wains loaded with weapons, supplies, food, and ale—all the things needed by an army on the march.

He watched as the nearest soldiers saddled their horses whilst the wagon riders whooped and hollered their oxen and ponies into noisy movement. Another hour passed as the winter sun climbed the ridge behind him. Olen waited until the last soldier had vacated the ravine's valley. Then he stood in one fluid motion, easing the cramp in his legs.

He needed to warn his people—and fast. Olen returned to the spot where Loroshai waited in the sunshine. He saddled and mounted the horse and bid him trot northwards along the edge of the ridges away from the ravine. After several miles the terrain flattened out, returning to the familiar carpet of blue-grey grasses and pale winter sky.

Olen turned west. He was well north of the host by now. He steered Loroshai closer and soon spotted the distant, endless train of wagons wending across the steppe lands. Again he tried to count their number but it was impossible. At least they were moving slowly; Olen guessed it would take them many weeks to reach Rorshai. With that last thought in mind, the lone rider spurred his war beast to quicken his trot. Olen was desperate to get back, but he must needs pace himself. Loroshai was one of the finest horses owned by the Yellow Clan, but even he needed rest and breaks from the arduous journey ahead. It had taken Olen thirty days to reach the foreign river. It took him twenty-three to return.

During that entire journey, the words of the Seeress echoed through his head. "He is coming via a dark road. You must be ready! He is the harbinger and the war cannot be won without him."

"How will I know him?" Olen had asked her.

"By the length of his sword and the smell of destiny that surrounds him," she had answered. And so Olen rode.

***

Rogan froze as he saw the distant trail of dust rising up to greet the afternoon. Could it be? Then he smiled, recognising the rider as their own beloved Olen, his war chief and eldest son of the Yellow Clan, or the Tcunkai (thinkers), as Olen's father the Kaan liked to call them.

"Teret! Your brother comes and he looks in bad need of ale!" Rogan yelled laughing at a dark-eyed woman who was crouched behind him in the stockade, milking a cow's teats into a wooden bucket. The woman stood, wiped her comely face with a sleeve and after hurdling the fence came and stood beside Rogan. Teret's face lit up when she saw her eldest brother guide his lathered steed into the corral.

"Brother! We feared you were lost! It's almost two months since anyone has seen you. Where have you been?" Teret ran forward to hug Olen as he slipped exhausted from his saddle. The smile fled from her face when she saw the worm of worry eating at his brow.

"What is it? What have you seen?" Teret's dark eyes reflected his worry as she threw her brown arms around her brother, noting how weak and thin he appeared. "You need rest," she told him.

"There is no time!" Olen shoved his sister back. "Take care of Loroshai, Teret. He needs sustenance and rest—and lots of water.

We ride out on the morrow!" Teret made to question her brother but his bleak gaze left the question in her mouth. Obeying, she turned and led the big horse towards the stables behind the homestead.

Olen turned to Rogan.

"Summon the clan! We fare south in the morning."

"South?" Rogan scratched an ear. "That's Anchai country—they'll not like us trespassing." The Anchai were known as the Red Clan, due to their love of blood sports and troublesome nature. They kept themselves aloof from the other tribes. The Anchai had settled the land north of the great arm of mountain that thrust east from the High Wall ranges and marked the southern borders of Rorshai. "Why south?" Rogan pressed.

"Because that's the direction he'll be coming." Olen thanked a youth who had just appeared with a large flask of ale. He downed the flask and sent the boy for another. "From the mountains," Olen added—as though that explained everything.

"Who?" Rogan's eyes were saucers. No one came from the mountains these days. There was rumoured a pass but the Rorshai steered clear of that region—even the Anchai. Word was that secret way beneath the mountains was haunted by an unknown terror.

That evening Olen spoke before his father, the Kaan, and the thirty war chiefs of his clan. Olen told them of his dreams, his journey to see the Seeress (many paled hearing this), and the long hard trek across the steppe lands. Nobody spoke whilst Olen recounted what he had witnessed, first from the river and later looking down into that ravine. Olen was respected here. Even the Kaan had learned to listen to his eldest boy. But it wasn't just that. Olen had the Dreaming.

"War is coming," Olen told them. "A pivotal strife unlike any other. The clans must be summoned at the Delve!"

"Good luck with that," wry Rogan had muttered under his breath. Olen's word might be respected by his own clan, but the shamans and head clan of the Delve were unlikely to be affected by his passionate words. Moreover, they probably wouldn't even listen.

"This stranger? The harbinger of war?" The Kaan leaned forward in his heavy chair and stared deeply into the fiery blue of his eldest son's eyes. "What did the Seeress say about him?"

"That he comes from the southlands, but he's no southerner. And that he brings with him a destiny that even he cannot comprehend. And hinted he was a Longswordsman and man of few words. He journeys with another—a younger brighter soul."

"A name?"

"Corin an Fol."

Early next morning, Olen of the Yellow Clan led his hundred horsemen south toward Anchai country. They passed the Red Clan's lands during the starry dark of night, thus avoiding certain conflict. Two days later, the hundred reached the folds of a mountain leading to a crack in the rock from which darkness yawned like a smoky mouth.

The hidden pass. Or the haunted pass, as most there liked to call it. There they fixed camp, waiting until the appointed moment when the stranger would appear. In his tent, Olen was late to sleep. Sometime ere morning he must have dozed, only to wake minutes later to the sound of urgent thunder rolling out across the grasslands far to the east.

On instinct, Olen rolled out of his blanket and eased his way out of the tent. Away east the thunder growled and boomed like prophesy. Olen nodded in silence to the watchmen posted at the edge of their camp. Uneasy, they watched their leader stride off into the gloom. Olen walked toward the rolling doom of thunder. A mile away from their camp were only open sighing grasses and a brittle breeze lifting the long shadow of his untamed hair.

It was then that Olen saw Him. The owner of the thunder. Far out across the plains He strode, a giant figure, eyes blazing and dark cloak billowing like a cloud behind Him. For an icy instant Olen felt that heavy gaze fall upon him. Then the giant was gone, storming off into the distance. Olen paled; it did not bode well to see Borian the Wind God whilst alone in the night.

Chapter 2

The Dragon

Tamersane crouched uncomfortably on a boulder and surveyed the darkening skies above with little relish. Snow was coming. And to think that only a few days earlier they'd been sweltering in the desert heat. He stole a glance at his companions, wondering why everyone was so damned grumpy this afternoon.

Bleyne stood yards away, whittling at a stick and brooding under the leaden cloud, whilst Zallerak was muttering incomprehensible expletives as he gazed morosely at the mountains behind them.

Corin an Fol and the young Prince Tarin stood glaring at each other and saying nothing. The prince was all sulks and scowls, whereas Corin simmered on the edge of boiling point. Tamersane, usually so jocular, just stared at the two of them with world-weary eyes. Tamersane didn't know why he currently felt thoroughly miserable. Nor did he care—he just wallowed in it.

It was approaching evening on the third day since their crossing the Liaho River, and already their time spent in the Permio Desert seemed an age ago to Tamersane, the young Kelwynian. They were gathered together on the barren crown of the Fallowheld, a raw-capped tooth marking the southern end of The High Wall—the chain of heights warding the Four Kingdoms from the wild eastern lands beyond.

Behind Tamersane, the closest of those peaks loomed down on them out of the murk, its lofty crown already lost in snow cloud. Tamersane hated winter. Just why they had climbed this bloody hill was beyond him. Another Zallerak thing. Who were they to question him? The bard had insisted in his usual annoying way, and so they'd spent most of that chilly day trudging up the steep slopes, so that they could loaf about shivering in this cold, grey, remote and windy place, and wait for snow to arrive.

And now Corin and the prince had fallen out again. The argument had started back in the desert after Ulani's departure. Tamersane missed the King of Yamondo. Ulani of the Baha would have knocked some sense into the pair for sure, or else he'd find something funny to shatter the ice.

If only Tarin hadn't mentioned Lady Shallan. Prince Tarin had known the Morwellan beauty from state visits in Kella before his father's untimely death, and he made it eminently clear that Corin, a "lowborn from the backwoods," was unworthy of her attentions. Corin had come close to skewering the prince. Instead he'd settled for a tongue-lashing, rendering Tarin as spoilt, arrogant, and obtuse. And the cause of all their troubles. Currently they were beyond words, just glaring at each other in mutual animosity, as Tamersane watched on gloomy, with the chill damp seeping into his aching joints.

"Looks like snow coming tonight." It was an obvious statement, but Tamersane thought someone had to make an effort, and he wasn't really up to more expansion at the moment. Corin and the prince ignored him; Bleyne grunted and scratched an ear. Zallerak turned and awarded Tamersane a sharp glance. He looked irritated and edgy. Nothing new there.

"You said something?" the bard snapped at Tamersane. "Snow?

It's fucking winter, what do you expect? A brief time ago you were griping on about the desert."

"Well, so what if I was! I for one don't see why we had to trump all the way up this bloody hillock," complained the Kelwynian. "I mean, it's not as if we can see a lot now we're up here, apart from snow clouds and snot dripping from our noses."

"Here, eat this and stop whining." Bleyne tossed a lump of meat across to the Kelwynian. Tamersane snatched it out the air, wiped his chilly nose and chewed mournfully. Corin and Tarin, both hungry, postponed their hostilities until after supper.

Nobody spoke as they chomped and sucked their way through the dried goat meat. It was the last of Barikani's desert fare and had served them well, but Tamersane was thoroughly bored with it. He longed for the fine cuisine of the Silver City. It was past time he went home. Good ale, warmth, and laughing lasses.

Let Zallerak deal with prince and crown. Bleyne, Corin, and himself had done their part. Or had they? That uncertainty was part of the reason Tamersane felt so edgy. Being on top of this freezing hill helped not at all.

"So what's the plan then?" Tamersane asked Zallerak, after gulping down the last of his meat and belching into their meagre fire. "You kept saying we'll decide when we reach the Fallowheld. I'll tell you more when we're on top of Fallowheld. We'll know what to do once we crest yonder hillock. Well, here we are and very comfortable it is too. So then—what's the plan?"

"Things will be clearer in the morning," announced the bard airily. His left arm crooked the heavy crown hidden beneath his sapphire cloak. He'd not let anyone see it since their flight from the Crystal Mountains, which struck Tamersane as broody and ungrateful, but he'd refrained from commenting on the matter.

Zallerak was a weirdo; no other way to describe him. He was an Aralais wizard apparently. Big stuff back in the day. One of those legendary Golden Folk that Galed had always wittered on about up in Wynais. A rare survivor from a distant age. Very interesting, but all a bit beyond Tamersane's normal parameters. Hitherto the Kelwynian's primary concerns were women, ale, and writing songs, and reciting poetry—the latter two primarily for the purpose of wooing said women. But all that had changed since they'd left the merchant's house last autumn.

"Is it me or has it got colder?" Tamersane was aware he was the only one talking. He tugged his cloak across his chest, fidgeted for a moment, then stood up. Tamersane could stand it no longer. Someone had to break the current mood pervading over this company.

"So. We're making for Wynais at first light." It wasn't a question.

"Eh?" Zallerak blinked at Tamersane. Beside him Corin picked his teeth with a grubby nail and brooded into the fire. Tarin watched him whilst Bleyne whittled his stick. No support there.

Tamersane launched a foot at a stone sending it crashing into the fire and getting their attention. "I want answers, Zallerak—you promised us answers! We have the crown and we've rescued Tarin. What's next?"

"You're welcome to accompany me to Car Carranis." It was the first time Corin had spoken in an hour. The Longswordsman looked tired and stressed, as though something were eating at him.

"Thank you—but no thank you. I intend to make for Wynais at first light. Bleyne? I know you're weary of all these shenanigans. Prince? How about you—coming with me?" Bleyne shrugged whilst Tarin looked to Zallerak, who now stood staring at the mountains again as though expecting them to speak. "Well, wizard—I'm waiting on an answer."

"Shut the fuck up!" Zallerak turned and snarled at Tamersane with a sudden viciousness that startled the Kelwynian to silence. "I'm trying to think. This rage inside me—inside all of us. It's growing fast. It's not natural. Something works against us! It's coming from the fog."

"What fog?" Tarin glanced up from his perch at the fire.

"That fog." Bleyne pointed north towards the haunch of mountain where a smoky darkness was rising over the slopes and swallowing pines. Tamersane noted how tense Bleyne looked. The archer's face was taut and his eyes wary and alarmed.

The Kelwynian turned and watched the darkness vapour through the vale between the Fallowheld's northern slopes and the shoulder of mountain beyond. The fog was spreading fast. Faster than it should. Within it a shape was forming. A vast, winged shape. Tamersane felt the small hairs rise on the back of his neck. This wasn't looking good.

To his left, he heard Corin slide Clouter free of its scabbard, whilst across to his right Tamersane saw Bleyne reach down in frosty silence, retrieve his bow from its perch by a stump, and nock arrow to bow. Beyond Bleyne, the horses were restless, bucking and snorting, and jolting at their tethers, where Tamersane had tied them to a thorny shrub.

They watched in awed silence as the shadow grew within the fog, its form becoming clearer and more defined. At last there was no mistaking it.

"Dragon," said Zallerak. "Now I understand."

***

"I have some bad news. Your former master is broken." Caswallon gazed triumphant into his fargaze crystal. Within its depth he could just make out the slits of amber—the eyes of the creature he had summoned. "Vaarg! Waken and join me! There is much to gain from our union. Morak and his cohorts are dead, blasted by that warlock who challenged him in Crenna. He must be more powerful than I anticipated."

The snake eyes opened just a touch. But more than enough to send a stab of malice through the void and lash Caswallon like a switch of willow across his forehead. He reeled and gasped.

The eyes were fully open now. "I WAS SLEEPING. YOU, MORTAL, WOKE ME."

"With good cause!" Caswallon steadied his nerves and gripped the arms of the Glass Throne, where he had taken to sitting of late, the Sorcerer's Nest being too chilly this time of year. "We are...allies. The warlock... I begin to suspect he is -"

"ARALAIS—YES I KNOW." Vaarg's eyes were half closed again. "AS I SAID, I WAS SLEEPING. I DO NOT CARE TO HAVE MY SLEEP INTERRUPTED BY FOOLS."

"I need your help, now that Morak has fallen. Gribble got back late last night. There is big news from the desert. A revolution—the sultanate has fallen!"

"WHAT CARE I FOR SUCH NEWS? BEWARE LEST YOU ANGER ME, SORCERER."

Caswallon steeled his nerves again. Dealing with Morak had been stressful. Vaarg was much worse; he could almost feel the heat of the dragon's breath filtering through the void that separated them and tingling in his own nostrils. And the last thing he wanted was another physical visit from the dragon; the previous one had left a ruined roof that cost a fortune to repair. "Gribble also informed me that the Aralais bribed the Smith into re-forging the Tekara. The crown is made whole again!"

A sound like storm rain on calm waters echoed up from the void. Somehow Caswallon knew the dragon was mocking him. "YOU SHOULD HAVE DESTROYED SHARDS AND PRINCE WHILST YOU HAD THE CHANCE."

"I know." Caswallon stared across to where Gribble squatted with grubby claws covering his ears. Gribble didn't much care for Vaarg. "It was an oversight. But that crown in Aralais hands could destroy all I stand, I mean, *we* stand, to gain!" The heavy laughter continued. Suddenly Caswallon had an idea.

"Great Vaarg, what is it you desire above all else? Tell me!"

"YOU THINK YOU HAVE THE POWER TO PROVIDE IT?"

"I can try. Tell me—please. Let me help you."

"VENGEANCE."

"Then I *can* help you!"

"HOW SO?"

"Golganak—the black spear. Your former master desired it so he could vanquish his foe. Well, I desire it also. And with that famed black rod I can destroy his enemy and your enemy utterly. What say you?"

"WHEN THE TIME COMES I WILL CRUSH THIS ARALAIS BEETLE MYSELF. I DO NOT NEED THE SPEAR. THAT SAID, IT MIGHT PLEASE ME TO AID YOUR AMBITIONS OUT OF SHEER CAPRICE, AND WIPE THE ARALAIS STAIN FROM ALL NINE WORLDS."

Caswallon felt a wash of relief flush through his veins. He was exhausted and his nervous system was barely holding out. "I would be honoured to have you as an ally, Lord Vaarg! My army already waxes strong, but with a dragon leading it..."

Again the grinding grate of distant laughter. "YOU, MORTAL, ARE TRANSPARENT. BUT NOW I AM CURIOUS TO RETURN TO ANSU, SEE WHAT YOU ARE UP TO. I HAVE NOT REGAINED MY FULL STRENGTH, BUT IT IS COMING. AND I HAVE FORTITUDE ENOUGH FOR A BRIEF ASTRAL VISIT BEFORE RESTING AGAIN."

"Then fly to the desert, Lord Vaarg, find the rebels and their Aralais master. Destroy them, and nothing can stop us!"

"I SHALL PAY THEM A BRIEF VISIT, YES. BUT ONLY TO INFORM THEM OF MY PRESENCE. THE ARALAIS IS CUNNING, AND I AM NOT YET FULLY PREPARED. BUT THE TIME IS DRAWING NIGH."

There followed a hissing sound like a distant frenzied kettle shedding steam. Caswallon's fargaze ball misted over and he struggled to see within. Then—snap! The connection was lost. Dragon and cave were gone; behind him, Gribble crawled out from under the table and squinted up at his master.

"Why did you have to invite him back, Mr Caswallon?" the Soilfin asked in plaintive tone. He had known Vaarg of old.

Caswallon leaned back on the throne; its cold crystal awarded him small comfort. The touch of that crystal was clammy on his skin.

Dead stone, its sheen was lost since the Tekara's breaking, like some once-glistening pebble bleached dry on summer sand. No matter, it served his purpose for now. Caswallon rubbed his tired eyes and watched Gribble pick his nostrils.

"We need Vaarg. Doesn't mean I trust him," he told the Soilfin. "Once I find the spear I can control the dragon. Vaarg knows not the powers I possess. Morak and his associates taught me much. More than they should have. I don't need them anymore, so it's convenient they are dead."

Gribble flicked a large booger across the throne room. "They were dead to begin with, Mr Caswallon. Best not rule them out yet." The Soilfin was twitchy this morning.

"You fret too much, Gribble. Are you hungry?"

"Of course." Gribble's stomach rumbled and his fleshy tongue slunk out between fangs. "Why ask such a stupid question? Have you booked my next flight?"

"You're scheduled for Kelwyn tomorrow." Caswallon looked peeved; the dragon had treated him with open contempt, and now Gribble was giving him lip. Soilfins had their uses, but Gribble had become impertinent of late. He had even dared to criticize his sending Derino down to Calprissa where the idiot got himself killed. "I need you to be discreet this time." Caswallon pointed a skinny accusing finger at the Soilfin. "I want to see what that little bitch-queen is up to."

For answer, Gribble hopped behind the throne and pissed in Caswallon's soil bucket. "I'm always discreet," the goblin yelled as he noisily filled the bucket. "I'm your master spy."

Caswallon let the matter go. He had more important issues to consider. The renegades would be returning from the desert by now: the Aralais wizard, Silon, and this Corin an Fol. They would have the Tekara whole and new with them, and useless Prince Tarin too. Gribble had found that knave Hagan lurking like a whipped hound among the corpses in the desert. From him, Gribble had learnt enough to wing east and witness the fall of the sultan, and the rebels parting with their allies in the desert. Gribble hadn't been back long, as he'd spent a good while digesting the remains rotting in the sun.

Another matter was Kelwyn. Despite Gribble's drivel, he, Caswallon, had done well down there. Perani himself had led his army through the gates of Wynais at midnight, and the traitor Tolranna had let them in. Perani held the Silver City; he'd hurt few as yet, awaiting his lord's word and the venomous arrival of the bitch-queen, Ariane. She would doubtless take the bait—stupid hot-head that she was.

And then there was Kelthara. That city had rallied of late, and now a group of surviving nobles had dared speak out against him whilst shored up behind their high walls. With Perani down in Kelwyn and his Groil ranging that countryside seeking the queen's rebel army, Caswallon had to let Kelthara be for the moment. It irked him and he wished he'd crushed that city like he had Kella. Another mistake. But all these were small issues that would be ironed out during winter. One thing really bugged him: Golganak the spear.

Caswallon had long studied Urgolais lore and learned that the spear could be used by a mortal wizard, if he possessed sufficient spell-craft and mind strength, which Caswallon now believed he did. Caswallon suspected the spear to be hidden in the catacombs of Ulan Valek. Morak had tried to locate it but had failed.

Caswallon also suspected that Morak, his former mentor, lacked the resources to delve deep in the catacombs of Ulan Valek in his current astral form. But Rael Hakkenon, fresh from his defeat at Calprissa, should prove more than ready for the task. Caswallon had already sent his spies out to find the Assassin, whom he believed was still at large on the mainland, most of his fleet having been sunk off Calprissa and Port Wind.

With Golganak in his control, Caswallon would cement the final piece in this game. Aided by spear and Urgolais lore, he would unlock the keys to immortality, his greatest desire, and establish his place as lord of this world, Ansu. At that point he would do away with dragon and Soilfin, but for now they had their uses.

Caswallon yawned and leaned back in his stolen throne. The hall was silent, Gribble having departed to the dungeons for a snack. Not much down there of late, the Groil legion having eaten most the prisoners. On impulse, Caswallon wiped the steam from his globe; once he could see within again, he cast his fargaze south until he found the dragon.

Chapter 3

The Hidden Land

The fog was all around them, choking their breath and freezing their bones. Tamersane yelled out, but his voice was lost in the gloom. Meanwhile, ahead, the darkness loomed over them. Inside it, a great winged beast crouched, darker than the mist surrounding it.

A dragon? He had heard Zallerak say that, before the fog swallowed his voice. Tamersane knew enough about dragons to know they were indestructible and paradoxically, until now, extinct. It wasn't the best news to discover that at least one had returned from extinction and chosen them for its first meal.

He heard muffled yells close by and glimpsed a sword in midair; most likely it was Clouter but it was impossible to tell. The fog— or dragon's breath—was clouding his vision, but the winged shape seemed in no hurry to rend them. But then Tamersane remembered another thing about dragons. They loved mind tricks. This one seemed no exception; Tamersane felt alien panic shaking his body. He swiped about with his sword, cutting air and yelling. Shadows rushed at him and he dimly made out Groil faces—doggy snouts, slavering and dribbling. Tamersane swiped and yelled and the shadows faded from view.

He tripped, rolled, and regained his feet. More shadows surrounded him. Tamersane swung the blade, and again it met nothing. Phantom Groil; it seemed the dragon was working on his fears, then. Then Tamersane froze as the metallic sound of alien laughter broke through the fog like a falling rockslide shatters the surface of a frozen lake.

The dragon spoke.

"ARALAIS! THIS IS BUT A COURTESY VISIT FROM CHAOS. WE WILL MEET AGAIN SOON, AND I WILL REND YOUR TWISTED SOUL ASUNDER!"

Tamersane was dimly aware of a muffled reply from nearby. He guessed it was Zallerak who spoke but couldn't be sure. The metallic laughter had resumed and the dragon's breath deepened to blackest night. Tamersane lost view of the winged shadow; he heard the thunder and drum of those wings as the dragon took to air.

Tamersane heard yells, more shouting, and a brief clash of steel, and he glimpsed more Groil shapes squeezing in through the blackness. He charged one, swinging his blade. Nothing. Glimpsing another, Tamersane sped forward, swiping and yelling, his earlier rage back now that the fear had subsided with the dragon's departure. He swung again and the Groil shapes faded.

Then he saw a large one looming in front of him, its dogface occluded by murk. Tamersane yelled and shoulder-charged the creature from behind. He heard a surprised grunt, saw a flash of steel, and then cursed as sudden pain lashed into his upper arm.

Tamersane's hapless flying tackle had pushed both himself and his target over from where they just stood, at the northern rim of the Fallowheld. Tamersane's foot caught a rock. Again he tripped, but this time he kept falling: rolling, tumbling, and crashing down, helter-skelter among rocks and twisted shrub.

As he tumbled, Tamersane saw the big Groil falling close by, its sword still in its claws. That sword looked familiar. It was at that point that Tamersane realised he had just attacked Corin an Fol and come off the worse for it.

He fell and Corin fell close by one another. The Fallowheld's flanks were steep and treacherous, and the two men tumbled for long minutes. Tamersane's arm oozed blood and his head spun as the slopes and thorns raced up at him. Crunch. His head struck a rock and he lost all consciousness.

***

Tamersane awoke to the sound of a struggling fire and the sharp cold of a starry night. He blinked, cursed at the pain in his arm, and then saw the shape hunched close by. Corin an Fol appeared none the worse for wear. He looked at Tamersane with that mournful lugubrious expression he so often wore.

"What the fuck happened?" Corin pulled a thorn from his forearm and spat in the fire. "I saw Groil in that fog. I heard growling and shouting and then some fuckoff great winged thing flew over my head. Next up, my new best friend attacks me from behind and pushes me off the bloody hill."

"Sorry," mumbled Tamersane, nursing his bleeding arm and looking despondent. "I was a bit confused."

"Did I do that?" Corin noticed the oozing slice gaping across Tamersane's left bicep. It was black with debris and soil and needed prompt attention.

"I...think so," Tamersane smiled weakly. It was safe to say he wasn't feeling his best.

"Then I'm the one that's sorry." Corin stood and walked over. He leaned down, examining the wound he'd given his friend. "You've got shit in that, I'll have to scrape it out before it festers. Even then, you might still catch a fever. I'm sorry, Tamersane, truly I am."

Tamersane chuckled weakly. "Don't be. I attacked you, remember. I thought you were Groil."

"Thanks for the compliment."

"Sorry." Tamersane managed a faint grin as Corin cut a thin

strip from his shirt. He poured a few drops of water from his gourd, fortunately still tied to his waist, and began wiping soil and mess from the wound.

"So what just happened?" Corin asked again as he washed the wound clean and tied a fresh slice of shirt around it. "That's better, you should be all right."

"It was a dragon." Tamersane laughed at his predicament, sliced by his own friend. "You saw that dark shape?"

"I saw something, and heard a lot of heavy growling shit. Whatever it was I knew it must be big."

"The others?" Tamersane glanced around, realising Corin and he were alone.

"Fuck knows?" Corin sat beside him and poked the fire with a stick. "I looked. Shouted up. Nothing. And when the fog cleared I climbed back up to the crown. Took me over an hour. But I found Thunder, though the other horses had gone."

"Where's Thunderhoof now?"

"Behind you eating grass."

"Oh...good."

"Not really. We have one horse and no companions. No food and enough water for a day at most, though this country should award streams."

"So what do we do?"

Corin poked the fire again. "We fare north, find a cut through the mountains and make for Car Carranis."

"Isn't that rather vague? I mean, Car Carranis is hundreds of leagues distant. What are we going to live on, field mushrooms?"

"No, I had a bad experience with those a while back."

"What then, earthworms? I've heard they're nutritious."

Corin shook his head. "Belmarius's army is somewhere ahead. I suggest we catch them up. A force that large won't be moving over swiftly. You agree?" But Tamersane had fallen asleep. Corin gazed down at his friend's wound. It was deep, with fresh blood already soaking the shirt tourniquet he'd tied. It was a miracle he hadn't sliced the arm off.

Corin cursed himself, although it hadn't been his fault. He'd seen shadows in the fog too. One moment he'd been glaring at Prince Tarin and Zallerak, then that mist had come—and with it rage and fear. He wasn't sure about Tamersane's dragon notion, but something had attacked them, doubtless some fetch of Caswallon.

And now here they were. And Tamersane's arm wound was going to need proper attention before long. If only Bleyne were here. Corin had almost expected the archer to appear during the night. But nothing. He and Tamersane were alone in winter wilderness. Corin hoped the others were alive, but no point dwelling on that. Besides, he was parting with them in due course. It just hadn't happened the way he'd planned it. He yawned and stretched. Meanwhile night faded, stars dimmed, and a slow pale sun peeped out from a shoulder in the mountains.

Corin wandered over to check on Thunder. The big horse was standing motionless in the morning. Just another day dawning for him. When Corin got back, Tamersane was sitting up and nursing his arm.

"How is it?"

"Painful, but I'll be fine."

"Good. You can ride Thunder and I'll walk alongside. We won't cover much distance in this terrain, so you might as well get your strength back." Minutes later Corin had saddled Thunderhoof and Tamersane was seated pale-faced on his back. Without further ado Corin commenced leading horse and rider through a tight clump of trees toward the knees of the closest mountain.

The woods closed in as they threaded along what looked to be a deer path. Corin scowled at the trees, expecting weird things to peek out at him. It wasn't just paranoia: it seemed to happen whenever he ventured through a forest.

"I'd love to know where we are," Corin muttered, then stopped and checked on horse and rider. Tamersane looked grey but managed a smile. "What's your geography like?" Corin asked the Kelwynian.

"I'm good west of the mountains, ask me anything."

"We are not west of the mountains."

"You have me there," Tamersane grinned. "I would say that we appear to be in some big old forest. It reminds me of Beechborn Woods, but that's miles away and I don't see many beeches here, mostly oaks and ash."

Corin nodded and led them on again. Every now and then Tamersane would try to say something witty, but Corin knew his friend was struggling with the pain in his arm. Tamersane didn't have long before that wound would overcome him. Corin closed such bleak thoughts from his mind and walked on.

He stopped when a figure emerged from the trees. A tall man he appeared, thin and gaunt, old and stooped, clad in gown and hood. The stranger held up his hand palm outwards as Corin glared at him. One fine day, Corin said to himself, he would walk through a wood without any otherworldly interruption. But not today apparently.

"Who is that?" Tamersane croaked behind Corin.

"I am called Feroda." The old man's voice was akin to the autumn rustle of leaf on dry soil. "And you are in my forest."

"Just passing through." Corin's eyes narrowed as his right hand found Clouter's hilt.

"You won't need that." The stranger pushed back his hood revealing a face that looked both ancient and handsome. There was a bluish tinge to his skin and Corin remembered the treacherous Nix in that other forest months ago. He stood his ground whilst behind him Thunder snorted and Tamersane slouched in saddle. Warily horse and men watched as the stranger wandered close, stopping a few yards in front of them.

"I mean you no harm. Though you trespass, I can see it is not by design, but rather dark happenstance."

"Dark what?" Corin reluctantly let his fingers fall from Clouter's hilt. "Who are you, old man? Are you a faen or something?"

"Faen?" The old man made a strange sound that could have been a chuckle. "No, I'm not of the faery folk, though they dwell hereabouts. You would know me as an Aralais. One of the Golden race that lived here long ago."

"You don't look like an Aralais." Corin's eyes narrowed again as he glimpsed a flash of annoyance in the old man's eyes. Big blue eyes, he noticed now. And the hair showing strands of gold amongst the grey.

All we need—another bloody Zallerak.

"You are familiar with my people." It wasn't a question. The figure before them had folded his arms and his gaze had become cold. "How so?"

"He's younger than you, goes by an odd name—Zallerak." The old man shrugged. "I know of no such individual."

"His real name is Arollas," Tamersane managed from his saddle. "Arollas the Golden." On hearing that name the old man blanched and his eyes took on a hostile glare.

"You must leave! You, trespassers, are not welcome here. Go swiftly before I summon the others!"

Despite their predicament Corin was intrigued. "I said we knew this Zallerak, I didn't say he was a friend of ours. Truth be told he's one of the most arrogant twats I've ever come across.'

"He is my enemy." Feroda pointed at Corin. "Therefore you, mortal, are my enemy also."

Corin shrugged. "I don't give a toss really, we're not planning on staying for tea. But do tell me why you hate this Zallerak, I mean, Arollas."

"He betrayed our people, gave our treasures and lands away to you mortal weaklings. We had defeated the old foe, and though exhausted were triumphant. But Arollas chose to throw our victory away. Go now, for my anger burns within me!"

"Wait." Corin took a step forward and the old man backed off a pace. This Corin took as an encouraging sign. It appeared they'd happened on some grumpy retired warlock that had a grudge against Zallerak. Entirely understandable—but why take it out on them? Obviously the old boy didn't get out much.

"Listen to me. I don't like this Arollas any more than you do, and he's up to some mischief. He used us in the desert to help him re-forge the shattered crown. He said he was doing it for us, but I know he plays a different game."

"The Tekara is whole again?" The old man's face softened a touch. "You were there, in the vaults with Croagon?"

"I was. I witnessed the whole bloody thing. Croagon re-forged the crown, and Zallerak, with the Smith's help, blasted Morak back into the void."

The old man smiled at that last statement. "Arollas has worked on you, that I see now. Morak and his kin—they are not wholly to blame, despite their loathsome qualities. Arollas doubtless exposed them as villains and himself as valiant saviour."

"Something like that." Corin nodded and scratched an ear. "Well... it's been nice chatting and we'd love to stay. But my comrade here is wounded and we need to go find help. You don't appear over hospitable."

Feroda glanced up at Tamersane who was now looking quite ill. "I give him three days." Feroda saw the glint in Corin's eye and backed off again. "There is destiny about you," Feroda said to Corin. "Darkness stalks you, I can see that. Though I believe you to be innocent of its design.

"I will do nothing for your friend. Why should I? Whether he lives or dies depends on chance. But I will aid you in leaving my country, for I want not your stain to linger here. And I don't care for strangers wandering lost in my forest."

"Which way?" Corin's eyes were steel. He had little liking for this creature before them.

"Continue on this path. It leads north, now that I have tweaked it. The way is very long, but I will shorten it as only I can. By nightfall you will reach a wall of rock, pierced by a tunnel. Enter within and depart this hidden land."

"I don't like tunnels." Corin glanced back at Tamersane who appeared to have nodded off. But what choice did they have? His friend needed help and that wasn't on offer here. Feroda said nothing, so Corin pressed further. "What's beyond the tunnel?"

"Rorshai, a land frequented by clans of horsemen."

"Are they friendly, or is that a stupid question?"

Feroda snorted. "No one is friendly east of the mountains. You are in the wilds now, boy. Arallos cannot help you here. Oh, and beware of Darkvale, I can smell her musky scent upon you."

Corin blinked as a sudden shaft of sunlight stabbed his eyes momentarily blinding him. "What?" Corin shielded his eyes and blinked again. Feroda the Aralais had vanished. All about the wood lay quiet and pensive.

Corin said not a word, this sort of thing being the norm for him these days. He turned, saw Tamersane was asleep, nudged Thunder's bridle, and the big horse clumped behind him.

Feroda had spoken truly. Just before sunset, the path led through a deep grove culminating in a craggy wall of limestone. On closer inspection, a crack allowed a way in. Corin muttered to Thunderhoof and the horse stood silent as his master ventured inside the crack and took stock of the darkness within.

Sconce light revealed smooth walls and a passage that ran arrow straight into dingy distance. Corin was reminded of the labyrinth under the Crystal Mountains. This place had a similar feel to it. Not an encouraging thought. And who had lit those torches lining the walls? Best not dwell on that.

Corin emerged back into the waning light. Thunder cropped grass as Tamersane watched miserably from his back. "I dreamt we had a visitation in the woods and some creepy old fella put a spell on me."

"No dream." Corin reached across and inspected Tamersane's arm. It was puckered and black. This boy did not look well. Corin cursed Feroda, convinced the ancient shit could have healed Tamersane easily, had he a mind to. No point fretting about it now. They needed to move on, get through this suspicious-looking tunnel, and hope not to get skewered by Rorshai on the other side. It was not a big ask really.

"How are you feeling?" Corin looped Thunder's reins around his wrist.

"Terrific." Tamersane winked at him.

"Well, just sit tight, we'll get through this tunnel and go find help. Maybe a pretty lass that will work on your arm," Corin smiled back at his friend. Some chance. But at least his glib words had caused Tamersane cheer. His friend was smiling now.

"Lead on, lead on," the Kelwynian said.

And so Corin led his horse and its rider into the smooth passage ahead. He closed his mind to the weight and darkness and focused on moving forward. Tamersane muttered something about how considerate folk were in these parts by lighting their way. Corin didn't respond. Every nerve in his body warned him that at any moment something ghastly would leap out at them. Or else that that creep Feroda had contrived their death in this eerie passage.

But nothing happened. After two hours' walking, Corin stopped and checked on his friend. Tamersane slumped asleep in his saddle. Corin shrugged and turned to survey the darkness behind them. He frowned, glimpsing shapes moving in the distance.

What's this?

Corin rubbed his eyes but the shapes remained, merging into silhouettes of figures as they closed the distance from behind. Tall and manlike, in a weird, twisted kind of way. The nearest and tallest appeared to have horns sprouting from his head. Corin heard whispers and strange urgent sounds.

He didn't hesitate, but swung his lean shanks across Thunder's back to sit astride behind his friend. Thunder took the hint and seconds later the big horse's hoofs clattered on the smooth stone as he gathered pace through the tunnel.

Corin, glancing back, saw the shadows fade into the murk. He could still hear them calling out with alien voices. Were they calling him or speaking amongst each other? It didn't matter, twenty minutes later the tunnel opened into a wide-open plain watched on by a large silver moon. Stars studded the firmament above, whilst to either side shadowy slopes revealed great heights of what must surely be The High Wall.

All of this was wasted on Corin. Instead he focused on the scar-faced horsemen urging their steeds towards where he and his horse and his sleeping co-passenger waited. Tamersane stirred and opened an eye.

"What's happening?" he asked Corin.

"Nothing good," the Longswordsman replied.

***

The traveller watches from the lakeside. He sees the disturbance in the water, feels the angry cold fall upon Him. Reels at the sudden blast of gale lashing Him from every direction. But He is an island, constant and calm as the tumult rages about him. Hail strikes the slatey surface of the lake, ridging its water into ranks of wave. Like a liquid army they fall upon the traveller. Oroonin smiles: this brother always likes to make His presence known.

The lake's water churns, and its midst becomes a spiral and cones up as the wind fashions it into weird shapes and patterns. It takes on the form of a man, huge and strong, marching toward the traveller from the centre of the lake.

Oroonin watches nonplussed as Borian of the Winds strides towards Him, his wayward brother back from His tours of the cosmos. Bored with His game, Borian allows the water to return to the lake. He looms wild and golden-eyed above His elder brother. He is near naked save only a tricoloured kilt, His long hair spiked in four corners. The wind god had returned to Ansu at last.

"What kept you?" Oroonin glances about at the arid terrain surrounding this place. There were no trees here, though none could have survived Borian's latest blow. He had felt it coming for hours, blasting west from distant Shen, wreaking havoc through the wet fields of Rundali, shredding the stilted homes of the river folk of

Tseola, ripping through the forests of Laregosa, and finally arriving here in Ptarni, beneath the Urgo Mountains.

"I said, what kept you?" Oroonin stood perched like a wary crow on a slab of rock washed by the lake's blue-grey tongue. He stared up at His brother, His one eye unfazed by that angry golden gaze.

"I WAS IN A DIFFERENT DIMENSION, MILLENNIA AWAY. I WAS HAVING A GOOD TIME, UNTIL I GOT YOUR SUMMONS, OLDER BROTHER. THIS HAD BETTER BE IMPORTANT LEST I STOMP ON YOU!"

"You are not in my league, Borian. You never were. You and Telcanna were ever-petulant siblings. You haven't changed; You're still blowing bollocks and bullshit about with Your noisiness. I haven't missed You a jot, and wouldn't ask for Your attendance without good reason. But We have a situation evolving here in Ansu. A certain issue that prompted me to call this crisis meeting."

"WHERE TO?" Borian glares down at His brother.

"Telcanna's blue castle. You know the one, it's just outside Deranii, the seventh world."

"I HATE THAT FUCKING PLACE. TELCANNA IS SUCH A SHOW-OFF." Oroonin raises a brow at that and watches as His violent brother starts stomping about and kicking up more gusts above the water. "SO WHAT HAS HAPPENED, CONNIVER? WHAT'S THE POINT OF THIS CRISIS MEETING? WHY SHOULD I ATTEND AND NOT RETURN TO MY DISTRACTIONS?"

"Oh, stop that," Oroonin mumbles a rune-chord and Borian's spiteful breeze slumps into a limp flutter. "You brother, are on the committee. Things have to be done right in this corner of the universe. It's not chaos here yet, you know."

Borian stamps a foot, causing a small earthquake in some distant corner of the world. His lips part, but Oroonin raises a finger and wags it at His brother.

"We are holding council in three moons. You will attend, as will my wife, Her latest lover, Croagon—He's free by the way. Simiolanis, Argowui, and the others. There's been a development. He's back."

Chapter 4

The Rebel Queen

Tarello ducked as the sword swept over his head and stuck in a beam, joining the other blade already embedded there. The queen glared at him, dark eyes flashing and hair wild and free. The innkeep had departed at the first sign of her rage, as had the few locals and any soldiers present, the exceptions being the taciturn Jaan, who now led the surviving remnant of Captain Darosi's Raleenian volunteers, and Squire Galed, the queen's closest friend and longtime companion.

Jaan winced as the queen lashed out with her foot, sending a chair spinning into the fireplace. The new Raleenian captain exchanged glances with Tarello, who shrugged and patiently waited as Ariane vented her fury. Her captains knew this rage had to pass before they could make any suggestions.

At last, after twenty minutes of spitting, cursing, kicking, and sword-swiping, knife-hurling, and general riotous behaviour, Ariane, Queen of Kelwyn, slumped exhausted into the leather chair the innkeep (Maryl) had fussed to get her, him not being used to royalty in his midst, let alone foul-mouthed, furious royalty.

Tarello waited for a moment then pulled a chair alongside the fireplace, close (but not too close) to his queen. At his nod, Captain Jaan followed suit and motioned Maryl (who had deemed it now safe to reappear) to get them some ale and tea for herself. Together the two captains waited as their leader sat staring into the fire. It was another twenty minutes before she spoke.

"They have desecrated my city! Whilst I wasted time in Calprissa, those bastards slipped inside Wynais and took control. My instinct told me something was wrong. I thought I was being shrewd but instead have played right into Caswallon's hands."

"Queen, how could you know?"

Ariane raised a hand to stop him and Tarello pursed his lips. She was taking this very badly, blaming her judgement for the fall of her capital and home of the Goddess's shrine. The Silver City had fallen to treachery and deceit, and in Ariane's opinion it was all her fault. An opinion neither Tarello nor Jaan subscribed to.

"I sensed there was something wrong in Wynais before we left," she said after a quiet moment. "But my primary concern was Calprissa, and now look what saving that city has cost us. My people inside those walls. . . . Goddess alone knows what that villain Perani has done."

"I doubt he's done anything yet, Ariane." A quiet voice reached her from the corner of the room, where smoke half occluded the small figure seated with a book between his hands. Like the captains, Galed had deemed it prudent to wait out Ariane's tempest. But now he spoke up with quiet confidence. Galed had changed since Calprissa; the death and slaughter he'd seen there had hardened him, and though not a fighter, he was no longer content to let others push events.

"I mean, Perani is no Derino. He's clever and not one to overreact. He'll await word from his master before committing any atrocities within Wynais."

"And what if he's received that word already? You all know how much Caswallon loathes me."

"Which is precisely why he'll bid Perani keep the city intact and stand easy with its people. He wants to give you false hope, queen. Lure you into attempting to recapture Wynais."

"Galed's right." Tarello leaned closer to the fire, his blue gaze intent on the flames. "Caswallon knows you're a hot-head."

"Have a care, captain." Ariane's eyes burned into Tarello's, but her captain held her gaze. After a moment she sighed and bade him continue. "You are right, patience is not my strong point, but I rage inside, Tarello."

"We all do, my Queen. But we have to get our heads around this. Attacking Wynais will achieve nothing. Caswallon and Perani are inviting you to do exactly that. Once our force enters the wide fields around Lake Wynais, it will be vulnerable to ambush."

"Aye," Jaan cut in, his dark eyes hungry and violent. "Perani will have kept most his army outside Wynais. I suspect there's just enough of his scum inside those walls to intimidate and bully. The rest will be lurking in the hills and countryside around, waiting for word of our arrival."

"Jaan's right," pressed Galed. "Caswallon's winning so far; he has only to wait until you enter this new trap he's devised."

"All right, gentlemen, I take your point. But what other choice have we?" Ariane nodded thanks as red-faced Maryl mumbled and delivered a piping pot of tea with best china, freshly polished and dusted and placed on a chipped silver tray. He lingered edgy until Tarello waved him off with a gruff, "Leave us, good fellow."

"I am not prepared to sit by and let my principal seat of power crumble beneath our enemies' feet!" Ariane stamped her own feet. "Direct action is our only option, but I concur we need to be artful about how we proceed."

"Before we do anything we need to know the facts." Tarello gripped his ale mug and took a swallow. "What do we actually know? We've only heard rumours the city has fallen. But what of the defenders' fate? Were they hoodwinked by the traitor into aiding his treachery, or simply butchered behind the walls? And what of Belmarius's Rangers? Are they gone too? We need answers, my Queen. Clarifications and certainties before we take one step toward Wynais."

"What do you propose, Tarello?" Despite their situation, Galed managed a smile from his shadowy station in the corner. Captain Tarello was proving a staunch asset. He'd never noticed the man before Calprissa, he was just another soldier in Yail Tolranna's shadow. But Tarello was proving himself not only competent in battle but a shrewd commander too. Galed felt at ease in his company, it was nice to have peace of mind in one quiet corner of your brain. Besides, the queen liked him.

Tarello slouched in his chair, the heat of the fire making his eyes water, and he sweated beneath the heavy winter cloak he still wore. "We play cat and mouse, counter their cunning, and dare Caswallon at his own game."

Galed and Jaan smiled as the queen nodded slowly. "Go on," she said, wincing as the tea found that exposed nerve in her tooth again.

Tarello leaned forward, his face flushed with eagerness. "We steer close, engage on our terms, and then run when they give chase. We know the terrain, they don't. We can swoop in and strike, then withdraw before they have their breeches up."

"First we need to learn where they are." Galed placed the book on a table and rubbed his hands free of dust.

"Scouts." Tarello took a long pull at his ale. "I have some keen-eyed lads that would love the chance to sneak up on that scum."

"Dangerous work," said Jaan, "but as you say, your boys know the terrain around that city."

"Perani is no fool." Ariane's tongue wedged the gap in her cracked tooth. "He'll have all his camps guarded and secure. He'll also have his own scouts out searching for us."

"Which will make it interesting," grinned Tarello. Ariane's face softened as she watched the captain gaze defiantly into the fire. There was wildness inside Tarello that reminded her of Corin an Fol. Her mind drifted for a brief moment until she slapped a palm on table.

No time for that nonsense.

With her other hand, Ariane placed her teacup on the adjacent table and then arched her fingers in front of her mouth. The men waited as their queen gave thought to their suggestions.

At last Ariane nodded and clapped her hands, announcing a decision made. "We are three days from Wynais and Calprissa is far behind us. How soon before these volunteer scouts can be activated, Captain Tarello?"

"I'll get to it right away," responded Tarello. "I'll have a dozen riding west ere first light."

"Good. We'll await their word before we make our next move. Once we know where the enemy camps are we can commence our guerrilla campaign. From then on we will rely on speed and reliable info. We'll enlist all we can from villages about and send those who cannot fight east to help the war effort in Calprissa. I will leave a guard in that city, for it will serve as our headquarters during this war. For war this is, gentlemen—full on." Ariane stood and dusted down her leather shirt and trousers. She looked happier now her mind was set on a plan.

"I'm to my bed, we've much to do on the morrow. I suggest you turn in early too." Ariane bid the three men goodnight and then made to vacate the taproom. As an afterthought she turned and smiled at them.

"Thank you my friends, for your wisdom and support. I am lucky to have you. And you, master Maryl." Ariane flashed a grin at the innkeep who beamed in return. His queen had paid him a compliment. Maryl was the first to enlist in the morning - as a cook, though, not a scout.

Tarello and Jaan watched as the queen departed the room. "She's the best," Tarello said and Jaan smiled at the evident adoration his fellow captain had for his queen. As for Jaan, he was a Raleenian but now saw himself as a Kelwynian too. Queen Ariane had a way of getting to men's hearts.

Galed, who alone of the three knew the queen well, was comforted too. It was only two days since they'd received word of Wynais's fall. Two horrible days, what with Ariane leading her battered force helter-skelter toward Wynais, and everyone bar her knowing they were rushing to their deaths.

But she'd worn out her rage and had listened to her captains at last. Despite the terrible odds, Galed was warmed by an unusual glow of optimism. "I'm getting soft in the head," he muttered, making sure the other two couldn't hear.

***

Valentin stood atop the hill gazing down on the smoking corpses of Groil. Over thirty lay dead—another good day for the Rangers. A week had passed since the messenger had brought word of Wynais's fall.

Valentin hadn't wasted time; he'd sent word west to Calprissa, though he knew not whether that city still stood. And he'd ordered his Rangers lie low and scout the terrain, trying to glean just how many enemies were out there. Was it another raiding force that had got lucky creeping into Wynais? Or was this a full-on invasion? Valentin suspected the latter to be true.

The chief Ranger held a dim view of Kelwynians. These southerners were not known for warriors as were the stout fighters of Kelthaine, where his regiment the Bears hailed from, not that he'd been up there for years.

Kelwynians were soft and their young queen naïve and rash. Oh, she was brave, sure. But no match for Caswallon and Perani. Valentin had not been happy when Belmarius ordered his Rangers escort the young queen back to Wynais. He would have preferred to ride alongside his commander as he always had in the past. But Valentin was a loyal soldier and a stout fighter, a veteran of the Permian troubles.

So they were caught betwixt Perani, Groil, and Caswallon's rumoured hunger for the queen's young person. Small wonder Wynais had fallen: Caswallon was a master at placing spies in the right place and then letting them work on would-be turncoats. Kelwynians, in Valentin's opinion, were easy cloth to warp and stretch.

That was part of the reason why he'd kept his boys out of the city. And thank the gods he had! Valentin had argued with their captain Tolranna about how best to defend the city. That prick didn't have a clue, so Valentin had left him to it.

Since then the Rangers had scoured hill, slope, and forest, picking off Groil and the occasional ex-Tiger caught with his pants down. This last batch of Groil had been roaming at will through deserted fields looking for victims to kill and eat. But all local inhabitants had wisely fled after news of Wynais. Valentin's lads had caught up with the Groil and butchered them at will, the third party in as many days. Doubtless tomorrow would bring more.

A warning curse to his left.

Valentin turned and watched as a rider appeared through the woods, a half mile below where he and his chief scouts stood. As one they dropped to lie belly-flat on the wet cold turf. Valentin watched the rider thread his horse along the banks of a nearby stream. As he approached the foot of the hill from where the Rangers watched, the rider urged his horse pick up its pace and made east toward Lake Wynais, hidden behind a fold of hills three miles distant.

Valentin heard a soft sound. Arac had nocked arrow shaft to bow and waited on his word. Arac was the finest archer in the regiment. He could take the rider easily from here, despite the gusty breeze and drizzle.

Arac glanced at Valentin who shook his head. "Let's see where this one is heading," Valentin told the archer. "He doesn't look like one of Perani's boys."

"He looks like a proper tosser." Arac hawked and spat phlegm on the damp ground.

"That he does." Valentin grinned and watched the rider amble along the stream without a glance up in their direction. "If he's a scout he's a crap one. More like some country yokel on a jolly."

"Want me to follow him?" Arac grinned, revealing his three remaining teeth.

"Yep, but be gentle. He might be a tosser but he might know something. Take Arne and Lusty Darrell." Arac nodded and winked at two other men lying close by. They nodded too and vanished behind the hill slope to Valentin's right.

***

Doyle rode with his head down, watching for Groil tracks. He'd seen a few earlier and they'd scared the shit out of him. Four nights had passed since his crazy decision to volunteer for scouting duties. He'd been flushed with pride back at the camp when the queen herself had bestowed her royal blessing on him, and Captain Tarello had promised him promotion to corporal on his return.

But now, here alone in the wild, with the weird howls and screeches during those awful nights, Doyle felt very alone. Particularly since his mates, the other scouts, had vanished in fog the day before. He hadn't bargained on being alone.

He was seventeen years old, from the streets of Calprissa, and had rashly enlisted with Ariane's freedom force when she'd stormed out the city a week ago. Now he heartily regretted that earlier decision. Too late.

Doyle kept his head down as Tarello had advised. That ploy worked until both rider and horse crashed into the net. Doyle yelled out as a rough hand knocked him from the horse and other hands rolled him tighter in the ropes, until he was gasping and gaping and hanging by his wrists from deftly tied knots.

A big ugly brute leaned over him, balding, a round scar (caused by a bottle in Doyle's opinion) circled his right eye and he displayed three brown teeth. "He looks harmless," someone said from behind where Doyle hung hooked and trussed like market day pork.

"Are you a Groil?" Doyle's tongue felt dry and he had a warm wet sensation seeping his thigh.

"Fucking Groil?" The big man spat at Doyle. "He thinks I'm a fucking Groil!" Doyle heard soft laughter and wondered why what he said was the source of amusement. He hoped they wouldn't cook him; he'd heard such horrible things about Caswallon's doggy soldiers. But whether they were Groil or not didn't seem to matter as they all shared the same nasty habits.

A tall rough-looking character with a longbow slung across his back appeared and slapped the big man hard across his back. "He has a point, Lusty. You're ugly enough to be a Groil."

"Fuck off!" More chuckles followed.

"What do you mean to do with me?" Doyle wished he could reach his sword but the weapon had been taken deftly as the brigands had lashed his body.

"I suspect we'll probably eat you," said the big man—Lusty. At that point Doyle passed out.

When he came to, Doyle heard the crackle of flame, which caused him great concern. He blinked an eye open. Night had fallen. He was in some sort of camp and three figures were cooking something in a pot over a rudimentary fire. At least they'd untied him from the rope net they'd caught him with. And the pot did not look large enough for him.

"He's awake," someone said. Doyle groaned as recognised Lusty shuffling toward him out of the dark. "Just getting the vegetables ready," Lusty grinned down at him. "How would you like an onion up your arse?"

"Cut the crap, Lust, the boss is here." Doyle recognised the rangy archer's voice.

"You got him?" Someone new spoke with sharp authority. Both archer and big ugly answered, "Yes boss."

"Good. Bring him over by the fire so I can see him." Doyle wriggled and cried out as Lusty hauled him to his feet and dragged him over to the fire as though he was made of feathers. This was not looking good.

Lusty shoved Doyle to the ground. The boy rolled and glared

up at a stranger who watched him calmly from a seat constructed of burlap and twisted wicker. A hard-faced, intelligent-looking man, long hair tied behind his back and dark sardonic eyes surveying Doyle as though he were the latest catch in Calprissa Harbour.

"Who the fuck are you?" The man's voice was rough, as though he smoked too much pipe weed.

"D-Doyle, I'm a scout."

"Is that right?" The newcomer gazed coldly down on Doyle as his men chuckled behind. "I think you are a spy, D-Doodle. Some wretch in Caswallon's pay, at large in the land creating mischief."

"Not so, I'm a loyal scout serving Queen Ariane!" Doyle yelled the queen's name and wished his voice hadn't sounded so squeaky. Even so, it gave him a modicum of courage. "You are in her country, so you had best be careful."

More laughter. "Don't tell me there are more scouts of your dangerous nature and evident skills lurking about this countryside?" Hard face almost cracked a smile. Almost.

Doyle blinked suspiciously. "Are you taking the piss?"

"Yes, Doodle, I'm taking the piss. Now sit up and tell us why you are here and how you've managed to keep your head on your shoulders with Caswallon's creeps patrolling the countryside."

Doyle blinked and struggled to his knees. He had no idea who these men were but obviously they were not friends of Caswallon. Things were suddenly looking better. And things improved further when Lusty appeared, ruffled Doyle's worried head and shoved a plate of hot beans in his shaking hands.

"Eat up, Doodle, you're part of the team now."

After his meal, Doyle told the strangers everything he knew.

***

Dazaleon crouched as water dripped on him from above. His head still throbbed from the beating he'd received two days earlier. They'd stormed Her temple—Perani's men. He'd floored four with his staff, but the others had knocked him senseless—though not before Dazaleon saw what they did to Her effigy.

He'd watched choking in pain as they had tossed ropes up and hauled down the stature of Elanion. He'd felt the mosaic floor shudder as Her graceful features tottered into the stone, exploding and splintering all around, spraying him with marble shards and rubble. Once the Goddess effigy had fallen they turned on the other gods with hammers and hooks, until each and every one was pulled down to ruin. It was at that point that Dazaleon lost consciousness.

He'd woken in pain, discovering himself lashed to a chain hook, which kept him upright and prevented any further chance of sleep. But that was of small account to Dazaleon. Sleep brought dreams, and the only dreams he could expect would be filled with sorrow and condemnation. He had failed, and now his queen had lost her city.

Perani's men had told him Ariane was dead. "Buggered and butchered outside Calprissa's walls," were the words they chose. Dazaleon knew they were lying. But what chance did she stand now Wynais had fallen? A rebel queen chased from every corner of her country. Word was Calprissa had fallen as was to be expected, though before his capture Dazaleon did hear a rumour that the over-proud Derino was dead—something to be thankful for.

Perani had paid visit during the last night, accompanied by guards bearing torches. The general had surveyed Dazaleon with cold silence.

"You will pay a high price for this felony," Dazaleon had told the general. Perani had smiled and motioned the guards set upon him again until his aching limbs and chest were bloody with belt welts and shallow cuts.

"You, priest, are soft in the head like the rest of your people. For years Kelthaine has protected your silly little country. Caswallon would have continued to do so had not your immature queen acted so hostile toward him. Well, Ariane has deserted you and her city. It was one of her senior officers that came to his senses and let my soldiers inside your walls."

"A traitor." Dazaleon mouthed the word like venom between his bleeding swollen lips.

"An opportunist, and someone you know quite well, I believe." Perani smiled ever so slightly.

Dazaleon pulled his ravaged body erect until the ropes cut into his wrists. "Who?" he demanded.

Perani's smile broadened. "Yail Tolranna. The new Lord of Wynais; I am just smoothing the way for his transition."

"I don't believe you."

Perani shrugged. "What care I for what you believe, high priest? You have failed; both your goddess and your queen have left you here to rot. A sad story, old man."

"The Goddess blast your bones, Perani of Kelthaine! Listen to me when I tell you that you are marked for violent death. And soon! You have committed the unthinkable, and there is no way back for your blighted soul."

"Maybe so." Perani's hard gaze narrowed. "But you, Dazaleon of Wynais, are a fool and will shortly be a dead fool. Come!" Perani signaled his men. "Leave him here to rot in his self-gloom. I've more important matters to attend." Perani waved his men follow him back down the dripping, torch-lit passage of Wynais's only oubliette.

Since then Dazaleon had been left to his thoughts. Tolranna? A traitor? It beggared belief. But then Yail had been acting odd of late. Very edgy and prickly—though he'd never been easy company, unlike his younger brother Tamersane.

Dazaleon had put that down to his new responsibilities as Captain of Guard. That and fretting about his queen, who Dazaleon knew Tolranna loved. So why betray the queen you love? What kind of madness had overcome Yail Tolranna? Despite his discomfort and pain, the sheer grief from Perani's words wore Dazaleon down until exhausted, he slumped upon a deep, turgid sleep.

***

While Dazaleon slept uneasy in the dungeon below, Yail Tolranna paced the walls of Queen Ariane's spacious and deserted courtroom. Tolranna could find no rest. He was torn by guilt at what they'd done to Dazaleon. Perani had promised the old man would be treated with dignity. Instead they had set upon him and hurled him in the oubliette. Perani had just laughed when Yail protested.

"Shut up, lest you join him," the hard–eyed general had said. Since then Yail had watched on as Perani's ex-Tigers swiftly and brutally curtailed any would-be rebellion. There were no killings that Tolranna had witnessed, but a deal of beatings and other nefarious behaviours. The Kelwynian defenders were promptly relieved of their weapons and explained who the new boss was. Like it or die—the only choice they got on the matter.

"I thought I'd find you here." Perani's broad frame showed between the doors of the courtroom blocking the light from without. "Still moping, Tolranna? You should be pleased, since I've done all your dirty work."

Yail watched as Perani strode across the courtroom and took his seat in the empty throne. "I've often wondered what it's like to be a ruler. Some men crave it. Not me, too many responsibilities. I already have enough of those." Perani rubbed his palms along the arms of the throne. "Apparently, you are one such, yes?"

"No, Perani, I'll not let you twist my actions. I did what had to be done to save my people, since their queen deserted them."

"The queen that you love? I heard she's dead. But if she's alive she'll want your head on a plate. And I don't blame her. You're a strange one, Tolranna. A coward methinks."

Yail turned and resumed his pacing to and fro. "Are you going to release Dazaleon?"

"No," Perani smiled. "You are."

Yail relaxed visibly hearing that. He slumped his shoulders and stopped his pacing, instead leaning out from the closest window ledge and watching the city below. Behind him, Perani jumped to his feet with a fluid grace that would shame a man half his age.

"Do you know Caswallon sits on the Glass Throne, way up in Kella?" Perani's voice was chillingly quiet.

Tolranna turned, awarded the general a quizzical glance. "What of it?"

Perani shrugged. "Just saying. Thrones are dangerous places to sit, Tolranna. I'd have a care if I were you."

"You were the one sitting just now. And I told you I acted out of need! I do not desire power, but someone has to rule Kelwyn. I appreciate how powerful Caswallon has become, unlike Ariane. I don't want him as my enemy. It's common sense!"

"I don't like thrones. And I don't like kings either." Perani joined Tolranna by the window and watched down on the city below. "And I don't much like you Yail Tolranna. Turncoats are the worst of men."

Tolranna made to reply but froze seeing the dagger in Perani's left hand. Before he could react the general spun the blade around his fingers and thrust it point deep into the wooden windowsill an inch from Tolranna's index finger.

"You will need this for your next task." Perani bid Yail tug the knife free of its purchase in the wood.

"I don't understand."

"I said you are to free Dazaleon. So... go and free him. Open his veins and let him escape his miserable existence."

"I...cannot...do that."

"Why not? You've betrayed your country and your queen. Why not your high priest too? It's a pattern. Besides, Caswallon demands a show of loyalty from his preferred new ruler in Kelwyn."

Tolranna's face had blanched to ivory. "I will not do this thing. I am a man of honour! Dazaleon is the wisest of men."

Perani's hand snapped out with cobra's speed, his stubby fingers deftly twisting the dagger from Yail's grip and then sliding the blade to rest under the other man's chin. "You will kill your high priest, Yail Tolranna, or else I will take your life instead. It's your choice." Perani pricked the soft flesh under Yail's chin and a spot of blood showed on the window ledge. "You understand me?"

Tolranna nodded.

"Good. Once that job's done you're free to handle this city as you like. I have a rebellion to crush up in Kelthara. But I'll leave a few lads to keep an eye on you. Caswallon will be keen to see how his new protégée in Kelwyn is doing.

"Now, take the knife and do the deed, and we can all be about our business." Perani let the dagger drop. It landed point down in a crack between stones. Seconds later, the general had left the room. Tolranna sank to his knees and wept. Once his tears ran dry, he retrieved the dagger and took urgent steps down to the oubliette below.

***

Dazaleon watched Tolranna enter the dingy room where he stooped in chained pain. The High Priest saw the self-loathing in Tolranna's face and knew what was coming. But like Perani he had small pity for this boy.

"Perani got you to do his dirty work, didn't he?" Dazaleon noted how Tolranna's face was wet with tears. "Best get to it, boy. You don't want to upset your new masters. They are not the forgiving type."

"Dazaleon...Lord, I respect you more than any other. I didn't want any of this to happen. Ariane's wildness has left me no choice."

"There is always choice."

"Not for me." Dazaleon watched as Tolranna slipped the dagger from his belt and held it at his throat.

"I weep for you soul, Yail Tolranna. Truly it is lost."

"I know," Yail replied as he plunged the dagger point deep into Dazaleon's neck and slid the edge across, allowing the high priest's blood to jet forth, splashing walls and assailant until they glistened crimson in the torchlight.

Chapter 5

The Dead City

Smoke veiled the southern skyline, darkening the leaden horizon to inky blue. Above her head, a skein of geese wended south beyond smoke and fallen city. Nobody spoke as they watched Fassof steer the skiff into the reeds and lash a swift stay to a knotty bush. Shallan stared with glazed eyes as her five companions vacated the boat amid shuffles and grunts—mainly from Taic and Sveyn. Zukei glanced back at Shallan, who still perched anxious on the wet bench.

"You ready, Duchess?" Zukei's voice was a frog croak through the reeds.

"Yes." Shallan's reply was barely audible. Zukei nodded approval and turned. Within seconds the dark-skinned woman had vaulted from the skiff leaving Shallan there alone. She shrugged, struggled to her feet and with heavy heart and limb clambered ashore.

They were three weeks out of Calprissa. Far away, Corin an Fol and Tamersane gazed out at the wide plains of Rorshai. West from there, Queen Ariane draw her plans against Perani in Wynais, and somewhere south of that the lost prince Tarin, his mentor Zallerak, and the archer Bleyne wandered the wilderness.

Shallan knew nothing of these matters. Theirs had been a long cold voyage with seas worsening and gales buffeting the timbers. But they'd encountered no pirate craft, neither any trader or else fishing skiff. They had been alone on the ocean, this world's troubled events happening elsewhere.

Shallan had kept herself busy writing a journal, learning sheet and sail craft, and even aiding Ruagon in the galley—anything rather than dwell on the events back in Calprissa. There her father had died and a part of her soul died too. She didn't think about the Assassin, still at large somewhere. Nor did Shallan dwell overlong on Corin an Fol, the man she loved. It was too painful—the thought that he might be lost too, despite cheerful Barin's assurance otherwise.

She had smiled once during that voyage when they raised the cliffs of Fol—Corin's homeland. During that sunny afternoon, Barin had made her laugh recounting his first meeting with Corin in the Longswordsman's town called Finnehalle. They'd rounded cape Fol that sunset and had steered east into the night, and as those cliffs darkened so did Shallan's mood.

After that the rains had come, washing timbers clean and driving her below decks. Slate skies had brooded low over the land in the distance. They'd passed the hills of Kelthaine surrounding Kashorn harbour, the village rain-obscured from view, though Barin told her what had occurred there too.

After that, the high ridge of cliff known as the Strain had flanked their south, a grim cloud-wracked wall. Beyond that waited poor troubled Morwella, her fallen land. They'd sailed close to Irodo Island, where Shallan had spent long sunny summers as a child. She felt a memory like the island, passing as mist to the north as they sailed by.

Then the Strain fell away and they veered south into Vangaris Bay. That had been yesterday afternoon. Barin had bid Fassof hide *The Starlight Wanderer* in a deep cove, hidden from without by pine and bluff. From there the land-bound party had sailed Barin's skiff south for several hours until she lay to, close to the pale stones of silent Vangaris. It had been Shallan's idea to come here despite Barin's protestations.

"I cannot pass the city without knowing if any of my people yet live, Barin." Shallan's cold expression left no room for argument. Barin was sympathetic but considered it an unnecessary risk to enter the city.

"There might still be enemies within," he'd warned.

"Even so, I will do as I must. I am Duchess now, at least until I find out if my brothers still live. Zukei will protect me; you others have done enough already."

"Shallan, I—"

"Please, you do not have to do this, Barin. Your home lies north away, and I know you must be missing those girls."

Barin had snorted derision through his nose. They'd been through this several times. "Me and these lads are coming, lass. Mrs Barin would flatten my earholes were she to discover I'd let you roam these parts alone, or with just Zukei helping you," he'd added quickly, seeing the glint in the fiery woman's eyes. Zukei had pledged her aid to Shallan after Calprissa. Though worlds apart, these women were fast friends.

Zukei stood with Fassof now as the mate untied the line and vaulted back on board the skiff. Shallan wasn't sure if she'd imagined it, but it seemed that Zukei's hand had brushed the mate's arm before she turned away.

"You take care, Fierce Eyes," Fassof grinned at Zukei from the deck of the skiff. The young woman glared back at him.

"What's that to you skinny man?" Zukei's lips parted to reveal the briefest hint of a feral grin.

"Nothing really."

"Oh, yeah?" Zukei's grin broadened and Shallan wondered if she'd been missing something these last weeks. Now Barin's bulk closed the gap between her and the other two.

"Give my love to all back home." Barin waved the mate get going. "Tell Marigold I'll be back by spring. In the meantime we've a castle to defend." Fassof waved and guided the skiff back into deeper water.

Barin awarded Shallan a thoughtful look. "Still want to put yourself through this Duchess? It's not going to be pleasant."

"I know," Shallan nodded tersely. "And thank you for tolerating my quirks. This isn't your fight, Barin."

"It is now. Besides, Redhand will be out there somewhere. My cherished foe and I have a debt to call, and I suspect we'll get a chance during the fight at Car Carranis. But one city at a time. We'll wait till dusk, it won't take long in this gloom."

Two hours later, Barin had led them through the reeds hugging the south side of Vangaris Bay, until three miles farther, and under the cover of moonless night, the city hinted shapes in the middle distance.

At a word from Barin, Zukei flitted ahead. She was gone a half hour and Shallan was starting to fret when her lean face appeared inches away and made the duchess jump. Zukei's expression was grim.

"They are all dead," the dark woman whispered. "Butchered like cattle at market. There are women...children. You do not need to do this, Shallan."

"Oh, but I do. They are my people, Zukei."

"Any barbarian scum still around?" Cogga's hard face loomed out of the murk. The ship's grumpy carpenter had insisted on accompanying his nephew Sveyn and Barin's nephew Taic, whilst insisting someone had to keep an eye on that pair. Barin hadn't objected. Cogga was a tough bastard and very useful with a knife.

"I didn't see any." Zukei still stared at Shallan. "Nothing alive there. It's a dead city." Shallan didn't respond.

"Well let's get on with it." Barin waved Zukei forward whilst smiling valiantly at Shallan. "Lead on, Fierce Eyes!" Zukei flashed him a grin; she liked this new name granted her by the Valkador sailors.

Vangaris reached out to them through the gloom as the party of six stole silent and moody toward the hidden gates. When these came into view Shallan held her breath and stopped for a moment. Barin glanced her way with eyebrow raised.

"I just need a minute," she told him. To their right the slow churn and thud of dark water hinted at shadows beyond. Ships, their shapes shifting in and out of vision. They were close by the harbour and still nothing stirred.

With a toss of her head, Shallan passed beneath the creaky gateway, the two iron gates hanging wide ajar. The others followed, Zukei scanning their rear like wolf stalking shepherd.

And so they entered Vangaris, six silent figures, faces grim and mouths dry. Barin loomed tall beside Shallan, his kind blue gaze watching her as much as the silent dark surrounding them.

A clatter of metal on stone saw them reaching for their blades before stopping when a rangy hound lurched into view, growled at them and then skulked back into the night. They walked on and slowly the horror of this dead city began to unfold.

There were bodies lying everywhere: maimed, broken, limbless, some partially burned and charred. They was no order to the carnage Shallan witnessed during that slow silent climb toward castle and keep, above and beyond—her former home, and the seat held by the Dukes of Morwella since the ancient times of Jerrel of Galanais, their patron.

Shallan was grateful for the murk and heavy atmosphere of winter night, for were she to witness such horror under a bright sun she knew she would crack. As it was she said nothing as her stride briskly carried her up toward her former home.

But she saw more than enough to set a fire of rage within her belly. A woman half naked, her legs thrust wide apart and her mouth open with teeth bared in silent scream.

The body of a man clutching a knife, his head nowhere in sight. A family—their bodies scattered and torn like rag dolls in a gale. It were though a rabid murderous beast had fallen upon Vangaris, slaying all within its path. The rage growing within her, Shallan picked up her pace until even Barin puffed at her side. Behind her friend, the grim shapes of Taic and Sveyn shuffled and muttered, whilst Cogga scowled and glared to their rear. Behind him the feral-eyed Zukei loped like a hungry she-panther ready to pounce at any moment.

Shallan reached the barbican that allowed passage to the castle inside. The portcullis was wedged up by trunks of ash and the drawbridge covered with the bodies of slain guards. As she crossed, Shallan glanced down at the smoky waters of the moat and wasn't surprised to see the dark shapes of bodies floating face down in the filthy water.

She pressed on, her strong legs pumping as her stride crossed the green sward leading to the keep. Again the gates were open, and the hollow dark of that grim building's interior hinted at what lay within.

Shallan stepped forward but Zukei blocked her path. "I'll go first," the dark woman told her. "There might be surprises within." Shallan nodded and followed Zukei inside the keep of Vangaris castle, the four men closing the gap behind. Now Barin took the rear, his bulk blocking the half-light of the dead city beyond.

They passed a hall to the left where more corpses sprawled like drunken sleepers at a feast. Zukei claimed the stairwell and sprinted up into the black; the young woman had her strange sword—the Karyia fashioned in mystic Shen—in her left hand, thrust up and out like a needle in front, whilst the Ptarnian throwing axe was balanced between the bony fingers of her right hand.

Up they wound, passing Shallan's room. Briefly she glanced inside, saw the glass broken and curtains wet and flapping in the night breeze. For an instant Shallan saw the duke, her father, standing there and staring hard at her, his dead eyes cold and distant. She walked on, closing that side of her mind, there being no room for weakness today.

But it was when they reached the library that Shallan's iron will nearly shattered. This had been her solace as a child. Alone and ignored, girl Shallan had spent hours in this room, reading parchments and daydreaming. Even now she could picture her mother seated in a corner, smiling with those kind sad eyes as her silent daughter stared at the words beneath the crackle of torchlight. There had been so many scrolls, and even some books (rare indeed) piled high on shelves flanking the walls.

Now there was nothing but damp ash and ruin. It became obvious as Shallan's eyes adjusted that the works had been piled into a heap and then set ablaze. As she stared at that ashen lump, Shallan felt the silent rage tearing her apart. She needed to kill and hurt and maim. She needed revenge.

A noise to her left. Zukei pounced and something sobbed in reply. "Steady girl," Barin waved Zukei back as he gazed down on the wretched shape huddled at the edge of the ash heap. "Can you speak?" Barin loomed over the shape. It moved, grew legs and arms and now resembled what must have once been a man, though the burns and scars on his body and face left little flesh untouched.

Shallan, looking down, recognised Gerrenus, her father's chief librarian and scribe. At that point her knees gave way and she sank in a heap to sit alongside the ruin of a man she had once loved.

"Gerrenus." The ruined face turned her way, the scars and torn tissue cracking as the former librarian tried to speak.

"Vile ghost...leave me, let me die without these dreams! Now you appear before me as the girl I once knew, Shallan, my lord's blessed child—though I know her to be dead."

Shallan brushed her lean fingers against Gerrenus's face and he shuddered as one kissed by a spider in a well. "Gerrenus, I live yet. I am no spirit, but flesh and blood! And I would know who did this vile thing to you, to our library, and to my people."

Gerrenus coughed and they waited, the men terse and tense and Zukei wide-eyed and pensive watching the door.

"They came in their ships, tore into the city like starving men falling on fresh cooked meat." Gerrenus coughed again. "I..."

"Take your time, old fella." Barin's eyes were kind, though Gerrenus gasped when he saw the yellow-haired giant looming over him.

"Barbarian, you've returned." Barin's expression hardened.

"This is Barin of Valkador." Shallan's fingers stroked the wisp of hair still clinging to her old friend's scalp. "He is my friend and a sworn foe to the perpetrators of this villainy. Gerrenus, my dear, you need not fear any more, but please continue your bitter tale."

At Barin's nod, Taic kneeled and pressed his flask into the old man's shaking hands.

"It ain't water." Taic grinned his gap-tooth smile. "I'm Barin's nephew," he added, seeing the terror written on the old man's face. "All mates here," Taic grinned.

Gerrenus nodded slowly and allowed the younger warrior hold the flask to his lips. He took a swallow, coughed again, and then took another. A ghost of a smile left his lips, "That's good," he said, and even Zukei was filled with admiration for the brave spirit pervading the battered wreck of this tortured man. "Very good."

"Finish it," Taic told him. "I need to give me liver a rest. It's yours, old man." Taic thrust the flask harder into Gerrenus's crusted palms then stood and went to watch the door near Zukei. "Too quiet here for my liking." Taic grinned at the woman, but Zukei ignored him.

"We were warned but didn't listen," Gerrenus croaked. "The duke got away, they say, his sons still at large in the woods outside Car Carranis...they do say. So the dead tell me."

Gerrenus coughed then took a long pull at the flask. He sighed. "Mercifully many escaped the initial horror and fled into the wilderness, though even then it was rumoured to be crawling with wolfheads and barbarian filth. Hopefully a few made it to the castle in the south."

"We are bound for Car Carranis," Shallan said. "We will gather and aid any folk we find. I will avenge this abomination, Gerrenus. This I pledge to you."

"Dear child, you are but a headstrong girl banging your head against the tumult."

"I'm not without skills, and my friends here are the greatest of warriors. I'm no wallflower, Gerrenus." Shallan smiled and stroked the wreck of his face.

"You never were, child." Gerrenus coughed again. A rough nasty sound announcing he didn't have long. "Just misunderstood, which... considering your father..."

"My father is The Horned Man. He is faen." Shallan's eyes narrowed as the battered scribe nodded slowly.

"I have always known, it was your sweet mother told me before the sickness took her. She swore me to silence. But, yes, I knew you to be the daughter of Cornelius Zawn, a leader among the faen people. A powerful being sometimes known as The Horned Man. He dwelt for a time in the woods close by."

"We better go," Zukei hissed from the door. "There are men coming this way bearing torches."

"How many?" Barin bulked through the door and scanned the castle below.

"A dozen, it's hard to tell. But they are making for the keep."

"Corgan."

Who?" They all turned to where Gerrenus now lay choking. "He said he would come back once he had spoken to his master."

"His master?"

"Daan Redhand."

Barin leaped across the room to glare down at the ruined old man. "Redhand is here?" Gerrenus choked and coughed again but he still gripped the flask in his trembling hands. Slowly he raised the pewter container to his lips. He drained the contents and smiled, "Good—so good! Now the ghosts can carry me away."

"Gerrenus?" Shallan gripped the old man's arm and shuddered as a chunk of skin crumbled like ash paper under her touch. Gerrenus didn't notice. He was already dead.

"Twelve, you reckon?" Cogga motioned Taic and Sveyn to silence whilst Zukei slid behind the door. They listened. Within seconds the sound of heavy shod feet and laughing filled the darkness of the passage below.

There were actually fourteen. Not that that mattered; the first thirteen died inside a minute, Zukei's Karyia puncturing holes in throats, as Sveyn and Taic's axes clove heads from shoulders, whilst Cogga's hurled knives did for the three that tried to leg it back downstairs. Barin didn't bother to unhook his axe; he knew his crew needed to vent some steam. Number fourteen was unlucky however. The leader Corgan: Shallan wanted him alive.

Chapter 6

The Tcunkai

Tamersane winced as winter sunlight speared his eyes, but after a grunt he managed to raise his good hand to shield the glare. He blinked and gulped and quickly regretted his decision. They were surrounded by a knot of very serious looking foreigners on shaggy horses.

Smallish in build and dark-skinned, they sat their steeds as though born in the saddle. Rorshai Riders. Not the best news really. Across the mountains in Kelwyn this lot were feared, mainly as horse thieves, but rumoured also as cutthroats and evil-tempered raiders. They'd never been near Wynais as far as he knew, but there were stories of trouble in the villages closest to the mountains. But it wasn't those rumours that concerned Tamersane. It was the expression on these riders' faces.

They wore scars like badges, chevrons on cheek and forehead, deep furrows dyed yellow, red, and blue. Their eyes were pale blue, which was strange considering the darkness of their skin. They wore large golden hoops in their ears, their sleek black hair tied back in long pigtails or braids swinging below. And their sinewy forearms were adorned with spirals of silver, bronze, and gold. All in all they looked an unpleasant lot.

Most were garbed in dark leather, though some wore chain mail and the odd one sported a helmet. All wore woollen cloaks dyed honey yellow, and each rider had an array of weaponry, comprising curved sword, a nasty looking whip with lead weights attached to the end, several babe-hilted throwing knives strapped on their broad leather belts, whilst across their backs were slung the infamous Rorshai horse bows. These boys were legendary archers. Tamersane closed his eyes as the pain shot up his arm again. He felt Thunder shuffle and heard Corin grunt back at him.

"I'll handle this," the Longswordsman said.

"Yes, please do," Tamersane muttered in reply as he tried to keep his ailing body on Thunder's sweaty saddle.

Corin watched as a rider urged his beast free of the group. Hawk-faced and whip-lean, this horseman's keen blue gaze probed Corin and Tamersane as he guided his horse in slow circles around them. Corin folded his arms and waited for this inspection to reach some kind of conclusion. At the moment it didn't look promising.

"You are Corin an Fol." A statement not a question—it came as a surprise on this already eventful day.

"Of course I am," Corin replied and the other man smiled at his answer. "Why wouldn't I be?"

"You may know us as the Rorshai." The rider leaned forward from his saddle and pinned Corin with his questioning eyes. "This is our country and you and your friend, Longsword, are trespassing."

Corin's arms remained folded. "Well, if it's any consolation, we never planned this visit. We just sort of ended up here. And…it's been a trying sort of day, thus far. My friend has a dodgy arm that needs attention and I already grow bored with this conversation. So… Please advise: are you going to skewer us with arrows or let us pass? At the moment I don't really give a toss which."

Some of the riders scowled when they heard this, and a broad-set older man urged his beast forward to glare down at this impertinent foreigner with the huge sword slung across his back.

"I ought to cut your throat to teach you manners, stranger. You are addressing the eldest son of the Kaan!"

Corin shrugged. "I hope you're quick with that knife." A dagger now showed in the older rider's fist. "You'll need to be. But I meant no offence—just been a long day, and I'm a tad irritable, if you get my meaning."

The older horseman glanced askance at his leader beside him who was now smiling. He frowned but stowed the dagger back in his belt. "Are you sure this is the right idiot, Kaanson?" The leader nodded and slid like quicksilver from his horse, waving the older man's protestations off as his boots settled even on the rocky ground.

"Excuse Rogan," the leader said as he approached Corin with outthrust hand. "He's old and crotchety. I am Olen Kaanson. We," he spread his arms wide, bidding his horsemen relax, "are the Tcunkai. The Yellow Clan." A soft thud announced Tamersane impacting the turf as he slumped free from Thunderhoof's saddle.

"Tamersane!" Corin leaped across to where his friend lay unconscious. "Can you help him?" This last to Olen who stood behind Corin as the taller man knelt and checked Tamersane's pulse.

"I stabbed him with Clouter," Corin mumbled. "I thought he was a Groil. Now I fear he's done for."

"He doesn't look dead." Rogan squinted from his saddle.

"Not dead, just buggered. Are any of your boys physicians?" Corin smacked Tamersane's face and his friend's eyes blinked and opened.

"I don't feel too good," the Kelwynian told him.

"We're going to get you sorted. This is Olen, he's our new best friend."

"Hello." Tamersane blinked at the short, hard-looking man with the weird blue eyes standing next to Corin and gazing down at him like a man prizing a cow at market. "I like the scars," Tamersane told him, then passed out again.

Olen turned and awarded Rogan a look. "Teret?"

"She has the skill."

"Who?" Corin was looking at Rogan now. He had that sinking feeling.

"My sister," Olen told him as Rogan dismounted and crossed to where Tamersane lay.

"He'll not last," Rogan said as he examined Tamersane's swollen hand. "You did this thinking he was a Groil?"

"Yes. You know of the Groil?"

"Only from children's stories." Olen was staring hard at Corin. "Our old folk told stories of ghouls that ate human flesh. Groil they called them. So they actually exist?"

"They do."

"What happened?" Olen's shrewd gaze pinned Corin.

"Shit happened." Corin looked mournful. "Where is this sister of yours?"

"Back home in our camp, two days ride north of here."

"Two days? He'll not last that." Corin's heart sank; he would never forgive himself if Tamersane died. "Is there no one here that can help?"

"I can clean the wound properly. Looks like you botched it before." Rogan shouted to another rider who yelled someone else bring boiling water and clean cloth.

Corin looked pained. "I did what I could, didn't have a lot of resources."

Tamersane yelped back into consciousness as Rogan carefully scrubbed the ooze and filth from his arm. "Here lad." Rogan had retrieved a gourd from his saddle and held its nozzle to Tamersane's mouth. "Drink this, it isn't water."

Tamersane took a gulp and then coughed and spat it out. "That's fucking disgusting!"

Rogan winked at him. "It is an acquired taste I'll grant you, but be a big lad and drink up. Twill give you strength." Tamersane did as he was told amid gurgles, scarcely managing to keep the disgusting fermented creamy stuff down, whilst Corin loomed over his friend looking pensive.

"What is that...stuff?"

"Fermented yak milk, most efficacious." Rogan capped the gourd and looped its cord around his belt. "Your boy should survive a few hours now. It's hard to die with that taste in your mouth. That's if the Anchai don't fill him with arrows."

"Anchai?" Corin looked worried again.

"Our neighbours; they live hereabouts and don't like strangers," Olen replied. "Actually they don't like anyone, but in particular strangers. Don't worry," he added seeing Corin's concern. "Rogan's blend is strong; that lad will be out till nightfall, and then we'll away north back to camp."

"What about these Anchai?"

Around midnight Corin received an unwelcome answer to that last question in the form of a red-fletched arrow buzzing an inch from his left ear and thudding into a lone ash tree. They had been riding for several hours at a steady trot. Both Olen and Rogan accompanied Corin, the men thundering behind, and Rogan sharing his mount with the slumped sleeping Tamersane—the Kelwynian not having surfaced from his fermented yak milk-induced slumber.

Before leaving, Olen had questioned Corin some more, and seeing no other option but to trust these Rorshai, Corin had recounted his wild capers down in Permio. Olen and his men had been captivated if a little bemused; Rorshai seldom left their own lands.

Then as they had ridden rough fields through darkness, Olen had told Corin of his own journey, the Ptarnian invaders heading west, and, more relevant to Corin, the Seeress's announcement of his own pending arrival.

"You didn't seem overly surprised that I knew your name," Olen had said while admiring Thunderhoof with his horse-savvy eyes. His own beast, Loroshai, was smaller but sleek and smooth, whereas this great warhorse, Thunderhoof, like his rider, had a battered, ungainly gait. That said, he was a strong-looking beast. "He is a fine horse, by the way."

"He's an old friend."

"Raleenian?"

"Yep, gift from my ex-boss."

"Nice gift, but you evade my other question." Olen glanced sideways at Corin with those unsettlingly shrewd eyes.

"Let's just say that during the last few months things have been a touch weird, so nothing surprises me anymore. That said, I'm glad of your help, friend Olen."

Olen hadn't replied, his attention diverted by the knot of angry horseman piercing the gloom ahead, the lone red-fletched arrow announcing their approach.

"Anchai. This is unfortunate." Olen leaned out from his saddle and whispered in Rogan's ear, "Take this sickling to my sister, and tell everyone at camp we need gather the clan. I will deal with these Anchai."

"They are treacherous bastards, Kaanson." Rogan's eyes narrowed, scanning the mustering horsemen ahead. He gauged they were outnumbered at least three to one, though there could be more Anchai riders hidden by the darkness.

"I'll handle it. Just go!" Olen urged his beast forward and held his hands wide in parley; he was greeted by hisses and curses ahead. Rogan cursed, but eased his horse back as the other riders guided their own steeds forward.

Rogan, after making sure he was unobserved, urged his mount cut left and make for a shadow of woodland a half-mile away. Once there, he downed a huge gulp of yak juice and dug his heels in, prompting the horse make speed towards the looming shadow of The High Wall in the east. Rogan drove the horse hard, arriving at the Tcunkai camp just as dawn gilded the rime-clad fields and revealed the towering heights of The High Wall beyond. Teret was waiting, the concern clouding her neat features as she watched her old friend and his dormant passenger arrive. In her heart Teret knew her life would never be the same again.

***

Corin reached back to slide Clouter free from its harness. "You won't be needing that," Olen told him. "The way to get through this, stranger, is to keep your lips together and do nothing. These Anchai will want to kill you, but I will persuade them otherwise."

"I hope so," said Corin, not convinced. He didn't like this sort of thing. His creed had always been: attack, holler, beat the fuck out of everything within reach, and then run or ride like heck. Simple but effective. That said, he had to admit that mantra didn't appear an option at this moment. So he did as he was bid and waited until the shadowy hostile riders loomed into view. What followed was an exchange of pleasantries Corin could have done without.

It was hard to make out their faces in the dark, but he could tell they were Rorshai: they had the same short wiry build and hard, staring, pale eyes. But this lot were a touch gothic and dramatic to Corin's mind. Most had their hair curled and twisted up, and then starched stiff into weird formations, whilst a few had fashioned theirs into greasy twisting spikes. They all had scars, but seemed to favour diamonds and circles on their cheeks rather than the Tcunkai's precise chevrons.

Corin watched a lone rider approach through the gloom. This one had three red teardrops tattooed beneath his left eye, and a red scimitar tattoo framing his right. He wore chain mail, blood red in colour, and at his side a skinny scimitar showed hilt and scabbard studded with rubies. He didn't look the friendly type.

"Greeting, Sulo," Olen allowed his hands drop to his side. He was all smiles and confidence. It was wasted on the other rider.

This Sulo character loomed close and pinned Corin with his tattoo-marked eyes. "You, Olen, dare the anger of Borian by bringing this stranger into our country. I got word you were off on some foolish caper, crossing our lands without permission. An act of war,

Tcunkai!"

"Not so, Sulo." Olen matched the other's hostile stare with measured calm. "Necessity. The Seeress bade me ride south to meet this man on the appointed hour. He is the one."

Sulo laughed hearing that. "You are a child, Olen. He is the one? The Seeress told you that? I think you were dreaming, you Tcunkai were ever moon gazers. Soft and stupid."

Olen refused to be goaded. "Let us pass, Sulo. We seek no provocation here."

"And yet you trespass, and worse bring an outlander to our country. I'll let you pass if you hand him over so we can roast him slowly over a spit and offer his foreign soul to Borian."

That... is not going to happen, Sulo."

"Can I say something?" Corin reached for Clouter again.

"No you can't." Olen bade him sit tight. "You had best let us through, Sulo."

"And why would I do that?" The Anchai leader's eyes narrowed. Despite his fierce hostility he was curious why Olen would chance riding through his country, a reckless and provocative act that was strange for the Yellow Clan.

"Because I intend to let this man speak at the Delve." A gasp sounded from both groups of riders. Olen's men knew nothing of this and were as surprised as the Anchai.

"Your mind has broken, Tcunkai. The Delve? They will tolerate no foreigner at council. As soon as you enter they will take him off your hands and gut him open, then they will skewer you for such heresy. The Delve is sacred, Olen. You ride to your death!"

"Maybe." Olen watched as Sulo paced his horse back and forth. Beyond, a thin strip of light announced dawn's approach. "But the news I bring, like this stranger, cannot wait. So let us pass or try to stop us, it matters not. Destiny rides with this stranger. We are part of his song now, and our homeland will soon be under attack.'

"I've heard enough." Sulo wrenched the scimitar from his saddle and sliced it down toward Corin at lightning speed. Corin blinked; the blade passed an inch to his left, as Sulo swung around yelping, then pitched from his saddle, a red-fletched arrow stuck clean through his right wrist. Corin winced. Bleyne would have been proud of that shot.

The apparent archer urged his beast forward, a horn bow gripped in his right palm. This one was young and good-looking for an Anchai, even allowing for the red and black lightning tattoo splitting his face from left brow to right jowl.

"Greeting Arami," Olen said. The new rider glared at him with scarce less loathing than Sulo had. The aforementioned was crouched close by squinting in pain as he gripped his wrist with his good hand. "Nice of you to intervene."

"Sulo was over hasty," the young rider said.

"I'll kill you, Arami," Sulo said. "You might be our mother's favourite but I'll still kill you!"

"Shut up." Arami was summing Corin up with his cool blue eyes. Corin saw a different sort of enemy before him. This one would still kill him, he'd just consider which way best and take his time.

"So what now?" Olen held Arami's gaze, as behind them Sulo snapped the arrow shaft with a chop from his left hand. Without a word he tugged the broken shaft through the hole in his hand and then wadded the hole with his shirt. Corin couldn't help but admire the bastard. That must have hurt.

"We accompany you to the Delve, friend Olen." Arami's smile was frosty. "You said there was no time to waste. And I for one will enjoy the reception you receive bringing this outlander along."

"I ride by Morning Hills first to gather my people."

"No, you ride alongside the Red Clan, Olen of the Tcunkai."

The two men looked at each other, no give in either. But eventually Olen shrugged.

"So be it then, Arami. You shall be witness to my account."

"Looking forward to it." Arami motioned his men to file alongside the Tcunkai; neither clan would tail the other. Corin glanced down at the acid-eyed Sulo, who said nothing as he watched them leave. Moments later he'd vaulted back on his horse and galloped west at speed.

"He will kill you," Olen said.

"Not if I kill him first," grinned Arami. Riding between them, Corin decided that things could only get better. Two days later, they reached the Delve, and instead things got worse.

***

He woke to the sound of cows lowing and the pungent smell of fresh shit. He opened his eyes and gasped in horror, discovering the shit stink came from the evil-looking paste covering his right arm. In disgust Tamersane reached down with his good hand. A woman's voice stopped him.

"Leave it!"

"But it stinks!" Tamersane complained. He tried to turn but discovered he was held fast in some sort of wicker cot chair.

"Small price for recovery," the woman said. Whoever she was sounded waspish. "Sleep, stranger, and I return in two hours. I have chores and already have spent too much time with you. The cattle need tending."

"Nice that you care," Tamersane muttered. He didn't get an answer. He glanced around as best he could. It appeared he was in some sort of barn, the sides open and the cold blast of winter air stinging his ears. Away off to the right were mountains. A grand view if you liked that sort of thing. At the moment Tamersane didn't.

The woman must be some local cow wench, doubtless ugly as her stock and worse tempered. Still, his arm did actually feel a little better. Tamersane was weak though, and not a little confused. He thought about Corin for a minute and then nodded off again, the wind rattling his ears.

Next time he woke, the woman was staring at him with something sharp in her hand. "You look tolerable," she said. Tamersane blinked water from his eyes and focused on the young woman leaning over him. She was actually quite attractive in a horsey, hard-eyed, shrewish kind of way. Short of body, dark tan, small breasts, long smoky black hair tied in a tight no-nonsense pigtail. Large, weirdly pale blue eyes dominated an oval face, dusted with light freckles arrayed around a sharp nose. No beauty, but definitely worth a quickie in Tamersane's estimate. There was also a small bird tattoo on her left cheek, which for some reason Tamersane found rather appealing.

"What are you staring at?" The woman frowned down at him. "Are you simple in the head?"

"No, but I think I'm in love." Tamersane flashed her his gorgeous smile. That always worked with these rustic wenches.

"I think you are soft in the head," the woman replied and left him alone again. Tamersane blinked. Strange lass. He didn't dwell on the matter as sleep claimed him again. When he woke next time it was dark and very chilly.

Close by, a crackle of flame showed orange as several shapes crouched over the fire. Two were playing what might generously be described as music by scraping a thin stick across strings tied to some bowl thing. The healing woman appeared again, appraised Tamersane's condition and chewed her lower lip. "You hungry?"

"Yes, but I'd settle for a wet snog." Tamersane tried his best grin again.

The woman's bright blue gaze flashed with irritation as she wondered why Rogan had delivered this injured lunatic into her care. "If you can walk, come sit by the fire. I'll bring you some broth. You can sit and be quiet and enjoy the music."

"Oh, is that what that is? I was unsure." The young woman turned and showed him her back. Tamersane took a deep breath and heaved his body up. He felt dizzy, slightly sick, and not a little wobbly in the legs. That said, he shuffled over to the bonfire easily enough and slunk into a surprisingly comfortable wicker chair. The three men already seated around the blaze ignored him. One of them Tamersane dimly recognised as Rogan, the old git that had given him the filthy yak juice.

"Hello," Tamersane smiled at his new companions. "This is

cosy." They didn't acknowledge him, just gazed despondent into the fire. "Has somebody died?" Tamersane added after a moment.

The young woman leaned over him and shoved a hot bowl of steaming something in his hands. "You talk over much," she told him as her pigtail tickled his nose.

"Just trying to be friendly," Tamersane replied and then sneezed into his broth. The healer chewed her lower lip again and rubbed that sharp nose.

"You are a strange man."

"Well, at least tell me your name, sweet nursemaid." Tamersane sneezed again.

"I am Teret and I am not your bloody nursemaid." To his right Rogan chuckled, and the other men grinned like loons.

"You've a lot to learn about Tcunkai women, stranger." Rogan winked at him. Tamersane shrugged. He decided to let the matter rest for the time being and instead changed tack.

"Thanks for bringing me here, old chap," he smiled at Rogan who shrugged in reply. "But where is here, exactly? I'm a bit confused."

"You are at Morning Hills, the winter camp of our people. Teret is Olen Kaanson's only sister, and he is very fond of her. She is skilled at medicine, and you, stranger, owe her your skinny life. You might show some appreciation and stop fucking about."

Tamersane felt a bit ashamed after that. "I think she's lovely," he told Rogan unaware that Teret was standing behind him. "Just a bit fierce."

Teret felt a flutter of a smile soften her lips; she turned and walked back to her tent where more tasks waited.

Meanwhile, Tamersane quizzed Rogan about the Anchai and what would happen to his friend Corin. He decided he liked Rogan, who had a bluff honesty about him.

"That I do not know. Dangerous business; that Sulo's a tosser. Unpredictable and violent, but Olen can handle his type."

"He is your leader then, this Olen?"

"No, but he is the Kaan's eldest son and he has the Dreaming."

"The Dreaming?" Tamersane's face stiffened. Gone was his easy smile as he thought about Queen Ariane and wondered how she fared in his own country. It had been so long since their departure at Vioyamis.

"Olen believes your friend to be the fulcrum—a hero long foretold that will arrive on the eve of the greatest war mankind will ever endure."

"Oh yeah, that sounds like Corin." Tamersane scooped the broth into his mouth. It was very good. "Always the centre of everything chaotic. Bloody good bloke, though, I must say."

"Olen will take him to the Delve."

"What is that?"

"It's a cliff dwelling where we hold our secret war councils and matters of state. It's also where the shamans and seers prance about naked in drug-induced trances."

"Sounds like fun."

"It's not." Rogan glared into the fire. He alone had Olen told about his plans. He knew the risk the Kaanson was taking chancing the Delve, but he also believed in his leader enough to back him all the way. "He'll come here once he's dealt with those Anchai morons, then we'll up camp and make north for the Delve."

"Me too?"

"No, boy. One foreigner at the Delve is dangerous. Two would be madness. You will stay here with Teret and the cows."

Tamersane felt sleep approaching as he carefully placed his empty bowl on the ground. "Do you think she'll warm to me?"

"I doubt it," replied Rogan and shuffled away to take a piss.

Later Teret took seat by the fire and thoughtfully sipped fermented milk from her wooden mug. As she sipped she studied the face of the stranger asleep in his wicker chair, whose name she'd learnt was Tamersane.

Upon a strange whim she stood, reached over him and placed a soft warm kiss on his lips. He didn't stir. Teret grinned evilly and drained her mug. She returned minutes later, checked Tamersane's wound, and satisfied, tossed a blanket over him. Then she wandered off and wrapped her lean small body in her cot and blankets. Within minutes Teret was asleep.

Chapter 7

Tigers and Hares

"It was a dragon. Now shut up and let me think." Zallerak was seated on a cold flat rock overlooking a steep gorge lined with ancient beeches. Prince Tarin stood with arms folded staring at the rushing river far below, his eyes bleak and his lip set in moody obstinacy.

A few yards to the right, Bleyne the Archer gazed across at the southern rim of Beechborn Forest. The autumn leaves had gone now, and the trees stood stark and wuthering, like grim sentinels watching them from the north. Two days had passed since the horror on the Fallowheld. Nobody had spoken about it much until now.

But now Tarin wanted answers. He'd only just recovered from his argument with Corin an Fol. Then the terror and fury on the Fallowheld had rendered him silent for the last two days. Two days in which Zallerak—crowish and grim—had urged Tarin down from that bleak hill and onto the Great South Road, which they had kept to until reaching the forest today.

Bleyne had scanned Fallowheld's flanks for signs of Corin and Tamersane. He'd also looked for the missing horses to scant avail;

the beasts could be miles away by now. He had found boot tracks down at the northern base of the Fallowheld where clumps of pines led up to the first great mountain comprising The High Wall. One man—most likes Corin judging by the size of the feet.

Bleyne had wanted to investigate further, but worry for prince and crown led him back up to the top of Fallowheld. From there he'd spied the tiny shapes of Zallerak and Tarin drifting along the ribbon of the Great South Way. Nice of them to wait.

Bleyne had joined them an hour later. When he'd told all he knew, Zallerak had shrugged.

"Corin will doubtless make for Car Carranis as he intended. Tamersane too, if yet he lives. Nothing we can do about that now." Bleyne had noted how unconcerned Zallerak appeared. He'd keep both eyes on this warlock, he decided that day.

And so they'd walked in silence, Bleyne scanning road ahead and bushes either side, Tarin sulking and chewing his lip, and Zallerak striding ahead with hostile glares and intent purpose. They'd camped that first night by the road then pushed on early before dawn crested the slopes parading their east.

The second day witnessed the walkers repeating their roles as they wandered north along the empty winter road. Then, on finally reaching the edge of Beechborn Forest, Tarin had snapped like a spring breaking free of a wheel.

"What if that *thing* comes back? Or more Groil?"

Zallerak had shrugged, gazing down at the river below. He turned to Bleyne, ignoring the prince. "We need to cross that river before nightfall and enter yonder wood. Beechborn is large, it will hide us until we reach the southern wolds and Atarios."

Bleyne nodded. "Silon needs to be informed of the attack on Fallowheld. We need to know what we're up against."

"I know what we're up against, archer, hence my mood of urgency. Groil and dragon. Master Caswallon has upped his game. Now we've two good hours before dusk, so let's press on!"

That night Tarin had raged at Zallerak, his former awe of the wizard torn away by dread and fear of what had happened to them on the Fallowheld.

"How do you know it won't find us in the forest? And what about those Groil things? Have you got a plan, any ideas at all?"

"Yes I do, now be silent and go to sleep."

"I need some bloody answers, Zallerak! You've played me for a fool for too long!"

"Which is entirely as you deserved. You have a long way to go, Prince Tarin, before you can win back respect from myself or any other. And—lest you forget—you owe me your life. Some gratitude is called for, but if you cannot manage that then keep your lips together."

Tarin withdrew to his blanket but decided on one last try, changing tack. "Well, at least tell me what our plans are so I can contribute."

"Contribute? You?" Zallerak snorted, and over in the corner Bleyne raised an eyebrow. "Bleyne hunts, keeps us from starving. I ...*think*. I'm currently working these problems through my weary mind. You, prince, can help by shutting the fuck up. But as far as our plans so far, we make for Atarios. From there we will gather news of Queen Ariane, and Caswallon, and alert Silon to petition for more Raleenian aid. I suspect he's back in Vioyamis by now. Then it's north into Kelwyn and war. Does that help?"

Defeated, Tarin had nodded and rolled into his blanket. He wasn't happy but would let things pass for the meanwhile.

***

General Perani rolled free from his blanket as the sounds of shouting and crackle of flame drove sleep away. The camp was under attack? It beggared belief. But he could hear fighting and men's death cries in the distance.

Perani grabbed the candle lamp and threw his cloak across his shoulders to rebuff the cold. Next he strapped his sword belt to his waist and stumbled over to the tent flap. He wrenched open the tent's canvas doors tearing the buttons off in his fury.

"What happens?" Perani yelled at a man rushing at him through the night.

"Riders, my lord! Raiders, they've broken into our camp at the south side and put torch to several tents!"

"Saddle my horse!" Perani raged at his aide who had just stumbled bleary-eyed into view. "Quickly man!" Within minutes Perani was astride his mare and guiding the beast through his camp amid shouting, chaos, and clash of distant steel.

But despite his speed Perani was too late arriving. The raiders had struck fast and faded like ghosts into the night. They'd left over a hundred dead, stolen forty horses, and set fire to over a dozen tents. Perani, raging and shaking in fury, was greeted by his second, Gonfalez, a note clutched in his gloved hand.

"They left this," the heavy-set Gonfalez told him, passing a scrunched piece of parchment into his fist. Perani smoothed the parchment flat and studied the contents, whilst his second steered close and held a torch for the general to see. It read thus:

Perani

This was but a courtesy call. We will be back for more serious work soon.

Tarello

"Who is this bastard?" Perani growled at Gonfalez who glared back at him through the gaps in his helm. Behind them men were rushing and putting out the flames still blazing through some of the tents.

"Queen Ariane's new warlord," Gonfalez barked back. "One of the 'heroes' of Calprissa. This Tarello has taken the war to us, general. Caswallon will not stand for this!"

"Caswallon doesn't need to know, Captain." Perani glared at his second. Like Derino before him, Gonfalez was ambitious, and Caswallon made it very clear you were only as good as your last job. Thus Perani's hand was forced and his customary cautiousness abandoned. "We will deal with this Tarello bastard swiftly and then put an end to Ariane's little army. It is time for direct action."

"Caswallon's spy said for us to hold fast in this camp and let the Groil flush out the rebels."

"The Groil are fucking useless! They failed at Calprissa and they will fail in Kelwyn. They're good for scaring smallfolk and eating peasants, but when it comes to real fighting they lack discipline and imagination. These bastard Kelwynians have proved both more resilient and smarter than I expected. Ariane is headstrong, so I believed she would fall into our hands at Wynais. She hasn't taken the bait. Someone—maybe this Tarello—held enough sway to caution her otherwise. We have underestimated the situation, Captain. Now we need to act fast to gain the upper hand again."

"What do you propose, General?"

"We break camp and ride south at first light. I'll send a small unit to aid the garrison at Wynais, but that city can look after itself now the troublemakers are dealt with and Tolranna knows his orders." Perani scrunched the parchment into a ball and sent it flying into nearby torchlight.

"The army moves south, Gonfalez. We will flush out this Tarello and his queenling inside a month. Time we finished this. Caswallon can have Ariane, but I will roast Tarello over slow coals—that I vow!"

Gonfalez didn't reply. Later he bid an aide write Caswallon coded message via bird, informing him of Perani's latest decision. It paid to keep in with the top draw, just in case Perani got it wrong.

Scarce three hours later, Perani's entire force (bar the three hundred guardsmen he sent to Wynais and a skeleton crew left at the camp) had crossed the River Kelphalos and was hastening south towards the Great South Road, having received rumours that Ariane's rebels were now stationed within Elglavis Wood south of Wynais.

***

"They're on the move!" Valentin watched with spy-glass in hand as the horde from Kelthaine swarmed down the Great South Way.

"How many?" Arac stood beside his leader as they watched from the hills flanking Elglavis Wood.

"Hard to say, perhaps twenty thousand." Valentin slung the scope in his belt and slapped the archer's shoulders. "We need to alert Ariane soonest. Failing that, maybe we can draw them away from the wood, buying time for the queen to spring the trap. Take Lusty, the boys, and Doodle McNoodle and go find the queen. I'll keep watch on our friends."

Arac nodded and swiftly departed to grab the Ranger's newest recruit.

"Where are we going?" Doyle asked him as Arac tossed over a flask of water.

"To find your queen," the Ranger grinned. "We've a busy few days ahead."

"Oh, good," Doyle managed as he struggled onto his horse, his face pale and worried.

"Cheer up, Doodle!" Arac grinned at him. "We Rangers revel at fighting, it's what we do best!"

***

"They've taken the bait." Tarello led his fifty riders down from the hills south of the Kelphalos River. "Looks like the whole army's on the move. Guess I must have pissed Perani off," he grinned at his companion rider.

Jaan didn't grin back. "We were lucky, Tarello. They won't be caught off guard again. And now Perani will hunt us down like a raging bear in springtime. And for what? A few slain enemy and several burnt tents?"

Tarello was unswayed by Jaan's opinion. "We struck the first blow. Perani's pride is dented, and Caswallon, when he finds out, will not be happy. It's a psychological masterstroke, Jaan."

"Let's hope we don't pay for it later today." The Raleenian spurred his horse faster as did Tarello beside him. It was already afternoon when they reached Ariane at her camp deep inside Elglavis Wood. They found the queen seated on a log drinking piping tea while a rangy archer and a younger man addressed her.

Ariane glanced their way as Tarello and Jaan dismounted and ordered their men go eat and see to the horses.

"Looks like you've stirred up a hornet's nest," Ariane smiled wolfishly. "Well done gentlemen. We now have at least twenty thousand comprising Perani's entire former Tiger Regiment hurrying our way."

"You said to get his attention." Unperturbed, Tarello flashed her a grin. Close to the queen, Squire Galed was fretting that they should be breaking camp and moving while they had the chance.

To his right sat a smaller figure, his young face flushed with excitement. So far this warrior life was suiting Cale well. His studies had been postponed. Instead he'd been working on his sword and knife skills. He'd wanted to accompany Tarello (whom he admired) and Jaan (whom he was slightly nervous of) on their bold venture and had been a bit grumpy when the queen put her foot down. But now Cale was beaming at the likelihood of the big battle coming their way.

But Cale's optimism was shared by few surrounding the queen. Most voiced Jaan's view that the raid had been rash and had brought the full fury of Kelthaine down on them before they were ready to withstand it.

Ariane was undaunted. She'd received word via pigeon from Vioyamis. Silon had persuaded the castellan of Atarios to send a thousand lancers north, all hungry, apparently, to avenge their comrades who fell at Calprissa. Jaan was delighted hearing this news as was his friend Tarello.

"A thousand Raleenians!" Tarello slapped Cale's back as he took seat on another log by the campfire. "We'll send Perani packing, master Cale. And lancers too!" Tarello flashed a grin at Jaan.

"A thousand Raleenians," Ariane repeated slowly. "We have, what? Three thousand in our entire force: mostly volunteers from around the country, recruits from farms, veterans of Calprissa, and those lucky few that escaped from Wynais.

"Jaan's men are few and Valentin's Rangers only comprise four hundred - that against a force of twenty thousand professional warriors renowned for their savagery and ruthlessness. And that's without including the Groil still at large in their hundreds roaming throughout my kingdom. Let us not get carried away, gentlemen, nor should we seek to take on Perani in the open."

"What do you propose, my Queen?" Tarello chewed tenaciously at a sausage and wiped his mouth. The raid had been hungry work and they hadn't eaten since.

"We ride forth with enough men to lure Perani south and away from our camp. We keep ahead of him but close enough to goad him on. We'll make sure Atarios knows Perani's moving south, so at some point we can liaise with the lancers to meet up and turn about, striking Perani hard, then breaking free before he can throw his entire army against us. Guerrilla tactics, gentlemen. That is how we will win this war."

Later Galed sat alone with Cale and the queen. Tarello and Jaan and their men were snatching sleep whilst Valentin's Rangers (who had arrived at dusk) kept watch on Perani's movements. Latest word was that the Kelthaine army was camped ten miles north of Elglavis Wood. Doubtless they would break camp at dawn and sweep into the forest hoping to catch Ariane unawares and annihilate her smaller army.

Galed watched Ariane as she poked the fire with a stick, her dark eyes fierce with concentration. "You've come a long way, my Queen," Galed told her. "Your father would be so proud."

"I hope so." Ariane dropped the stick and looked up, a single tear glinting beneath her left eye. She still so missed her father. She missed Corin an Fol too, and Barin and the others. Tarello and Jaan were good men, and Galed her dear friend. But they were not legends like her father had been, or like Barin and Corin were becoming. "I often wonder what he would do were he here."

"Everyone loves you." Cale's face was flushed redder than normal. "You are the best queen in the world."

"And you've known many, young sir." Ariane cuffed Cale's curly head. "But thanks for your support."

When Tarello and Jaan returned from their rests Ariane held brief campfire council, announcing she would lead a force of fifteen hundred riders out of Elglavis Wood. There were protestations at her leading this fleeing army but she waved them down.

"Perani needs to know I'm running from him. That way he'll throw his full force against us and will let Elglavis alone. Tarello and Jaan will accompany me, as will Galed and Cale." (The latter beamed hearing this.) "We are hares before wolves."

"Tigers," Tarello cut in.

"Tigers." Ariane smiled. "Those tigers are no match for our crafty hares. And," she added, "While we are keeping Perani occupied I've a task for you Rangers." The hard-faced Valentin nodded from across the campfire. The chief Ranger joined her whilst Arac and crew kept watch on the enemy.

"Name it."

"I want you to retake Wynais under cover of night. Are your boys up to such a task, Captain?"

Valentin grinned nastily. "It's what we do best, my Queen."

An hour before dawn, Arac and a puffing Doyle crashed in upon a dozing Ariane and Galed, still both at the campfire.

"They're on the move!" Arac yelled, "heading for the forest!"

An hour later, Perani whooped in delight when his scouts announced that riders led by the queen herself were fleeing the woods, making southwest for the road. The chase was on and the little queen's short reign nearly over. With a roar, Perani ordered his captains bid their men turn about and resume their march along the Great South Way.

***

About this time, in a musty tavern in the shady side of Atarios, a quiet figure in the corner watched and listened as he sipped his rough brandy through parched lips. Watching and listening had kept him alive these last few weeks, that and the odd bit of throat slitting and coin pilfering.

His body still ached from the beating he'd got down south, but his head burned with vengeful schemes that kept him strong, and more importantly, alive.

Hagan smiled as he listened to the soldiers talking discreetly in the tavern. They were Raleenian lancers and they were heading north tomorrow to go assist the beleaguered queen of Kelwyn.

But it wasn't this news that concerned Hagan. He couldn't give a toss about Queen Ariane, having had more than enough from her at Kashorn harbour three months ago. It was their other gossip that kept Hagan's ears pricked.

"Dragon," the older lancer muttered. "Can you believe it?"

"Sounds like tosh." His friend gulped at his tankard and yelled the innkeep for another. "It attacked this warlock on the Fallowheld? Sounds like total bollocks to me."

"Me too, Garral, but I heard that tosser prince talking to the castellan. I heard other things too. Guard duty was uncommonly interesting last night."

"Weren't you sworn to secrecy?" Garral sipped his whiskey, not overly happy that Zane was telling him all this. But his young friend was full of conspiracies this evening.

"Just us here." Neither man had taken time to notice the hard-eyed figure in the dark corner furthest from the fire and half hidden by a pole. They were soldiers in their own city, confident and proud— particularly the younger one. "Besides," Zane continued, "the prince blurted it out so loud anyone within a mile could have heard."

"Heard what?"

"They have the crown, Garral. The fucking Tekara. All repaired and good as new. I reckon that Caswallon's in trouble now." Hagan had frozen hearing that. So that's why everyone had been so excited down there in the desert. Prince Tarin alive and well and hanging out with this foreign wizard, and him having reforged the crown down in Permio! Hagan hadn't had much time to focus on events beneath the mountains. It had taken all his concentration to stay alive during that unfortunate visit. He tuned his ears harder to the men seated by the fireplace.

"Things are happening, Garral." Zane had the upbeat confidence only the young and unworldly possess. His companion was more reticent.

"So are they taking it to Queen Ariane?" Garral washed the brandy around his mouth; he had a head cold and the strong liquid warmed his shivers. "Sounds a bit daft. I mean, are this wizard and the prince coming with us in the morning?"

"I don't know," Zane grinned, "but why would they stay in Atarios when there's a war going on up north?"

"But won't they need someone to wear the Tekara? I mean, a crown without a king is pretty useless. And I don't see any potential kings stepping up to quarrel with Caswallon. You've heard the stories from Kella, Zane. It's bad up there."

"Maybe this wizard bloke knows somebody. Look, it's got to be good news hasn't it? Cheer up, Garral. Caswallon's had it easy up till now. But now we have sorcery back-up too."

"The only thing I know about sorcery is to stay as far from it as I can. Come on, we need to get back or you'll drink too much and feel shit in the morning. It's a long ride to Kelwyn. Wizards can't change that."

A moment later the two lancers drained their drinks, thanked the landlord, and left the tavern filled with their own theories on what would come of these exciting events.

Hagan watched them leave with a cold smile on his face. He ordered another brandy from the innkeep and claimed their former place by the fire. He felt better—much better. If Tarin was here, then Corin must be around too. But this time he'd need a hand dealing with old longshanks.

But who to call on? Actually that was obvious. Hagan's smile deepened as he recalled how someone else owed Corin a debt. A man he knew, and feared were truth be known. But a man with special skills and devotions, ensuring he would stop at nothing to see Hagan and himself avenged. That following morning, Hagan Delmorier stole a horse from a stable and rode northwest for the coast. It would take some time to find the one he sought, but he deemed the trip well worth it.

Chapter 8

The Road to Car Carranis

Shallan felt sick to the bone. The dead city around her, poor Gerrenus now departed, and the corpses of the recently slain lying strewn and bleeding across the room—that combination of stench and horror left her reeling and shaking in the corner, her guts churning in a cocktail of rage and revulsion.

Zukei sat cross-legged over their prisoner. It hadn't taken Corgan long to break. He was a hard man, but Zukei had some very dark skills. Now Corgan lay sobbing and screaming for the woman to let him be. Zukei grinned at him and lowered the knife again. Another scream.

"Enough!" Shallan could stand no more. The man had told them all he knew. He'd screamed it out, but Zukei wanted more. "Stop!" Shallan yelled at the warrior woman, and Zukei glared back at her.

"I thought you wanted vengeance, Duchess? Someone to pay for these atrocities?"

"I know, and I did. But this isn't right, Zukei. We don't have to sink to their level."

Zukei shook her head. "Pity is for the weak. Harden your heart, Duchess. This one might have more to tell us. I've only really just started."

"Shallan is right." Barin loomed over from the shadows. "And we've spent too long here already. Time to vacate this fallen city, we've a journey to make. So slit that bastard's throat, Zukei girl, and let's get moving."

"As you wish." Zukei's thin blade slid along the supine man's throat. Corgan choked, spluttered, kicked out, and then lay still. Shallan turned her gaze away.

The man hadn't told them much, but what he had told them was all they needed to know. Redhand had been and gone. It was he who had been responsible for the sacking of Vangaris. His father, King Hal, and Redhand's other brothers had initially attacked the city but waited for the king's eldest son to join them. After Daan's arrival they had departed southeast for Car Carranis. Redhand had told them of his meeting with Rael Hakkenon in Crenna, and how Caswallon had wanted Morwella destroyed: house, ship, farm, and family.

And Redhand was at Car Carranis now. He'd left this Corgan with just a shadow crew watching the ashes of Vangaris. Zukei proposed they flush the other Leethmen out of their rat holes in the city, but Barin said they had scarce time for such recreation.

At his word, they left the keep behind and made for the southern gates, which like the northern ones stood broken and ajar. After that they crossed the stone bridge spanning the River Falahine and left ruined Vangaris far behind.

Shallan never looked back once. Vangaris was dead and Morwella dying. A city of ghosts and a country of shadows. But she would focus on what lay ahead rather than behind: Car Carranis, war, and the distant hope of finding her love again.

Night found them camped in a forest. It was chilly and wet but Barin dared not light fires. So they managed with what little sleep they could and were up and moving an hour before sun-up. They stayed close to the road but dared not travel on it. This made their progress slow, but Zukei, also skilled in scout work, found shortcuts and deer paths which gained them back some ground.

Two days passed with the six fugitives flitting through woods and fording streams. Their way wound up ever steeper, and the bleak heights of eastern Morwella loomed close. Beyond them lay Leeth and the Disputed Realm, whilst to their north the Gulf of Leeth glinted greyish-blue through gaps in the trees.

It was during the morning of their third day after leaving Vangaris that Taic emerged from the path ahead, a finger raised to his lips in warning. The young Northman had been ranging ahead with Zukei and had spotted movement on the road.

"What is it?" Barin frowned at his nephew whilst Shallan and Sveyn took a breather.

"Brigands I'd say. A score or more ranging east along the road."

"Leethmen?" Cogga had emerged through the trees. Barin had bid his ship's carpenter act as tail man, ensuring they weren't followed.

"No, these look like Morwellans." Taic nodded as Zukei slunk into view. "Here she is," Taic grinned. He liked Zukei, though mostly she ignored him.

"There are twenty-two." Zukei folded her brown arms and leaned against a tree. She slipped a dagger from her belt and started cleaning out dirt from beneath her nails. For some reason this fascinated Taic and Sveyn. "They are ill-equipped and shabby. I can kill them if you want," Zukei offered.

"Let them be." Barin glanced at Shallan who shrugged agreement. "They might be refugees of Vangaris, like us making for Carranis. And even if they are scumbags, there might be more. Keep an eye on them, sweetness; don't let them get too far ahead but don't get too close either."

"I know how to fucking scout." Zukei glared at Barin and disappeared into the woods again. Taic, chuckling, trotted after her. Cogga flashed Barin a grin.

"Don't you just love that girl?" he said.

"Hard not to," replied Barin.

Throughout that afternoon Zukei and Taic appeared at odd times to report on the Morwellans, who for the most part seemed content to follow the road without much care if they were being watched. Zukei held their tracking skills in contempt. Aside that, the road steepened as they turned south and left the Gulf of Leeth behind. Ahead and close loomed the first great heights of the mountain range that surrounded Car Carranis. Betwixt these ranges the road wound and threaded, a pale worm half hidden by pine and briar.

Their way got tougher and at last there was no alternative but to take to the road. Shallan panted as the stiff climb led up through pines, the frosty chill choking her breath.

An hour before dusk, Taic came running into view. He looked alarmed.

"What is it now?" Barin had that dubious expression he reserved for his nephew alone. "Wood goblins?"

"Big feet!"

"What?" Shallan and Barin replied at the same time.

"Foot prints. Huge with claws!"

"Elephant?" suggested Cogga.

"Don't be silly." Shallan's eyes showed worry and alarm. "Bears maybe?"

"Nope. These prints are man-shaped but bigger than any frigging bear's. There's something nasty out there uncle."

"Where is Zukei?" Shallan demanded, now worried for her friend.

"Following the tracks up yonder hill." Taic pointed to where a cluster of crags frowned down upon them above the pines a half mile east of the road.

"Get her back here," snapped Barin, for once irritated with Zukei's tenacity. "This isn't some beast hunting expedition. Whatever it is, hopefully it will stay up there and leave us alone. And what of our friends further up the road?"

"They're setting up camp two miles ahead. I was going to tell you that."

"On the road?" Cogga looked askance. "Are they unhinged or merely overconfident?"

"They look exhausted," Taic shrugged. "Like men who have nothing left. They've lit a fire and spread blankets a hundred feet from the road. We had no trouble spotting them."

"So what do we do?" Shallan felt edgy and strange. The small hairs were rising in the nape of her neck. Something wasn't right here.

Barin nodded. "I feel it too. Something's out there. We'll wait for that daft lass to re-join us then we'll steal up the road, get ahead of those Morwellan fools and hopefully leave this bad region behind."

Moments later, Zukei slunk into view, her expression grim. "There's an old settlement up there just past those rocks," she told them. "I found human bones—they weren't that old."

"More footprints?" Barin scratched his ear and wished he had an ale handy. He felt thirsty this evening. Thirsty and grumpy.

"Yes lots, they trailed off toward that mountain." Zukei pointed to where a dark shoulder of rock showed pink in the evening light.

"Well I don't see any reason to linger here a moment longer," Barin said. "Let's get some miles behind us while we still have light." The others agreed, and they filed back onto the road and commenced jogging while their energy lasted. Zukei scouted the camp. "They are asleep!" she hissed them forward. "Not even a guard posted, the twats!"

They passed the place where the Morwellans were sleeping and continued on. The road was even steeper now, winding ever up into the mountains, and the air bitter chill. Barin and Zukei led them on, walking at a punishing pace despite the climb. Shallan's legs ached and her heart thudded in her chest. But she didn't complain, just wanted rid of this place.

They crested a rise where the wind whistled around their ears and a knot of stubby oaks creaked close by. Aside that they were on a level plateau, a shoulder that during daylight would award fine views north and west.

"We'll settle here," Barin announced. "It's chilly but hard for someone or something to spring us without us spotting them first." No one complained about that decision. They were all exhausted; even Zukei looked tired, and apart from Sveyn (who took first stag) were all sleeping huddled within their blankets inside an hour.

The screams woke them an hour before dawn. Shallan blinked, shivered, and rolled free from her blanket. What the...? A sound like crushing logs exploded somewhere below, followed by more screams and then silence. Nobody spoke though all were thinking the same. Those Morwellans had just had a visit by the owner of the big feet.

"Shall I go and investigate?" Zukei asked Barin, who shook his head.

"Are you nuts?" Sveyn was shaking. One thing Shallan had noted about these tough Valkador men, they didn't do spooks. Anything unnatural seemed to unnerve them. Both Taic and Cogga looked gloomy, whilst Barin was chewing his beard.

"We stay put," he said after a moment. "All of us. The last thing we want to do is get lost in the dark. This is wild country and Car Carranis still a good two days' hike."

"Would that we had bloody horses," muttered Cogga. They sat tight as night deepened around them. It was bitter cold, and a white half moon glinted through the trees. Shallan dozed, her head nodded forward, and with a jolt she snapped awake. Someone watched beneath the trees.

"Cornelius? Father—is that you?"

A shadow slipped behind a rock. She heard a soft sound, turned and saw him standing there. The Horned Man.

"Daughter, you are in peril." The words were leaves brushing stone; she couldn't see him—just a shadowy shape in the gloom. "There is great danger for you here!" The voice seemed to come from far away. Close by her companions made not a sound.

"I feel it, but what is it?"

Just then an almighty crash erupted somewhere close below,

something bellowed, and then another crash and the sound of thundering feet approaching at large shook the ground.

"Father!" Shallan hissed but the shadow of The Horned Man had vanished into the night.

"Flee!" His voice came to her like wind over water. Then Shallan cried out as something knocked her over. It was Taic, his blue eyes wild as he unslung his axe.

"What the fuck?" That was Sveyn.

"Barin!" Zukei yelled.

Then the monstrosity fell upon them.

It was huge, violent, and fucking ugly. Those were Shallan's first impressions. They leapt inside her head about the same time that she dived for cover behind a log, her companions taking similar evasive steps. Shallan's brief glimpses hinted at huge gnarly head, greenish oily skin (which glistened in the moonlight like slime in a trough), shaggy black hair, and huge sinewy torso. It was naked save a belt and short woollen kilt, and below that oak-broad stout legs stomped and kicked as their owner roared and bellowed.

"It cannot be!" Shallan heard Cogga shout to her left.

"I thought they were extinct!" That was Sveyn, closer to her right.

"What is it?" Taic, somewhere behind her, his voice hoarse and muffled.

"A fucking troll." That was Barin, who stood with feet braced and Wyrmfang grasped in his fists. The troll (if that's what it was) came crashing toward Barin, and for the first time since she'd met him, the master of *The Starlight Wanderer* looked small to Shallan. The greenish creature was double Barin's height and so broad it looked squat. It carried a huge tree stump as a weapon, which it now swung down at Barin.

He leapt back out of range just as Zukei danced free of a rock and hurled a knife at the brute's chest. The blade bounced off that hide and the creature hardly noticed. Zukei slipped the Ptarnian axe she'd acquired in Calprissa into her left palm. The troll lurched down to grasp her but she danced between its legs and chopped hard at the sinews behind its knees. This time black ooze showed as her axe cut through that leather-hard flesh.

The troll kicked out at Zukei with a yard-long foot, sending her flying. Another knife bounced off its head as Cogga rolled into view, then Sveyn, yelling and spitting, ran at the monster and swung his axe hard between its legs.

That didn't work too well; the troll brought a knee up and sent Sveyn skyward. Taic nocked an arrow to his bow and let loose. The shaft stuck in the side of the troll's head. The troll shook his skull, bellowed, and scratched its ear.

Then Barin strode forth with Wyrmfang in full swing. The troll batted the double blades aside with one massive fist and sent the other one hammer-hard toward Barin's face.

Barin dived clear, and as he rolled swung up again with the axe, this time scoring a long bloody wound along the inside of the troll's thigh.

About this time, Shallan remembered her horn. She snatched the great curved tusk from her blanket and put it to her lips. She blew three times and the troll grinned at her.

Shallan swore and tossed the horn away, reaching instead for her bow. She had the troll's full attention now. It lumbered toward her, still grinning; she counted at least three teeth in that gaping mouth.

Barin swung Wyrmfang and caught the troll behind its right knee, just as Cogga reappeared to slam Sveyn's discarded axe into the monster's left ankle.

The troll buckled, but as he sank to his knees a table-sized fist sent Cogga spinning over a rock. Moments later, Zukei, Taic, and Sveyn (all remarkably still in one piece) mustered into a tight group and advanced heroic toward the troll amid expletives, hissing, and wailing (this last from Sveyn who had lost it again).

The troll yawned and showed them his back. The monster tried to stand but his legs were bleeding badly. The troll looked puzzled but didn't have long to think for Barin had climbed on his back and now had both hands around the troll's foot-thick neck.

And so the troll hugging began. Later Taic would embellish that fight to scare the children, saying how Bad Uncle Barin single-handedly defeated the troll in a show of strength. It wasn't exactly like that.

But something happened to Barin that made Zukei and company freeze and Shallan drop her bow. As she watched awestruck, it seemed to Shallan that Barin's face was changing; she shook her head but the image stayed with her. Gone was her friend, replaced by a huge snarling bear that tore and heaved at the troll's exposed neck.

The troll reached back and grasped Barin's beard. It tugged, and a huge blonde tuft came free. Barin let go a hand and with his fist slammed upward into the troll's nose. It landed like a missile between each nostril and made the troll sneeze.

The troll reared its head back, butting Barin in the face breaking his nose, but bear Barin didn't flinch. Instead he roared, his fury eclipsing the troll as his arms locked around its neck again and his teeth tore into its dinner plate ear.

The troll backed up against a boulder and brought his full weight against Barin, crushing him against the boulder, but Barin sank his teeth harder and the troll's ear fell off and rolled like a giant field mushroom into a rock. Barin spat out black blood and choked as the troll's weight bore down upon him, but his nail/claws tore into the troll's eyes until the creature had to lean forward, and Barin dropped to the ground, taking deep breaths.

The troll turned and swung a fist at Barin. The Northman blocked with both forearms and then shoulder charged the troll's neck. But the troll shook him loose and batted Barin's head with a paw, knocking him rolling across the rimy ground.

The troll looked about for his tree trunk but found it not. Again he tried to gain his feet. He looked puzzled by his handicap but didn't have much time to think about it as just then Zukei's skinny Karyia punctured a hole through the back of his head, the point emerging like a steel viper from inside his mouth. The troll was dead before he hit the ground.

What followed was silence and grunts of pain, these coming from Cogga who had just limped into view. Shallan took stock: Zukei stood wolf-wary over the troll's hill-heavy corpse, as if she expected him to leap back to life any minute. Taic was seated close by nursing his head, and Sveyn was dribbling and chewing his axe behind him. Barin had rolled to his knees and looked pale and battered. But at least he looked like Barin again. Gone were the bear visage and phantom claws.

Shallan shuffled across to her big friend. She gazed down at him shaking her head in wonder; sheepishly he grinned back. "Hello," he said.

"What happened to you?" Shallan was struggling for breath in the cold. "It were though a huge bear had taken your place. Barin, who are you?"

"A victim of spell craft. I'd sooner not talk about it." Shallan said nothing further as Barin gained his feet and shakily reclaimed Wyrmfang and stowed the mighty axe back in his belt loop.

"So," he said. "A troll. Who'd have believed it?"

"Caswallon?" Shallan wrapped her blanket around her shivering body. She felt utterly exhausted.

Barin shrugged. "I don't know. Trolls were rumoured to exist when I was a lad. Way up beyond the Forest of Enromer in Leeth. No one I knew had ever seen one, let alone this far south. But days grow darker, Shallan."

They rested that morning, allowing the winter sun to warm their aching bones. Miraculously no one was badly injured. Taic had a sprained ankle, Sveyn a clicking jaw and cracked lower rib. Zukei sported a long nasty looking slice under her left eye, which she insisted was nothing despite it still bleeding. And Barin had his broken nose and a mournful expression.

"I can fix that," Zukei grinned at him.

"Er, no...I'd rather you didn't." Zukei pounced on Barin before he could grumble further. She slapped her left palm against the crooked bridge of his nose whilst ramming a knuckle into the other side. There came a nasty crunch.

"Fuck!" Barin's eyes crossed and ran water for a moment then cleared. "That hurt!"

"You will mend." Zukei left him to look at Taic's ankle.

"Hello gorgeous!" Taic winked at her.

"Oh shut up," Zukei replied.

They rested until midmorning and then ventured back out onto the road. Glancing back, Shallan saw large birds circling the skies a mile away. Doubtless buzzards waiting to feast on her unfortunate countrymen below. Those birds left the troll corpse well alone. Some things were too foul even for carrion.

Their progress was slow. Taic limped and Sveyn was hurting, but by nightfall they reached a high place shouldering the mountains.

"I know this spot," said Barin who had travelled this road in his youth. "We're only a day from the city now. The road starts descending after this, before climbing and then immersing in a wood. Beyond that lies Car Carranis."

The following morning, Shallan shrugged free of her blanket and gaped at the stunning panorama. Away north, the glint of water hinted at the Gulf of Leeth, and to the west patrolled the dark hills of northern Kelthaine and the faint glimmer of what must be the River Falahine threading north to Vangaris. Southward, the road was lost beneath stone and woods. Beyond these a single tower pierced the morning sky. Car Carranis. Their destination was in sight at last. They reached the rear gates at dusk. But it was morning before anyone came to open them.

Chapter 9

A Fork in the Road

"How far is it?" Corin leaned forward in his saddle and patted Thunderhoof's neck; the big horse was sweating despite the chill. Ahead and to their left, the great slopes of The High Wall reared majestic. All about them a blue-sky day lit fields and woods to honey brown. Rorshai seemed a fair country, mostly comprising pastures, small woods and shallow valleys where tinkling rock-strewn streams hurried down from the mountains.

"We shall arrive ere nightfall if we keep up this pace." Olen's sharp eyes glanced at Corin. "How fares your horse?"

"He's knackered like me, but we've been through worse."

Olen grinned. "I dare say." It was the second day since the stand-off with the Anchai. The Red Clan rode a mile west, the hard-faced Arami setting the pace. Now and then he steered close and glared at Olen and Corin, Olen would raise hand in greeting and Arami, frosty-eyed, would turn away.

Last night they had set up rudimentary camp by a stream, the Anchai keeping their distance, but staying close enough to eavesdrop.

Olen had paid them scant heed. Instead he'd asked Corin about the days the Longswordsman had spent down in Permio—a country he'd heard much of but had never seen.

"We Rorshai are not travelers; we keep to ourselves. We are few in number and our country far ranging. That said, I myself have journeyed far." Olen had told Corin about the Seeress and his discovery east across the plains.

"Ptarni?" Corin had heard the name somewhere before, and he was alarmed of Olen's account of the warriors he'd seen. Just what they needed—more enemies. He'd slept fitfully that night, half expecting a recovered Sulo, or else the hostile Arami to emerge out the dark and stick a knife in his throat. Corin was happy to see the sun rise that morning.

They rode until noon, then stopped by a stream where the horses drank and the rival clansmen sat their beasts glaring at each other. A few dismounted and washed their faces in the stream. Corin shrugged off Thunder's back and went scrambling for some dewy grass, up by a pasture where it grew long and lush.

He had a full armful and was about to turn back when a shadow crossed his path. Arami sat his horse with bow in hand and blue gaze hostile. "You are a confident bastard, straying from the camp." Arami nocked an arrow to his bow. Corin watched him in silence. Arami grinned, then he leant back in the saddle and arced the bow skyward. He pulled back and released. Corin watched the arrow disappear into the sky.

"You might want to move," Arami smiled at him.

Corin smiled back. He counted: one, two three, four, five and a half. He dropped the grass and slid Biter free from his belt in one fluid motion, at the same time stepping backwards, then slicing hard from left to right, splitting Arami's arrow shaft in two.

Arami stared at Corin in amazement as the northerner slammed Biter back in its sheath and knelt to scoop up the grass. "You, laddie, are not in my league," Corin told him. "Now if you don't mind, my horse is hungry, so piss off." Corin wandered back to where

Thunderhoof waited with his hooves in the stream. "This is good shit," Corin told him and Thunder snorted.

"That was rash." Olen joined him. The Kaanson had been consulting with his closet men when Corin had slipped away. From a distance, he and his companions had seen what happened. Behind their leader the men gazed at Corin in awe and not a little admiration. There were looks coming from the Anchai too. Corin grinned; he liked making an impression.

"You have some skill with a blade," Olen said. "But that could have gone wrong rather easily. Arami doesn't fuck about."

"Neither do I," Corin told him. "And I've no time for tosspots trying to prove themselves to their men. If that young twit pulls another stunt I'll slice him open like a sack of meal. I've a war to fight and a lady to find." Corin hadn't mentioned Shallan before, and Olen's eyes widened with curiosity. "I'll tell you later," Corin said.

Olen was right. As the sun sank crimson behind The High Wall, the land levelled ahead and a wide open plain spread across to an outthrust of the mountains, running east for over seventy miles. "That's The Long Fend," Olen announced, pointing north at the dark slopes blocking the horizon. "A spur of The High Wall, it protects our country from what lies beyond."

"And what is that?" Corin wondered, but Olen shook his head and would say no more on the matter. Instead he guided his horse left and followed the road toward a deep cleft where the spur met the mountain chain.

"The Delve lies ahead." Corin saw that the Anchai had picked up their pace and were cantering forward away from the Tcunkai. "They want to get there first, spread the good news."

"Hadn't we better catch up?"

"No rush, the Council won't receive us until tomorrow. So tonight we can get drunk and fuck around."

"Isn't that a bit dangerous?" Corin didn't like the idea of getting drunk amongst a bunch of headhunting Anchai.

"Oh, it's what we do at the Delve. And don't worry, fighting is prohibited amongst the clans within the compound surrounding the Delve."

"I suppose that's good." Corin urged Thunder pick up his pace as the other riders began trotting towards the approaching wall of mountain ahead. "But what if some rash fellow like that Arami, or else another Soli decides to break the rules and stick a knife in you —or more likely me?"

"They won't. And it's Sulo, and yes, you will see him again. He's not a quitter, that one. But we're safe at the Delve, though not at the Council. The Council makes the rules, you see. They don't like the clans scrapping, hence any such behaviour results in the felon being stripped, lashed to four horses, and then torn apart."

Corin winced. "That's a bit harsh."

"Maybe so, but there aren't any scraps. So, friend Corin, enjoy yourself this evening amongst the clans. Learn what you can about our people but keep your wits for the morning. The Council are tricky, and most won't like you overmuch."

"Nothing new there." Corin patted Thunder's neck. "Nearly grub time old chum."

As light faded, they crossed the smooth flat plain, at last reaching the base of the mountains. Ahead Corin could see tents and what looked to be a big fence spanning across their path.

"The Horseshoe." Olen told him that was the name of the fence, as it resembled a horseshoe in shape and curved out from the rock walls in a big half circle. "Everything within lies under the jurisdiction of the Delve."

"So are we here?" Corin asked Olen as they thundered through the open gates, entering the stockade of tents and cluster beyond.

"No, this is the camp area for visitors, aides, and merchants. It's where we'll spend the night. The Delve itself lies ahead."

"Where? All I see is rock?"

"Keep looking!"

And Corin did, and just as last light faded from the plain, he saw a huge flat ledge that appeared suspended in the sky two hundred feet above the camp they were now riding through. "The Delve." Olen grinned at him. "That ledge leads to caverns where our sacred councils are held and the seers perform their rites."

"How do we get up there—fly?"

"Don't fret, there is a rope! Come Corin an Fol, these are the Tcunkai tents, reserved for my clan when at Delve. Here we will find sustenance and liquor. There are also wenches that might be interested in you, despite your appearance."

"Just an ale and natter will do fine," Corin said, staring at the ledge suspended off the mountain arm ahead. A rope to access that didn't look promising. That night, Corin tried not to enjoy himself and also tried to stay away from the harsh white stuff which Olen told him was triple fermented yak milk of finest vintage. It tasted like venom. After his third glass Corin yawned, watching the wenches dance around the fire. Two months back he'd have been dancing with them. Not a pretty sight. But Corin an Fol had changed; he now knew his wenching days were over forever. He wasn't sad, and it was still nice to look at the beautiful women for a while, at least until they all merged into one as his vision got muddy. Would that Tamersane were here though.

You are missing out, my friend.

* * *

Actually, as he currently viewed the situation, Tamersane wasn't missing out at all. The young woman, Teret, though a tad grumpy and dour, was very attentive. Her looks were tolerable, Tamersane decided, and when she smiled (this did happen occasionally - in a fierce pole-cat kind of way), she actually looked quite pretty. She did possess a sharp tongue and had a slight odour of stale horse about her. She was some healer, though.

That first day, Teret had scraped Rogan's vile ooze out of his wound. That had hurt but Tamersane hadn't shown it. For some reason he wanted to impress this woman, though he had no notion why. She'd cleaned the wound up nicely and then applied some different stuff that had stung like shit. Again he hadn't flinched—well, only a little bit. After that, she'd been checking his arm on the hour, pouring broth into his mouth, though he was perfectly capable of applying it himself, and chuntering in his ear.

Tamersane tried to remain affable, but his glib comments and witticisms were rewarded by grunts and shrugs and the occasional quizzical stare.

"You are an odd man," Teret told him one time after she'd rubbed some fresh milky ooze into his wound.

"What is that stuff?"

"A mixture of yak urine, vinegar, and milk of magnesium." Tamersane wished he hadn't asked. "It will dry up your wound and enable swift recovery, as long as you let it rest and stop messing about like you always do."

"I think you are very nice," Tamersane had told her as Teret scratched her ear, glared at him, and stormed off to feed the cows.

Such was farm life. It didn't do much for Tamersane. He'd watched folk (mostly women) passing to and fro, amid curt nods and brief comments. Behind him were tents, their canvas flapping in the breeze, whilst ahead the broad sweep of green fields melded into distant woods with The High Wall's peaks parading beyond. It was a fine view, though chilly. Tamersane had asked to be put inside, but the healing woman had said the fresh air was good for him.

As he sat there and watched morning fade into afternoon, Tamersane let his mind wander. Off to the right, a group of boys were kicking some object back and forth and yelling. Now and then one of them would punch another in the face and a fight would follow. This would lead to intervention by one of the women and usually another beating to both fighters from said woman. The men strolling about seemed intent with purpose; most were middle-aged and wore stiff beards. All ignored Tamersane.

He gazed to his left where a stockade fence hemmed in yaks (ugly great hairy things), horses and cows, and the odd sheep bleating vacant. Chickens scurried and hopped about whilst sundry lazy dogs yawned in the sunshine.

Tamersane wondered what had happened to Corin; their parting and the ride here with Rogan was all a bit vague. Even dimmer was his recollection of what had occurred on the Fallowheld, before Corin had injured him.

A dragon, or something huge that looked like a dragon, had fallen upon them together with phantom Groil, one of whom had turned out to be Corin. After that, things were even more confusing: the fall and his pain, their wandering through those creepy woods. And then that grouchy weird old man—Feroda—Tamersane barely recalled the name. Following that, a race through a tunnel full of shadows and whispers. And now this lot. The Rorshai.

They seemed friendly enough in the main. Some of the children smiled at him and the odd young woman (and a few of the older ones) gave him sly appraisal. Tamersane just sat there, nodding off, waking up, grinning at everyone, then nodding off again. Evening saw Teret striding towards him with purpose and serious stare. She had been away much longer than usual.

"You awake?" Teret's blue gaze appeared inches from Tamersane's face.

"Yes, of course," he blinked. "I was just going through things in my head. It's been a busy few weeks. Nice to get a chance to sit and peruse."

"Good." Teret cast a critical eye at his arm. "That looks better. Now you need to sharpen up, stranger, for the Kaan has demanded your presence in his tent this evening."

"The Kaan?"

"The leader of the Tcunkai Clan." Teret looked at him as though he were stupid. "Olen's father, my father too—though by a different mother."

Tamersane wasn't sure what to think about that. "What does he want with me?"

"To interview you, interrogate you—maybe torture you." The

slight twist of a smile hinted at a wicked sense of humour.

"That isn't funny."

"You need to shed those stinky clothes, ugh—you must have had them on for months. You can wash outside my tent. I'll scrub you, make sure you're respectable." She beckoned him follow her to a small tent close by the cow shed.

"Toss those clothes outside the tent." Teret pointed at the open flap. "You will find fresh ones inside. Go on...strip." Tamersane just watched her in pensive silence.

"What's the matter?"

"It's a bit exposed here," he complained. "Can't I go inside the tent to change?"

"I need to scrub you out here. Stop fussing and take off your clothes. I shall be back with hot water, soap, and bucket. I expect you to be naked when I return." Teret stomped off toward the cowshed whilst, grumbling, Tamersane did as he was told.

She returned with another young woman. Both carried buckets, whilst Teret had some evil-looking brush in her left hand. They grinned at his nakedness. The other woman looked him up and down for way too long in Tamersane's opinion. "Not bad, Teret—for a foreigner."

"This is intolerable!" Tamersane felt his face redden despite the cold. And despite the cold he was aware of a bit of action below. Both women were grinning now.

"On your knees," the other woman said. Tamersane closed his eyes and kneeled. He gasped as hot water engulfed his head and shoulders. Then the scrubbing began. To say it was ruthless was an understatement. Groil would have been gentler.

Tamersane was pink and sore when they left him to dry off and dress in the new clothes Teret had supplied. He was also acutely embarrassed, a new experience for him, and not one he'd want to repeat, particularly as not only Teret but her evil friend too had each spent several moments fumbling his privates in a most indecent way. These Rorshai women were shameless.

Teret appeared inside the tent. "Sorchei likes you," Teret told him. "I wanted a second opinion, someone experienced, and Sorchei has been married over five years, whereas I am single."

Tamersane blinked at her. Was he missing something? He was usually so smart around the fairer sex. "Oh, that's good then," he managed for want of anything better to say.

"She's a second cousin," Teret added as if that explained anything. "You ready?"

"Raring to go."

Teret raised a brow. "Good. Then follow me!"

The woman led him through a maze of tents and corrals leading up to a rise where a larger tent, supported by four tree-thick poles paraded yellow in the breeze. It was the first time Tamersane had got a proper look at the camp called Morning Hills.

The Tcunkai camp was bigger than he'd expected, a cluster of tents, fences, and timber outbuildings, and through the middle, a wide gurgling stream. Outside, a broad warrior glared at their approach, his huge tattooed arms folded, and at his side a heavy tulwar. The guard nodded at Teret and without a word pulled back the tent flaps, allowing the young woman and her companion to enter.

It was spacious inside, lamps lit the corners, and thick rugs covered the floor. Tamersane blinked and glanced about until Teret bid him sit cross-legged by a pole and wait. It was only then that Tamersane realised this tent was curtained into several parts, thus even bigger than he'd thought. Teret kneeled beside him, and together they waited in silence for several minutes.

At last a deep voice bid them enter. Teret stood with fluid grace whilst Tamersane awkwardly shambled to his feet. Ahead, the curtains were pulled back and Tamersane recognised Rogan's tough features staring at them beneath a lantern. Rogan grinned and ushered Teret and Tamersane inside the inner tent.

A large figure was seated on a broad rocking chair, smoking a pipe and fussing the floppy ears of an ancient hound that lolled sleepy at his feet. The man looked to be in his fifties, with a wide-set frame, and his heavy-set face wore a lugubrious expression. He looked at Tamersane with lazy eyes: they were shrewd jet beads, and Tamersane noted that this was the first Tcunkai he'd seen without blue eyes.

"Take your seat." The Kaan's voice was as heavy as his face. He looked bored, but Tamersane knew that laconic gaze was summing him up. "I trust your arm improves?"

Tamersane nodded, looked around for a chair and seeing none evident, took to sitting cross-legged on the rug again. Teret remained standing, as did Rogan and another thin-looking warrior who had just arrived and now glared at Tamersane in an unfriendly fashion. Tamersane smiled at the newcomer. There's always one miserable bastard.

"I'm mending fast, thanks to Teret here." Tamersane smiled at the healer, who for her part kept her cool gaze focussed on the tent wall ahead.

"She is a good healer." The Kaan puffed at his pipe and fussed his hound again. He leaned back and yawned. "Well, farlander, how best may I serve thee?"

Tamersane was a bit taken aback by the formal tones. He scratched his head. "To be honest, I'm not entirely sure. My head's in a bit of a muddle," he said after a moment. Close by, Rogan grinned and Teret flashed a smile. Meanwhile, the glaring man kept glaring. "It's been a hectic few weeks, and I don't know where to begin."

"At the beginning." The Kaan pulled at his pipe, sending a sweet aroma washing through the tent. It reminded Tamersane of Yashan, their guide in the desert, who had favoured a similar habit.

"It's a long story, and a tad complicated." Tamersane's nose itched. He was tempted to pick it but deemed this not the right time. Instead he smiled at the Kaan in vacant fashion.

"Is he soft in the head?" This from the skinny man with the hostile expression.

"A joker, I believe." The Kaan smiled ever so slightly. "And a man who hides his cunning behind a smiling mask. Relax, Dilani, not every farlander is our foe." Dilani said nothing. Neither did he relax. "My attendant has no love for strangers," the Kaan told Tamersane. "He doesn't like his own family much, come to think of it. Do you Dilani?" The Kaan chuckled slightly whilst the thin man's gaze slipped sideways. Tamersane would have to watch his back with that one, he decided. "Now," continued the Kaan, "bring sustenance and brew, there's a good fellow. We have a long evening ahead."

Throughout that night Tamersane remained crouched and very uncomfortable as he recounted events west and south of The High Wall during recent months. He started with his meeting Corin at Waysmeet Village in distant Kelthaine and continued through to their victory against the sultan down in Permio. He filled in as best he could around Corin's other adventures, as it was his friend that seemed to interest the Kaan most.

"This is the one the Seeress told Olen to await?" This to Rogan.

"Aye, Kaan, a Longswordsman and redoubtable fighter by the look of him," Rogan replied.

"That he is," added Tamersane. "The finest warrior I've ever known, though a touch grumpy on occasion." He went on to explain how Corin was cursed by visitations of various divinities and had a weird kind of death wish. The Kaan was most interested in this.

"Your friend is at the Delve. That will be touch and go, but if he is who Olen thinks he is, and how you describe him, then I daresay he'll survive their questioning. You see, Tamersane of Kelwyn," (this was the first time anyone had mentioned his name and Tamersane was a bit shocked) "we Rorshai are not overly trusting of strangers. We need to vet you out. So. Enough of this Corin. What of you, Kelwynian?"

Tamerlane shrugged. "I haven't really thought about it. But I suppose I'll head back to Kelwyn and seek out my cousin, Queen Ariane. See how she fares against the usurper in Kelthaine."

Teret's eyes widened. She hadn't known about his connection to the queen. She also looked a bit disappointed, Tamersane couldn't help noting.

"Yes, perhaps that's best." The Kaan had noted Teret's expression also. "But not until spring. It's too hazardous to cross the mountains this late in the year."

"Or else I could go and join my friend at the Delve." Tamersane glanced sideways at Teret.

"They would kill you." She pinned him with those large blue eyes. "You are not your friend."

"Then I guess I'll just have to chance the mountains in winter. They need me in Kelwyn, and there's nothing for me here."

"You are an arrogant man." Teret's eyes were daggers, but from his seat the Kaan chuckled.

"Come farlander, we've grilled you enough this evening! You must be weary. I'd have got you a chair but I wanted to see the mettle in your loins."

"Thank you."

"Go now." The Kaan waved him and Teret leave. "We will speak more over the coming days whilst we await news from the Delve concerning the Ptarnians."

"Ptarnians?" Tamersane glanced back before leaving the tent.

"An army, apparently heading this way. Good night!"

Teret walked silent beside him as Tamersane tried to gather his thoughts. It had been a peculiar few days. And now he came to think about it, he didn't have a clue what he wanted.

Kelwyn and Ariane would stand or fall despite anything he did. Sure, Corin could use his help but that seemed out of his hands now. Then that left staying here. They seemed amicable enough, apart from the hostile attendant whom he would keep two eyes on. And then there was Teret, walking silent and moody beside him.

She said not a word until they arrived at a tent. A different tent, Tamersane couldn't help noting. "Get some sleep." Teret turned and faded into the night. Tamersane ventured inside, found a nest of blankets strewn across the floor. The Tcunkai clothes he wore itched so he stripped, and within seconds was fast asleep.

Tamersane woke in alarm to the soft touch of a warm hand caressing his manhood.

What the...?

"Is it really that bad—the prospect of spending winter at Morning Hills?" Teret smiled at him from the dark.

He was about to reply but she stopped him with a kiss. After that he got quite enthusiastic. "Be mindful of that arm," Teret laughed as he pulled her close.

That following morning, Tamersane reflected that staying at Morning Hills until Spring might prove prudent. Besides, he needed to get his strength back.

Chapter 10

Greystone Bridge

"How close are they?" Ariane sat her horse next to Tarello as her captain held the glass to his left eye. The glass was a gift from Valentin that had proved invaluable thus far.

"Three miles and closing. It's going to be tight." Ariane nodded as her captain continued to scan the road behind. She knew the detachment had left Atarios but she didn't know when. It was still twenty leagues to Greystone Bridge where she had arranged, via pigeon, to meet them. Once there, their combined forces would hold the bridge against Perani, do as much damage to his army as possible, then cut and run into Raleen, hopefully tempting the enemy to follow. But, as Tarello just said, it was going to be tight.

"Ready for the next push?" Tarello shoved the glass in his belt and yelled the riders forward again, whilst Ariane gazed back along the road.

She could just about see the first riders coming into view as they raced south along the glistening ribbon of the rain-washed road. Dark-clad horsemen gaining fast. Time to get moving. If they held their pace they would reach Greystone Bridge at dusk, allowing just enough light to set their trap. Ariane doubted Perani would stop for darkness with his prize so close. She turned her horse about and urged it speed back down the hill. Once there, Queen Ariane joined the others and galloped along the Great South Way as afternoon deepened.

***

"He has done what?" Caswallon viciously hurled his wine glass at Gribble who ducked and hid behind a large urn. After a second, he dared show his goblin face again to leer at his boss. Mr Caswallon was in a rare bad mood today.

"Abandoned his post, yes, yes—I know it's naughty. Give me a break, I'm only the fucking messenger," Gribble sulked. During the last few weeks Caswallon had become more and more volatile. It was almost as bad as working for Morak, his old boss back in the good old bad days.

Morak had been prone to incinerating things that irritated him, several of which had included Soilfins. But at least he had been predictable in his nastiness. It was consistent. This mortal wizard was all moods and scowls with the occasional treat sent his way.

Trouble was, Caswallon was obsessed with three things. First, acquiring the spear Golganak, which Gribble was familiar with and didn't really want to see again—ghastly thing that it was. Second, crushing Kelthara, and they had rebelled again a few days ago and now appeared to have a more concerted leadership. The Groil Caswallon sent had been slaughtered, and his new boss was beside himself with fury.

The third issue was Bitch-Queen Ariane, who continued to evade Mr Caswallon's generals—dim lot that they were, in Gribble's astute military opinion. Derino had messed up big time, and now Perani seemed to be losing the plot—abandoning his post and all. Bound to piss the boss off that. Mr Caswallon employed the wrong people. Gribble had considered putting his name forward for general but hadn't wanted the responsibility.

Gribble had just got back from the Perani camp, which had been almost deserted, save for a few guards. He'd flown on to Wynais, but that wasn't much fun because he wasn't allowed to eat anyone in that city—part of the tenuous arrangement between Caswallon and the turncoat Tolranna (though things would change shortly, Caswallon had informed him with one of his rare smiles). So Gribble decided it best to watch and wait, at least for the time being.

Caswallon, ignoring Gribble, slunk back in The Glass Throne, his coaly eyes smouldering like hot acid. Gribble, deeming his timing right, grinned and hopped over to snatch a fresh wine glass from the crystal bench gathering dust to the throne's right. He twirled the decanter daintily with his claws and filled two generous glasses, taking the first to Caswallon.

"Perani better succeed else I'll have his head on a plate. I will not be gainsaid, Goblin."

"Of course not. You are the boss. Perani needs to shape up. If I were he I'd —"

Caswallon raised a hand as though he was swatting an invisible fly. "I do not need your counsel, Goblin."

Gribble looked pained. "Well, you know I'm always here for you. You haven't got many friends Mr Caswallon. But please don't call me goblin."

Caswallon's face softened. "You are loyal, yes. And I do appreciate that, Gribble." Gribble purred like a malfunctioning engine. "And yes, I am misunderstood—always have been. It's just that someone strong has to take the helm. Rule the realms and maintain order. Kelsalion was weak—he had to go. By having him murdered I was merely being proactive."

A dark cloud settled outside, accompanied by the noise of something heavy crashing into the wall. Somewhere close by glass shattered and voices screamed.

Caswallon paled. *Not again!* He'd just had the roof repaired.

For his part Gribble slipped behind The Glass Throne and stared bug-eyed at the winged shape manifesting outside the window like a thousand-ton bat. Vaarg the dragon was paying another social call.

Caswallon shrank back in The Glass Throne as Vaarg's huge triangular head smashed through the double doors opening into the throne room, knocking them free of their hinges and onto the floor.

"I'M BACK."

"So I see." Caswallon gripped the throne's crystal arms with his bony fingers and somehow held his nerve. "Do you always have to be so bloody destructive?" Last time the dragon dropped by, it had cost him a roof. This time it looked like the entire iron wall of the palace had fallen in alongside the doors. Caswallon shivered as the chilly breeze found him from outside.

"I FOUND YOUR REBELS, WARLOCK."

"Did you grill them to charcoal?" Caswallon maintained hold of his wine glass and just managed to get the contents down his throat before the dragon replied, his great voice shaking the ceiling and sending a crystal chandelier crashing to the floor.

"NO. MY BELLY IS NOT HEATED YET. I'VE ONLY BEEN AWAKE A FORTNIGHT. IT TAKES TIME TO REACH THE CORRECT SETTING. BUT I GAVE THEM A FRIGHT ALL THE SAME."

"I would have preferred if you'd grilled them."

Gribble stuck his head out from the side of the throne. "It would have been better, yes, they are very dangerous." He ducked back out of view when the dragon's dinner plate eyes turned his way.

"I STOPPED BY TO INFORM YOU OF YOUR ENEMY'S IDENTITY."

"Go on."

Vaarg's tongue flicked out across the room, knocking the decanter off the chest and spilling claret on the expensive carpet. Caswallon winced, whilst Gribble scurried over to lick up the mess.

"ARALLOS THE GOLDEN. HE HAS RETURNED."

"That's not possible. The Aralais are gone, Morak told me so." Caswallon paled. No wonder he'd been blocked in his mission to crush the little queen and find the missing prince. An Aralais. No—the Aralais. Arollas the Golden was the greatest sorcerer of his time, though that was over a thousand years ago.

Vaarg's massive eyes mocked the mortal wizard now shivering on his stolen throne. "IT IS OF SMALL ACCOUNT. I HAVE VOWED TO OBLITERATE HIM AT THE APPOINTED TIME."

"Oh, that's good," Gribble muttered, now safely back behind the throne.

Vaarg ignored him. "ANY NEWS OF THE SPEAR?"

"I'm working on that." Caswallon's mind was everywhere.

"WORK HARDER. I WILL RETURN ONCE I'VE RESTED, AND I WILL BRING MY FIRE."

"Something to look forward to," Gribble couldn't help saying as Vaarg's huge head retreated back through the hole in the wall it had created. Minutes later, dark wings drummed the sky, and the shadow of the dragon vanished from the afternoon. Caswallon stared at Gribble and the goblin stared back; neither enjoyed these unannounced visits from the dragon.

"I met him on that boat before I got skewered." Gribble chewed a nail thoughtfully.

"What?"

"That Arallos fellow. Thought I'd recognised him from somewhere. Very tall. Got big blue scary eyes."

"Why didn't you report that back to me?'

"I forgot."

Caswallon pulled his cloak tighter around his shoulders and bid the goblin go get a flask of brandy - something stronger than wine was called for now. When Gribble returned, the goblin and his master sat staring at the hole in the wall. He'd have to get the builders back. Just another day in Kella City.

Meanwhile, in the south, Perani sensed victory was close.

***

"We must cut them off before they reach that bridge!" Perani yelled in Gonfalez's ear. The general and his second stared down from the hill as their troops filed by, rank upon rank of spear carrying hard-faced former Tigers. A mile ahead his cavalry— two thousand strong—were closing on the queen's pathetic force, just visible in the distance.

Perani was anxious. Light was fading fast, and they should have caught up with Ariane by now, but somehow the little minx had stayed ahead. It was though she was tempting him on, or else playing him for a fool. Perani had the nasty feeling trickery lay ahead, but he calmed his nerves and snatched the spyglass off his second.

What could possibly go wrong? The little queen was running scared, hoping to reach Raleen. And so what if she did? Raleenians wouldn't help lest they brought down the wrath of Caswallon. Nope, thought Perani, this irritating business would be sorted inside an hour—two at most. He cast an urgent eye at Gonfalez, who nodded and together they filed down to re-join the rest of the army below.

***

Ariane urged her beast to greater speed. Beside her, Tarello yelled encouragement at the riders following, amongst them Cale and Galed, pale-faced and ready for this day to be over. To the west, the sun sank like a huge brandy ball behind the shoulder of a rock. Ahead, the rush of water on stone announced they drew close to the River Glebe, where Kelwyn bordered Raleen.

Directly ahead, and clearly visible despite the rapidly fading light, Ariane spotted the stone walls marking Greystone Bridge, the only safe place to cross the Glebe between mountain and ocean. She spurred her mare on one last time. "Go girl—we're almost there!"

Ariane's riders clattered onto Greystone Bridge just as Perani's vanguard thundered close behind. She gazed about wide-eyed; there was no sign of any Raleenians, and away south the road dwindled empty into evening.

Ariane cursed and dismounted, allowing her beast respite. "Form a shield wall!" she yelled. "We have to hold the bridge for as long as we can!" Tarello leaped down from his horse and shouted orders as the Kelwynians and Jaan's Raleenian Lancers hastened to block the bridge from the approaching foe. The general's first riders were scarce a hundred yards distant. In the fourth row, his ginger head buffeted by shields and the armour of his companions, Cale felt a little bit sick. It seemed very apparent that they were about to receive another hiding.

"Keep your sword low and shield high," Galed hissed in his ear, though Cale knew what to do, and in his opinion was a much more accomplished warrior than his friend.

He grinned at Galed. "Here we go again!" Then Perani's force fell upon them in a clash of steel, screams, and kicking horses.

***

"Order those horsemen about!" Perani growled. It was useless wasting cavalry where his foot soldiers would serve better. "They're trapped," he snarled at Gonfalez. "If they break and run, the horse boys can have another go, run them down the other side of the river. If they prefer to stay on the bridge, we'll fill them with arrows."

Gonfalez nodded and shouted an officer to order the archers to get ready. "They cannot hold long, General! See, even now our boys are forcing them back." As Perani watched, his cavalry wended back up toward where he and his staff waited on the hill.

Down at the bridge, he could make out the dark figures of his spearmen making ground onto the bridge. It was tough fighting down there, but it would soon be over.

Perani smiled for the first time that week. At last the situation was playing into his hands. The smile ran away from his face when a huge explosion rocked the left wall of Greystone Bridge, sending stone crashing down into the hurrying Glebe below.

"What the fuck just happened?" Gonfalez yelled in his ear. Perani didn't respond because down at the bridge all manner of craziness was going on.

***

Cale shrank back as the weight of the press pushed him and his companions further back along the bridge. The queen's men had done well. Cale couldn't see from where he was, but there were over two hundred ex-Tiger veterans gored and bleeding at the north end of the bridge.

The alliance had taken casualties, too. Although the Raleenians' lance work and their stoic defence taking advantage of the bridge's limited width had served them well, three score had fallen, and double that amount bore wounds, including Tarello, whose face was torn by a large gash that impaired his vision and forced him to clamber back through the ranks to seek aid.

Jaan stood with the last of his Raleenians. Just over a dozen lived yet. As at Calprissa, they'd taken the brunt of the fighting. Cale could hear Jaan yelling and urging his men stand their ground despite the overwhelming odds crushing down against them.

Someone took a hit to Cale's right. A big Kelwynian, he crashed down on Cale with an axe buried in his head. Cale rolled, somehow got back to his feet. He saw a warrior leap through, dressed in black and wielding a short handled battle-axe in one hand and a mace in the other.

Galed leapt across the big warrior's path. The man swatted down with his mace, sending Cale's friend and mentor sprawling. Cale screamed in rage. The ex-Tiger turned toward him, his mace already swinging. Cale trapped the weapon with his shield, yelling as a sharp pain lanced through his arm from the jolt. He clenched his teeth and thrust hard at the enemy's face.

"Bastard!" Cale spat at his foe and the warrior rounded on him again, this time with the axe. Guttersnipe instinct and speed saved Cale that day. He dived low, somehow kept the sword in his hand, and as he fell, Cale twisted and shoved the blade hard up, stabbing the big man in the balls.

The ex-Tiger yammered and pitched to the ground, soon to be

crushed and trampled by his companions, who were on the verge of breaking through the Kelwynian defence.

Cale gulped and closed his eyes. Somewhere near he heard a woman shout, and he smiled, knowing that his queen still lived. But not for long, thought Cale—not for long. That thought hardened him.

"No!" Cale wrenched his eyes open. "It's not going to end like this!" He tried to tug the sword free from the corpse's body but got buffeted sideways. He stood, tripped, and rolled again. For the briefest second Cale saw Galed's pale face beneath a tide of rushing feet.

Cale yelled again, then a blast like thunder shook the bridge, jolting Cale forward until he crashed into the side of the stone wall. Another blast ripped through the bridge, but Cale didn't hear that one because he'd already lost consciousness.

***

Prince Tarin jumped and clung on to his ears as another one of Zallerak's blasts sent stone and men flying everywhere. Beside him the wizard was grinning like a madman. "I love pyrotechnics!" Zallerak yelled at him as he tossed a third one at the mangled panicking mess that was Perani's prized veterans fleeing the bridge.

"You're killing our friends too!" Tarin shouted back at Zallerak who was rolling another "grenade," as he called it between his palms and getting ready to hurl it.

"Shit happens." Zallerak grinned at Tarin as he threw the grenade. Another loud blast, and a large part of the nearside wall of Greystone Bridge crumpled away and pitched like fiery meteors into the tossing Glebe far below.

"They would all be slaughtered by now if it weren't for me. Sometimes you just have to make sacrifices for the greater cause."

"But don't you even care?" Tarin had never seen Zallerak like this before; it was like some random, reckless joy was eating him. Meanwhile, on the bridge and banks surrounding, darkness had fallen, delivering total chaos.

"Stop!" A woman's voice yelled from close by. Tarin glanced up at the bridge and saw his cousin Queen Ariane staring daggers down at them. "Zallerak, you've done enough! Let the archers pick them off from the south bank!"

Tarin was not sure what had happened, but it seemed evident that Ariane had some how linked up with the Raleenian reinforcements and already detailed their archers to get some arrows moving.

"Oh, very well." Zallerak rubbed his hands free of the acrid dust clinging to them. "Greeting, Queen Ariane, lucky I happened along—heh?"

"You could have warned us." Ariane was striding toward where Zallerak stood on the south bank, now surrounded by archers from Atarios, all busy launching shafts into the fleeing dark mass spilling out onto the north bank. They didn't really have to aim, as there were thousands of men trapped over there.

Perani answered with his own archers, but these couldn't see anything, and most of their shafts hit their own men too. At last, the general had to order them stop. As night dwindled, so did the fighting, and it wasn't until dawn that anyone either side of the river could make sense of what had happened.

***

At first light, Perani was rewarded by a sight that made his stomach growl: the corpses of his soldiers strewn in piles surrounding the north bank. Most had fallen victim to arrows, many fired by his own men. The bridge beyond was a mess of bodies and broken stone. It still stood, but a large chunk of its west wall had disappeared into the river.

None of this concerned Perani. What did concern him most passionately was the lack of any enemies on the far bank. Not a soul stood there. It were though his men had been torn apart by an army of ghosts. Ariane and her renegade army had disappeared. His returning scouts had already informed him the road south was empty.

"What do we do now?" Was it Perani's imagination, or was his second smirking? Perani stared hard and long at Gonfalez until the other dropped his gaze.

"We cross that bridge before it topples into the river," Perani said. "Then we find that little queen and we kill her."

An hour later, Perani's force crossed Greystone Bridge and filed into Raleen. The die had been cast. There was no going back now. Perani knew Caswallon would have his hide for abandoning Kelwyn, but what choice was there? He had lost nearly five hundred men at Greystone Bridge, barely a dent in his huge army, but still a deep dent in his pride.

This was personal now. There was no other place for Ariane to cross the river, and if she hadn't fled for Atarios (and his scouts insisted she hadn't), then that left two choices: the sea or the mountains. The ocean was too far, so that meant the mountains.

During the next week, Perani lost another three hundred men to archers hiding above in rocks. He did get close enough to see they were Raleenians. So the bastards had allied against him. So be it. The hunt was closing. Perani led his force deeper into the folds of The High Wall and winter's worst.

Chapter 11

The Walls of Car Carranis

They waited beneath the shroud of pines and stared morosely at the huge grey walls ahead. Nothing stirred save the odd crow arcing and barking through leaden morning skies. Silence. No sign of movement on the walls above, and the gates remained locked. It was colder than yesterday, and all of them were stiff and battered after the business with the troll.

At last Barin could take no more. His patience shredded by cold and grumpiness, he stormed out of the cover of trees where they'd spent that chilly unexpected night.

"Car Carranis, this is Barin of Valkador! Let us in before we freeze out here, quickly else I'll tear your gates apart and break some heads! Bastards," he added under his breath, then turned and grumbled his way back to where Shallan watched shivering with the others.

To Shallan, it seemed to be getting colder by the minute, then when she felt the soft wet kiss of the first snow flake dampen her cheek, she decided she too had had enough.

"I'll deal with this." Shallan gave Barin a flat look and then clambered up on a rock awarding a better view of the bleak line of wall ahead.

"What's she doing?" Taic's expression was mournful.

"What she should have done an hour ago," Zukei replied. "I could be by a warm fire eating sausages instead of freezing next to you tosspots."

Shallan untied the horn from her belt and hoisted it to her lips. She blew once, long and clear, sending a score of rooks chattering into the grey above.

No one came, so Shallan blew again. After six more blasts and a resulting hoarse throat, she was relieved to see the tiny figure of a guard or someone running along the walls.

"Hey you—Buttitch!" yelled Barin. "Hurry up!" But it was still another two hours before they opened the gates.

***

From the walls of the Car Carranis, Lord Starkhold surveyed the enemy camp as he always did during the morning hours. No great change. The only real difference was that now the entire Gap of Leeth was filled with tents instead of only half.

A month had passed since the barbarians had arrived, and bar the odd shouting match, nothing of any great import had happened.

King Haal appeared content with his earlier plan to wait this game out, starve the city, and break through when the defenders were too weak to put up a fight. Since that first attack he'd realised the archers could make a mess of his warriors.

Leethmen didn't like getting skewered by arrows. A sword in the gut or a knife through the throat, that was a warrior's death. Archers were cowards, and to perish by an arrow was considered ignoble. Hence he'd received few ready volunteers. Not that King Haal and his sons were in any great rush to sack Car Carranis; they'd already enjoyed a month of wenching, drinking, and torturing any poor strays still roaming the countryside. They knew they had only to wait and the city's resolve would crack like an eggshell under the strain.

Starkhold knew it too. Time was an iron chain dragging his people down. His expression dour, he lifted the flask of brandy to his mouth and sipped small sips. It was all about control. Discipline. Their stocks were fine for now, but he'd rationed his men and so needed to set a good example. Besides, Starkhold rarely partook. But this morning was damp and chilly with fresh wet snow whitening the skies. A soul-sapping brandy morning, thought Starkhold, as he took a second sip then stopped when shouting announced another coming his way.

Captain Ralian, his second in command, was sprinting toward him.

"What is it?" Starkhold's eyes narrowed. Ralian looked excited.

"There are people at the back gate, and apparently a lady blowing a horn." Ralian smiled thanks when his leader offered him a shot of brandy.

"So? A few refugees survived the hazards of the passes. What of it?"

"They are not refugees, Lord. A guard heard the horn blasting from the woods. Some racket he said. The fellow took a look and reported back that a huge barbarian was yelling to be let in."

Starkhold looked alarmed. So the enemy had found the secret door, despite his scouts' attempts to keep it hidden. This was grave news indeed. "One of Haal's sons."

"That's what I feared," Ralian smiled fiercely. "But it's not so."

"Go on."

"The guard reported to his team leader - Porlos, I think it was. Anyway, Porlos or someone sent a squad to the back gate to investigate. They challenged the strangers outside, and after hearing their story reported back to me. There are only half a dozen or so, two of whom are women."

"Well?" Starkhold was getting impatient. It wasn't like Ralian to vex him with small news. "I fail to see the significance of —"

"I gave out word to let them inside," Ralian blurted.

Starkhold's expression darkened. "That was rash, captain."

"I don't believe so, Lord. One of the men is Barin of Valkador, and the woman blowing the horn, the Lady Shallan of Morwella."

"I see." Starkhold took a longer sip at his brandy. "Well, you've certainly piqued my curiosity, Ralian. I shall have to call in on these new arrivals. Where are they now?"

"In the barbican at the far side. The other woman—a wild thing apparently—insisted on being fed at once."

Starkhold scratched his ear. Never a dull moment in Car Carranis lately. But this did change things. Barin of Valkador, of all people. Starkhold (who had spent a deal of time in Leeth during his younger years as a mercenary) knew the story of how Barin and Daan Redhand had become bitterest of blood foes, both vowing to carve a blood eagle on the other's back. A half-smile cracked his lips apart. Played right, this might yet prove useful.

Barin of Valkador's presence in the city could be just the spark to prompt the Leethmen into doing something rash. And Shallan of Morwella? He'd thought her dead alongside her father back in Vangaris, and yet here she was at Car Carranis, alive and well, and with Barin of Valkador of all people. Strange. Starkhold sighed as he remembered what had happened just a week earlier. It would not be easy telling the noblewoman about her brothers.

***

Shallan watched in wary silence as the three men entered the room. The first was a hawk-eyed officer, his apparel precise and his armour gleaming. This one looked like a coiled spring, his eyes hungry for news. The second man was clearly a guard, helmeted, clad in mail, and hefting a long halberd across his left shoulder.

The third man was different. Small in build, whip-lean, and erudite, his manner both confident and stiff. Dark eyes and weathered face marked him as a southerner, Raleenian most likely. He wore a blue cloak over battered mail, his lips were narrow, and his eyes held that world-weary, knowing look.

Here, thought Shallan, was a coil that had long lost its spring. His hair was dark with a dusting of grey like ashen dead fire. His beard was short and precise. It was this one who addressed them first.

"I am Starkhold." The dark shrewd gaze swept over them with cool curiosity. "I am in charge of this stronghold."

"I remember you." Barin leaned against the wall, his massive arms folded. "I saw you in Grimhold long ago. Mercenary you were then, as I recall."

"That was then, Lord Barin. And yes, I remember you too, as the fiery giant from Valkador who so upset the young princes of Leeth." Starkhold smiled ever so slightly.

"Not without just cause," Barin growled.

"That I do not doubt." Starkhold's cool eyes studied the companions: three Northmen lounged in chairs close to the fire; close by, a wild-looking young woman, with eyes like coal and skin deep nut brown, looked on in unfriendly fashion. A killer this one, Starkhold had no doubt. The other woman needed no introduction. Rumour of Shallan's pale beauty had reached Car Carranis years ago.

"You have eaten, I trust, and are rested?" He didn't wait for a response. "I'm intrigued, not only by how you got here, but perhaps even more by why you chose to come. Car Carranis is under siege."

"Not the back door, apparently." Barin was still sore about being left outside.

"We abandoned this side of the stronghold, needing all our men elsewhere. You will see what I mean when you enter the fortress main, some four miles south."

"Four miles?" Shallan was astounded.

"Even so, Lady Shallan." Starkhold's cool gaze rested on her for a moment then flitted back to Barin. "So. Do tell me why you chose to come to Car Carranis to die."

Shallan crossed her arms and awarded Starkhold a bleak look. "We do not intend to die, General. We have come through a lot, seen the ashes of Vangaris, and fought battles in the south. This fortress will hold, Starkhold!"

"Will it?" Starkhold raised a brow. "I admire your confidence, my lady. That might change when you gaze out from our southern walls."

"How many of my people are here? Tell me, General. Did any survive the slaughter in Morwella? And," she paused, "what of my brothers, live they yet?"

Starkhold shrugged. He settled into a chair next to the fire, facing the three Northmen who watched him in silence. Behind him, officer and soldier shuffled and waited.

"This is difficult for me." Starkhold rubbed his hands close to the flames. "There are many Morwellans here. Too many, if truth be told, as they need feeding and most are either too young and too old to fight, or else women and therefore unable to do so."

"Some women fight, old man," Zukei spat like a lynx from the corner. Starkhold acknowledged her with another shrug.

"I daresay, but my point is we have too many mouths to feed in this city."

"What of my brothers?" Shallan, like Zukei, had decided not to like this Starkhold over much.

"I was coming to that. They are fled."

"Fled? They are not cowards!"

"No. But they are fools. The three led a party of good fighting men from my walls under cover of darkness, against my strictest orders, their aim being to take out the king himself, thus cut off the head of the beast. I warned them against such a rash and foolish venture. Despite my words, they stole from the city and took a hundred fighting men with them."

"Well, what became of them?" Shallan had that crushing feeling that she already knew the answer.

"We're not sure," put in the young officer, who appeared much more sympathetic than his overlord. "Though we suspect they've been captured, my lady. They're brave lads and fiery too, and when they saw what those bastards did to that girl..."

"What girl?" Shallan's stomach was turning and she was feeling faint. Just when she thought her heart had taken all the hits it could. Now this.

"They tortured a poor lass outside the walls. A score or so took part. It —"

"Enough Ralian, such details are irrelevant. This is war." Starkhold's hard face revealed nothing. This Starkhold was one cold bastard, Shallan decided.

"But we don't know they're dead, do we?" Barin loomed from the wall. Like Shallan and Zukei, he had no fondness for Starkhold's attitude.

"They are alive for certain," Starkhold replied. "Haal will pick a time to end their lives, doubtless in front of the walls for all to see. Such is the way he plays things thus far. I am sorry, my lady. But truth will out."

"Then we rescue them!" Zukei snapped at the general.

"And join them on the gallows pole," Starkhold laughed without mirth. "You are a naïve girl."

Zukei's left hand found her kariya's hilt and she tugged, but Shallan stopped her.

"Enough Zukei! The general is right; such rash action would merely play into the enemy's hands. Now kindly leave me, all of you! I need time to be alone!" Zukei looked askance at Shallan, whilst Barin hung his shoulders and the other men looked awkward. Starkhold nodded and rose from the fire.

"Take your time. Ralian and this soldier will accompany you to the fortress main when you are ready. They will wait within earshot. I take my leave from you for the time being." Without further word Lord Starkhold turned briskly on his heels, raised his hand, and bid his men follow him out the room.

After a few awkward moments, Taic nudged Sveyn's arm, and together with Cogga, the three slunk out into the corridor that led to the barbican where Captain Ralian and the guard had pulled up chairs beside a table.

"Fancy a game of dice?" The captain asked them. This Ralian at least was making an effort, thought Taic, as he pulled a chair alongside.

Barin looked at Zukei who shrugged and made to leave the room.

"No stay, both of you please." Shallan bade them take seats with her by the fire. "I need your thoughts and wanted that...man out of the room. I do not like him."

"He's a bastard," nodded Zukei seizing a chair and grinning at Shallan, happy to be part of her conspiracies.

"He is, however a fine tactician and reputable soldier." Barin squatted into a chair way too small for his girth. It was a sight that made Zukei giggle like a girl and Shallan manage a wan grin. "Bloody thing's uncomfortable," Barin snorted. "Well lady, what are you thinking—how to rescue your brothers?"

"There has to be a way, Barin. You and Zukei have taught me how to fight. There has to be a way to save them. But I don't want Starkhold to know."

"He'll not know from us," hissed Zukei. "Let me go, I can slip inside their camp under the cover of darkness, silence their guards and lead them out. Such contracts were once my profession."

"I know, but if we do this, we do it together," Shallan said. "They've been gone a week. That's a long time to be a captive of Leeth. You saw what Redhand did in Vangaris."

"I know Redhand, Shallan. He will not damage your brothers permanently. Starkhold's right about that much. Redhand and his father will use them at some key point in some foul manner. Until then, I suspect they have them strung up for sport somewhere in their camp."

"Which is small comfort, Barin." Shallan struggled to her feet. "Spread the word to Cogga and the others. We'll discuss this further tonight once we know the lay of this city. And Barin...make sure Taic and Sveyn keep their lips together."

"They will," Barin assured her, and feeling slightly better, the three left the room and were met by Ralian and co in the barbican.

"Ready to see the city, my lady?" Ralian flashed her a grin.

"Ready as I'll ever be, Captain. Lead on!" And so they began the long cold trudge back to the inner walls of Car Carranis.

She'd always assumed Car Carranis was huge, but the reality was beyond her wildest imagination. Ralian (whose empathy and social skills were in pleasant contrast to his commander's) informed her that the entire rear side of the city had been abandoned for nearly a hundred years.

When Starkhold arrived, one of his first acts had been to destroy the empty buildings that spread between the outer rear walls and the inner walls, thereby creating a killing zone. Should any enemy (very unlikely as few folk even knew it existed) find the back gate and break through, they would be exposed and trapped by archers watching from the inner wall.

During the long peace of the Tekara, Car Carranis's population had depleted, as most folk preferred the warmer climes around Kella City and Kelthara. So what remained was a third of the original fortress city, the walls of which were now looming ahead.

"We scarcely patrol the outer wall," Ralian explained as they approached the second barbican that led into the occupied part of the city. "I send a scout out every now and then just in case any of the bastards have found a way up to the gate. It's sheer from the east and west, with the only access across the mountains. We've had some refugees find that door like yourselves, but most came before the horde arrived outside the main gates."

Shallan explained that Barin, who was striding ahead of them, had known about the back gate from earlier days, but had expected it to be manned.

"We are spread too thin." Ralian smiled sadly at Shallan. "I'm sorry that you come to us at such a time, my lady."

"I appreciate that Captain. I would that your general shared those sentiments."

"Judge not Lord Starkhold too harshly. He is a good man. Strong, though pragmatic and dour. He has seen much horror in his time, and little surprises him."

"And he will doubtless see more yet. Lead on!"

As the inner barbican loomed close, Shallan saw evidence of earthworks, trenches, and all manner of spikes and barbed wires, strewn about to slow an invading force. Ahead of the walls, a wide muddy moat with floating ice covered the ground from east to west. Its eastern end was stopped by the base of a mountain wall; the west end was walled by stone, outside of which there was a sheer fall of two hundred feet.

A large drawbridge spanned the moat leading through to a heavy portcullis, with murder holes and arrow slots all forming part of this second and much larger barbican. Barin strode toward the drawbridge like thunder. A guard yelled challenge but Ralian raised his hand and Barin's pace remained unchecked.

"What's with him?" Zukei asked Taic as they walked behind Shallan and the captain.

"He wants to see the enemy camp," Taic said. "Uncle Barin gets a bit stressed when he knows Redhand's about."

"What happened between those two?"

"It's a long story—I'll tell you one day." They watched as Barin's bulk disappeared inside the barbican. Minutes later Shallan, Zukei, and Barin's men followed Ralian and the guard through the barbican and arrived in winter sunlight to gaze on the city of Car Carranis.

Shallan's first impression was how stark and bleak it looked. She remembered Calprissa with its gardens, harbor, and white glistening walls. Car Carranis was greyer and grimmer than any place she'd encountered. There was scant beauty here. But there was strength.

Everywhere she looked, Shallan saw barracks, paddocks studded with archery butts, and fighting pits. She saw stables and tanneries and taverns and armouries—all the drab grey of winter cloud.

Ahead loomed the great walls that famously overlooked the Gap of Leeth. To her left, a mile away at least, a shoulder of mountain shielded the city from attack, whilst on the other side, the walls terminated at a natural cliff face, a sheer drop of over two hundred feet, looking down on the tiny ribbon of the main route threading between the city and distant Vangaris—the way they would have come in more peaceful times.

As Shallan walked beside Ralian, she was aware of many eyes watching her. Not only soldiers, gazing curious from street and tavern, but civilians too. Most she suspected were her countrymen; these gaped wide-eyed at Barin and then at her and her friends.

At last she reached the base of the great wall. Looking up, Shallan saw that Barin had almost reached the ramparts over sixty feet above.

Ralian rested a polite hand on her shoulder. "Are you sure you are ready for this, my lady? It's not an easy sight to digest."

"I want to see what we are up against, Captain."

"Very well, but mind your feet on the steps, some are quite worn." Zukei's dark eyes flashed at Shallan who smiled slightly in return. Clearly Captain Ralian was unaware of whom he addressed. Shallan was a huntress these days, not a "my lady." It was a humourous moment in an otherwise bleak, scary day.

Snowflakes danced around Shallan's face as she crested the parapet walls and joined Barin to gaze in horror on the army waiting below.

"Looks busy," Taic said as he joined them. Shallan felt her heart shrink inside her chest like a fragile bird trapped in a shrinking cage. She hadn't know what to expect, but the sheer magnitude of what massed below drove the new warrior inside her far away for a good few minutes. Zukei's face was arid.

"Take a long time to kill that lot," she said.

"There must be a million murderers down there." Shallan steadied herself against the parapet wall. How could they ever survive these odds?

"Nope." Barin awarded her a savage grin. "'Tis only a hundred thousand or so, don't fret, lass!"

"But this fortress—mighty though it is—cannot hold back that storm, Barin. That's only common sense. I realise now that I've brought you all here to die, as Starkhold said. I'm sorry—I really am." Shallan felt giddy as a wave of fear, loathing, and dread washed through her.

Barin rested a meaty hand on her shoulder. "You're too hasty lady. I'm not planning on dying here and nor should you be. Not dying yet—eh, Taic...Sveyn?"

"Nope," Sveyn grunted whilst Taic grinned at his uncle. "Not until I've learnt to beat you at dice!"

"What say you, Zukei?"

"Death is just another gateway." The dark-woman shrugged as if the question was irrelevant. "Everyone passes through, and even the gods must fade in time. What matters is how you shine during the time you're here. That said, I do not intend to die on the end of some fat barbarian's sword."

"Oh, well that's good." Barin looked a bit puzzled by the extent of Zukei's answer; he'd been expecting nothing more than a grunt. He smiled at Shallan. "You see, no one else in this little crew is planning on ending their days at Car Carranis. So stop moping, lass. Instead let's find a dark quiet place where we can discuss in private how to rescue your reckless brothers."

Shallan reached up on her tiptoes and kissed Barin's beard. "Thank you," she said.

Afternoon waned and snow settled on the camp inside, whilst beyond the walls and all across the Gap of Leeth, dark fires blazed like a million eyes winking around the tents of the Leethmen. Shallan gazed out on the enemy for over an hour. Barin had departed below for ale, as had Taic and the others. Zukei remained, though she said little. Shallan's peruse was interrupted by a small voice.

"You're pretty." A girl stood behind her, perhaps nine or ten years old. She was dressed shabbily and looked thinner than she should. Despite that, her eyes were large and blue and her smile rather cheeky.

"Hello." Shallan reached down and parted the girl's tawny thatch so she could better see her face. "And so are you!" Shallan winked at the girl who giggled back. "What's your name, sweetheart?"

"Sorrel."

"That's a pretty name too."

"It's a plant," the girl snorted as though she didn't approve of being named after a plant. "What's your name?"

"I am called Shallan."

"Is that a plant too?"

"It might be—I'm not sure."

"She's a very special lady. And an important one too." Zukei's dark eyes flashed warning at the girl.

Sorrel blinked and hopped back when she saw Zukei. "You're scary." Sorrel didn't look scared however. "Not from ,round here, are you? You look half savage."

"Cheeky little bitch." Zukei made to swipe the girl, but Sorrel jumped sideways and stuck her tongue out, and Zukei laughed at her. "You are a little survivor—I'll give you that."

"Where are your parents, Sorrel?" Shallan licked a finger, leaned down and wiped a smudge of muck from the girl's left cheek. "That's better."

"Dead." Sorrel glared back at her.

"I'm sorry, sweetheart. My parents are dead too. Have you any family here?"

The girl shook her head. Later, Shallan discovered that she had been one of a large party of Morwellan refugees that had fled the countryside south of Vangaris during the raids by Hagan's mercenaries before the arrival of the Leethmen. Sorrel's family had been murdered during that time, a debt Shallan vowed she would repay Hagan Delmorier, should ever she see him again.

"Well, Sorrel, how would you like to shoot a bow and throw knives and punch things that attack you?"

"Very much!" Sorrel grinned up at Shallan, revealing a missing tooth.

"Good!" Shallan winked at Zukei. "Can you show this one some tricks?"

"Excuse me?" Zukei wasn't impressed by Shallan's proposition. "I'm not a fucking magician."

"That's rude!" Sorrel pointed a grubby finger at Zukei.

"Yep, and you had better get used to it if you want to be a warrior and not a little madam." And so things passed, until evening found Shallan and Zukei huddled in the gloomy corner of a tavern with Barin, Cogga, and the other two. As for young Sorrel, she was in her cot down by the stables. Her dreams that night were fighting dreams of warrior maidens despatching big hairy men with sharp pointy things.

Meanwhile, in the far corner of the tavern, Barin clung to his tankard like a broody hen, his face despondent and wan. "There has to be a way to get outside these walls without anyone noticing."

"Fly?" Zukei suggested unhelpfully.

"And we can hardly bribe the guards at the main gate. They're all shit scared of Starkhold." Cogga looked miserable too. Everyone was for a night raid on the enemy camp. A bold cunning plan to rescue Shallan's brothers and maybe gut a few Leethmen too. But it wasn't a promising start when they couldn't find a way out of the fortress without waving a flag announcing their departure.

Shallan felt weary and sleepy. She glanced about the gloomy tavern. It was one of three taverns in this part of the fortress, and like the others, mostly empty due to soldier duties being doubled and Starkhold's rationing of ale. Barin was still grumpy about having been restricted to two pints only, which he had complained to the proprietor wasn't enough to wet his lips.

As they hunched brooding, Shallan noticed a hooded figure sipping ale at the far end of the room. She hadn't noticed him before, and it looked like he'd just come in from the cold. The man caught her eye and grinned at her, and Shallan recognised Captain Ralian.

"I think we've been rumbled," she said, rubbing her tired eyes. It was depressing to know that there was nothing she could do to help her brothers. Barin and Cogga's suggestions as to how they vacate the fortress undetected had verged on the ridiculous, and now it seemed their ruse was discovered by the shrewd eyes of Captain Ralian, who'd just happened to come along.

"May I join you?" Ralian pulled up a chair before anyone answered. Shallan wondered why he hadn't joined them earlier but had instead sneaked at them from the far corner. Could no one be trusted these days? "I hope your room is adequate, my lady?"

"It's fine, yes—thank you."

"When do you expect them to attack, Captain?" Barin rubbed his nose and sneezed. He now suspected he was getting a head cold brought on by lack of sustenance.

"Hard to say—they are in no great rush. They've built siege towers a-plenty and have a stack of ladders, so they could attack tomorrow. But it's like their king wants to break our resolve. Every morning he shows us trophies."

"Trophies?" Shallan's face darkened, thinking of her brothers.

Ralian nodded and changed the subject. «The soldiers are worn out with this endless waiting. There's too much time to think and not enough ale to drink. They're good tough lads, but morale is ebbing fast. They need a victory—however small. Some kind of heroic stunt pulled against the foe. But who could do such a thing?»

Shallan's eyes narrowed. "You've been eavesdropping, Captain Ralian." The others pinned him with their eyes until Ralian shrugged.

"Forgive me, my lady - yes. And you others too, but I make it my business to know the mood in this city. I knew you'd want a way out so you can save Tolemon, Vorreti, and Danail. They are fine men and I wish there was something I could do to help."

"But instead you spy and then report us to your superior," Zukei hissed at him. Beside her, Shallan was almost in tears after hearing her brothers' names for the first time in weeks.

Ralian's lips tightened. He clearly had no fondness for Zukei. "I am loyal to my lord, yes. But I am also aware that we need to do something—and fast. This city is rotting from within.

"Starkhold thinks we just have to hang on. I disagree. We—or rather you, with my clandestine assistance—need to pull something off that will enrage Haal enough to attack our city head on while we are strong enough to fight back. A winter of this stalemate will break our resolve—despite what Starkhold says."

"So what do you propose?" Barin leaned forward, trying hard not to trust this fiery-eyed young captain.

Ralian grinned. "I will see that you get through the front gates myself."

"What about Starkhold?" Shallan now worried that Ralian was putting his life in danger for her and her brothers. She was so weary of people offering their help without her being able to help them back. "You said he was a dangerous man."

"That he is, but he also needs his officers in one piece." Ralian barked a wry laugh. "Let me worry about Lord Starkhold, my lady." He turned to Barin. "When do you intend to do this thing, to raid the enemy camp?"

Barin stared at Ralian for a long moment before answering. "Very well—I trust you. You seem like a good lad. Early tomorrow night. That will give us time to plan and prepare. Say, an hour after dusk."

"Who is participating?" Ralian motioned the innkeep over. "My friends are a special case, and this big fellow very thirsty. See he has as much ale as he needs tonight."

"But the Lord General?" The innkeep's expression was bleak.

"Do it!" The proprietor grumbled back to the taproom and minutes later arrived with fresh ale and some more food for all of them.

Barin grinned. "I like you lad, you've got the right attitude." Shallan still wasn't sure if she trusted Ralian, but he seemed genuine, and what choice did they have?

"So," repeated Ralian. "Who are tomorrow's heroes?"

"I will go," announced Barin. "Zukei will accompany me as will these two dopeheads," he motioned Taic and Sveyn, who grinned and nodded as if he'd announced they were going on a fishing trip in summertime.

"Cogga here will stay with the lady and serve as her bodyguard should we not return." Cogga nodded, though he looked disappointed.

"I am going too." Shallan cut through their easy smiles like wire slicing cheese. "This is my affair."

"Don't be ridiculous, Shallan." Barin wiped froth from his beard. "You will stay here with Cogga and the captain to protect you. You are the Duchess of Morwella, for fuck's sake."

"And they are my brothers out there, and if they yet live then I shall save them and bring them back!" Zukei raised a brow, Barin scowled like thunder, and Taic and Sveyn kept grinning. Cogga sighed whilst Ralian stared at Shallan with renewed respect.

"Forgive me, my lady, but Lord Barin is right. You must stay here—the enemy camp is no place for a woman." Before he could move Zukei's dagger left her hand and pinned Ralian's cuff to the table. "What the —" Ralian gaped as a second knife slammed into the tiny gap between his third and index finger.

"What do you have against women?" Zukei glared at Ralian, who looked stunned by the knives and the speed they'd appeared.

Barin grunted in his beer. "Enough nonsense, Zukei, the captain is our friend. Put those bloody daggers away and apologise to the captain for startling him."

Zukei complied in silence. After she stowed her knives, she steered close to Ralian and whispered in his ear. "Sorry—it's a sore point."

Ralian nodded quickly. "I get that," he said.

"Listen up." Eyes turned her way as Shallan stood and rested her hands on the table. The others excluding Ralian, now lost in thought, watched her in silence. "I am going. Tomorrow. Into the enemy camp. Once there I will find and rescue my three brothers and anyone else those cunts hold captive." Ralian looked up, clearly shocked by the Morwellan lady's choice of words.

"I've seen what they do to prisoners." Shallan held their gaze. "I *am* Duchess, but I'm also a warrior and a leader. It's time I started acting like one!"

"Pardon me lassie, but this is ridiculous!" Barin's face was reddening by the minute. "It makes no bloody sense at all."

"It makes more sense than Barin of Valkador walking into the camp of his arch-enemy," Shallan countered. "I know your temper, Barin. You might take out a hundred of them, but in the end they will bring you down, like hounds surrounding a bear."

"I will not allow that to happen. I have made up my mind, gentlemen. I will do this thing. Zukei will be with me, Taic and Sveyn too—and Cogga if he's willing. But not you, Barin, you I will not sacrifice."

Barin looked like he was about to explode any minute. It was Cogga who spoke next. "I don't approve of Lady Shallan's attending the raid, but that's not down to me. Nor is it down to you, Barin. The lady knows her own mind and she's right about you entering that camp—very bad idea."

"I'm done with this farce." Barin stood, knocked the table over, leaving the others to dive for the precious ale, and left the tavern. At a nod from Cogga, Taic followed him out the door, keeping a healthy distance.

"Fuck!" Cogga had snagged Barin's ale tankard and he drained it. "You know he's pissed when he leaves good ale. Too good to waste," he grinned at Shallan who was shaking at her own anger as much as Barin's. "Well," continued Cogga, "if we're going to pull this off we had better start planning."

"What about Barin?" Ralian was watching the door half expecting Barin to return and smash the table with an axe. Part of him was glad this crew were leaving tomorrow night. Part of him wished he could go too.

"He'll come round," Sveyn said. "But uncle's right. If he sees

Redhand or vice versa, big shit will happen. Best our leader stay out of that camp. Is there any more ale?"

There was more ale and it was brought speedily. The innkeep had witnessed both Zukei's nimble fingers and Barin's fury, and he wasn't about to protest again. They were served late into the night. At one point, Barin returned along with Taic and sat the far table in silence. Eventually, he joined them. An hour before dawn they had a plan, which could possibly work. Barin was the only one that didn't like it, but he admitted the reason was because he wasn't a party to it.

"Are you all right?" Shallan asked her giant friend quietly, just before seeking her room.

"Just promise me you'll return safe, for if you don't I will walk into that camp alone and kill everyone I can."

"I will return Barin, I promise. It's not my destiny to die yet—despite what I said this afternoon. My instinct... something tells me I've yet work to do. Besides... Zukei will be there."

"I will keep her from their steel." Zukei flashed Barin a grin.

Barin nodded slowly. "I know when I'm defeated. You women go get some sleep, you'll need it. And Shallan." She turned her head one last time.

"Corin will never forgive me if you get hurt in any way. He's on his way here lest you've forgotten."

"I haven't forgotten," Shallan smiled. "I shall await him alongside you, my dear old friend." She bade Barin and Zukei good night, and minutes later was fast asleep in her cot. Just before she closed her eyes, Shallan pictured Corin as she'd last seen him at the gardens in Vioyamis—so long ago it felt.

You had better hurry, my love.

Chapter 12

The Delving

To say his head hurt was an understatement. Olen was an evil man that had misled his new friend into drinking an entire jug of the fermented yak brew, resulting in his head being on fire and his vision a blur—which wasn't ideal when trying to hoist oneself up a swaying rope in the freezing rain. At least he'd left Clouter, Biter, and his mail and clobber below. Not his idea—weapons in any form were banned from the Delve.

Corin was dressed in borrowed hide. It made a change from his customary leathers and mail, which were currently getting scrubbed and oiled by one of the lackeys in the camp under Olen's instructions. The hide trousers and shirt were light and comfy, but failed utterly to rebuff the chilly wind and soak of drizzle. All in all a miserable morning.

The knotted rope swung and danced around as Corin heaved up hand over hand. Olen laughed as he looked down seeing Corin struggle. "Nearly there!" He grinned and Corin scowled up at him. It was another full ten minutes before Corin crested the top and rolled on his back, gasping like a stranded whale on a desolate beach.

"What is the matter?' Olen loomed over him, whilst Arami stared at them from a distance. The Red clan had mostly stayed below in camp, but Arami and three others had decided to attend the Delve, mostly so they could berate Olen and his companion. Olen had brought two men, leaving the rest of his riders below. The Delve was serious business—most preferred to stay away.

"My head is thumping," Corin complained. He wished he was asleep with Thunderhoof down in those cosy stables. That horse got more breaks than his owner these days. "Why can't you people drink ale or something sensible?"

Olen yanked Corin to his feet. "Best not to lark around here, any sign of weakness will be set upon. Are you ready for the Delving, Corin an Fol?"

"The Delving?" Corin steadied his stance and took three long breaths. Mind over matter, he told himself. He glanced down from the ledge. Far below, the camp was stirring. Corin could easily make out the horseshoe fence and the corrals and gates and many tents scattered about. Again he wished he were down there.

"It's what we call our sacred meetings at the Delve. There are normally four a year, but this is a special occasion. No more joking, my friend, this is a war council we attend, and you are a stranger, which means you could be friend or foe depending on their perception. Go carefully."

Corin nodded and yawned and then long-faced followed Olen towards the caverns yawning in the distance. Arami and the other men had already vanished inside.

"I seem to be constantly dipping into caves these days," he addressed Olen's back but was rewarded no response. Corin thought of the road under the mountains from Feroda's Forest and before that, the long journey beneath the Crystal Mountains in distant Permio. That seemed a while back now.

The ledge was a huge flat shelf of rock defying nature as it thrust out like fungus on a dying tree from the mountain wall. To Corin's left, the closest slopes of The High Wall were lost in fog, though he could just discern the sharp points of legions of pines marching off into shadow. Above and to the right the peaks comprising The Long Fend reared and faded into distance like a row of frozen giants with pointy hats staring hostile in the gloom. Ahead, the cavern threatened to swallow them whole.

They entered within. At first Corin was impressed by the light. There were lanterns, sconces, and torches everywhere, and also wide pits where fires roared welcome warmth and banished the damp from within.

The next thing that impressed him was the cavern size. The roof above was smooth and domed and the vista before him wide and spacious—a natural amphitheatre carved and scooped clean by nature's mighty spoon. The acoustics were amazing. Corin could hear voices, and looking around realised it was Arami and his men whispering a good 20 paces away.

"So how do the wise and the old get up here? Surely not by that rope?" Corin asked Olen as they ventured deeper inside the cavern. Corin had noticed people in robes emerging and taking seats in a series of benches set into the rock below—the spoon's basin. The benches were set facing another ledge looming out of the back of the cavern. On closer inspection, it seemed suspended in air, hovering slightly—though Corin guessed the latter an illusion aided by his muddy vision this morning. Hover or not it was an eerie sight.

"No indeed." Olen walked with purpose and bid Corin stick close to his tail. "There are entrances leading down from the slopes of The Long Fend, but only the Council or seers can use them. Even I know not of their whereabouts. Warriors, servants, and any visitors must all access the Delve from the rope below.

"See those benches?" Corin nodded. "We are making for the front row. Just take a seat there and keep you lips together. I will do the talking."

"No problem." Corin wasn't in the mood for discussions at the moment. He followed Olen of the Tcunkai to the front row of benches and took his seat, glancing around as more robed figures emerged from deep corners lost to view. Corin saw men and women settle the benches. Most were older, some in their middle years and some verging ancient.

Then he saw the fighting men, the clans, with their tattoos, scars, and earrings marking their own particular clan. Last night Corin had asked Olen how many clans there were and the Tcunkai warrior had told him there were six. All wore colours: yellow, red, purple, brown, green, and blue; their names he struggled to recall.

The yellow Tcunkai were thinkers. The red Anchai were called Blood People. The purple Oromai were far rangers—these dwelt at the eastern end of The Long Fend. The brown Fadaya were dreamers, known for their seers, most of those wise men having come from this clan. The green Cortai were the horse breeders. And finally, the blue Pargai were the deep ones. These alone of the Rorshai peoples dwelt in the mountains in caves ranging east along the gnarly feet of The Long Fend.

The robed elders had coloured cords around their necks and waists displaying which clan they were from. Corin noticed many browns and blues, a few reds—these glaring evilly at him, and a couple of greens. But no yellows were evident save the two men sitting alongside Olen.

The sharp-faced Arami was already in deep excited discussion with two of the red elders. Both of these were looking at Corin with narrowed eyes. Corin pretended not to notice. More people emerged over the next few minutes, until the benches were filled and a great hush settled on the cavern.

Corin watched as a man walked out form the distant wall formng the cavern's rear. He was garbed in a long white gown, striped diagonally with the six colours of the clans. He took seat on a wide chair raised high to overlook the rows of benches. Corin could hardly make out his face, but he looked old and skinny.

There were six other chairs alongside, and now other figures appeared from the back to take their various seats. Corin saw one of them wore the yellow of the Tcunkai, and the others were decked out in their various hues.

"The Seers," Olen whispercd in his ear. "They head the Delving."

"The stripy one in white looks important."

"The Mage—oldest and wisest of the Seers. His word is law, and he alone overrules any clan's single wish." It was the Mage that spoke first. And it was Olen whom he addressed.

"Olen of the Tcunkai, your news has reached us and we are alarmed." Corin was impressed how the Mage's voice reached them where they sat. He might look frail, but the old boy had a fine set of lungs.

"You warn of an army," the Mage was saying, "of portents, of She we do not name. And now this stranger you have brought upon us. What of him? What is his story? Stand Tcunkai—speak your words!"

Olen obeyed. He dipped his head in respect to the Seers watching in silence from their chairs. "Wise ones and warriors, my father the Tcunkai Kaan requested this meeting after hearing my tale. My intent was to return and accompany him here, but these Anchai gathered were in a rush to gainsay my words, and so I journeyed with them instead of returning to Morning Hills."

"What news has so upset the Anchai?" The Mage turned to face the Seer garbed in red to his left. The man took to his feet and bowed at the Mage. This one was portly and deeply tanned. His face was oval and his eyes slightly slanted. He looked a tad oily in Corin's opinion.

"This Olen is an excitable youth," the red Seer pointed across to where Olen stood in silence. "And an alarmist. He twice crossed Anchai lands without asking permission—an act of unprovoked aggression. Young Arami here has told us of this stranger, a mercenary and a warmonger apparently. But the one foretold? That I doubt. And Olen's talk of an invading force approaching from the plains is ridiculous."

"You think I made it up?" Olen's face tightened.

"Silence!" The Mage stood and pointed at Olen. You, boy, address a Seer! You will show respect to Subotan lest we strip and beat you. Remember where you are, Olen of the Yellow Clan!"

Olen wasn't swayed. "Then you must beat me. But first know my words are true and that there is indeed an army bound hither from distant Ptarni."

"Liar!" Subotan jabbed a finger toward where Olen stood. "He is bewitched and needs urgent flogging! I suggest we punish this one now before he can utter more deception."

"You may continue, Olen. But choose your words carefully." The Mage bid the red Seer return to his seat. "Subotan, we will award him chance to spin his tale, whether fact or fiction, and decide his fate thereafter." Subotan nodded, though he didn't look happy.

Olen continued. "I rode east for many days across the steppes. I saw nothing until I arrived at a broad river and saw a city in the clouds. A distant realm hemmed by dark mountains."

All faces were on Olen as he spoke. Most were hostile, convinced he was telling some crazy yarn. But some were curious and one or two looked worried. The yellow Seer, a shaven-headed heavy-set man with large blue eyes, was watching Olen with evident pride. He alone was on this boy's side, Corin thought.

"I walked the bank until I saw some buildings on the near shore. I investigated and saw signs of wheel tracks and recent movement. The tracks led out into the open steppes. Curious and alarmed, I followed for days until I came upon their camp."

"What did you see?" The Mage folded his arms and gazed coldly down on Olen. "I suspect, an army of ghosts and shadows brought on by your foolish curiosity."

"They were real enough. Wainriders clad in weird armour and carrying long spears and other outlandish weaponry. They were breaking camp down in a ravine. I watched them depart amid bustle. Most wore strange helmets with chains hiding their faces, but one or two were bare-headed. These were narrow-eyed and dark of skin. I have never seen their like before."

"Ptarnians for certain." The yellow Seer spoke for the first time, his voice deep and penetrating. "Sounds like a raiding party."

"Too many for that," Olen replied. "They filled the ravine. This is a force bent on invasion."

"Invasion of what exactly?" Subotan scoffed and Arami laughed from his bench to Corin's right. "I mean where would they be heading? Clearly there is nothing for them here."

"I don't know. But I do know what I saw."

"But what prompted your journey? Why ride off into the emptiness? Did a madness aflict you, and if so why should we trust your wild story?" The Mage had taken his seat again and now gazed coolly at Olen with thoughtful eyes. "It was the Dreaming, wasn't it? You think you have the Seeing, Olen?"

"I have the Dreaming, yes."

"This liar should be horsewhipped bloody!" Subotan was on his feet again. "Only Seers have the Dreaming. He is mad or else a false shaman scraping alone in the dark. I say take him out and hurl him and the foreigner from the ledge."

"Maybe I should say something," Corin muttered, "since you are doing such a good job."

"Shut up!" Olen hissed down at him.

"So, you have the Dreaming?" The Mage's voice was laden with irony. "And what have you dreamt of? Invasions?"

"I dreamt of the man beside me. I dreamt he is the harbinger, the one long foretold. And I dreamt of war and loss and the end of all we care for."

"And these wild, doubtless drug-induced dreams drove you into the steppes. The wilderness where no one sane ventures? I am inclined to agree with Subotan. I think you are deluded, Olen, or else this stranger has cast a glamour on you. Which is it?"

"This is total bollocks." A rough voice to Olen's right.

The sharp intake of breath heralded silence in the cavern. All eyes were on the stranger. The tall, hard-faced warrior now stood addressing them. "He went to see the Mountain Seeress, who told him all about me and the Ptarnians. Now, I don't know rat shit about Ptarnians, but I do know enough about me to warn you that you are in for a rough ride and need to listen in to this Olen laddie and stop acting like a bunch of stupid twats." Corin sat down with a thump as hostile shock filled the cavern like steam.

"I think you've just arranged our execution," Olen whispered in his ear.

"Sorry, but someone had to stick up for you."

"Take this impostor outside and hurl him off the ledge," roared the Mage, beside himself with rage at being addressed so by a foreigner. "And arrest that fool too!" He pointed again to Olen, and suddenly the Delve erupted with yelling and confusion. Corin had produced a knife from his belt and calmly tossed it between his hands.

"I learnt long ago never to be entirely without at least some weapon," he grinned at Olen. "You can never have enough sharp things in this world." The Mage signalled the warriors present to close in and take the impostor in a rush. They leapt to obey but then froze as sudden chill filled the cavern. The torches and lanterns flickered and stilled and the fires roared high for a moment and then retreated back.

Someone had entered the cavern from without. Corin saw the scrawny shape of what looked to be a woman limping toward the high place where the Mage and his Seers looked on askance.

"You are not permitted here!" The Mage yelled at the woman but she ignored him as though he were invisible. She approached like a hunting spider, stopping to the left of the nearest Seer who shrank back from her in his chair.

"Elsbetha you are banned form this place! You —"

"You, Mage, are a fool and this is a Delving of folly. You have no vision and deserve to crumble like winter leaves beneath the storm that is coming. The stranger speaks the truth as does Olen of the Tcunkai. War is coming!"

She threw the hood back from her face and Corin saw a women

perhaps in her late forties, but with ancient eyes of the darkest blue they appeared almost black. She was thin beneath her robes and a fierce hunger seemed to eat at her. Her hair was very long and smoky dark and she wore heavy kohl that accentuated those terrifying eyes.

She was both frighteningly ugly and weirdly attractive. There was a feral lust shining in her eyes and Corin now realised who this must be: the witch who had warned Olen to meet him by the hidden pass. Corin recalled the washer at the ford, the last witch he'd seen, and shuddered.

The Mage approached her now with both hands pointing. She laughed, uttered a spell and the Mage's hands became bats flapping in his face. The other Seers took on the shapes of strange beasts.

Corin saw that Subotan now resembled a large fat ape and the Tcunkai Seer a two-headed donkey. The Mage cried out as the floor turned to hot liquid and rose up to cover his body. He fell and the liquid poured over him until he lay wriggling and shuddering on the cavern floor. The woman laughed again and her spell subsided, the beasts returned to men, and the Mage flapped his hands instead of bats.

Corin wondered if he would ever see a normal day again. The woman was looking at him now, ignoring the panic and furore of the crash of bench and rush of feet, as Seer and robed elders fled the cavern. Only the clans' warriors remained, though their faces were grim with fear.

The strange woman approached Corin from the dais, her gait awkward and jerky. She smiled cruelly. "Yes, you are the one. The fulcrum foretold. The harbinger of war." Then in a quieter voice she added, "You ride into peril, Corin an Fol. Seek your father in the mountains."

Corin wasn't surprised to see Skulde's harsh stare. "Oh, it's you again. Can't say I've missed you." The hag's face shifted to become Vervandi's golden smile, then her beauty crumbled like flooded sandcastles to become the girl child up that tree. Corin heard Urdei's childish giggles filled the cavern. The three nasty sisters were back in town.

"Be careful, lover boy," Urdei winked at him. "Your time of greatest peril is close. *She* is waiting. Even Vervandi cannot save you from *her*."

Then the vision passed, and Corin found himself gaping with open mouth at the sharp-faced Seeress called Elsbetha.

"Who the fuck are you?" he managed, watching the knife fall through his fingers.

"She is the Seeress of Silent Mountain," Olen muttered beside Corin. "She is forbidden here, as she is believed a witch and creature of the night. But Elsbetha is the one true Seer and my dreams guided me to see her."

"And my dreams led me to see you." The woman smiled coldly at Corin, surveying him from head to boot. He had the nasty feeling she could see inside his clothes and was about to make him an offer he couldn't refuse. "Relax," Elsbetha said, "there is another has claim to you, Longswordsman."

"You know of Shallan?" Corin felt a sudden rush of excitement. "How fares she?"

"I know not who you mean. I speak of another." Before Corin could respond, the woman turned away. She raised her voice so that those remaining could clearly hear her.

"You need to make ready, warriors. Your leaders have forsaken you and are no longer fit to rule. Instead it is down to you to decide and act. But do so swiftly!

"Even now riders hasten here. One from the east the other the west. The news they bring rides on ravens of war. This Delving is at an end, and there will there no other. Rorshai is at war!"

Without further word, the woman flicked the hood back over her head and limped off into the gloom behind the flickering sconces. Corin watched her go like a man recovering from a bad trip.

As the witch foretold, half an hour later, the first messenger arrived. Purple snake scars on his forehead announced him as Borasi, a chief among the far-ranging Oromai. "I come from our camp bearing grim news. The steppes are alive with strange warriors. They are marching northeast toward another army, camped in a valley near the dark wood."

"Another army?" Olen thrust his face into Borasi's. "More Ptarnians?'

Borasi shook his head. "No, these marched up from the south a week ago. A disciplined group, but small in number compared to the army approaching them."

"Belmarius!" Corin blurted. "We must warn him of this impending attack. He is our friend and ally," Corin continued, but got no further, for the second messenger had arrived and stood dripping wet in the cavern. It was Rogan, and the news he brought was dire indeed.

Chapter 13

A Twist of Love and Loathing

Tamersane emerged from his blanket and stuck his head out the tent flap as the drumming of hoofs thundered through the morning. It was early, the cold grey glimmer of dawn spreading in the east. He heard shouts, then a woman's scream.

Teret!

Tamersane hurried into his trousers and tossed a shirt over his shoulder, fussing at the buttons as he looked for his sword. There it was propped against the tent pole; Teret whilst tidying must have put it there.

His arm hurt this morning but he ignored the pain, grabbed the sword, and slid it fee of its scabbard, allowing that fall to the floor. Wild-eyed, Tamersane leaped out the tent and started yelling, just as something hard smacked him across the back of the head and he pitched forward into darkness. Such was the swift glory of Tamersane's morning. At least his intentions had been good.

When he awoke Tamersane was lying alongside a stream, Teret's concerned face looking over him. "Is he awake?" That was

Rogan his voice raw with emotion.

"Yes." Teret passed a gourd to Tamersane and motioned him to drink, which he did greedily. Only then he noticed the tears staining her cheeks.

"Teret—what has happened? I heard hoof beats and shouts then a woman's scream. I rushed out of the tent but then something hit me hard and I fell. I am sorry."

"You are lucky to be alive." Rogan crouched over him as Teret wiped spilt water from Tamersane's lips. "That was a cast bola, meant to stun and then snare you. But your attacker was over hasty, and my thrown knife punctured his lung before he could close on his quarry."

Tamersane blinked. "Thank you, friend. You must think me a crap warrior—all I do is roll around in the dirt these days."

"At least you tried." Teret's eyes were warm as they gazed on him.

"Where are the others?" Tamersane winced as he took a look around. They were seated beneath dark pines flanking the stream. Morning Hills was nowhere to be seen, though a distant trail of smoke gave out its location.

"Dead or fled." Rogan looked weary and bitter. "And the children taken."

"Who?"

"Sulo—who else? He must have gathered some of the reds to come pay a visit. Olen should have slit that bastard's throat."

"The Kaan?" Tamersane reached up and wiped a tear from Teret's cheek.

"My father is dead, my other brothers too, and my cousin who you liked. All murdered in their sleep by treacherous Anchai. Morning Hills is no more."

"Teret, I'm so sorry."

"Rogan saved us," she continued shaking her head as though in disbelief. "He was out hunting early and heard the attack. He hid your body and then found me with three of them on top of me."

Tamersane's face lost all colour.

"They didn't harm her—they didn't have time. Once they were dead, Teret and I returned to scoop you up and flee the camp. We lay low a mile away and watched them leave. I wanted to challenge them and take as many as I could, but Teret insisted I stay alive to warn Olen. So guess where I'm going?"

"The Delve?"

"Yes, the Delve. Some of the horses broke loose. They'll be around somewhere. Once I've reined one in I'll away. Olen needs to know about this, as does the Council."

"We'll come with you." Tamersane sat up and then spewed on the ground. His head thudded and his arm hurt again. But he was angry and determined to protect this woman and help their friend.

"No, I'll travel faster alone, and we've scant time to explain your presence at the Delve. Look after Teret and seek cover in the mountains.

"Don't linger here, that Anchai scum will most likes return when he realises Teret escaped. He'll scour these lands for miles until Olen returns to spill his guts on the floor. Now I'm off as there's no time to waste." Rogan showed them his back and commenced sprinting toward the thin funnel of smoke smudging the horizon. Soon he was out of sight.

"How do you feel?" Teret stroked his hair and smiled at him, and suddenly Tamersane was filed with love for this tough, self-reliant woman. She had lost almost all her kin to raiders and yet she was more concerned about him.

"Sore. But then I'm used to that. But more importantly how fare you, Teret? Would that I'd woken early like Rogan and managed to kill some of those bastards. But I slept somewhat heavy last night." He winked at her and she smiled.

"As did I too. Come on, we cannot linger here. Let's make for the mountains, there's a path way up that will award wide views and we'll be able to see when Olen returns or if the Anchai come back."

"What then?"

"We join Olen and help him kill Sulo."

"And after that?"

Teret frowned. "I don't take your meaning?"

"Olen rides to war with Corin an Fol. I've seen this happen before with Corin. I think we too should look to another path."

"There is no other path." Teret's mouth twitched and her blue eyes narrowed. "What are you talking about?"

"Going home," Tamersane winked at her. "My home—Kelwyn. I long to see it, Teret, and hear how my cousin fares."

"Your cousin?"

"Queen Ariane of Wynais."

"So you are noble born? I thought so." Teret looked troubled. "Then yes—you must go home, help your queen against her enemies. There is nothing for you in Rorshai."

"Just the one thing I never expected to find."

"And what is that?" Teret gazed down at the fields, her eyes sad and lost.

"My heart's desire."

"You are being foolish."

"Look at me Teret." She turned, and he smiled at her troubled eyes. "I love you and will not be parted from you."

Teret wrinkled her nose. "You are easy with words, and you are not hale of body; therefore you cannot be trusted."

"I am easy with words, and yes, I did have a bit of a reputation. But that was then. Truth is, I've always been looking for the right woman and have never found her. I'm not addled. My mind is clear as yonder stream, and I know what I want."

"You would choose a Rorshai cow maid over the high-born ladies of Kelwyn?"

"You are the Kaan's daughter, Teret, and therefore not your average milk maid." Tamersane rolled onto his knees and reached out, holding her face in his hands.

"Look, I want to return to Wynais and help Ariane fight that bastard Caswallon. That's my fight, Teret. But if you must choose to stay here, then I'll stay here too. One thing I will not do is let you out of my sight, Rorshai girl."

She kissed him then, long and hard. "Does that mean you're coming with me?" Tamersane asked after they were done fooling around by the stream.

"We had best get moving." Teret started off toward the fading smoke trail. "Like Rogan, we'll need horses and any food we can find for a long cold trip across the mountains."

That night, they huddled close by a small fire as the wild cries of mountain lions sounded in the distance. Above their heads, the pines were cloaked in snow and a white moon rolled free from a shoulder of rock. It was there by the fire that she told him she loved him.

Looking back on his life in later years, Tamersane never recalled feeling so happy as on that night beneath moon and pines, with the orchestra of wind and wild beasts snarling in the distance. By morning, they reached The Wild Way—the ancient track that ran the entire length of The High Wall Mountain Range. It was two days later when their troubles returned.

***

The three dead men sat their tables laughing and spilling ale. Hagan smiled, because the drunken fools didn't realise they were dead. But dead they were or would be shortly. He leaned back in his armchair stationed at the corner of the inn and watched fascinated as the newcomer took silent seat by the door, his back resting on a wall and his face, like Hagan's, hidden from view.

The man watched the three soldiers jostling and jibing until the inevitable happened. The nearest and biggest turned and noticed the hooded figure watching him at the door.

"What's your problem?" The big soldier demanded of the smaller hooded figure. "Where did you sneak from? Are you a spy listening in to our conversation?"

The newcomer said nothing, just stared, and Hagan noticed the slight hint of a smile brushing his lips. The big soldier leapt to his feet and approached the newcomer, a knife brandished in his right fist.

"Did you hear me?" The soldier thrust his knife toward the other's face in warning. The man smiled at him, then cobra-swift his left hand shot out, locking the soldier's wrist and pulling him forward onto the knife he held hidden beneath his cloak.

The soldier gurgled as his blood drenched the wooden floor of the inn. His two comrades cursed and leaped to their feet, their swords scraping free of their scabbards whilst their friend twitched on the floor. The nearest lunged and missed, the newcomer having leapt to his left and kicked the chair out from under his feet, sending it crashing into the third soldier's knees. This one cursed as he stumbled forward.

The second soldier swung again and again he missed. But this time his opponent got inside his reach and sliced his knife up along the man's exposed wrist, severing the veins. He dropped the sword and sobbed as his blood spurted forth.

The newcomer kicked him to the floor and faced the final soldier. This last one clearly was in no mood for a fight.

"Who are you?" the man gasped as he levelled his blade at the killer of his friends. A raucous night in a Port Wind Tavern had turned into his worst nightmare. The man facing him had green eyes and a beautiful smile.

"I am Death," the stranger said before dancing lithely inside the soldier's guard and opening his throat with a single sharp slice from his dagger. Then the killer turned to gaze at the second soldier, still sobbing as he clutched his spewing wrist.

He kicked the man again and then stamped hard on his neck snapping the bone. The second soldier twitched and then lay still. The soldier's killer reached over and poured himself a glass of port from the decanter supplied for the soldiers. He took a long swig and then smiled at Hagan.

"Took your time getting here," Rael Hakkenon said. He winced at the blood-drenched floor. "Bit of a mess here. May happen we should retire someplace quieter."

"May happen," nodded Hagan, and followed the Assassin out of the door. Minutes later, the innkeep crept back into the room. He'd heard who was in town and had taken no chances when he saw the hooded stranger arrive.

Rael knew Port Wind well from his raiding days. He led his companion through a tangle of streets until they reached a scruffy looking inn at the water's edge. "Care for a brandy?" the assassin asked Hagan.

Hagan nodded, and the two ventured inside to split a flask. After a long moment studying the deserted room, the Assassin turned toward his companion and awarded him his special look. "So. You have something to tell me."

"I do." Only now did Hagan notice the index finger was missing from Rael's left hand. His face was badly scarred too, and his nose — like Hagan's—had been recently broken. No small accomplishment to inflict such damage on the most feared man in western Ansu. "I have news of a certain party's movement."

"Why not impart that to Caswallon or his goblin?"

"I'm not in their good books. Besides I'm sick of that fucking goblin."

Rael nodded slightly. "That's understandable."

"I'll not work for Caswallon again. Not directly."

"Yes, I heard how you fucked up in the desert." Rael smiled at his brandy. "And now the Tekara is whole again and Caswallon hopping furious with this new wizard kicking up stink."

"And that's my fault?"

"Just saying." Rael sipped whilst his cool green gaze mocked Hagan. "So, tell me what you know, and I'll do all I can to get you reinstated with the big man in Kella City."

"Fuck Caswallon." Hagan slammed his brandy on the table. "I want revenge, Assassin—as do you!"

"For what?"

"For this!" Hagan fingered his badly broken nose. "That and

more besides. I want that bastard Longshanks, Corin an Fol, split open from toe to tuft."

Rael's cat eyes narrowed dangerously. "Tell me of this Corin an Fol. I heard you two were acquainted in the past."

"Aye, we were. Down in Permio during the wars. Corin and me shared some stiff times, back then."

"Back when you were friends."

"We were never friends." Hagan gulped at his brandy and belched. "We were allies in a bloody, stinking, fly-infested dangerous place. As northerners it made sense to stick together. And Corin does have certain skills with that five-foot meat cleaver he drags about.

"But this latest business with the crown," Hagan shook his head. "I've seen things—unnatural things. Something is going on here that is way bigger than any of us. The wizard is an Aralais, one of the golden people. I never believed in such folk and yet I've seen him and the other lot. They are all planning something very nasty in my opinion. And in some crazy way it seems to centre on Corin. Don't ask me how I know this—I just do."

Rael snorted into his brandy. "You've spent too long in that desert. I will terminate Longshanks and you can get me the lady. That way this partnership will work out for both of us."

"She sailed north with Barin of Valkador, making for Vangaris."

"I heard that city is no more."

"I heard that too. My country Morwella is overrun. Doubtless she will make for Car Carranis. As will Corin an Fol, I have good reason to believe."

"Then you had better pack your bags for a long journey."

"What about you?"

"I'll go see Caswallon, get the latest, then return to Crenna. Once there, I'll round up some heavies to join us at Car Carranis. And Hagan..."

"What?"

"Don't kill hurt Corin until I get there. Locate him and the lady Shallan. I want them both and I want them alive."

"And I want gold as well as vengeance—that way you and I will get on just fine."

"In the short term." Rael awarded Hagan his beautiful smile. He reached into a hidden pocket up his sleeve and produced a small pouch. "Thirty crannels—should keep you going for a while."

Hagan grinned and reached for the pouch.

Rael's good hand snatched it up before Hagan could retrieve it. "Don't for one minute, Hagan Delmorier, consider yourself in my league." Rael drained the brandy flask and stood up. "I bid you goodnight." He tossed the pouch on the table.

Hagan masked his shudder well and retained his blithe expression "My best wishes to Caswallon and the goblin!" Rael nodded and left him to his thoughts.

Hagan smiled. He didn't trust the Assassin for one blink, but they had a lot in common. On his own, he was a rogue wolf; sooner or later his luck, which hadn't been great lately, would run out completely and he'd be gutted in some alleyway. But with Rael alongside, and a new crew funded by him, plus the Assassin's men—things would be sorted at last. One small matter troubled Hagan.

Car Carranis was rumoured surrounded by a horde of barbarians. How to convince them he was an ally without having his throat slit? That was something to work on as he made his way across the winter hills of Kelthaine. But now for another flask of brandy.

Chapter 14

Night Raid

"A cold night, my lord." Ralian leaned forward and scanned the campfires winking in the fields below. By his side, Starkhold stood motionless and unyielding as the granite walls surrounding him. Ralian kept a calm demeanour, but inside he fretted. It was two hours before midnight and he needed his general to retire so he could get the gates open. "Going to get colder too," Ralian muttered.

"You know what I value most in this life?" Starkhold's grim bark cut through the evening as his grey eyes locked on his captain. "Loyalty." Starkhold smiled briefly and returned his peruse to the distant fires. "It has to be loyalty, Captain. Without trust we tumble into an ocean of lies."

"Indeed so, sir." Ralian rubbed his mittens and banged fresh snow free from his boots. "The men are steadfast; they will not break." He felt uncomfortable standing there in the bitter chill, blinking as fresh snow whirled in from the night.

"But others might." Starkhold turned and rested an iron-gloved hand on his second's armoured shoulder. "I need you to be strong,

Ralian. These newcomers will cause trouble—I feel it. They mean well but know not the situation. I expect you to keep a keen eye on both Barin of Valkador and the Morwellan lady."

"You mean the duchess?" Ralian's eyes glinted at the snow.

"She is just a girl, and therefore liable to do something rash. Barin too—with his arch-foe so close by." Starkhold stroked his beard and shook snow from his cloak. "I take my leave, Ralian. As ever, alert me at once should anything occur. And Ralian..."

"My lord?"

"I want those Northmen watched. They are as unpredictable as their cousins outside these walls. Redhand and Barin are related—never forget that!"

Starkhold awarded Ralian a bleak look and then nodded. "I bid you goodnight." Within minutes, he'd vanished into the gloom below. Ralian waited a good half hour until his aide joined him puffing on the battlements.

"You followed him?"

"Yes, Captain, the general has retired to his chamber. He looked weary—I doubt we'll see him ere morning."

"I pray that you are right, Farien. I do not like having to do this."

"The guard are with you, Captain. They await word on the gates."

"What of Lady Shallan and the others?"

"They are shivering in the north barbican, awaiting your signal."

"Then it is time we gave it! Alert the sentries, open the left gate just enough for them to slip out unnoticed."

"Your wish, Captain." Farien turned on his heels and climbed swiftly down from the battlements. After a worried moment hesitating, Ralian followed and watched as his aide entered the north barbican. Moments later, he heard the creak of gate and the soft thud of boots on snow. The die was cast. It was too late to go back now.

***

In the end, Sveyn had stayed with Barin. That boy's temper once roused could prove disastrous in the Leeth camp, plus Barin needed one of his men to seek out Fassof and his ship, should all else fall down. But neither Barin or Sveyn was happy about the decision. Both watched glum and silent as Shallan and Zukei and Taic and Cogga trudged away from the walls and were soon swallowed by night.

"Elanion watch over that lass," Barin mumbled stumbling over the words. "She is like a daughter to me." Barin blinked a tear from his left eye and cursed the fact he was getting old and soft.

Sveyn flashed him a savage grin. "She'll be all right. That Zukei will keep her from harm. She's a hella—worth a hundred of those bastards out there!"

"You are right, but I am not used to inaction. This waiting in the cold dark will wear me thin."

"What do you suggest we do to kill the time?"

"Get drunk."

"Is that wise?" Farien the aide loomed out of the doorway where he'd been lurking with open ears. "You are aware of Starkhold's ale restriction."

"Let it be, Farien." The aide shrugged indifference as Captain Ralian entered the barbican hall where Barin and Taic and a few guards lurked together with Farien. "I too feel the need for something strong this night, for the outcome—whether good or bad—will most likes change this war. So be a good fellow and go get the brandy." Farien nodded and departed without further word.

"Well, my friends, let us warm our weary bones as we conduct this dark vigil." Ralian raised his tankard of ale in one hand and the brandy flask in another. "Here's to the duchess and her brothers!"

**

They stole like thieves from the city walls, their boots crunching snow the only noise. The cold gnawed at Shallan's fingers and her feet felt like icy lead. But her heart was hot and beating fast, as fear, excitement, and anticipation pulled her every which way.

It wasn't long before the first hint of pointed tents blurred into view. Around their heads snowflakes danced and whirled, and

Shallan pulled her cloak hood low over her face, lest they impair what vision she had.

Zukei prowled like a questing panther, leading the way forward whilst threading through the chaotic cluster of tent and guttering campfire. Taic followed with axe and sword in hands and wild-eyed stare.

Shallan kept close to Taic's bulk. She gripped her horn at her waist with one hand whilst holding the bow with the other. She had a long curved knife in her belt—a parting gift from Captain Ralian. Last up, Cogga hoisted a double-headed axe and glared into the gloom; at his waist seven throwing knives glittered whenever they drew close to the fires.

Those fires were everywhere, winking at them like dull red eyes. Shallan dared not dwell on how many men lay sleeping close by and beyond. They saw no guards; mercifully the Leethmen were so confident they hadn't bothered posting any. For good reason, Shallan thought wryly. Only a crazy person would attempt something like this. But as she stalked with her companions deeper into the enemy camp, Shallan felt a wild freedom she'd never encountered before.

I am the huntress—let the hunt commence!

Zukei led them up and on through the maze of snow-clustered tents. She was confident and precise and knew when at last they drew near to their destination. Ralian's brave scouts had ascertained the location of King Haal's personal guard, over two hundred prized warriors who kept their tents close to the king and his sons.

These were on the higher ground rising north from the Gap of Leeth. Zukei halted on seeing a limp banner on a pole loom at them from just ahead. She flashed her teeth at it. "We're here," Zukei whispered.

They had reached King Haal's feasting tent. Zukei squatted low and bid her companions hustle close. Ahead, Shallan could just make out a circle of much larger tents surrounding a huge marquee. Ahead of that were raised three tall poles, each topped by a horse's skull. She shivered—no going back now.

"That is the feasting hall for Haal's chosen warriors," Zukei hissed in her ear. "That is where your brothers will be. Are you ready for this, Duchess?"

Shallan nodded, "I am." She glanced at Taic and Cogga, who nodded too. Taic winked at her, and she felt a wash of gratitude to these brave friends willing to die at her side.

"Let's do it!" Shallan hissed, and Zukei nodded. The dark woman sprang to her toes and motioned; they followed her in silence toward the looming canvas. They entered the feasting hall and froze in the entryway.

The first thing that hit Shallan was the smell: a pungent combination of red smoking faggots, spilt ale, stale farts, and wet dog. Shallan blinked back tears brought on by the stench. To her right, Taic held back a sneeze, whilst behind him Cogga fastidiously wrapped a kerchief around his nose. Zukei ignored the aromatic blends as she took stock. Eventually, Shallan's eyes accustomed to the heavy atmosphere and moist gloom. She looked around.

There were a few lanterns hanging from canvas and pole. These cast winking shadows on shaggy prostrate figures. Some lolled from benches with dripping tankards still in hand. Others snored supine on tables, whilst most lay strewn about the floor, many of these with their brawny arms wrapped around a half-naked sleeping wench.

Hounds lolled and blinked, as lazy as the rest. Taic unravelled the small package he'd carried under his cloak. He grinned and tossed the sausages at the hounds, which blinked, stood with wobbly legs, and then went to investigate. Zukei signalled them to follow her deeper into the hall.

Shallan shuddered as she tripped over the legs of a prostrate warrior. She froze as the man stirred, blinked, and then rolled over and commenced snoring again. She moved on, stealing cat-lithe through the muggy atmosphere of the great tent.

Ahead were more lanterns set from transoms lashed to two large beams. Behind these on a chair slept a great chieftain, his greying beard long and filthy and his hair a tangled mess.

A horned kettle helm shadowed his face, but Taic whispered in her ear that this was none other than Corvalian Cutthroat himself, King Haal's second son and feared more than any other except perhaps his older brother, Daan Redhand.

But Shallan's gaze rested not on the sleeping barbarian prince. Rather her eyes were on the three unconscious figures hanging limp from the transoms, with cruel ropes lashed around their bleeding wrists. Shallan almost gasped out loud when she recognised her brothers, but covered her mouth and suppressed any sound. They were long-bearded, filthy, and wretched to behold. Shallan mouthed a silent prayer.

There they hung unconscious, like pigs trussed at market: Vorreti, Danail, and the oldest, Tolemon. Shallan felt sick with rage and worry. Lived they yet? She watched in dread silence as Zukei stole close and glanced expertly at each prisoner. At last satisfied she turned to Shallan and nodded. They are alive, that nod told her. Shallan almost collapsed with relief.

Elanion be praised - now let us away to safety and warmth!

Within minutes, Zukei and Cogga's knives had freed the captive brothers and dragged them to the ground where they lay stone-still in exhausted slumber. The nearest opened an eye, saw Zukei, and made to yell, but the black woman covered his mouth with a calloused palm. Shallan steered close and knelt beside her waking brother.

"Vorreti. It's me, Shallan. Can you understand me?"

Vorreti's eyes widened in disbelief, but eventually he nodded, and Shallan bade Zukei free his mouth. "This is Zukei... these others are Taic and Cogga. They are my friends aiding in your rescue. Do you understand?"

"Shallan...?" Vorreti's voice was half croak, half whisper. "How came you here?"

"It doesn't matter," replied Shallan, whilst Zukei enquired if he was strong enough to walk. Vorreti nodded that he was.

"Time we weren't here." The dark woman flashed her eyes at

Shallan. And then in relief Shallan noticed her other brothers stirring too. She approached them in hushed whispers and after a moment they too announced they could stand.

"Yes, let's get moving," Shallan nodded at Zukei, then froze as one of the dogs broke out in a fit of howly barks.

"What the—?" Taic glanced to where a large hound had finished its sausage and now stood glowering and slavering at them.

"Silence that fucker!" hissed Zukei, and Cogga reached for a knife. But it was already too late, for now the other hounds had joined in, and soon the racket woke everyone in the entire marquee.

Zukei didn't hesitate. She growled at Taic and Cogga to assist Tolemon and Danail in fleeing the tent. Vorreti had grabbed a sword from a nearby drunk and announced coolly that he was fit to fight. Time froze as the tent's occupants stirred into dozy motion. On his seat the big prince blinked and yawned.

"What the fuck is happening?" Corvalian Cutthroat said, his voice crow-rough and angry. Then the fighting started.

"Get them outside!" Zukei yelled at Taic who blinked and nodded in return. A warrior loomed large and angry in front of Taic. Taic ducked beneath a wild swipe from the Leethman's blade and butted his head into the warrior's nose, cracking it like an eggshell and sending the man sprawling on his back.

Zukei spat like a lynx, her Karyia a blur in her left hand and the throwing axe chopping and hacking in her right. Already a half dozen sleepy warriors lay groaning and gurgling with severed throats and sliced ears.

A warrior roared at Shallan, two big greedy hands reaching out for her. Vorreti's stolen sword ran him through, but another grabbed her wrist, whilst a third struck Vorreti from behind with a shield. Vorreti rolled and kicked up as his adversary dived on top of him. Together they rolled and grappled on the tent floor.

Shallan's attacker grinned as he pulled her toward him, his eyes shining with lust. She found her knife and pulled it free with her good hand, slicing up and in. Shallan cut open his belly and broke free of his grip as the Leethmen gasped, watching his guts spill free.

Everywhere hounds yapped and growled, some attacking their own ale-fuddled masters, only now coming to their senses. Cogga reached the door flap and tossed Danail through. "Keep moving!" he yelled at the brother. "Don't stop!" Danail nodded and faded off into the night.

Taic reached the door with Tolemon in tow. He ducked as a thrown axe thudded into the pole a inch above his head. "Follow your brother," Taic yelled at Tolemon, "I'm needed inside."

"I can fight!" Tolemon yelled back, but then more warriors emerged yelling and Taic was forced back inside the tent and Tolemon was lost from view. Taic shoulder-charged a giant axeman bearing down on Cogga. Taic grappled the axeman's legs, tripping him, whilst Cogga sliced along his throat.

"Go!" Cogga hissed at the younger Northman. "Steal some horses and retrieve those brothers. I'll help Zukei and the duchess!"

"You need me in here!"

"Just fuck off!" Cogga ducked as a cast spear flew over his head. Taic caught the spear's shaft, spun it around his arm and launched it back at the sender, puncturing a deep hole in his chest.

"Sure you can manage without me?"

"Yes!" yelled Cogga, cutting and stamping and slicing his way back to where the real fight was happening. Reluctantly, Taic fled the tent. Within minutes he had purloined some steeds from the nearest corral. Fortunately the commotion erupting inside the marquee was muffled by the heavy blanket of snow settling deep all around. Taic found Tolemon and Danail crouched around the back of a tent.

He freed a horse, tossing the reins to Tolemon. "Take the hint and piss off!" Taic told him and watched as both brothers hurled themselves onto the horse's back. Soon they were gone amid hoof beats in the night. Taic lashed the other steeds to a pine stump and waited.

A boot impacted Shallan's face, pitching her on her back. A huge man loomed over her, and Shallan recognised Corvalian Cutthroat grinning down on her with long-hafted axe clutched in both hands.

"Who are you, warrior-witch?" He kicked out, striking Shallan's legs as she struggled to roll over. Then Zukei was on him, spitting, biting, and slicing with the Karyia.

But Corvalian was a veteran of a thousand hand-to-hand fights. He cunningly evaded every lunge and twist and stab Zukei tenaciously provided. He at last was a foe to match Zukei's steely skills.

She cut and sliced hard at Corvalian's face, knocking the horned helm free of his head. He caught her wrist and twisted, until Zukei yelped and dropped the thin sword. She swung the Ptarnian throwing axe but Corvalian's ironclad forearm knocked it from her grasp. He kicked Zukei hard in the belly and she doubled over in pain.

Shallan found her feet, and gripping the horn with both hands (she'd lost the knife when he'd knocked her to the floor), she smashed it hard into the back of Corvalian's head. The warrior prince swore, shook his head, and without turning, sent an elbow back cracking into Shallan's chin. She saw stars and fell again.

Vorreti had just despatched his opponent with a slice of his knife. He clambered to his feet and rounded on Corvalian who just laughed at him.

"Think you a match for me, boy?" Corvalian's right fist telegraphed toward Vorreti's head, but just then Cogga arrived and slammed a shoulder against the prince, knocking him sideways. Meanwhile, Zukei had recovered and, after regaining her Karyia, recommenced slicing and hacking at any limb within reach. Corvalian chewed his beard as the madness took over him.

"Who are you, bastard?" he roared at Cogga, who staggered to his feet and leered back at him.

"I'm Barin's right hand man, so start shitting yourself, Leethman!"

"You're Barin's man? What the fuck are you doing here? Don't bother answering, let me skewer you instead!"

Corvalian reached back and retrieved his war axe perched by the seat. He swung hard and fast at Cogga's face. Cogga leapt back, but not before the axe scored a long furrow across his forehead and through his left brow. Cogga blinked blood from his face and snarled back the pain. But he couldn't see, and now Corvalian was swinging down on him again.

The axe went wide. Corvalian yelped as Zukei's Karyia needled into his wrist an inch above his right hand. The big prince roared and tugged the blade free of Zukei's grasp whilst smacking her over the head with the axe's shaft. Zukei saw stars but hung on. She produced a knife and leapt to attack as Corvalian pulled the Karyia free from his punctured wrist and again grasped the axe in both hands.

The flat of the blade sent Zukei's knife sailing across the marquee. Zukei blinked, the prince loomed over her, axe held high for the final blow. Zukei blinked again. The axe fell, but again that blow went wide, as Shallan's recovered knife stabbed hard and fast and deep up into Corvalian's exposed groin. The warrior prince gasped and groaned and sank to his knees as agony tore into him, and his berserkergang faded as he realised he was overcome.

Shallan twisted the knife, and Corvalian screamed. "That's for Vangaris! I only wish you were your brother, but his time will come too!" Corvalian made to reply but his mouth filled with blood and his knees gave. Zukei stepped over him and sliced the Karyia neatly along his throat. And that was the end of Corvalian Cutthroat.

Vorreti gripped Shallan's arm. "Thanks for coming, sister, I always knew you were the strong one!" Her youngest brother smiled at her and only then did Shallan notice the knife lodged in his side.

"No! Vorreti!"

"I've got him." Taic's bloodied face loomed close. "Best we get moving, duchess!" Cogga slung the limp Vorreti over his shoulder and staggered toward the distant tent flap. Close by, Zukei had reclaimed her axe and now fell upon any still living in the marquee. A man made to slip outside and sound the alarm. Zukei's tossed axe split open the back of his skull.

A second man made it through but his yell was cut short as Taic's slung knife tore into his throat. Cogga's head emerged from the tent. "Where are you?"

"Here—waiting for you lot!" Taic hissed from the corner of the tent.

"Horses?"

"I have four and they are spooked!"

"Nicely done!" Cogga grinned as Zukei and Shallan appeared through the tent flap. They found Taic and the steeds. Cogga hoisted the prone form of Danail across his saddle and sat behind. Taic, Zukei, and Shallan each claimed a horse. Within moments they were ready to vacate the camp.

Then three horn blasts sounded the alarm. One warrior had managed to evade Zukei's questing Karyia. It was he who ran head-long into another, larger tent hidden behind the marquee. Here King Haal lay sleeping with a leman clutched in both hands. The king's guards leapt up as the warrior entered yelling.

"Corvalian is dead!" yelled the man. "Corvalian Cutthroat is slain!" Within an hour, the entire army of Leeth stirred into angry life like a twenty-mile-wide ants' nest. But they were too late. The night raiders had escaped the trap.

They cleared the outskirts of the camp just as the first warriors emerged yelling and cursing out of the dark. These hurled spears and nocked arrow to bow, but they couldn't see much in the snowy gloom, and those they cursed as the murdering horse thieves were soon lost to sight.

Ralian opened the gates as Shallan and company thundered in. "My brothers!" Shallan yelled at the captain.

"They are here!" Ralian motioned toward the barbican. Shallan dismounted and ran inside. Soon Taic and Cogga joined them as did a very relieved and drunk Barin and Sveyn. Cogga yelled Ralian to get a cart for Vorreti who was slumped across the saddle of the horse.

"How fares he?" Ralian asked the Northman.

"It don't look good," Cogga replied and sprang from the horse to join his friends. Last in was Zukei, who'd been scouting their rear.

"We've stirred up a hornets' nest!" She grinned down at Ralian.

"I thought you might—but I'm glad to see you dark-eyed lady!"

"I am glad to see you too, Captain!" Zukei flashed him a rare smile as she vaulted from her horse. "How is the Lady Shallan?"

"She is well, but her brother..."

Zukei nodded and vanished inside the barbican. Shallan looked up as she saw the dark woman enter. She smiled weakly, but Zukei could tell she'd been weeping. "How is he?" Zukei's tough, bloody face was lined with concern.

"He is dead," Shallan said. "Vorreti is dead." Beside Shallan, her two older brothers knelt in sorrow and said nothing. "He was ever the brightest of us."

"He died fighting and has kept his honour," Tolemon said stiffly, and retired to a corner where Farien poured him a brandy. Outside the walls, the muffled sounds of horns and drums pierced the snowy quiet.

"Well," said Barin after they'd all listened to the noises for a moment. "Looks like we're in for a rough few days."

Ralian told off some men to seek out physicians to look over the wounded. Danail and Tolemon were weak and starving; aside that, they were not in bad shape. Taic had some stitches sewed along his head and Cogga too. Zukei wouldn't allow anyone near her. She stitched her own face back together and then swallowed a whole flask of brandy.

By dawn, everyone was back at his or her proper station. Shallan slept exhausted in her bed, as did the men from Valkador. Zukei alone sat wakeful and staring at the fire outside Shallan's room.

Ralian watched as dawn revealed a mass of figures lined up outside the walls. He sighed. It seemed at long last the real battle for Car Carranis had begun. A sergeant approached him from the distance.

"Captain!" The man's voice was urgent and worried beneath his helm.

"What is it?"

"You are to accompany my soldiers at once!" The sergeant's brisk strides brought him alongside Ralian, who now noticed a squad of spearmen approaching at speed.

"What nonsense is this?"

"You are under arrest," the sergeant puffed inside his helmet.

"On what charge?" Ralian's eyes were hawk hard as they pinned the sergeant.

"Three charges: insubordination, subterfuge, and treachery."

"Treachery? This is absurd!"

"Treachery," the sergeant repeated. "The punishment for which is death. I am sorry, Captain. These are the general's specific instructions."

"Starkhold wants me dead?" Ralian laughed out loud as they lashed his hands behind his back and led him down from the walls. "You are mad! Aren't there enough enemies outside?" They tossed Ralian in the deepest oubliette where he shivered and waited. It was a full day before Starkhold paid him visit.

"Choose your death," were the only words the general awarded him.

Chapter 15

The Kaan Rides Forth

The face within the crystal mirror was both inhuman and beautiful. Symmetrical features were dominated by purple eyes and blade-lean nose. Slightly arched brows and soft brown skin was surmounted by wispy hair of smoky crimson. The lips were full and lush, and these now opened to reveal perfect ivory teeth—each one filed with precision to a razor sharp point.

The young man bowed his head to the face in the mirror and the face smiled back.

"You have done well, Callanz. You and your forefathers have served me with devotion over the years. And for that service you, young Emperor, have been well rewarded."

Callanz bowed again—deeper this time, his tanned face and dark narrow eyes fierce with concentration.

"My Lord Morak, we of the Ptarni race will always be loyal to the Urgolais overlords. Your mountains overlook our city just as your counsel guides our every thought. My forefathers served you well, as you say, but I wish to do better than they. I've read the signs and seen the portents. Ptarni is ready, Great One!"

Morak's eyes narrowed, and his smile faded like smoke over water. "There is much to do, and you are yet young—even for a mortal. I cannot keep this form long; my strength is badly depleted as my other self lies trapped in limbo. You, Emperor, have the means to free it."

"The ruined castle? I've already sent an army west to probe and report back. They have provisions to set up permanent camp within sight of those other mountains and await your command."

Morak smiled again. "That is well. You will need all three of your imperial armies during the next few years. I have been deceived by a servant, and my old enemy has returned. Twice now, he has gotten lucky. There will not be a third time."

"What is it you wish of my people, Great One? They are yours to command, as am I." The young emperor shifted on his knees and wiped his face. It was so hot in the Dark Room—the place reserved for astral communications and certain special sacrifices. The place where he and his ancestors had always consulted their god and mentor—the Urgolais Witch-Lord known as Morak.

Morak's visage faded in the mirror. "My strength fails—I cannot hold this guise. I need Golganak, and I need your soldiers to obtain it for me, Callanz. I still believe it to be lost beneath the ruins of my old home, but when I searched I found it not. But my time was brief back then, and the cosmic balance set against us.

"Things have changed. Victory draws close, Callanz. The one true lord of Ansu has awoken—the Shadowman will reward all his loyal servants, especially the Urgolais who have ever stood close to him.

"With great Cul-Saan whole again, the Urgolais will return to their original power and form. We were once beautiful like the vision you see before you, but the Aralais hated us, and their witch-spells twisted our form into creatures of unimaginable horror.

"We were branded as evil ones, and they, our envious cousins, became the golden folk. Ill did they serve us back then. But they paid a high price, for when we sought out the Shadowman before His fall, He aided us well, and our enemy was torn apart.

"But we also were worn out, and then your distant kin arrived from a land called Gol, and through their intervention the Aralais were saved. Their leader was ever crafty. Arollas knew he was spent and that the only way for him to survive was to invest in these new mortals—hence he gave them the Tekara and Callanak, his two greatest artifacts, to protect their realm and enable him to vanish into retirement. There he could lick his wounds and scheme fresh schemes.

"Callanak is lost, which is well. That sword alone can undo us. But the crown has been found—and worse, remade by the blind fool, Croagon. Arollas struck when he knew we were weak. I had misplaced trust in a mortal wizard who had shown great promise. But this Caswallon has deceived me. My servant, the dragon Vaarg, informs me Caswallon desires the black spear for himself and is already planning a mission to Olen Valek to retrieve it.

"He must not get that spear! He already has too much power, and with Golganak could put an end to our return to rule. You, Callanz, will send your finest fighters into those western ranges. Find my old city and delve deep within. I will do all I can to aid you from any sorcery. But I am weak without my spear!"

Callanz shuddered as Morak's beautiful face blurred and warped into a blackened mask of horror. He gasped as feverish eyes of lamp-yellow glared back at him, the face surrounding them burnt and roughened like ancient charcoal. His nose was swollen huge and thrust out so it resembled the snout of a hound.

"Yes, look well, young mortal." That strong voice had faded to a croaky bark. "I show this image so you can understand my ancient hatred. The Aralais did this to me. They blamed it on my spear, but it was their sorcery that tore my flesh from my body and altered my shape. My kin suffered likewise—you cannot imagine the pain we have endured since that abomination was worked upon us."

Callanz coughed and felt sweat stream down his face. He wanted to take his leave but dared not depart until his master allowed it. "We will find Golganak and Vaarg, and with his help we will seek out this Arollas and break him, or at least bring him to you so you can destroy him once and for all."

"That is well, Emperor. Now I leave you." Callanz watched as the twisted warped face in the mirror shrank and darkened and faded back into nothing. Smoke filled the mirror's surface, and a bitter cold filled the Dark Room, freezing the sweat on the young emperor's brow.

Callanz rose to his feet, wrapped the golden robe tight about his shivering frame, and then walked briskly from that hallowed place. Later that day, Emperor Callanz addressed his people, informing them of his new plans for expansion in the west.

"We hold the east," he told them. "All save distant Shen pay tribute to our tax collectors and slavers. But that is not enough! My father and his father before him created this empire, but I, Callanz, will make it greater yet. There is a land in the west. A land of legends. A land of riches. And a land ready for the taking. Already my first army approaches its boundaries, and soon the ravens of victory will return with good news!"

Callanz sat back in his golden throne and smiled as the million-strong throng below roared and clapped approval and adoration for their lord and emperor. That night there were many sacrifices in the ancient groves. Ptarni would soon be the greatest nation in the world.

***

The camp was deserted save a few dogs wandering and sniffing at discarded offal. The wind blew bitter from the east, and Corin an Fol watched with a sour expression as his new friend Olen of the Tcunkai walked among the ruins of his people's camp at Morning Hills. With him was the hotheaded Arami, who had taken great pains to distance himself and his people from the atrocity surrounding them.

Arami had offered Olen his sword and bid the Tcunkai leader—
now the Kaan—remove his head to save the honour of his Clan. "We
the Anchai are warrior-fierce and proud. But we are not murderers
and neither are we cowards. Take my head as payment for what that
mad dog Sulo did."

Corin had watched in fascination as Olen had accepted the
sword and held it to Arami's neck. The young Anchai leader hadn't
flinched once. Nor did he close his eyes, until Olen threw the sword
on the dirt and turned away.

"I do not want your death," Olen had told him. "Not yet anyway." That had been yesterday afternoon, whilst they were deciding
who and how many warriors would go where.

The Tcunkai were already small in number. Olen had his prized
two hundred riders, and they scooped up a few more hiding in bushes
and caves around the mountains. These, like Teret and Tamersane,
had evaded capture and were more than ready for vengeance.

That night, Corin watched and drank as Olen's people built a
large pyre and carried the Kaan's greying corpse over to it. Olen lit
the wood and the pyre took to flame. They sang dirges as the body
was consumed by orange flame.

Afterwards, Rogan approached his leader. "You are Kaan now,
Olen. You must tell us what to do. Do we ride on the red camp and
seek out and destroy Sulo and his scum?"

"Upon my honour, I will slay him!" Arami stepped forward.
"And from now on my allegiance switches from my own people to
yours, Kaan. The Anchai are tainted for ever, but if you will have us,
we here will prove loyal fighters at your side!"

"That is well-said, and I thank you and accept your offer." Olen's
cool blue gaze rested on Arami for a moment before returning to the
flames where his father burned. "Now I will have silence and solace
for a time so that I may mourn my kin."

Olen had lost two brothers and three cousins, whose bodies now
burned alongside his father. The new Kaan's face was ashen grim,
and after his last words he had taken himself off and spent the rest

of the night alone, leaving Corin, Rogan, and Arami of the Anchai to discuss their next options. But when Olen returned in the dawn his mind was made up.

"We ride east and we ride fast!" he told them as they consumed a cold breakfast by the dying embers of last night's fire.

"What of our vengeance? What of Sulo?" Rogan's eyes were bloodshot. He'd drunk heavily last night and was still savage to catch up with Sulo. "And what of Teret and the Kelwynian? I said for them to wait and then join us when they saw you return to Morning Hills."

"Teret must look to herself." Olen waved a dismissive hand at Rogan, whose face was flushed with emotion.

"Tamersane will protect her," Corin said, shuffling uncomfortably in the chill. Close by Thunderhoof snorted, announcing that he was ready to be away.

"He had better, or I will cut him open from neck to bollocks." Corin let that be; clearly Olen was in no mood for compromise this morning. "And Sulo can wait too. He's a dead man; he and his rabid pack of curs cannot hide anywhere that I won't flush them out. But that pleasure must needs wait. Our country's survival is more important than our vengeance, Rogan. We have to take the fight to these Ptarnians, we must catch them unawares whilst they roam lost and weary in the wilds."

Rogan nodded. "As you wish, but at least let me return to where I last saw Teret and the westerner."

Olen nodded, "Be quick about it. We ride within the hour." Rogan vaulted onto his horse and thundered toward the nearest fold of mountain without further word. Corin watched his horse kicking up dust into the distance.

That left Olen and Arami and their riders, who still kept a wary distance from each other despite their leaders' new alliance and pledge. Corin could tell that some of the Anchai were not over happy about Arami's offer. More trouble for later he suspected.

"So what is the plan?" Corin asked Olen as the Kaan mounted his black stallion Loroshai and bid him trot back and forth to shake off the cold. "Do we join Belmarius?"

"We ride the Long Fend and kill any raiders we find. Other warriors from the clans will find and join us when they hear what happened at the Delve. But we won't wait for them. I need to see where this horde is going. I alone have seen the size of it."

"But why attack Rorshai?" Corin could see the dust returning and was relieved that Rogan was on his way back. But there was no sign of him having anyone with him. Corin surmised that Tamersane had persuaded the woman to journey west to Wynais. If anyone could persuade a lass to cross The High Wall in deepest winter it was Tamersane.

"I suspect those murderers were scouts, or else a small raiding party. Where their real destination lies is hard to guess. Permio? The Gap of Leeth?"

"I bet it's Kelthaine," replied Corin. "Via the Gap. Maybe the Ptarnians you saw are Caswallon's new foot soldiers."

"I doubt that." Olen watched as Rogan thundered toward them. "Their country is far away, Corin an Fol. The force I saw looked more than ready for a long campaign war. Something they've been planning for years." Corin wanted to say more but Rogan reined in his horse alongside.

"I found tracks leading up into the mountains—nothing else."

Olen nodded. "Then let us be off," he said. "Are your lot ready, Arami?"

"We are Kaan!"

"That's good! Tell them to keep their steel sharp and heads sober. We ride to battle!" With a thunder of hooves and storm of dust, the riders of the Tcunkai and Anchai cantered free of the valley that had been Morning Hills.

They rode apace for many hours, eventually passing the Delve. Here they collected three hundred assorted warriors from various clans. Many more joined them as that day fell to dusk. They camped beneath the arm of the Long Fend. In Corin's estimate they now numbered nearly two thousand horsemen. Not a lot against an army the size Olen had spoken of, but surely enough to make a dent.

Corin smiled as he unsaddled Thunder and rubbed down his back and legs. In the days ahead they would find Belmarius, or at least some sign of his camps. Then Corin would part company with his new friends and fare north to Car Carranis with the Bears. Somehow he would get inside that fortress and find his beloved Shallan waiting for him. Simple really.

Get ready lady - I'm on my way!

It took three days' hard riding to clear the Long Fend and enter the wide lands beyond. During that time they passed ruined camps and saw evidence of raiding and looting.

Kerante, the heavily moustached leader of the Oromai, the purple clan, met them where the last folds of the Long Fend dwindled to stubby hillocks. Kerante had with him five hundred riders, all brimming with rage at the damage done to their homes.

After that they had turned north. Olen and Arami rode ahead scouting the way. They reported back no sign of the enemy, but instead announced there were tracks showing a large force of foot soldiers and some horse had passed this way several days earlier.

Corin could only hope that was Belmarius's Bears, though he had expected the general to be further north by now. Maybe the same marauders that had plundered eastern Rorshai had attacked him too? That thought was cause for concern.

The fourth evening found them camped among the ashes of Greywoods, a high plateau of trees awarding sweeping views of the wild country surrounding it. Corin watched from beneath the wind-scoured limbs as light faded in the east.

That way, the ground fell away and smoothed into what looked to be an endless sea of grass, the Ptarni Steppes. The terrain to the north was similar, and Corin began to fret about what had happened to Belmarius. He had expected to see more signs of movement by now. What tracks they had found had vanished in the stiff brush, or else were buried beneath the blanket of freshly fallen snow.

Their camp was bitter chill. Olen dared light no fires. Corin was struggling to sleep when he heard the soft sound of boot on soil. He rolled to his feet in one motion, his hunting knife in hand.

"'Tis only I." Olen stared down at him, framed by creaking trees and a wide wandering moon. The Kaan's eyes were wild as the night sky glinting through those wintry limbs. "I grow restless—care to walk for a time?"

Corin nodded. He was restless too. On a whim, Olen walked deeper into the Greywoods with Corin close at his heel. It was eerie, and Corin was reminded of his dislike for woods at night. Or really, in the day time as well. He turned once, sensing something watching him. It was just an owl; its huge eyes blinked once at Corin, then the bird took to wing in silent flight.

"Something's brewing," Olen muttered as they reached a clump of broken stone path leading up to a higher elevation. This they climbed, and after several minutes' panting, broke free from the forest's breezy crown.

It was bitterly cold, and a fresh wind stiffened, numbing Corin's ears. "Borian is about in the land." Olen studied the grey shape of land beyond the western fringe of the forest. "I can feel His violence brewing all around us. The Wind God is hungry for battle!"

"I too feel something," Corin nodded as his breath steamed into the dark. "An uneasiness, like we are close to a place of great peril." Together they waited as night dwindled and a red sky shone through the trees at their back.

"Time to move on." Olen tugged Corin's shoulder. "The men will be wondering where we've got to." Olen turned and started back down toward the nest of trees below.

Corin made to join him then stopped. "Wait!"

Olen gazed back at where Corin stood looking hard into the west.

"What is it?"

"There's something down there. Come look! Your eyes are most likes sharper than mine!"

Olen re-joined him, and together they scried the wide grass-lands below, which slowly revealed themselves as the sun's winter rays filtered through the trees.

"I see men marching west on foot," said Corin his hands shielding his eyes. "They are making for that distant forest. They appear to be in a hurry."

"That is because those over there are after them." Olen guided Corin's hand along the fringe of wood until he spied a much larger troop of soldiers also marching at speed into the west. These wore brightly painted armour that glinted gaudy in the sunlight.

"Ptarnians?" Corin squinted at his friend.

"For sure."

"Then that other lot must be Belmarius's Bears. They must have been attacked in the night. We have to help them Olen!"

Olen nodded. "We'll return to camp and lead a scouting party west, find out what we are up against." Corin sprinted behind Olen as the Kaan crashed through trees on his way back to camp.

"Where the fuck have you been?" Rogan grumped at Olen as his Kaan broke through the waking camp. "We thought you'd been taken by night spirits."

"Finding the enemy," replied Olen. "I need a hundred riders willing to join Corin and me in riding out and taking a closer look at them. The rest of you will stay hidden lest we fare into a trap."

Arami was first to offer his services and Rogan second. "You stay," Olen told his old friend. "Keep an eye on these Anchai and post sentries throughout the woods. We'll need updating on any enemy movement."

"How many Ptarnians are down there?" Rogan pulled his pouch from his saddle holster and took a swig of yak milk.

"They were too distant to be sure, but I suspect several hundred, pursuing a force half that size."

"They are making for that distant forest," Corin told Rogan whose face blanched at his words.

"What forest would that be?"

"There is a great wood nestled beneath the mountains. I saw it in the distance. A deep dark wood it appeared, even with the sun flooding the countryside surrounding it."

Rogan exchanged glances with Olen, who nodded. "We don't go near that wood," the Kaan told Corin. "We'll ride just close enough to see what is going on, then we'll turn back and be on our way. I suspect that's a Ptarnian scouting party that caught your friends unawares. Their main force must be north of us."

"What of General Belmarius?"

Olen shrugged. "Hard to guess. Perhaps the Ptarnians ambushed his Bears during the night and what we saw is all that remains of their force."

Corin shook his head. "Belmarius is no fool to be caught out like that. But whoever is down there will need our help from those Ptarnians."

"Not if they are making for that forest."

"Why so?" Corin stared hard at Olen.

"Because that forest is cursed, Corin an Fol. It is not named Darkvale for nothing."

Darkvale.

Corin shivered as an icy tingle settled along his spine. He recalled that someone at some time had warned him about Darkvale. Why, who, and when? Too late to worry about that now. An hour later, Corin left the camp with Olen and a hundred volunteers, among them Arami of the Anchai and Kerante of the Oromai. It was later that morning that they caught up with Belmarius.

Chapter 16

The Fury of Corin an Fol

It didn't prove difficult. All they had to do was follow the heavy boot tracks leading from east to west, and then make for where the birds were circling high in the winter sky, their small black shapes studding the grey ahead. There was no snow this morning, but a chill wind soughed relentless from the steppes.

Corin shivered; no amount of wool or leather could rebuff those icy probing fingers. Perhaps Olen was right and the Wind God was close. Certainly there was a grim atmosphere to this region. He hoped that wasn't the case; he'd seen enough deities recently to last a lifetime.

Closing the gap, Corin saw ravens swooping and diving in the lowering skies ahead; with them, the larger shapes of buzzards could be seen gliding down, some settling out of sight in the distance. Corin steeled his heart; this didn't bode well. Olen caught his eye and nodded grimly. There were more tracks now, evidence that a great many feet had marched this way since last snowfall.

They rode apace for several miles, at last slowing down as they reached the base of a low flat hill. Above this mound, the ravens croaked and mocked them. Olen reined in, motioning his men follow suit. Corin patted Thunder's back and then blew on his hands, enabling movement to return to his fingers.

"No point in us all riding up there!" Olen yelled through the wind. "Corin and I will take a look. Arami too. Kerante, best you stay here and keep watch for any movement on the steppes whilst we investigate."

The Oromai leader nodded quietly, and Corin noted how the Purple Clan's Kaan seemed content to follow Olen's lead. Kerante watched as the three riders split from the pack and urged their steeds up the gentle rise of the hillock.

A huge lone oak stood like a mighty guardian at the top of that climb, its bare branches blackened and crowded with the squawking cluster of carrion birds. From those stark limbs, the birds observed the three riders' approach with baleful glares, then as one, they took wing and screamed at them from above.

Corin felt an icy shiver run along his spine. He had a very bad feeling about this. Wary-eyed, the three approached the tree. On closer inspection, they found the trunk was hollow, with a great split running down its entire length, those crow-deserted limbs reaching out like creaking black fingers as the wind whipped up a gale around the tree.

Crows, rooks, and ravens shrieked down at them, as Corin and Olen and Arami guided their horses closer to the great oak. The tree was dead, and so was the man hanging from it.

Without comment, Corin eased his long limbs from Thunderhoof's back and ventured toward the oak. He gazed up at the bulky figure swaying in the wind and his heart sank like a brick tossed down a well when he recognised the bluff honest face of General Belmarius, renowned leader of the Regiment of Bears.

The general swung in his armour, creaking and swaying. His eyes were gone and half the hair on his scalp was missing. Corin stared up at Belmarius's lifeless body in silence, and as he stared it seemed to him that his whole world was crashing down around him. Belmarius was dead, and Corin's dreams of reaching Car Carranis and Shallan were shattered into dust.

Behind him, Olen slid from Loroshai's back. Knife in hand, he scaled the tree, reached out across the limb and sliced the rope above the dead general's head. Belmarius's corpse thudded onto the soft snow beneath it. Arami watched on wild-eyed, whilst Corin scarcely blinked.

"Belmarius?" Olen had sheathed his knife and shimmied down the tree. He studied the corpse.

Corin didn't respond. He seemed as one frozen in time.

"What ails him?" Arami yelled at Olen as the Kaan remounted his horse to survey the area past the tree. "Did he know this man?"

"Aye so, best we leave him be for a moment and take a look around." Arami nodded and the two Rorshai left Corin standing silent in the icy wind, his face white and his eyes cold as northern seas.

Beyond the lone tree was evidence of a large camp. All around it were strewn the hacked and maimed bodies of men. There must have been several hundred. Many were big warriors, moustached and clad in rusty armour, though most were smaller in build, their armour shiny and painted in bright colours and their pointed helmets covered by face chains.

Olen leaned down from his horse and with his scimitar eased back the mask-chain of a dead warrior. The corpse-face staring back at him was dark-skinned and lean, with narrow sloping eyes the colour of coal. Olen had seen faces like this before when he'd spied down on the army in the ravine far to the east.

"Ptarnian." Olen slid his sword back in its scabbard. "They must have crashed in on Corin's friends whilst they were sleeping, despite their being veterans."

"Even so, they sold their lives dear." Arami scanned the bodies as he sat his horse. "There are twice as many Ptarnian dead here."

Olen nodded that he'd seen enough. He motioned Arami return with him to where Corin stood statue-still beneath the tree.

"Nothing we can do here," Olen told the Anchai. "Best we head back to Rorshai. This was only a small part of the army I saw. I guess most have headed north making for the Gap of Leeth. These must have been stragglers or else maybe scouts."

"What of those we saw earlier making for the forest?"

"I expect they are already dead, alongside those they were pursuing. You know that forest's reputation?"

Arami inclined his head without further comment. They reined in, seeing Corin still standing and gazing as one struck blind and fey into the wind. Behind him the big horse Thunderhoof stood dark and silent as his master.

"Has he lost his mind?" Arami muttered. The young Anchai warrior was anxious, as he too sensed a wrongness in the atmosphere. Olen shook his head and motioned Arami wait while he spoke with Corin.

If Corin noticed the Kaan appearing beside him, he made no sign, but stood stiff and silent as a man frozen, or else struck dumb by sudden lightning.

"A hard-fought battle took place here," Olen said, his deep blue gaze resting on the frosted corpse of the illustrious general. "His Bears did themselves proud. Judging by the fallen, they defended their camp against a force much greater. The Ptarnian dead heavily outnumber theirs."

Olen reached out and gripped Corin's shoulder. Still his friend didn't respond. "Come Corin—it serves no purpose us remaining here. Best we return to the Delve and make ready for a long winter campaign. Most of those raiders have fared north but I daresay they'll return."

"I didn't know him well." Corin's stony gaze brushed over the ice-crusted corpse of Belmarius. "But he listened to my counsel, and because of that he lies dead and frozen here today. A brave man." Corin spat into the wind and the spittle flew back in his face. He didn't notice.

"I heard he was a shrewd battlemaster who would only listen to someone whose advice was sound. You are not to blame here, Corin an Fol. No man may outlive his wyrd."

Corin turned and smiled at Olen. There was no mirth in that grin, only irony. "Looks like I'm going to Car Carranis alone. Which way is north?"

"You are talking like a fool!" Olen yelled in his face, trying to promote any kind of response that would free his friend from his self-loathing. "You wouldn't last a day out there alone. I told you these dead Ptarnians were only a part of a much larger force. And if by some miracle you evade their scouts and reach the Gap then you'll find it filled with a hundred thousand barbarians. Even you, Longswordsman, have no chance of reaching that city alive."

"We had no chance with Belmarius's boys helping me," Corin replied, his gaze still on the general. "But I don't give a shit about chance. I will find a way through and I will enter that city fortress and find the woman I love. No god, spook, goblin, or fucking army of men can stop me."

Olen's hands dropped by his side and his face grew grim. "Then I can do nothing for you, Longswordsman. My responsibility lies with my people. I like you Corin an Fol, I really do, but I'm not prepared to sacrifice my men in some crazy suicide scheme. Either you come back with us, or you fare north alone. I am sorry."

Corin hadn't been listening. Instead his expression had changed, his face now lit with savage joy. "We can avenge them! Those men we saw earlier heading west, we can kill them and save Belmarius's survivors before they get trapped in that forest!"

"Forget it! They are dead men already! And I daresay those Ptarnians chasing them will perish also. No one of sense goes near that wood, Corin. Darkvale is death!"

Corin smiled at Olen again. "Didn't I just hear you say that no man may outlive his wyrd?"

"That doesn't mean he should rush headlong to greet it."

But Corin still wasn't listening. His mind was set. If two armies blocked the north, then he'd find another way through. A secret way and a road he'd used when stationed in Point Keep.

The Wild Way—the old path threading the mountains' spine would serve to bring him close to Gap of Leeth without being apprehended. This time of year it would be deserted and the only thing he'd have to worry about was sourcing enough food and fuel for warmth—something he'd done all his life.

Easy. That way Corin could catch up with any stray easterners and kill them and also join with any remnant of Belmarius's men that had survived. No matter the odds and no matter the outcome. He was Corin an Fol and he was bound for Car Carranis. Nothing else mattered. Simple. Why had it seemed so difficult before? Corin grinned and his eyes took on a feral gleam as he felt the battle madness surge into his veins.

"I bid you farewell Rorshai!" Corin raised a fist to Olen and Arami who watched in stunned silence as the Longswordsman vaulted onto Thunderhoof's back and yelled his horse gallop full pelt through the chaos of camp and corpses and down the hill to the snow-covered grasses beyond.

"He rides to his death!" Arami shouted. "A brave and foolish man." He shrugged and followed the Kaan back down at a slower pace to where the others waited on their horses.

Olen's face was bleak as he guided his horse to join Kerante. "Where is Corin?" the older man asked.

"Gone." Olen would say no more on the matter. "Time we departed," he muttered instead, and made ready to address his riders. But before he could issue his orders, Olen froze.

Clear as the day surrounding him, he saw her standing there, just for the glimmer of a second. The Seeress of Silent Mountain. There she stood, her eyes accusing and her bony fingers pointing at him. Even now her husky voice echoed around his head

Corin an Fol is the fulcrum—the Chosen One. You must not abandon him!

Olen gasped and blinked, and when he opened his eyes she was gone. Though she had vanished, he stared at the place where he'd seen her for several long seconds, his body shaking and mind hard-wired. Men shuffled and fidgeted on their horses, and some exchanged puzzled glances, though most eyes were on the Kaan. Arami steered close. "You were saying?"

"Nothing." Olen squinted up at the sky. "Looks like more snow coming," he mumbled to Arami, whose expression was beyond quizzical and concerned. In a quieter voice he added, "I've just seen her."

"Who?"

"The Seeress. She was standing watching us just over there."

"Are you certain?" Arami's face blanched and he turned to stare to where Olen inclined his head.

"It was she. I could hear her voice inside my head, telling me we cannot abandon Corin. That we have to help him."

"Then we are dead men too," Arami growled as Olen turned to face his riders.

"Rorshai, you now face a choice. Ride forth with me or ride home. A vision of the Dreaming has come upon me and I now know what I must do. But it is no comfort knowing."

"What are you talking about?" Kerante of the Oromai yelled, "Speak up! What vision? What's weighing you down, Tcunkai?"

"The Dreaming—the Seeress. She spoke to me. He who has left us is the chosen one, and here we sit as he rides like a madman to his death."

"Who?" Kerante again. "You are talking nonsense, Kaan!"

"He means the stranger, Corin—the man's lost his mind and is riding bewitched toward Darkvale Forest!" Arami yelled.

"And I am riding after him," said Olen in a flat voice. "As I now know I must."

"Why?" Kerante's voice was joined with several others there.

"Call it destiny," Olen replied. "None of you need accompany me, but I ride to rescue my friend ere he ends himself in yonder wood. And you, Kerante, can avenge yourself on those Ptarnian dogs still living should you wish to."

"I'm coming with you!" Arami steered his horse in a circle. "If this is what the Seeress wants, then we must comply!"

"This is madness," Kerante shook his head. "But I will ride with you and see this thing through, though I fear your infection has spread to me also and my senses have I lost."

"Then let those who will ride out with us today!" Olen spurred Loroshai forward into the murky grey of fresh snowfall, whilst his grimacing Tcunkai warriors mustered around their Kaan. Behind them rode Arami and his Anchai. After a moment, Kerante roared, "Vengeance!" and spurred his beast forward, and soon after, all one hundred volunteers galloped full speed behind the Tcunkai Kaan. One turned back at Olen's shout, his task to return to Rogan and let the army know their latest decision. Olen doubted not that they'd all be dead before Rogan got that message.

***

Corin's mind surged as he urged Thunder on mercilessly, digging in his heels, making the big horse speed into a deep cleft that led down and then opened on a wide vale framed by shadowy trees in the distance. Darkvale.

Ahead was a column of soldiers hurrying on foot with spears. Beyond them, a smaller group mustering heroic at the edge of the woods. Both groups appeared agitated and uneasy, as though they were unsure what to do.

Corin hardly noticed them. Instead he laughed as the berserkergang (that wild northern rage) tore through him, shaking his limbs and rattling his mind. He wanted to kill, cut, and maim—destroy all in his path. It mattered not how many they were. Corin would avenge Belmarius, and then he would fare north along the mountains, and all the gods and spooks in Ansu could just try stopping him. He had Clouter and Biter and his wild untapped rage. He was fury and he was death!

Gone was Corin's reason and gone any thought of Shallan—save a seed deeply embedded that gave him distant purpose. It was as though something alien and cruel had gotten inside his head and was feeding his inner fires. He felt an uncanny, potent force giving him strength and anger beyond any he'd known before. This was no common rage but rather an inferno that threatened to unhinge this mind.

A face took shape in his head as Corin rode. The face of a woman, beautiful and perfect and stunning in a way that made Shallan look plain, and Vervandi dull as dishwater.

The woman was smiling at him, promising warmth and love and an end to all his woes. Her green eyes and full red lips urged him hurry, and around her perfect face, smoky black hair floated in slowest motion.

You are close…

Her voice was silk-soft and sultry. It stirred his loins and dizzied his head. Corin felt his memory blur and his vision dim. The trees ahead blurred too, and the sky was shrouded by sudden heavy snowfall, the flakes descending so thick that Corin could scarcely see at all. It was as though a cloud of gloom had risen up from before the forest, fogging his senses as well as his vision.

But Corin cared not, as the mystery woman was inside his head now, yelling that he kill and kill and kill, and guiding him to where the Ptarnians struggled and panicked in the sudden violent snowfall.

Corin laughed as he crashed upon them, a deathbringer swinging a great Longsword. Men cried out and were hewn, or else trampled by Thunder's mighty hoofs. Corin laughed and swung Clouter, caring not who he struck, and Clouter's steel dented as it smote armour alongside mail and steel.

Spears thrust up at him, but he sliced them away. He glimpsed odd-shaped helmets and heard muffled yelling, then screaming as he slew those who yelled. Hack and slice and stab and hew! Corin's rage burned within him until he thought he was on fire.

He heard distant shouts—a man calling out his name. Corin didn't register—he just kept lashing out with Clouter as the blizzard densened to blinding fog, and even the shuffling, shouting shapes of his enemies were lost to view. A man grabbed at his feet. Corin brought Clouter's wolf pommel down hard splitting the attacker's skull through his helmet. Never had he felt such strength.

Corin laughed and swung Clouter again. He had claimed a dozen more lives when he felt Thunder shudder and jolt as something struck the big horse's side. Thunderhoof reared and lashed out with his hooves, tossing his rider to the ground. The big horse whinnied and then crashed to lie still. Corin landed badly on his left elbow, snapping it like a rotten twig. He felt no pain, but the hand hung useless at his side and Clouter was nowhere to be seen. Neither was Thunderhoof.

Corin snarled and slid Biter free of its scabbard, as armoured figures lurched out at him from the fog. He laughed at them and sliced Biter through steel and flesh, his alien strength unstoppable. A man sobbed as his guts spilled free. Corin laughed again and closed in with Biter, killing two more men before a sharp blow struck the side of his head, knocking him forward, his vision blurred.

He rolled and lashed out with a foot. A helmet looked down at him then disappeared. Corin heard muffled shouts. Again a familiar voice called out his name. Then, like a tapped faucet, the fiery flow and strength and rage fled his bones. Corin stumbled and fell, rose half-blind, and stumbled again.

Corin heard more voices amid angry shouts and the urgent clash of steel. His strength had deserted him, replaced by an icy stab of fear clawing like a rodent inside his belly. He had to escape this place. Something inside him knew it was a trap. Corin ran and stumbled and ran again, but the fog inside his head and all around him closed like a net cast over him. He heard a voice—*her* voice—bidding him seek her deeper in the forest.

I will save you, but you must come find me!

"No!" Corin feared that voice now, and he winced when he saw the woman's green eyes gazing at him through the murk. Those jade lamps were laughing at him now. Corin ran, tripped, and righted himself with a tree branch. He shook his limbs into motion and then froze, as looking up he saw her standing there smiling at him.

Why are you afraid, when all I offer you is love? Come—my home lieth deep inside this forest. There you will find warmth and wine and love, and all your troubles will dissolve. Come visit me, Corin son of Fol!

The driving flurry hid her from him again, and Corin gasped as sudden pain tore into is left arm.

"Can you help me?"

He heard soft laughter drifting through the snow. Despite his senses warning him to flee, to Corin's addled mind it seemed he had but two choices: stay put and freeze and die, or else seek out the promised respite deeper in the forest.

He lacked the strength to go it alone in the wild now that he was wounded, his horse gone, and his berserk rage dried up. And he had reached the forest's shroud, and something within its shadowy mantle assured him that was where he was meant to be. And she waited—the green-eyed witch—her eyes glowing with promise of all his desires' fulfillment.

Behind him, Corin heard harsh shouts, and turning, could just make out the blurry shapes of men rushing at him from the gloom. He lacked the strength and will to fight, but a sudden urgent desire fuelled movement back into his limbs. Mind made up, Corin rushed headlong into the darkness that was Darkvale.

"Corin, wait—do not enter the forest!" He turned and briefly glimpsed Olen's blanched features through the fog. "Save yourself!" The voice faded as wind and storm carried Olen and reality far away.

Farewell Olen.

Corin turned and slung Biter back into its scabbard so that he could grip his wounded arm. The pain was screaming at him now, as was every warning bell inside his head. What madness had fallen upon him?

Again he heard the crone's voice by the river as she washed her bloodied rags. "You ride into peril, Corin an Fol." But it was too late. Already the mistress of the forest had cast her nets upon him.

End of Part One

Part Two

The Wild Way

Chapter 17

The Forest of Nightmares

Olen stood at the edge of the forest of Darkvale, the whirl of snow-flakes dancing past his face. The blizzard was easing at last, and he could make out the shapes of dark pines rising like ice spears into the distance.

Close by, Arami knelt by Corin's horse, attending the wound on the beast's flank. They had found Thunderhoof staggering around riderless, a cluster of corpses lying at his feet, and a cast spear protruding from his right flank.

"He'll mend," Arami said after removing the shaft and cleaning the wound with Thunder hardly making a sound. "He's as tough as his master."

Olen nodded and watched as Kerante loomed out of the white. "Still no sign?" Olen enquired as the Oromai Kaan slipped from his saddle and dusted snow from his purple cloak.

"Nothing." Kerante's expression was grim. "No tracks, sign, blood, or anything—just more Ptarnian dead scattered about, but no Longswordsman." Kerante's scimitar was crimson; he'd been mopping up the last of the Ptarnians they'd found. "What say you—do we keep looking?"

"Aye so." Olen's eyes were on the trees scarce twenty yards to his left. "Though I fear we'll have scant success, and suspect he has fallen victim to the evil residing in that wood."

"We have to try!" Arami rubbed his mittens and stamped his feet. The young Anchai had a renewed respect for Corin and now saw it as his personal quest to find the missing Longswordsman. "At least the Ptarnians are all dead. But what of the other lot, Corin's allies?"

"Disappeared too." Olen watched as a lone raven settled on the closest pine and glared their way. He shivered; there was something strange about that bird, and Olen got the strong impression someone watched them from somewhere close.

"We cannot linger in this witchy place. If Corin's entered that wood he's on his own. If he's who the Seeress says he is, then maybe he'll pull through. In the meanwhile, let's comb for tracks going the other way."

The Rorshai riders spent the rest of that dreary day searching for signs of Corin an Fol and found nothing. Olen blamed himself; if he had followed after Corin at once then perhaps he could have saved his friend. He had spied Corin twice in the distance as they drew near the wood but had been disoriented by the blizzard and had lost him again.

The Rorshai had killed a great many Ptarnians. That hadn't proved difficult, as the marauders had been cold and confused and evidently terrified of the forest surrounding them. And Olen could understand their dread as he cast a bleary eye toward the trees again. There was real malice in there, and every bone in his body bid him flee while he still had breath.

But they stayed close till nightfall, then retired a mile away and risked a small fire as it was bitter cold, but at least the snow had stopped. Soon a pale moon winked silver through cloud, spreading its gaze on the dale surrounding them, but not on the forest beyond.

That was when Olen saw him—the rider in the sky. The ancient horseman by some called the Wanderer, he hurried forth a dark storm, his hounds baying overhead and a host drifting silent behind him.

The Wild Hunt was abroad.

Olen's riders gazed up in horror as the grim vision tore across the night sky. The Wanderer blew three times on his ghostly horn and then, even from that distance, those watching by their campfire could feel the heavy gaze of his single eye.

The Wanderer pointed his spear toward them and then swung it around, whilst guiding his eight-legged stallion to face north. With a final horn blast, the host rode high, passing overhead and fading into the distant shadows of The High Wall.

It might have been his imagination, but Olen thought he glimpsed the faces of the dead Ptarnians he'd spied that morning rushing behind the Wanderer's hounds. With a distant boom, the host vanished, and the moon rolled back behind cloud.

The following morning, a pale sun spilled a modicum of warmth on the white dale and moor surrounding the dark forest, brooding a mile to their north. Olen walked among his men alongside Arami and Kerante. The vision last night had terrified them all—except Olen, who now had a grim determined set to his jaw.

"So what do you propose?" Kerante asked him while they were breaking camp. "Back to Rorshai?"

Olen shook his head. "That was a message from the Skyrider last night. He is faring north for war and bids us do the same. Corin—should he survive Darkvale—will make for Point Keep, the old fortress, and we will do the same."

"What of the Ptarnians?" Arami had overheard their conversation.

"We kill any we find." Olen smiled grimly. "Their main force will be far north of us by now, and if we stick close to the mountains we should avoid their scouts. "Come, alert the others we're riding out. Once we join Rogan and the rest back at the Greywoods we'll fare north. What say you, my friends and comrades?"

***

The aging king slumped on his throne and watched his handsome son gesticulating enthusiastically in front of him. Callanz had all the fire that his father had lost years ago. His eldest now called himself Emperor and flaunted the title openly in front of his father. It was common news throughout court that Callanz was waiting for King Akamates to drown himself in drink. That wouldn't take long, Akamates thought with a wry smile, as he watched the fire glint in his son's eyes.

"Father, we have heard from the first expedition. Pashel Akaz has reached the western ranges. I received coded bird this morning. We can commence the invasion within days!"

"What of the Urgolais?" Akamates let his smile fall from his face. Callanz had an unhealthy enthusiasm concerning the dark brethren. Akamates and his fathers had served and sacrificed to the Dog People as had been their duty, but his son was unusually ardent in his passion for offering blood.

Callanz had big dreams. It had been his suggestion and persistence that had led to Akamates bidding one of his three great armies march west into the barbaric lands beyond the Great Plains.

What lay there was of scant interest to Akamates. He—like his forefathers—had been more than content with subjugating every kingdom surrounding Ptarni and bringing them to heel. Only distant Shen had been powerful enough to rebuff their forces.

But this wasn't enough for Callanz. A month ago he had spilled into court, the blood of his last sacrifice dripping from his forearms. "Morak has spoken to me!" Callanz had addressed the court rather than his father. "He says there is a land of vast wealth and treasures rotting beyond the plains. A kingdom ripe for the taking, for its people are lost and their gods forsaken."

"What say you, Father?" Callanz had turned and addressed the king, now he had the whole court buzzing. "Those lands parade the western ocean. Once they are ours, we will command the seas as well as most this entire continent. Too long have we sat on our heels!

This last comment was addressed to the crowd, but Akamates knew it was just another stab at his kingship. For forty years, Akamates had ruled as fairly and wisely as he knew how, but that wasn't enough, in his son's opinion.

The news that the deity Morak himself had spoken of these lands had caused such fervour that Akamates' only choice had been to give his son his blessing and bid the entire Second Army, under command of the capable Pashel Akaz, range west across the steppes.

Now Akamates drained his wine glass and smiled his thin smile. That had been a month ago, and this was the first word Callanz had received from that army.

"What next, Emperor?" The king bid a slave pour him more wine. He slumped back further in the throne and showed his teeth to his preening son. Callanz held the court at his every word. Callanz was loved by the gods and loved by his people, whilst his father was a dry old stick taking too long to die.

Callanz's dark eyes flashed annoyance hearing that title. "The people chose that title Father—not I." Then his face brightened like a child receiving an unexpected gift. "But don't you see, this is a chance for Ptarni to become the greatest realm that ever was?"

"That ever was?" Akamates coughed into his wine. "Your ambition might prove your undoing, Callanz. That or your trust of the Dog-People. Ever have we steered a wary course with them, and yet you go full out to sate their every desire."

"Father, I —"

"Go ahead, sack yonder kingdoms, slay and enslave whomsoever you can. And then what? Swim in that foreign sea? Catch cold? The Urgolais will have their price, Callanz, and it will be a high one."

"That may well prove the case." The Emperor's eyes narrowed to cunning slits of coal. "But they need us too! Morak seeks his old spear—Golganak. With that returned, he would regain his former powers. I have promised to deliver it to him, and in return, he will ensure that Ptarni rises to become the greatest Empire since the days of legendary Xandoria—that fabled, fallen kingdom rumored to lie across the sea from Shen."

Callanz stopped as his father rose from his seat of indolent power, spilling crimson wine from his heavy gold chalice and dropping the cup to clatter and roll on the mosaic floor at his feet.

"It appears I have sired the greatest of fools!" Akamates roared at his son. "That spear is as evil as its master! And while he has been without it we have always managed to appease him. But with it, he will use us as his puppets and then destroy us. He will obliterate Ptarni or else enslave our race when he is done. Morak despises mankind!"

"But Father —"

"You, most wretched son, have sold our people to the Dog Lords, and without my permission. I am still king here! Go now, Callanz. Leave my realm whilst I still have the strength to banish you from it!"

Callanz stood for a minute staring defiantly back at his father. "As you wish... King." The smirk smeared his handsome face and mocked his father. "But I am the power in this 'Kingdom,' and soon you will be dead!" Callanz laughed then, and turning on his heels, swept his golden cloak behind him and briskly vacated the palace.

Akamates felt both strength and anger fade from his limbs as his son departed. He sank back on the throne and supped hard at the new chalice that had quickly been replaced at his table. So the spear would soon be loosed, and the time long foretold was finally upon them. He was almost glad he wouldn't live to see it.

***

The wood's thick tapestry was dry and warm after the bitter chill of the wilderness outside, the pines so dense and close no sky could pierce their mantle, and neither could any determined snowflake reach that dense carpet of needles far below.

Corin walked as one lost in a dream. His arm no longer troubled him, and all fear, fatigue, and chill had vanished the minute he'd ventured deeper into the forest. Darkvale—the name meant little to him. Someone, somewhere, had said something about it. So what? She was waiting for him somewhere within its midst—the woman whose warm promises he felt inside his head and whose smiling green eyes he saw through the trees.

He heard her sultry tones as he hurried beneath the drooping limbs of willow, birch, and creaking alder—the pines having given way to older, heavier trees. She whispered more promises to him, beckoning him hurry to claim them, her voice soft as willow brushing soil.

There were no paths in this forest, but Corin threaded his long limbs betwixt briar and thorn, hardly noticing as they tore deep into his flesh. He walked into darkness, the trees closing in as if listening to his hurried breath.

At last he reached a glade containing a small pasture, ordered and neat. Corin saw cows grazing and a lone sheep rubbing its back against a fence. A peaceful, gentle scene. Canes were tied in wigwams with beans descending and bees buzzing noisily around.

It was hot, the snow long forgotten, and a bright sun sent golden shafts of light into the surrounding trees. Ahead rested a cottage, small and thatched with low chimney and steady smoke drifting up into the blue. At its door stood the woman, her arms folded and and the loveliest smile on her lips.

She beckoned him approach, and Corin almost tripped with eagerness to reach her. There she stood, tall and slender, her tanned ankles and arms hinting at greater delights hidden beneath her deep green dress. She wore a smile like other women wore silk, and her eyes were the green of polished emeralds in firelight.

As one stupefied with drink, Corin fell into her arms, and she closed her net around him, soft and strong and silent. Snap! Her full lips brushed his, and to Corin it felt that he had never kissed a woman before. Gone was his memory, his purpose, or his reason for existing, all extinguished by this witchy woman's kiss. She kissed him again and then smiled, letting her hands drop to caress the stirring he felt below.

"Come inside," she told him. "I have been waiting for you."

"Who are you?" Corin heard himself mutter, though his lips trembled and his words were but echoes lost in that enchanted place. And though he hardly cared for an answer.

"Someone who knows you well, Corin an Fol, and someone who can heal your pain like no other could even attempt. I have many names," she told him as she placed a slender arm in his and led him to a leather chair parked easy by the glowing log fire.

"You can call me Maife; it's a name I bore in my younger days. Come, Corin, sit by the fire and let me heal your weariness. You have come a long way and achieved much, though little reward have you received. Scant appreciation, save only hints and innuendoes from those who have used you. And they have used you ill. You deserve better, Longswordsman."

As she said the final words, her soft hand slipped inside his trousers and eased his tension within. "Love me!" Maife's voice was husky in his ears and her breath hung over him like honey wine. "It has been so long since a real man entered my domain, and I have been so very lonely cooped up in this wood."

Corin groaned as she worked her hand up and down expertly. He reached beneath her dress, sliding his fingers up her thighs, but then she laughed and pulled away. "Later," she promised. "First you must rest, and to rest properly you need good strong ale."

"Ale," Corin smiled, and before he knew it she'd produced a brimming cup of beer and leaned to placed it in his shaking hands. Corin smiled as her smoky hair brushed his face. He leant forward to kiss her again, but she backed off.

"Drink it." Maife's smile fell away from her face. He didn't notice, but her eyes had hardened to urgent jade glints.

So drink it he did, and moments later, Corin slumped into a deep and troubled dream—if dream it was, for the visions that flew at him were hideous and real.

***

He woke inside his dream, his laced eyes blinking in total darkness. Outside, an owl screeched, and something large clawed at the timbers of the cottage. Corin shivered, and looking down, he saw that he was naked, and in horror he noticed there were signs and shapes cut shallow into his flesh. He cried out, and the woman loomed close. Her hair no longer smelt of honey, but stank of decaying death.

"You are mine now." She smiled, but there was no kindness in her face. The visage gazing down at him was infinitely beautiful and quintessentially cruel. "Corin an Fol, brave and valiant warrior. The Chosen One—they said. The fulcrum and a new hope! But you are none of those things. Instead you are a fool, weak and easy as any other man."

Corin tried to rise, but her hand slapped him back hard on the chair. Those fingers burnt his naked flesh like glacial ice. Their icy touch sapped all strength left in his veins.

"It was my task to trap you and keep you for a while, at least until I grow bored. And I do get bored most easily!" She laughed in his ear and Corin screamed silently, feeling her long broken nails scraping deep inside the soft flesh of his inner thighs. The woman called Maife laughed. Corin kicked out at her but his feet found no target. The woman had vanished. A show of motion drifted by the door, a shape that faded to grey like day-old ashes in the gloom. He heard distant laughter like wind chimes in a gale.

Light fled the room then, and dark things rushed at him. He heard screams, the clash of steel on steel, and as his eyes adjusted to the gloom, Corin found himself inside a broken roofless shack with man-size cobwebs glistening in the moonlight. The dark winking owl perched on a beam, its eyes green as emeralds.

Corin tried to rise, shout out, and break free from the dream in any way he could. But his words would form no sounds and his body felt weak and cold as though invisible chains cut into his skin. His flesh crawled and shivered, and looking down in horror Corin saw there were tiny grey things scurrying up his legs, whilst others crawled around his face, occasionally settling to bite his forehead and cheek. And all the while that metallic laughter filtered through from the chilly black outside.

The scene shifted. Corin stood beneath a city's great walls, a pile of corpses all around, and a cloaked figure approached with a long black spear held aloft in both hands.

Corin felt the corpses stir at his feet and gasped as they reached up and tugged him down through the soil. The cloaked figure loomed over him, and Corin screamed as the black spear skewered his flesh, and all strength, will, and courage leaked out from his veins.

This is not real!

A small voice reached him—maybe it was his own voice, but he couldn't tell.

Do not surrender to the dream—THIS IS NOT REAL!

Corin wrenched his lips apart in a silent scream. "Help me!" The words scurried like rats from the room, and above his head Corin saw a shadow growing like a huge bat and hanging over his bleeding body. Looking up, he cried out as Maife's feral eyes bore like beetles deep inside his head.

But suddenly Corin was aware of another shadow, a warm shadow of copper and gold filtering into his dream. A voice he recognized broke through the dark. "He is not yours, cousin! You must release him—you have no right holding him here!"

The bat-like shadow folded its wings and stretched along the walls, becoming a spider. As it crawled, Maife's whispers followed it like the noisome buzz of blowflies on a corpse. "You trespass, Vervandi. You have no power here. This is *my* realm!"

"But he is mine, and his destiny awaits him. You have no sanction here, Undeyna. It is you who trespass, dark cousin who so long ago betrayed the light!" The shadows met and intermingled, Corin felt a tingle all over his body as the fusion in the air erupted like plasma inside his head.

The faint shadow of Vervandi flickered as the greater spider shadow surrounded it and smothered its honey glow to black. A bell tolled, and a silent scream fled into the night.

A crashing thud revealed Vervandi lying prone at his feet like a broken doll, twisted and torn. The spider/bat shape folded and dropped to the floor, becoming Maife again. In her left hand was a dagger, long and black and twisted. It shimmered slightly in the gloom. She crouched low over Vervandi's prone form, and yanking her head back by her copper hair, scraped the blade along her white throat. Vervandi's blood oozed out, soaking Corin's feet.

"Now it's your turn." Maife's smile at Corin was as twisted as her knife. She leaned low over Corin's struggling body and plunged the knife hard into his belly. Corin roared as the red pain tore open inside him; even in his dream state he felt his consciousness fade and his butchered self float like a cloud above the oozing wrecks that were his and Vervandi's bodies.

A sound broke through his pain, driving it into the background. The long doleful note of a horn. Corin felt his inner self crash back inside his body. He opened his eyes.

Silence. Vervandi was gone. Gone too were the other woman and the gaping rent in his belly, the shapes cut in his flesh, and the crawling creatures. Corin gasped out loud with relief. He heard a croaky chuckle coming from somewhere close. Corin shifted his body until he saw who stood in the doorway with arms folded, surveying him as a butcher studies hides.

An old man, but no stranger to Corin. He watched the Wanderer stoop low beneath the broken doorway at the entrance of the shack. A single damning silver eye fell upon Corin, and then the Huntsman crashed through the room and swept Corin's body up in his iron-strong arms as though he were a lamb.

"Am I still dreaming?" Corin asked, as the Wanderer summoned his eight-legged horse, and after tossing Corin over the saddle, clambered on Uppsalion's back and bade the mighty deathsteed carry them up to the night skies above. "Am I dead?" Corin felt the chill of winter night return as that silver gaze fell upon him again.

"You live." The voice was a blunt saw scraping metal. "Your time has yet to come, Corin an Fol," the Wanderer told him. "But come it will."

"Where are you taking me?"

"To meet your father." The Wanderer raised his great horn to his lips and blew a long cold note. Corin felt an icy rush of air followed by a sense of falling through dark, then the cold soft touch of snow settled all around him, blanketing his fall.

Corin opened his eyes and blinked in bright sunlight. The Wanderer had vanished. Instead, Vervandi was seated close by on a large flat stone, Clouter gripped in her slender hands. Corin almost wept to see her lovely face.

"I thought you were dead." He struggled to rise, but his body ached so much he fell forward on his face.

"Almost I was, and it pains me that I owe my Father the debt of saving me and yourself alike—because he always has a price."

"Your father is the Wanderer?"

"The same. You are alone now Corin, I cannot aid you here. But at least you are free from her clutches. I suggest you go seek warmth in a cave and rest up a while."

"Must you leave me?" Corin felt a sudden urge to hold this woman close. Vervandi, his first love, the mystery woman who had saved him from self-destruction after losing his kin. He had learnt not to trust her, but his heart cried out for her now.

She read his thoughts and smiled. "Would that I could, but then, I thought you loved another? Besides, I must depart—I am much weakened by my encounter with Undeyna."

"The wood-witch—she said her name was Maife?" Dimly Corin remembered that. "Is she slain?"

"Even my Father lacks the mandate to slay Undeyna. Maife was once a cousin of mine, but the Shadowman stole her soul and she serves Him now. Her punishment for that betrayal was to be fenced inside that grim wood until the end of time. You were warned to stay clear, Corin—lucky are you we were in the area."

Vervandi stood briskly and tossed Clouter to the snow at Corin's feet. "Take your sword and go forth before night brings fresh dangers. We are still close to Darkvale; neither of us should tarry here. She cannot leave that forest but there are Dark Faen hereabouts who will hunt you in her name."

"Who is my father, Vervandi?" Corin felt a sudden wash of shame flushing through his veins. He had forgotten Shallan and now was filled with urgent purpose to resume his journey north. But the Wanderer's words still echoed in his head. Past time that riddle was solved. Feeling stronger, Corin rolled to his feet and seized Clouter with both fists, feeling power to hold the sword again.

"He is close." Vervandi smiled and turned away. "I can say no more. Farewell beloved!"

"Where am I?" Corin yelled at her departing shadow.

"You are on The Wild Way. North lies Point Keep and Car Carranis and the woman that you think you love." Vervandi's slender form faded from view behind a rock. Corin rushed to follow her but she had vanished in the sunlight. Instead, he gazed down at a wide sloping side of The High Wall. Far below and to the south a distant threatening gloom hinted where Darkvale lay. Aside that, the bright day fell on glistening snow and flanking mountains marching shoulder over shoulder. Corin shook movement into his limbs. He stretched his muscles, pushing off against the rock, feeling stronger than he had any right to. It was only then that he recalled how he'd broken his arm after falling from Thunderhoof's back. Corin stared at the arm and tested it in wonder. Had that been a dream too? Enough thinking; he needed to get going whilst the day allowed progress and warmth.

Corin strode along The Wild Way, not stopping until dusk, when mercifully he found a cave and took much needed rest. Corin was beyond exhausted, and he couldn't begin to comprehend what had just happened to him.

He knew that a madness had come upon him after seeing Belmarius's corpse swaying in the wind. After that, he recalled little save hearing Olen's anxious shouts and Thunderhoof's whinny of pain as he threw Corin from his back. "Poor Thunder," Corin muttered as he struggled to light a kindling fire. "You were a grand old lad. I'm so sorry."

Corin felt the tears well up in his eyes as he thought of his great warhorse slain. He'd lost his friends and his horse, but at least he had his life. Whatever that was worth. But Shallan waited. He would cling on to that thought. She waited in that fortress, and he would come. He had survived something he didn't understand. That meant they needed him—the Wanderer and His team. That was no small comfort in this lonely place. Sure, they'd play him to their tunes, but they needed him alive. And as long as Corin still drew breath then he would find Shallan, and together they would carve out a life in this crazy dangerous world called Ansu.

And he did love her, despite what Vervandi had said. With that last determined thought, Corin's eyes closed and he sank into a deep and mercifully dreamless sleep. Which was just as well, because when he woke the cold press of steel was hard against his neck.

Chapter 18

Reunion

Teret called out a warning as the archer's head appeared from the bushes ahead. "Ambush!" she yelled as Tamersane ducked in his saddle, feeling the whoosh of the arrow racing close above his head.

Shouts followed, and Tamersane, yelling and swearing and flapping his arms about, wheeled his horse around, and commenced galloping frantically back down to where she waited tense astride her own saddle.

"Outlaws!" Tamersane hollered in her ear as his horse thundered past hers.

"Yes, I noticed." Teret crinkled her nose and briskly urged her beast follow Tamersane's.

They had been traversing The Wild Way for two days and had seen nothing living save one hungry-looking fox and a brace of squawking quail running and jumping ahead of them. It had snowed heavily most of the time and they had made slow progress, but Tamersane had taken cheer when he recognised a part of the ancient track.

Here the land fell away to the right, awarding deep views of the snow-clad slopes and timberline now far below them. Beyond and behind them in the far distance, they could just make out the neat white folds of Rorshai fields miles away.

"I've been here before," he'd told her. "The road splits several miles ahead, the left fork dropping down steep to Wynais. It's a difficult descent, but at least we'll have sanctuary when we get there."

Instead what they got was an ambush.

A half-mile down from where Teret had spotted the archer they ran into more trouble. A dozen armed men with spears were blocking their way ahead.

"What the fuck?" Tamersane screwed his eyes against the glare of bright sun on snow. "These look like Raleenian Lancers out of Atarios, I'd recognise those outfits anywhere!"

"What are they doing up here?" Teret slipped a knife into her left hand and made ready, lest any man try hurting her lover. Other soldiers sprang out from the walls mounting either side of The Wild Way and joined those already blocking the road south.

"Buggered if I know." Tamersane smiled at Teret as they reined in and waited, which was their only choice as there was nowhere to go. "Don't worrit, sweetling—I shall handle this!" He grinned at her and Teret gripped the knife even tighter in her fist. A rider appeared behind the last lot of lancers and casually guided his horse through their cluster. He was garbed in heavy cloak with a deep hood hiding his features.

"Hello there!" Tamersane raised his palm and grinned. "All friends here!"

"Of all the bloody hazards in this wilderness, I never expected to encounter you, Tamersane of Wynais." A rough chuckle followed, and the rider reined in to stare at them from several yards distant.

"I know this man." The horseman bid the Raleenians relax their guard behind him. "He is cousin to Queen Ariane herself, though what he's doing up here with this Rorshai wench is beyond baffling."

"Show your face and quit smirking!" Tamersane didn't like

this stranger calling Teret a Rorshai wench. "This is the Lady Teret, formerly of Morning Hills. She is daughter to the Tcunkai Kaan—though the poor chap's dead now."

Another chuckle, and the rider pushed his hood back allowing the sunlight to fall on his face. Tamersane nearly fell from his horse recognising the hard tanned features and white-cropped hair of Silon of Port Sarfe.

"Oh, it's you!" Tamersane struggled to disguise his relief. Instead he blinked in the sun and tried not to look smug. "Well, if it's strange us being up here then what about you lot? It's a long way to Raleen. This merchant hails from Port Sarfe," Tamersane muttered to Teret who was looking both bemused and angry. "He is a friend and ally to our cause."

"A friend?" Teret glared at Silon and the surrounding Raleenians, not forgetting the arrow near Tamersane's head, and waved her dagger at them. Silon laughed and some of the spearmen chuckled. Teret hissed at them.

"Looks like you've found a lass who can handle you at last," Silon remarked. "Come on Kelwynian, bring your Rorshai lady, and we'll escort you to Herself."

"Who is Herself?" Teret's frown deepened. "Is there something I need to know?" Tamersane blinked at her.

"Queen Ariane of Kelwyn of course—she'll be most excited to see her wayward cousin." Silon rode forward and clasped Tamersane's arm. "Glad you're still alive laddie. Come on!"

They rode behind the merchant, who waved back the archers, these now appearing in their dozens from either side of the road. "You expecting company?" Tamersane asked Silon, who shrugged.

"It's a long story. I'll let Ariane explain."

They found the queen sitting on a rock drinking hot tea with a group of people gathered close. Tamersane grinned when he recognised Cale and Galed among the group. There were several Raleenians present and the rest were clearly from Kelwyn. Beyond where they sat and stood talking, a great number of soldiers lurked moody by horses, watching and talking amongst themselves.

Tamersane was amazed to see what appeared to be well over a hundred fighting men gathered either side of the place where The Wild Way forked and a second track wound left into rocks.

Ariane looked up as Silon rode into her rudimentary camp; as she glanced Tamersane she leapt to her feet, smiling and spilling tea.

"Cousin? Is it really you?" Teret watched taut-faced as Tamersane swung his legs free of his saddle and sprang across to embrace the young queen. Ariane was dressed in tight black leather trousers and long-sleeved navy tunic, topped with a white fur collar and cuffs. She wore a tawny wolf cloak, and from her pearl-studded belt hung two swords.

Teret waited in frosty silence as her lover and his queen kissed and hugged, a business that went on far too long in her opinion, despite Tamersane's earlier insistence that this dark-haired beauty was just a cousin.

"Doesn't it make you want to smile?" the man called Silon said beside her. Teret noticed the diamond in his left ear for the first time.

"No," she answered. "It doesn't."

"Tell me everything! Where is Corin? What happened to your hand?" Ariane fired questions at Tamersane as he sat on a tree stump a piping cup of tea clasped in his chapped hands. By his side, the woman Teret looked uncomfortable and edgy.

Ariane had smiled at her and bade her join them, but the Rorshai woman had only done so reluctantly and now chose to wear an aloof, disinterested expression, which Ariane could not help but find amusing.

"And who is she?" Ariane whispered in Tamersane's ear when Teret was looking the other way. Silon alone persisted in talking to the Rorshai healer woman, who for her part nodded a few times and responded in curt fashion to his advances.

Tamersane whispered back that this was the late Tcunkai Kaan's daughter, Teret, and explained how she had healed him from a nasty wound given to him by Corin an Fol. "An accident." Tamersane had waved a hand spilling tea. "I thought he was a Groil and attacked him."

"That was rather silly of you." Ariane had heard from Zallerak (whom, she'd informed Tamersane, was present somewhere) about the dragon's visit upon Fallowheld. "You were lucky to escape. But where is Corin?"

"He's with Belmarius, or else making that way; he has a bunch of Rorshai warriors with him—none of them seem to get on. They were going to some meeting at a place called the Delve, and then on to join Belmarius and make north for Car Carranis."

"And Shallan." Ariane smiled into her tea.

"I believe that's what drives him—yes."

Ariane took a long hard sip at her tea and placed the mug on the ground at her feet. "I do hope that Corin is not with Belmarius," she said in a quieter voice.

"Why is that?" Tamersane studied his cousin's dark eyes. Ariane's face was thinner than he'd last seen it when they had parted on the road near Vioyamis, well over a month ago.

"Because General Belmarius is dead." Tamersane's jaw dropped, and Teret, who had been listening despite pretending otherwise, turned to stare in disbelief at the queen's words.

"We came upon some of his men just yesterday, or rather some scouts I sent north did. They escorted them back here and I interviewed them. They are in a poor state, confused and very scared and unsure what happened to them. Zallerak believes they got entangled in Darkvale forest, so they are beyond lucky to be alive.

"Anyway, one of them had wits enough to inform us that Belmarius's camp was attacked at night by a large force of warriors they had never encountered before. Easterners he assumed—they wore chains from their helmets so they never got to see any faces."

"Ptarnians," said Tamersane and to his right Silon nodded agreement. "Teret's brother warned of an army approaching from the steppes. That must be them."

"Even so," the queen rubbed cold from her hands. "This man saw Belmarius fall to their pikes and spears. Soon after that, those Bears that could broke camp and fled with the remaining Ptarnians hard on their heels. After that, his account of things got confused so I let him rest with his fellows, who are sleeping in one of the spare tents. As I said they are in poor shape."

"What of my brother and the Tcunkai?" Teret's blue eyes bored into Ariane. "They rode out with this Corin you all speak of—this Longswordsman."

"The Kelthaine warrior from those Bears I spoke to never mentioned your people, so I assume they are still looking for Belmarius. Poor Corin, he will be devastated when he discovers the truth."

"That won't stop him," Silon said. "And now Tamersane—let's hear your story and then we will tell you why Queen Ariane's entire army is up here freezing in the mountains."

"That would be good to know." Tamersane turned to where Teret watched him, her face dark and unsure as evening fell suddenly upon them. "I owe everything to this lady," he told them, and began to relate the story from when he and Corin fled Fallowheld, their encounter with the weird Feroda, the journey through the mountains and the creatures that followed, and then the Rorshai and Rogan taking him to Morning Hills where he was healed by Teret and introduced to the Kaan. Last up, he spoke of the treacherous raid by the Anchai brigand, Sulo.

After Tamersane had finished his account, Ariane reached across and touched Teret's arm. "It seems I owe you a great deal. I'm fond of my cousin, though he has driven me to madness at times—him and his brother." Teret managed a stiff smile. "He is a good man."

"That he is, and now he has a good woman, and I for one am heartened to see that. Teret of the Tcunkai, you are most welcome here amongst the free army of Wynais."

In the bitter cold of that mountain night, Tamersane heard all about the war west of the mountains. Zallerak had joined them from some peruse he'd been taking, and Cale and Galed too. Cale was desperate to question Tamersane about Corin's whereabouts but got little joy from his answers. When the campfires were lit and food appeared, Prince Tarin emerged from a tent and sat beside them too. He said little and looked pale and thin.

"So Perani followed you into the mountains? I thought he was known for being cautious?" Tamersane chewed into a tough chunk of dried beef and crackly fat. Teret, beside him, was looking at Zallerak as though he were a serpent about to bite her. She had never encountered such a one before. For his part, Zallerak seemed out of sorts and hardly noticed her hostile surveillance. Nor did he contribute much to the current conversation.

"We dented his pride," Silon said. "I was late arriving at Greystone Bridge as I had other business to attend. But Zallerak and the queen and I had liaised via bird. I got there just before dawn, saw the carnage on the bridge, and watched as morning unfolded and Perani led his army into Raleen.

"I notified Zallerak and he deemed it shrewd to return and place more explosives, taking the entire bridge down and trapping Perani's army south of the river, lest he choose to return that way."

"Where is he now?" Tamersane couldn't believe that Perani had dragged his vast army up into the mountains.

"He's on our tail. We've encountered several scouts; hence your ambush." Silon smiled slightly. "But I almost feel sorry for Perani. He screwed up at Greystone Bridge and now has committed Caswallon's entire army to struggling behind us along The Wild Way. Had he kept his temper and ridden back north and re-entered Wynais, we would have been trapped up here in winter. Instead he's played into out hands, and Caswallon will know that by now. Perani's future looks fragile. Shame—he was once a good man before the darkness claimed him."

Earlier, Tamersane had heard how Wynais had been betrayed from within and that the traitor now ruled as Caswallon's puppet. "Who is this bastard?" Tamersane had asked, though no one had responded.

"So we have been playing cat and mouse in the snow," Ariane told him. "Keeping just ahead of Perani's army, and yet close enough to see what they are up to."

"What about Wynais?" Tamersane yawned and winked at Teret, who was wrapped in the deep folds of a borrowed fur coat. "Soon be bedtime—eh, love?" he whispered. Close by, Cale giggled as if he'd said something funny and Tamersane awarded the lad a quizzical glance.

"We have people working on that." Ariane smiled and informed Tamersane of Valentin's mission to get inside the city walls. "Hopefully, we will be welcomed home on our arrival and can slam the gate shut in Perani's face."

***

Captain Gonfalez shook snow from his gauntlets and held the letter up to the light. His man had just delivered it to his tent under the cover of darkness. It bore Caswallon's seal and he was shaking with excitement as he cut through it. The words read thus:

Captain Gonfalez,

In appreciation of your loyal attentiveness and devotion to our cause we promote you to Lord General of the Armies of Kelthaine. Your predecessor has failed us utterly and therefore lost our trust. I charge you to re- enter the rebel city and slay all inside, including the fools Perani posted there. After that, take the rebel queen and her little army and tear them apart—but leave her for me.

I will be sending my messenger south, and you will also have reinforcements including fresh Groil and other creatures. Once Kelwyn is finally under our control you must take the army north to Kelthara and destroy all in that city too. You stand to gain much by succeeding in these tasks, General. Your promotion is as of now and I do not wish to see Perani again.

C

***

General Perani gazed up at the moon and smiled. Strangely, he felt at peace tonight, at one with this crazy world. He no longer regretted his rash decision to pursue Ariane way up into the mountains.

He should have guessed that their ally the wizard would blow the bridge and block any quick return north. Since then, he'd lost countless scouts to archers waiting in the rocks above. And now he was committed to following Ariane's army through the mountains back down to Wynais, where doubtless the little minx had already planned a way inside the city, or else maybe the traitor Tolranna was a double agent.

Perani had badly underestimated that girl. Ariane had proved a brave and resourceful opponent and he quietly saluted her as he stood in silence beneath the questing moon.

It mattered not. He'd play the game out until its end, which wouldn't be long. He had failed Caswallon too many times now to expect to survive another winter.

Perani was hardly surprised to see the tall shape of Captain Gonfalez striding toward him out of the dark. "A fine night General." Gonfalez's eyes were shining.

"You have something for me?"

"I do indeed." Gonfalez's hidden sword sliced through Perani's belly, spilling his guts. Perani crumpled without a sound. Gonfalez stepped back and swung again and Perani's head flew from his shoulders, spraying the moonlit snow with scarlet drops.

So passed the former leader of the Tigers, once a proud and honest man who had fallen to the corruption of the Usurper.

Gonfalez grinned down at Perani's kicking corpse. "You know what they say about working for sorcerers, General? You're only as good as your last job."

Gonfalez wiped his sword on Perani's cloak and departed back to his tent. Late that night he heard the wolves howling and feasting under the moon. He smiled and rolled back to sleep. Tomorrow was a new start for General Gonfalez of Kelthaine.

Chapter 19

The Wild Way

"*What you got there?*" *a rough voice* called from outside the cave. Corin stared at the young man with the accusing eyes who was pressing the knife to his neck.

"Dunno—maybe a spy?" Another face appeared, followed by two others. All were bearded and hard-looking, their hair shaggy and long and their eyes wary as they gazed down on their prisoner.

"You got a tongue?" The man who had first spoken loomed into view. He was older, his tough face dominated by a badly broken nose and missing front teeth.

"Not one I'd share with you, Greggan."

"What did you say? How does he know your name?" The young one pushed the knife harder into Corin's neck, piercing skin.

"I'd stow that blade if I was you, Scaff, else you might end up wearing it. I know this man and he's got a nasty temper and a bloody great sword." Scaff looked baffled but after a moment he withdrew his knife and stood to join the others. Their prisoner rubbed his neck and glared at the younger man.

"I don't blinking believe it." Greggan shoved Scaff out the way and grinned down at Corin. "The terror of Permio has returned to join his old mates. Corin an Fol, where the fuck have you been?"

"He's Corin an Fol?" Scaff's face paled to the colour of the snow outside. "*The* Corin an Fol? The legendary Longswordsman who fought with the boss down in Permio, and him wot done for Taskala Swordsmaster high on Gardale Moor?"

"The very one," Greggan smiled, as the others gazed down at Corin with dubious expressions.

"Fuck." Scaff blinked and fiddled with his fingers. "Sorry about your neck, mate."

Corin ignored him. Instead he rolled to his feet and spat phlegm on the floor of the cave. "You got any food, Greggan? I'm starving."

"Oh, sure. Scaff, you young tosspot, go do something useful and make some porridge for our long lost laddie. And you Baley," this to the second bearded man on his right, "Go tell the boss what we found lolling idle in this cave."

The shaggy-faced Baley nodded and grinned fiercely at Corin before backing out of the cave. His companion, who looked just like him and whom Corin vaguely remembered was called Bonkers (and they both shared the nickname Strongarm due to their great strength), followed on without a word, but grinned at Corin just the same. That just left Greggan, who chose to take a seat on the cave floor next to Corin.

"You all right?" Geggan said, picking dirt from one of his better teeth.

"Not bad," Corin yawned. "How long will that shithead be with the porridge?" He really was feeling hungry now.

"He'll be back in a mo. Camp's close, and once you've stuffed your face the boss will want to see you."

"Who's the boss these days?" Corin scratched his neck and wiped a bead of blood on his sleeve. That boy Scaff had been a tad overzealous, in his opinion.

"Same as has always been."

"Halfdan?" Corin leapt to his feet and banged his head on the cave ceiling. "Fuck! Ouch, bollocks! But I thought he was dead? Murdered by the King of Leeth on contract to that bastard Caswallon. Fuck but that hurt!" Corin nursed his aching skull. "Halfdan's alive?" he added after a moment.

"He lives, as do about a hundred of us, by the skin of our elbows. We lost the city, Corin. The bastards found a way in and killed many of the lads before we could sneak out the back passage, if you pardon my expression."

Corin was grinning from ear to ear. He hadn't felt so happy since he'd left Silon's villa. "So Halfdan's really alive." He rubbed the bump on his head. "I can scarce believe it." Minutes later the nervous Scaff reappeared with a wooden bowl of steaming oats.

"You want a spoon?" Scaff handed Corin the bowl.

"No. Fuck off."

Scaff departed without hesitation and Corin shoved the contents of the bowl into his mouth with his dirt-covered fingers. "You got any ale in that camp?"

"Not much—the bastard Snake's got most of it." Greggan looked mournful.

"Who?"

"Vale the Snake, one of Haal's delightful sons. He's the viscous prick that took Point Keep from us while we had our pants down." It was apparent Greggan was still bitter about losing their fortress. Just then, Baley and Bonkers Strongarm showed their beards in the cave entrance.

"Boss wants to see him," Baley said to Greggan whilst his twin grunted agreement and picked his nose. Corin grinned; it was good to be back with his old crew again. The Wolves were ever the salt of the earth, far better than the dour Bears or the snooty stuck-up Tigers. The Wolves were always up for the craic. And he had thought them all dead. Things were finally looking up.

The camp was a hundred yards to the left of The Wild Way,

where a large overhanging rock awarded shelter from the raw east winds, and the shoulder of the mountain rose steep to the other side. There were wooden huts and sheds and a few tents, and a corral containing mounts, these stomping their feet and blowing steam into the cold air. Corin thought of Thunderhoof and his recent joy was dulled for a moment.

A man was seated by a roaring fire, his features hidden by a white mottled cloak and snowy hood. He was chewing at a rabbit leg and spitting its small bones into the fire. Greggan approached him and grunted in his ear. The man turned and awarded Corin a hard expression. Corin gave him look for look. It was years since he'd last seen this man.

"So, you live yet. It warms my heart to see you, Longswordsman." Halfdan was thinner than Corin remembered him and his close-cropped beard whiter. But his eyes were the same hard blue/grey and his lean face and sharp nose unchanged. The High King's brother—despite all the rumours, he lived and appeared in reasonable fettle.

"As my heart warms to see you, Lord." Corin stood with arms either side. Neither man smiled.

"No one has called me 'Lord' lately." Halfdan bid Corin join him by the fire. "Greggan, you twins, bugger off and leave me alone with this wastrel. We've a deal to catch up on." After they had departed Halfdan placed a hand on Corin's shoulder. He was smiling now. "I cannot express how happy I feel to see you alive and well, Corin an Fol."

"Likewise, the rumours said you were dead, but I always hoped..."

"We've come very close, and my own stupidity cost us Point Keep. The lads were worn out scouting on the enemy day after day. I decided on a feast and we all got hammered. My timing wasn't that great, as Vale the Snake chose that very night to crash in on us, killing the sentries and taking us unawares."

"But you escaped." Corin smiled; he had always liked Halfdan, who had guided him during his wayward days serving in the regiment.

"Aye—to my eternal shame. We lost a lot of men that night, and a lot more the day Caswallon showed his hand back in Kella City. The Wolves are few now, Corin."

"They are faring better than the Bears."

"How so?" After Corin had told him about Belmarius, the Wolf general's face grew grim. "He was a good man—strong and dependable. A sad loss and a heavy blow for us."

"I met him in Raleen at Silon's house—I liked him. But it's not all bad news.

I've found friends in the Rorshai. Olen, the new Kaan, thinks I'm some kind of 'harbinger of victory,' though I don't share his view."

"The Rorshai? Can they be trusted? I thought they were wild and crazy horse thieves?"

"Some of them are, but this Olen is a friend. A good ally against the foe."

"Which one?" Halfdan barked a bitter laugh. "There are several to choose from."

"I've got a notion about that; you might say it's a bit of a plan."

"As I recall most of your plans involve risk of slow, violent death. Tell me later of this plan. First let me know what's become of you. I see you still carry your swords and I trust you still have that gold brooch?

"It's at Silon's house. I forgot to pack it on my last trip."

"You still work for that merchant?"

"Funny you should say that."

During the next two hours Corin found himself recounting all his adventures to Lord Halfdan, starting with his leaving Silon's employment right up to the Tekara business in the desert, and finally rounding off with the Rorshai and his near-death experience in Darkvale.

Scaff, who seemed desperate to make up for his earlier behavior, was keen to serve at hand to bring Corin fresh stewed rabbit and even a large flagon of beer, at which point the Longswordsman almost forgave him—almost. Halfdan declined any ale and instead sat in thoughtful silence as Corin told his tale.

When he finally finished, Corin stretched out by the fire and yawned. "So as you see, I've been rather busy lately."

Halfdan said nothing; his face looked troubled and he appeared on the brink of tears, as though recalling some distant memory sparked by Corin's words. "I need a drink," he said at last and signalled Scaff, still perched close by, to go get ale and another for Corin. He waited for the boy to return and then bid Scaff out of earshot.

"This changes things," Halfdan said as he sipped his beer and winced as the cold liquid found a sensitive tooth.

"I thought you would be pleased, about the crown at least." Corin felt warm and fed for the first time in ages, and the ale was making him sleepy.

"Naturally I'm pleased about the Tekara being remade, but I wasn't thinking about that. I was thinking about you, Corin an Fol."

Corin shuffled uncomfortably. "So? What of that? I'm still he same. Just an ex-Wolf and recent mercenary who's not bad at poking people with sharp things."

"That's my point. You never were just those things. Yes, you have a talent for killing, as do most my lads—it keeps them alive. But you are very different from them."

"I do not understand you." Corin was starting to feel alarmed. He knew something big was about to happen—something a lot of people had hinted at.

"This is hard for me." Halfdan took a long gulp of ale. "But here we go. You, Corin an Fol, are different because you are noble-born."

"Bollocks."

"Not so, and not only are you noble born but you are the true heir to The Glass Throne. The High King's nephew. You are my son, Corin an Fol. There you are—I've said it."

Corin placed his tankard on a log by the fire. He slid Clouter free and commenced working his whetstone along its length, his face set in stony silence. Halfdan watched him until he could stand it no more. "Well? Don't I at least deserve a response?"

Corin shrugged, "All right, here's my response. I don't believe you." He shrugged again and returned to the sword honing.

"Yes, you do."

"Then why the fuck didn't you tell me before? All these years and I've never known who my real father is and the whole time he's been under my fucking nose!" Corin stood and hurled Clouter and whetstone onto the ground. He paced from the fire and then turned to confront his father. "Why?"

"To protect you." Halfdan struggled to his feet, stiff with cold and aching joints. "When I first knew, my prime worry was keeping you alive—my long lost baby son returned to me by some miracle.

"I knew nothing of your upbringing in Fol and neither did anyone else. But when I saw your scrawny face that day you first enlisted back in Kella City, I knew you for my son, and therefore the High King's true heir.

"But Caswallon was everywhere—even back then. I knew I had to keep your identity hidden, so if anything I was harder toward you than most others in the regiment, and bid Taskala treat you roughly. Of course that got out of hand, and again I blame myself."

"Because I killed him? So that's why I never hanged then?" Corin's laugh was bitter. "Excuse me while I go take a piss. This is all a bit much to swallow."

After he had drained his bladder Corin ventured back to the fire and carefully wiped Clouter free from the dirt he'd gotten on it. "So you've known all that time." Corin felt exhausted, as though all the air had been sucked out of him.

"I still don't believe it," he muttered after a moment.

"Story goes they found your naked tiny body on the beach a day after that cursed storm took my other child, and Kelsalion's eldest son. And the High Queen and my own beloved wife. That day the best part of me died.

"The villagers never asked any questions; you were a gift from the gods—that's what they told me. You see, I went to Finnehalle once I knew that was your home. I guess I dared hope my other son lived too, or even the High King's boy. The Innkeep at The Last Ship told me about the Crenise raid and how you, a mere stripling, had fought beside your foster father. I knew that had to be my son he spoke of."

So Burmon knows too. Corin made a small noise between his lips.

"But think about it. All this attention by otherworldly folk you've told me about. It's no great riddle. You, my son (Corin shivered slightly, hearing that), are crucial to this war, and for some reason it's a conflict of high interest to the powers that be. The Wanderer, Elanion, Vervandi, and Croagon—even this horrible Maife you've spoken of—all of them interested in you? Why? The Rorshai Seeress was right Corin. You are the fulcrum - the turning tide. I don't like that any more than you do, but its truth cannot be denied. You are destiny. The spinning coin of fate."

"I hate this shit."

"And then there's Shallan and Queen Ariane."

"What about them?"

"Well obviously, they both love you, and you're not that fucking good-looking. So they must have sensed something about you, a hidden layer you couldn't even see yourself."

"And I thought it was my rustic charm and the soap I rarely use." Corin managed a wry smile. "Guess I'll have to start calling you father."

"Please don't."

Corin stared into the fire and as he stared the tears at long last fell free from his eyes. Halfdan let him be and ventured off to check on his men. They left Corin alone that night, though on Halfdan's orders Scaff kept him well replenished with their low stock of ale.

"You feeling all right now?" Scaff dared ask when night was well underway.

Corin turned and awarded the younger man a long slow glance. "Yes, master Scaff, and you know why?" Scaff shook his head. "It's because from this day on we've turned a corner in this war. Because

I *am* Corin an Fol and for the first time in my life I know who I am. And Scaff," (Scaff nodded urgently) "no fucker is going to stop me from getting what I want. You got that?"

"Yes," Scaff nodded.

"Good. You can go now." Scaff went.

***

Dawn saw Corin up and ready. He'd slept exhausted in a tent without dream or worry and he felt alive and ready for the next big thing. Finding Shallan, then claiming his inheritance. Not that he wanted that, but it now seemed the logical next step to shaft Caswallon's plans. Ironic to think that the crystal crown was rightly his all along. But before all that there were a few things to tie up locally.

"How are you feeling?" Lord Halfdan looked tired as he greeted Corin. Beside the leader stood Greggan and the twins and a few others. They'd been discussing their latest situation.

"I'm fine." Corin flashed his father a grin fit for a former wolf. "I found it!" He produced the wolf brooch and pinned it to his cloak. "Must have been in my back pocket all this time."

"He's got a gold one!" Scaff appeared with a kettle for tea and was staring in awe at Corin's brooch. "They're rare, aren't they?"

"Very." Greggan cuffed his ear. "And he's Lord Corin to you from now on, boy."

"So, what's the plan?" Corin asked as he accepted a hot mug of tea and a biscuit from Scaff.

"We were waiting for you to tell us." Halfdan winked at Greggan, and Corin realised they'd all been talking about him. They seemed fired up and excited, as did all the men roaming about in the camp. Corin grinned; it was nice to be popular for once.

"Well, as it happens, I do have a plan that might just win us this war, and reunite me with a certain lady in the meantime. First I've a question - have we any birds?"

"You mean like a pigeon?" Scaff asked trying to impress.

"I don't care if it's a fucking parrot as long as it takes a message," Corin replied.

"We have pigeons," Halfdan told him.

"Then we will send one to Wynais City informing them of my notion, and can we spare a rider?"

"What for?" Greggan asked scratching his ear.

"There are several thousand bad-tempered Rorshai riders not too far from here, all wanting to wreak some havoc up north. They need to know Corin an Fol is alive and well and ready to play alongside. I need a durable fellow to ride to a place called the Delve. I'll give out directions."

"I'm your man," said Greggan. "I'll leave after breakfast."

"Ride south along The Wild Way," Halfdan told Greggan. "That way you can drop down into Rorshai without going near Darkvale. And keep your wits about you; Corin says some of those Rorshai are murdering bastards."

"That's actually good to hear," Greggan answered with a toothless grin, "because until now I thought they all were."

""So. Corin, what do we do next?" Halfdan sipped his tea and smiled at his son.

Corin grinned back. "You know the answer to that."

"Yes, I do, but I want you to say it."

Corin nodded. "We ride north along The Wild Way and return to Point Keep via the back door. We enter in and then murder every bastard in it. And that's us just getting started, my lord."

Chapter 20

The Fall of Starkhold

"He's done what?" Barin had the sergeant pinned against the wall and struggling to breathe. "Speak to me shithead, lest I pull your earholes off!"

"Barin, It's not his fault, the sergeant's just obeying his master," Shallan pulled at Barin's sleeve, and the Northman reluctantly let the red-faced sergeant slump to his knees choking whilst trying to recover his breath. Close by, Zukei eyed the sergeant evilly, her Karyia in hand, and he wished himself anywhere but here.

"He's to hang tomorrow on Starkhold's orders," the sergeant blurted out. "There's nothing I can do—or anyone else for that matter."

"Where's Ralian now?" Shallan asked.

"In the oubliette—last cell on the left. He ain't going anywhere."

"And where is Starkhold?" Barin boomed in the sergeant's ear.

"Out on the walls where they tell me the enemy are busy swarming for attack." The sergeant tried squirming to his left, determined to be somewhere else.

"Yes go," Barin growled at him and the sergeant sloped of and vanished at speed around a corner. "Well, seems I need to go and have a quiet word with Lord Starkhold, bend his ears a touch and suggest he change his mind."

"He won't." Shallan watched a squad of spearmen hurry by, making grim-faced for the walls. "Despite how much we need every fighter, especially officers like Ralian, Joachim Starkhold is not a forgiving man."

"Then we'll have to bust Ralian out ourselves," smouldered Barin. "You up for that Zukei girl?"

"Of course," Zukei grinned at Barin. "It's the sort of work I specialise in, and I can pick locks too."

But Shallan wasn't happy. "That will just get you pair hanged alongside Ralian. I'm sorry, but I don't know what we can do for him without crossing Starkhold and therefore putting ourselves in danger too. That said, there's no harm in talking to him, and I suppose we'd better see what the enemy is doing."

"I think you'll find they are attacking." Barin flashed her a bear grin. "Lead on, Duchess!"

As they approached the walls, the clash of steel on steel and shouts were easily discerned. Cresting the battlements, they saw how the king of Leeth had lined up his finest warriors outside the walls. These were currently yelling up insults, yelling at each other, and striking their weapons against their round shields.

Far more worrying to those watching were the twenty or so huge wicker-framed towers rumbling towards them from the woods, and beyond these were other contraptions, scorpions, mangonels, and such. They were shoddy in construction but there was no doubt they'd work.

"Looks like Haal's changed his tactics," growled Barin. "They must have kept those monsters hidden in the trees. I thought them too stupid for such constructions, but may happen Caswallon sent them sketch plans."

"We need to find Starkhold." Shallan turned her back on the

dismal sights and noises below. She asked a guard, who pointed east along the walls. Barin and Zukei strode beside her as they sought out the warlord.

"How are your brothers?" Barin asked her as he hoisted Wyrmfang over his left shoulder, just in case the boys below got excited and started hurling things at them.

"They'll mend. Danail is in good shape but Tolemon is torn by guilt at losing Vorreti."

"It wasn't his fault," cut in Zukei, who was prowling like a cat just behind them.

"No, but he's the oldest and blames himself for their capture. Tolemon is much like my father was—he takes too much upon himself." They found Starkhold gazing down from the walls with a group of officers gathered around. He looked up seeing their approach and barked a bitter laugh.

"So the heroes of last night dare show their faces on the walls. What now? Come to see the result of your boldness, Lady Shallan?"

"They would have attacked soon anyway." Barin loomed across and glared at the men surrounding Starkhold. "This waiting game was destroying your people's morale and your stores. You should be grateful to this lady and her commandoes. They pulled off a stunning raid and killed one of that bastard's sons."

"And thus brought the entire fury of Leeth down upon us. Do you not see those siege towers?" Starkhold held Barin's gaze in contempt for a moment and then returned to stare at the view below.

"And if you've come to ask for clemency on behalf of Captain Ralian you can forget it. The man disobeyed my orders and went behind my back. Worse, he put our city in danger."

"I take full responsibility for that." Shallan sidled around Barin's bulk. "I'll handle this," she told her friend. Zukei's hand rested on the pommel of her Karyia and her dark eyes glowered at the officers surrounding them. "It was my passion persuaded Ralian this raid was necessary, not only to free my kin but to raise morale in the city."

"You are a naïve, stupid girl." Starkhold rounded on Shallan.

Behind her both Barin and Zukei bristled but she bid them relax.

"That may be so," she smiled coldly at the warlord. "But surely not as stupid or reckless proud as a commander who locks up his finest lieutenant at the hour of greatest need."

"I think someone's in a hurry to see you, Starkhold." Zukei had been looking back along the walls and had spotted the sergeant from earlier sprinting madly toward where they stood, his face even redder than before.

"What is it?" Starkhold hissed at the man.

"Prisoner's gone—someone broke in to his cell. There's no sign of Ralian. He —" The sergeant lurched forward onto his knees as Starkhold's iron boot impacted his groin. He tried to stand but the warlord kicked him again, hard in the side of his head, knocking the sergeant sprawling.

"Incompetence and treachery!" Starkhold turned on Barin, who watched him with measured eyes. Shallan knelt and saw to the sergeant, who was bleeding badly from that last kick.

"You could have killed him, you bullying bastard!" Shallan spat at Starkhold, whilst Zukei squared against the other men.

But Starkhold laughed at her and brushed past where she leaned over his victim. "You officers keep me informed, and you three spearmen," this addressed to three marching past, who stopped and saluted, "accompany me down to the dungeons. Seems like if I want something done right, I have to do it myself." Starkhold left them without a glance, his eyes slits of granite, the three spearmen crunching behind him.

"Where you going?" an officer snapped at Barin as he made to follow, and another blocked Shallan's way. He withdrew when Zukei's Karyia prodded his neck.

"If I were you I'd keep your snouts out of our business," she told the man as Barin threatened to brain the other one.

"The sergeant's dead," Shallan said, though no one was listening. She stood and pushed the officers surrounding her out of the way, and like grim sentinels Barin and Zukei followed her back down from the battlements. Time to resolve this nonsense.

"Best let them go," one of he officers said. He had liked Ralian and was shocked by Starkhold's loss of temper. "Out of our hands now," the other agreed, and they turned to watch the latest from below the walls.

"So who's to blame for this latest act of rebellion?" Shallan snapped as she stormed through the city toward where Ralian had been held. "Or am I stupid to ask?"

"Cogga and the boys were bored." Barin looked sheepish. "So I suggested they rough up the guards and spring the captain loose. We need Ralian, Shallan."

"But we don't need Starkhold as our enemy as well as the hordes of Leeth." Taic greeted them outside the rusty doors leading down into the dungeons.

"Cogga and Sveyn have smuggled Ralian into our rooms, but master Starkhold and his lads are on their way there. Looks like trouble if you ask me." Shallan just glared at Taic and kept walking towards where they were stationed over the right. Taic shrugged and took to strolling alongside his uncle.

"She don't look very happy," Taic said and Barin cuffed him on the ear.

***

Ralian rubbed his freezing fingers together and drank deep from the water contained in the stone cup Sveyn had handed him. "You boys are in big trouble for helping me, but I thank you—though I suspect you'll join me at the gallows."

"Not without a fight." Sveyn fingered his axe and smiled.

Just then Cogga appeared. "Warlord's on his way and he don't look pleased." Seconds later Joachim Starkhold emerged into the room, a long sword gripped in his left hand and the three spearmen clustered behind him. Cogga laughed when he saw them. "You should have brought more than that, General."

"These will serve against dogs like you. If you've any sense, you'd flee the walls and join your friends outside. You Northmen are all the bloody same—treacherous bastards." Sveyn's eyes narrowed and Cogga's hand reached for a knife.

"Go!" Ralian hissed at the two. "Lest he kill you too!"

"And us?" Barin grinned evilly as he stooped into the room; behind him prowled Zukei, Karyia in hand, and last up Shallan, hovering by the door.

"Lord Starkhold," Shallan addressed the warlord as he glared at the Northmen. "This can achieve nothing. My friends were rash to intervene, but we all need Captain Ralian, and what good would executing him serve?"

"Orders are to be obeyed." Starkhold gazed down at Ralian. "See the dissension your treachery has caused, Captain. These troublemakers have used you ill. And now you have to die as a result." With dazzling speed that betrayed his age, Joachim Starkhold leaped toward Ralian, his long sword cutting air above and descending toward the younger man's neck.

Starkhold was quick, but Zukei was quicker. The intended blow was blocked by her axe whilst the Karyia slid hard up into Starkhold's kidneys and the warlord slumped to the floor.

"Zukei!" Shallan yelled, but it was too late, the axe having already sliced across his neck. Zukei gave her a wild look. "He called you stupid—I didn't like that."

For a moment everyone in the room gaped in silence, except Zukei who wiped her weapons clean on Starkhold's snowy cloak. The spearmen glared at her in stunned horror. Barin looked at Cogga and Taic and Sveyn shook their heads. Interesting afternoon for them.

Ralian stood shakily. "I blame myself for this," he told them. "But now that it is done I say we honour his passing and perform the rites quickly so we can get on with the business of defending this city. What say you?" This last was directed at the spearmen.

"We are with you," they said after moment's hesitation. Ralian was popular, and no one had wanted his death in the city. That said, they glared at Zukei as though she were a she-wolf. "But that one needs reining in," the nearest grumbled.

"Good luck with that." Taic winked at the spearman. Word reached the city that Lord Starkhold had suffered a fatal blow to heart—that after months of worry and responsibility, even his iron resolve had caved in, and the renowned warlord of Raleen had perished alone. No one believed the rumour, but no one challenged it either. They had other things on their mind. The siege towers were rolling towards the walls and the first real attack against Car Carranis had finally begun.

***

Miles to the west, the wind cried chill through the deserted streets of Kella City. Guards shivered on the walls, and at the gates the men never even questioned the lone rider as he gazed down upon them. They knew this man, as did most people in the realm—knew and feared him.

Rael Hakkenon steered his beast through the city, and as he rode he noted the mournful state of Kella. The city was almost deserted except for the large rats that scurried everywhere and got under his horse's feet. Skinny hounds loped and growled as he urged his mount trot on toward the palace where Caswallon held frosty court.

Trash and filth littered every avenue, and stench, despite the bitter cold, clogged his nostrils. He rode on dispassionate, passing ruined buildings where lone lamps hinted that someone lived within. It seemed that Kella City was now a place of ghosts.

Three huge Groil manned the doors leading to the palace. These blocked his way with heavy halberds crossed before him. A rush of wings, and Gribble settled nasty on a wall to their right.

"Oh, it's you," Gribble remarked, trying to look important. "Tell your boss Mr Assassin is here," Gribble squeaked at the nearest Groil, who grunted and made off into the palace. The Groil returned moments later and beckoned Rael enter.

The Assassin slid from his horse and tossed the reins at the second Groil. "See that she gets fed," he snapped at the Groil. "And I don't want any claw marks on her flesh, I need her to get to Car Carranis!" The Groil blinked. This was the first human that had dared address it so. Even Caswallon was wary around his Groil.

"Covering a lot of ground lately Mr Assassin?" Gribble dribbled from his perch on the wall.

"Shut yer face, Goblin." Rael glared at Gribble, who spat down at him as the Assassin ventured inside the palace. Gribble licked his wet mouth and hopped after the man lest he miss out on big news.

Caswallon was sprawled languid on the Glass Throne. Chin in hand with a large goblet of claret tipping and spilling in the other, his eyes were hooded and he looked half asleep. He wasn't. Instead he watched intently behind those half shut eyes as the Assassin and Gribble approached.

"What happened to your face?" Caswallon asked the Assassin, and Gribble giggled, not having noticed the scars and broken nose until now.

"Messy," Gribble commented, and Rael made a swat at him causing him jump back out of range.

"I've a few scores to settle, truth be told. I was badly let down by your crew at Calprissa. And that Morwellan bitch owes me a finger. No matter. I still have nine that I can shove up her arse. I am here to report and then move on to Car Carranis, where I believe the next big fight will happen. Hagan Delmorier is already there."

"Hagan is worse than useless." Caswallon sipped his wine. "That Morwellan has failed me three times now. If he shows his hide around here I shall have him lynched."

"As is your right," nodded Rael. "But Hagan also has a score to settle with this Corin bastard, so I figured he might yet prove useful, thus I gave him a contract. But you needn't be involved."

"Down to you, but I wouldn't put much faith in that fellow. But forget Hagan and Car Carranis. I've more important work for you, Assassin."

"Name it."

"Ulan Valek."

"Never heard of it."

"It's a ruined Urgolais fortress hidden in the midst of The High Wall mountain range. I believe it lies somewhere northeast of Wynais."

"Very nasty there," Gribble cut in helpfully.

"Yes it is, Gribble, and we'll need you to help the Assassin locate it."

"Bugger that—I'm not flying near that place. It's full of shadows and ghoulies."

"Most of which are the product of rumours." Caswallon waved the goblin be silent. "That fortress has been empty for millennia. That said, there is something there that I require more than anything else. An artifact for which I am prepared to pay a vast sum to the brave venturer that brings it to me."

"What artifact and how large a sum?" Rael's green gaze narrowed as he studied the fervour in Caswallon's eyes. "I am already rich."

"Two hundred thousand crannels to retrieve for me the black spear, Golganak, and deliver it here to the palace. That's the job."

"Bad idea." Gribble chewed the hairy skin on his knuckles. "That spear is best lost, don't want to see that again. Nasty thing."

Caswallon ignored that as he focussed on the Assassin. "And you will have help in the form of Groil and Vaarg the firedrake, who is currently resting and preparing to revisit the realm. He lives in limbo—it's a long way from here but dragons are fast movers. Besides he can shift through dimensions easily enough." The Assassin raised a brow at that and Gribble yawned, physics not being his thing.

"I believe our enemy, this Aralais sorcerer, also desires Golganak. Vaarg will deal with him, just as you and the Groil can deal with any others wishing to thwart me."

"I'm not interested, Caswallon. I've business in Car Carranis. Once that's done I'll return to my island. You can keep your crannels."

"You didn't let me finish, Assassin; you are ever too impatient."

"Go on."

"I was about to add that on top of that huge sum of coin, I will award you the Kingdom of Kelwyn, once the little queen's rebellion is broken. Perani, like Derino before him, failed, but I have a new and very promising young general who will soon get me results down there. What say you, Assassin? Do you like the sound of King Rael?"

Rael let a slow sinister grin spread across his lips. "It's actually quite fitting," he said.

"I thought so too," Caswallon smiled at him, whilst Gribble picked his nose and grumbled that he didn't understand. "Make yourself useful, Goblin! Go get food and wine for my dear friend the Assassin. We have much to discuss."

"I'm not a bloody waiter, and quit calling me Goblin." Despite his moans, Gribble departed to undertake said task.

"Vaarg knows where the ruined city lies, and Gribble can spy out the land for you. Golganak will take some finding, but I know it's down there."

"If it's there then I shall acquire it." Rael spat in his hand and thrust it towards Caswallon. The usurper frowned for a moment then shrugged and repeated the gesture.

"Deal done," said the Assassin. "I'll depart soon as."

"What about your vengeance?"

"I'll keep it safely stored like vintage wine to be supped later at my leisure." Hence on they turned the conversation towards other matters, as afternoon light filtered into the throne room and Gribble returned with fresh chilled wine.

Chapter 21

The Brothers

"Wynais is ours!" Silon stood at the entrance of Ariane's tent, a rare grin showing on his lips. "Valentin has taken the city and sent three of his men to inform you!"

Ariane threw off her blanket and ran half-naked to embrace Silon. "Now we've turned the tide!" She kissed him, and Silon's face reddened.

"My Queen, you need to dress and attend these fellows waiting by the quartermaster's tent."

"Give me five minutes."

Silon nodded and withdrew; he tied the tent flap back lest anyone glance in and see the queen in state of undress. A crowd was gathering near the aforementioned tent. Prince Tarin was there, sitting moody on a log. Near him were Tamersane and the Rorshai healing woman, and close by them stood Galed and Cale, talking excitedly to Jaan the Raleenian captain. Tarello was addressing the three riders that had come from Valentin. All turned as Ariane rushed to join them.

She studied the three rangers and was surprised to see the smallest was Doyle, a young Calprissan that had signed up with her army after the battle with Derino. "Doyle? What's this? Are you a ranger now?"

Before Doyle could respond, one of his companions, a tall rangy archer, took a step forward and bowed. "He's an apprentice ranger, my Queen, and not overly promising." The third messenger, a huge fellow, stood grinning and nodding.

"Well, never mind that. You have big news to tell me, so I'm informed."

"Wynais is ours, Your Highness!" Doyle blurted before either of his companions could speak.

"Shut up, Doodle—I was going to tell her that." Arac looked peeved.

"We scaled the walls under cover of darkness," Doyle continued, ignoring his older companions. "It was tough going and we were nearly spotted. But we slew the guards on the walls and stole heroically within."

"I don't remember you slaying anyone Doodle," Arac said.

"Enough, let him continue." Ariane nodded thanks as Galed handed her a piping cup of tea accompanied by a hot sausage in a bun. "I just need the overall picture," she said through munched sausage.

"There weren't that many soldiers in the city and no Groil. Perani had left only a skeleton crew, which we quickly overcame."

"What of my lord Dazaleon and the traitor we've heard about?" The queen's eyes narrowed seeing the worry on Doyle's face.

"Er..."

"Dazaleon's dead," Arac said. "Murdered by the same traitor Valentin has locked up in your oubliette, my Queen. Valentin questioned one of Perani's men under the hot knife. Bastard spilled the peas, saying that Perani had coerced said turncoat into doing for the High Priest. I'm sorry..."

Ariane felt the colour drain from her face. She stooped to sit on a log before her knees gave. Dazaleon dead. Her wisest counselor and dearest friend, and worse, murdered by Yail Tolranna himself. She held back tears and sipped her tea. Close by, Galed had his head in his hands and several others were stunned and ashen-faced at this news.

"Well, who is this sodding traitor, will someone please tell me?" Tamersane's face was red, he too had been fond of Dazaleon. All faces turned toward him now.

"What is it?" Tamersane's face darkened. "What am I missing here?"

Ariane took a deep breath and sighed. "The traitor is your brother, Tamersane. Yail Tolranna is in league with Caswallon. We captured one of Perani's scouts a few days ago and he told us every-thing before we slit his throat open. Tolranna's plan was to usurp my throne, just as Caswallon usurped Kelsalion's. I am truly sorry, cousin."

Tamersane's customary cheerful demeanour was obliterated by violent denial. "I don't believe it. The scout lied, my brother is no fucking traitor!"

Beside him, Teret gripped his hand with her own, her dark eyes moist with worry. "Tolranna loves Kelwyn more than anyone—and he loved you too! Perhaps more than he should."

"It's true, Tamersane—and now your brother's killed Dazaleon." Captain Tarello stood beside his queen and stared hard at Tamersane.

"I wasn't fucking talking to you," Tamersane sneered back at Tarello, who gave him look for look. Ariane stood and waved them settle lest this get out of hand.

"Enough, Tarello, what's done is done. Tamersane, cousin, we will deal with this when we reach the city. Hold fast till then. In the meantime, gentlemen, let us break camp and get moving. Remember, Perani is not far behind us, and it would prove idiotic should we let him overtake us just before we reach our city."

Ariane walked over to where Tamersane sat hunched and moody next to the Rorshai woman. Teret stared hard at the queen as she took seat on the log beside them. Ariane chewed her sausage and smiled bravely at Teret. The other woman's lip flickered but she failed to comment. If Tamersane noticed the queen then he didn't let on. All about them, soldiers were dismantling camp and loading horse and wagons—these recently made during their travail in the mountains.

Cale hovered close; he looked worried and upset on Tamersane's part. "What is it Cale?" The queen sipped her tea and motioned the boy speak with a curt wave of hand. "Haven't you chores?"

"Zallerak's missing." Cale grinned at Tamersane who had briefly looked up when hearing the boy's voice. Tamersane stared at the boy for a moment and then dropped his gaze. Teret slipped an arm around his shoulders.

"So? He's always mooching around somewhere. I'm sure he'll turn up at some useless moment. Now leave us and be about your day, Master Cale." Cale nodded, grinned at Tamersane again, and then went and joined the action where the horses were tethered.

"Always we were different," Tamersane said, staring into the dying faggots of last night's fire. "He was the serious one and I the joker. We fought, seldom agreed on anything. But we both loved Kelwyn and we both adored its queen."

"I know." Ariane glanced at Teret who—judging by her behaviour and looks and for some reason alien to the queen—apparently didn't much care for her. No matter— that was the woman's concern, not hers. "That may be part of the problem. I know Tolranna would never betray us without some coercion or twisting by Caswallon. And I know how ambitious your brother is—or rather was."

"He is no traitor, Ariane." Tamersane looked at Teret, who smiled at him.

"Wait till we arrive in Wynais," Teret said. "Then you can ask him yourself. He will be able to do that—won't he?" This to the queen.

Ariane forced a smile; this woman was trying her nerves. "Of course. And it's best we let the brothers sort this out between them, and before I have to make a decision on Yail Tolranna.

"In the meantime, cousin dearest, we have other matters to attend. Perani's going to pull some stunt before we arrive at Wynais, I am sure of it. So please swallow your outrage and fury until we are safe behind the city walls. Then you can do as you must."

Tamersane nodded. "It will keep," he said. "But I tell you this Queen, if Tolranna did betray you, then I'm going to fucking kill him myself." Teret shook her head and Ariane rested a hand on Tamersane's shoulder.

"It mustn't come to that, cousin—promise me that won't happen. Tamersane, your Queen is addressing you!"

"I promise," Tamersane muttered under his breath. "But he's fucking innocent anyway." Ariane glanced briefly at Teret.

"I leave him in your hands, Teret. See that he comes to no harm. I must away to other duties." Teret nodded and watched the queen depart with angry eyes.

Long hard hours later, the combined armies of Kelwyn and Raleen reached the base of The High Wall, and Wynais waited silver in the sunset. Ariane raised her swords for the final plunge to safety. She wasn't surprised to hear horns blasting in the woods behind. At least the bastards hadn't got ahead, but now the final chase was on!

***

Zallerak watched the young queen's army spread out into the green vale that stretched from mountain roots to city. Close by, he heard their pursuers crashing through briar and brush as they sped after her much smaller force. Zallerak saw they were gaining and frowned. He still had uses for the queen and her rebels, so with that in mind he set about working on a fog.

Within minutes the vale had vanished from view, and Gonfalez's army were stumbling about blind and confused in the trees, their leader raging at them. Men crashed into each other, horses blew and snorted, and fights broke out as sheer terror of new sorcery filled Gonfalez's soldiers, none of whom could forget the destruction and carnage at Greystone Bridge. The fog finally lifted, allowing Gonfalez, who sat his horse at the edge of the trees, to witness the last of the young queen's rebels slither inside her gates.

"So she has won Wynais back whilst playing us for fools," he said softly to himself. Gonfalez suddenly wished that Perani were still in command. He was in deep shit now, but best send a bird nonetheless.

Zallerak laughed as his handiwork confounded the army of Kelthaine. He watched Ariane's force slip inside the city and then turned back toward the steep climb that led back up to The Wild Way.

For several days, Zallerak wandered that path alone looking for what he sought. One morning, he stumbled upon a tight group of men laughing by a campfire. Zallerak recognised Corin an Fol and smiled again. Things were working out well in the main.

He made sure he wasn't spotted and fared north until he reached the forgotten path that led deeper into the folds of the mountains.

Here, the great peak Carfallan stared cold and remote, as Zallerak followed the wind-scoured track towards it. Close by Carfallan's shoulders, the trees gave way to a gloomy valley. No snow settled down there, and at the bottom the valley deepened to a sharp cleft.

Down there, Zallerak spied the hint of a dark tower. It appeared little more a twisted bent spike, jutting jaunty, like frozen lightning coming up from the ground. Beyond that dark spike, other towers lay broken and scattered, and crumpled walls and buildings showed in the gloaming.

Zallerak steeled his heart for the final confrontation. He knew this would be tricky—far more difficult than the business with the crown. But he felt strong again and well rested. So, summoning confidence and courage, the Aralais Wizard, by some called Zallerak, started the long bitter trek down towards the ruined city called Ulan Valek.

***

Valentin welcomed the queen with a smile as she led her army into the city. The chief ranger looked tired out, but a feral triumph lit his dark eyes. "My Queen, the city is yours." Valentin took Ariane's reins in hand and let her dismount. "It was surprisingly easy, like they were too arrogant to even imagine you planning such a coup."

Ariane nodded, her face grim, but she thanked Valentin with a stiff smile. "I owe you a great deal, Captain Valentin, but I'm afraid amidst our victory there is also loss."

Valentin nodded, "Dazaleon. I'm sorry—they say he was one of the wisest men living and a kindly soul to boot."

"He was that." Ariane dusted her trousers free of snow and watched as the last of her riders and scouts filtered in. There was still no sign of the enemy, which puzzled her deeply. That said, Ariane was relieved to see the gates fastened shut as the last runner sped through. "He was also my friend and counselor. But it wasn't Lord Dazaleon of whom I spoke."

Valentin arched a quizzical brow. "Am I missing something?"

The general's dead, Captain," Arac the archer blurted from his horse behind them. "Belmarius! Murdered near Rorshai."

"What?" Valentin's face blanched and he gripped Ariane's reins to steady himself. "What are you talking about, Arac?"

"Your scout tells the truth, though I did not ask him to speak." Ariane awarded Arac a cold glance, but he merely shrugged in response. "Lord Belmarius is slain. I am sorry for your loss. I met him in Raleen and knew him to be a fierce and forthright warrior."

"Rorshai horse thieves?"

"Unlikely. Tamersane here has spent some time with the Rorshai and I believe Corin an Fol is still with them. These were Ptarnians, Valentin."

"Ptarnians—I thought them a rumour, a myth?"

"Regrettably, they are real, and they appear to have allied themselves to Caswallon. Rumour is they've a large force making for the Gap of Leeth. I suspect they plan to join King Haal's already swollen army."

"Then surely all is lost!" Valentin, tough fighter that he was, looked crestfallen and bitter.

"Not so!" Ariane's eyes hardened. "We are winning, Captain. Those other battles are for later. One thing at a time. First we deal with Perani—that's a big enough job."

Valentin straightened. "You are right, my Queen. I'm sorry I spoke so shamefully."

"Apologies accepted, Captain. You are a good man and I'm lucky to have you. Now I suggest you go find those survivors from Belmarius's army. It will cheer them greatly to see their old comrades. They've been through a lot, Valentin."

"Thank you, my Queen, I'll go seek them out at once. Arac, Doodle, get the others!" The lean archer nodded, and behind him Doyle nodded too, happy to be included in the conversation.

Ariane watched them hurry off then turned to survey the streets of her city. People had been slow emerging, fearing another contrivance by Perani or some kind of trap, but now they were everywhere, calling her name and waving and clapping.

Ariane smiled, and she spent over an hour walking amongst them, despite her cold and hunger and desire to bathe and don new clothes. Her people had survived an ordeal, and they needed her now more than ever.

At last she reached the palace and entered weary within, Galed and Cale at her side. Cale was beaming from all the girls who had blown him kisses. Behind them Tamersane walked as one lost in dreams, his Rorshai woman close at his side. Teret didn't like it here: too many people, and very few with friendly eyes.

Ariane reached her chamber and doffed her long boots. Her maids hovered and fluttered around her like moths until she bid them scat. She filled a basin and soaked her feet blissfully for over half an hour.

A knock. "Who is it?

"Silon."

"Yes, do come in." Silon emerged behind her door and, after

closing it again, turned to smile at her.

"Ah…the simple pleasures are the best, are they not? He took seat on a chair near her bath and she splashed water in his face with her feet. But when he asked, "What of Tolranna?" Ariane stopped splashing, and her face darkened.

"I cannot put it off, I'll have to attend him this evening. What's too be done, Silon?"

"Just keep Tamersane away from him."

"Tamersane is all talk, he's upset and outraged and understandably so. But he loves Tolranna despite their differences. And I know he'll want to see him."

"Heed my counsel, Ariane. That would prove a mistake." Ariane let it go.

"Pass me that towel."

Silon did as he was bidden. "What of your maids?"

"I told them to piss off. They were chattering like squirrels and I needed to think."

Silon chuckled. "Yes indeed, and we need to talk about the next phase too. We've been lucky Ariane, but the net is closing. And another thing: Zallerak has gone."

"Are you sure?"

"He didn't enter the city, and nobody's seen him today."

Ariane dried her feet briskly and squeezed them back into stockings. She wished she had time for a full body soak but could scarce afford that leisure at the moment.

"What is he up to? Damn it, but we need him, Silon. What if Caswallon uses sorcery next time?"

"We'll just have to do our best without him. Zallerak's capricious, most likes he'll show his face at some point. I wouldn't worry just yet."

Ariane was unconvinced. "It's funny, he's been acting strange since we joined him at Greystone Bridge. Distant and aloof—even for him."

"Zallerak has always acted strange."

"Yes, but he's been shifty and furtive and not wanting to speak with anyone—not even Tarin, who sees him as a mentor."

Silon shrugged. "Time will out. Can I suggest council tonight in the throne room?"

"I can't avoid it - can I?"

"Not really." Silon folded his arms and rose to his feet. "I'll take my leave, Ariane. Go steady with Tamersane, and I'll meet you later when you call council."

"Yes, fine." Ariane had the nagging sensation that she had overlooked something. She was tired, that was all. She slid her long boots on and yelled her maids get her a candle and escort to accompany her to the oubliette. Best not delay what had to be done. But when Arianne reached the dungeons it was already too late.

***

Tamersane mooched and fretted whilst Teret's dark eyes flashed warning signals at any approaching them. His first reaction since arriving in the city had been to get seriously drunk. That he achieved without improving his mood. Rather it darkened him.

There was a worm swelling inside Tamersane's chest threatening to devour him. The words "brother" and "traitor" kept surfacing in his mind, and every time they did he would feel the acid bile of the worm's breath rise with them.

Teret sat in the cold tavern sipping on wine, which tasted like flowers to her, but at least had the desired soothing effect. Beside her, Tamersane stared into his half empty tankard saying nothing.

Teret gazed about. It was quiet and still. All the fuss of the queen's return had settled into the grim realisation that another army was encamped close outside the city. She'd heard people out in the streets shouting that Perani's entire force was camped nearby. Teret cared little about what she heard. What would be would be. Her prime worries surrounded her lover. At last she could stand no more.

"Don't you want to know the truth?"

"What?"

"About your brother. I thought you were going to confront him and at least allow him to explain his actions, or deny any wrongdoing. It serves nothing us sitting here with you getting wasted."

Tamersane turned and awarded her a long mournful look. "I am trying to forget him at the moment," he replied. "I'm tired, Teret. I need to get my head around things."

"And I say you won't achieve a damn thing sitting here moping and whining. Come, let's go visit and get this sorted out. Your countrymen might have drawn the wrong conclusions about your brother." Teret's first impression of Wynais and its people hadn't improved. She viewed them as soft suburban chatterers, which was not entirely fair.

Tamersane slurped his ale, wiped his mouth on his sleeve, and yawned in her ear. "Very well then, if only to have some peace." He tossed some coin at the innkeep and stumbled out into the cold afternoon light. "Too bright out here," he grumbled.

"You know the way?"

"Of course I know the fucking way, everyone knows where the sodding oubliettes are. And you can usually tell by the smell, even in this cold." He tromped through the streets with cloak pulled tight about his body and Teret clinging to his arm. She flashed him a smile and for a brief while he felt better.

After a sombre walk, they reached the creaky gate that led down to the dungeons. The three guards seated at table were dicing; they jumped up when they saw Tamersane. They said nothing but their eyes were wary. "All right lads, it's only me." Tamersane grinned and the nearest nodded, and Tamersane left them to it. Teret, glancing back, noticed how the guards whispered and muttered as they stared after them.

Tamersane grabbed a sconce from the wall. "Take care, it's slippery down here." He led her down a steep spiral stairway leading to another door. A fourth guard stood there yawning on his spear. He looked up surprised seeing Tamersane and the foreign-looking young woman. "You got a pass?" It was so gloomy the guard hadn't realised whom he was addressing.

"Shut up and unlock that door." Tamersane put his nose close to the guard's nose. The guard blinked, finally recognizing the queen's cousin, and hastily fumbled for his keys.

"Last cell on the left," he coughed helpfully. Tamersane and Teret ignored him and disappeared into the gloom. The guard rubbed his eyes, wishing himself in his favourite tavern and not stuck down here in the bitter chill and damp.

Teret chewed her bottom lip as she followed her lover past doors on either side. It was very dark down here and the cobbles beneath her feet were slippery with ice, whilst green weed slimed the walls wherever the sconces showed light. "This is a cheerless place," Teret said.

"It's meant to be, and it's rumoured a damn sight better than the dungeons up in Kella City, or Kelthara, and as for those in Kranek Castle, ask Prince Tarin about that. We in Wynais are more forgiving than those other folk, and these dungeons are mostly empty." They had actually been full recently but Valentin's rangers had slain the guards and freed the folk within.

"We don't have these places in Rorshai. If a man is charged with an offense then he has he right to prove his innocence with steel."

"What happens if he's a crap swordsman?"

"He dies."

They reached the last door on the left. Tamersane rapped his sword pommel on the heavy oak and someone grumbled inside. There was a rattle of a key sliding into a lock. The door creaked ajar. Another guard blinked at them. This one recognised Tamersane right away.

"I heard you were back." He lit a sconce on the wall and grinned at them. "I was just checking if he'd eaten his scoff. He hasn't and is asleep at the moment." This guard pointed to a cot at the far end of the dank cell where a shaggy figure sat hunched forward with chains holding his wrists. It was safe to say Yail Tolranna had looked better.

"Fuck," muttered Tamersane staring at the battered sleeping shape of his brother. "Leave us, good fellow."

"Is that wise?" The guard retrieved a long pike that he'd left resting on the wall. "And who's she?" Teret glared at him and the guard shrugged and slipped out behind the creaking door. "Shout if you need me," his voice echoed from outside the cell.

Teret stared at the grim figure hunched on the cot, the chains chafing into his wrists and the dark stain of blood crusting around them. "He doesn't look much like you." The sleeper groaned and opened an eye.

"Who are you?" Yail Tolranna blinked at Teret and choked. "Get me some water, will you?" Teret turned to Tamersane who lurched toward his brother.

"Drink this." Tamersane poured some water left in a bucket into a rusty cup and placed it at his brother's swollen mouth.

"Oh, it's you. Back from your adventures at last, heh?" Tolranna drank greedily at the cold water and choked and coughed spilling it down his front. "Wine would be better," he croaked. Tamersane knelt on the cot and looked hard at his brother. Teret watched them from the door. Outside the guard shuffled and muttered.

"Tell me this is some absurd mistake," Tamersane said at last, his blue eyes challenging his brother's brown glare. "Tell me they've got it all wrong. That Perani or some other bastard twisted the facts and somehow you ended up down here. Lie if needs be, tell me anything. But don't tell me you're a traitor. And don't tell me you murdered Dazaleon."

"Shit happens," Tolranna coughed again. "And usually to me. You, brother, always got the breaks whilst I got the responsibility. You, Tamersane, are a lightweight and I don't need to explain anything to you. And who's this wench you've brought to show me? Looks like a Rorshai bitch. You want to be careful brother lest you catch something."

"What happened to you?" Tamersane shoved a gloved hand hard under his brother's chin forcing Yail to choke again. Teret's lips were tight and her left hand rested on her dagger. Were this not her lover's brother then Tolranna would be dead by now. "I always admired you, brother. Always you were strong and steadfast and passionately loyal. I don't understand what has happened to you."

"I need to shit," Tolranna grinned at Teret. "Your wench doesn't like me much. Heh, wench, bring me the soil bucket, will you?" Tolranna chuckled bitterly.

"Teret, leave us a minute please." Tamersane urged her depart outside. "I need to get the truth from my brother, one way or another." Tamersane's earlier drunkenness had vanished. He appeared ice cold sober now.

"I'd rather stay."

"Just a few minutes, my love." Teret nodded and joined the guard outside. Tamersane turned to his brother. "Those manacles hurt, I should imagine?"

"So what? Feeling sorry for me, Tamersane? After everything I've done? Yes, I killed Dazaleon; he was weak and we needed a leader, and Perani told me if I didn't do it then he would kill me, and I couldn't let that happen, could I? So I spilt the old man's blood in this very room."

"He was like a father to both of us," Tamersane struggled for words, confused and baffled by what he was hearing. "What of Ariane, I know you loved her and yet you betrayed her too. Why?"

"Because she is a fool!" Tolranna spat phlegm over his brother's cheek. "It's because of her this country is on the brink of ruin. We cannot win this war, brother. Caswallon is too powerful. I knew this and brokered a deal to save us, though I could not save Ariane. And yes, I love her, I always have—but that's just the shit way my life is." Tolranna tugged at his hands until fresh blood smeared his wrists. "And I still need to shit."

"Guard!" The soldier peered in.

"What?"

"Unlock my brother's manacles, I'd not see him treated worse than a dog. Allow him to void his bowels and not foul himself."

"I have strict orders from Lord Valentin."

"And I am Queen Ariane's fucking cousin, so unlock his chains!" The guard grumbled into the room, producing his keys, and he thrust one into the hole at Tolranna's wrist. He turned it and the manacles snapped apart.

"Keep um, that way I'm not responsible." The guard thrust the keys into Tamersane's hands and vacated the room again.

Tolranna sighed as his hands were freed. "Thank you." He wiped the blood from his sleeve and licked it. Unnoticed by either brother, Teret slid back inside the room, her dagger now in hand.

Yail laughed as Tamersane placed the soil bucket by the bed. "I was joking little brother, just seeing how I could play you." He saw Teret smouldering by the door. "Pretty little thing, isn't she? Have you told her how many whores you've tupped? Does this girlie know what a total lush you are, little brother?"

Tamersane lashed out with a fist knocking Tolranna from the bed. "Shut up!" Turning he saw Teret standing over Tolranna with the knife, her eyes flashing in the dark. At a look from her lover she made to slide the knife back in its sheath but Yail proved quicker.

The former Captain of the Guard rolled and lashed out with a foot catching Tamersane under the jaw and sending him sprawling, then he swung to his feet and caught Teret's wrist, twisting it until she dropped the dagger. He threw her across the floor as the guard came rushing in, pike in hands.

Yail danced sideways and wrenched the long weapon from the guard. He reversed it sending the razor sharp point into the guard's neck. The pike man crumpled. Tamersane's sword was out, but Yail blocked his brother's half-hearted thrust and kicked him in the groin whilst making for the door. There Teret tripped him and he sprawled to his knees, but not before twisting the dagger up into her flesh.

Teret cried out as her own dagger tore deep into her bicep. Tamersane, seeing her hurt, surged to his feet and barrelled into his brother. For a time they rolled on the filthy floor whilst Teret gripped her arm and tried to quench the bleeding. At last Tolranna locked his brother's arms and twisted him beneath him. Crazy with rage, he lifted the knife.

Just then the door swung open, catching Yail from behind and pitching him over his brother, the knife clattering across the floor. Tamersane rolled free and retrieved the knife, Tolranna jumping after him. Red with rage Tamersane sliced out with the knife and shuddered as it slid hard into his brother's neck. Tolranna grinned at his brother and then slumped on top of him.

Tamersane clutched his dying brother and sobbed, all his rage evaporated. Then his eyes fell on the doorway where Queen Ariane stood in silence, the other three guards behind her.

Chapter 22

Point Keep

For four days they filed along the icy thread of The Wild Way, their breath steaming and fingers and toes numb with cold. During two of those days snow storms had made the track almost impassable, and sometimes they must needs shovel banks of snow so that the horses and few wagons they possessed could get through.

A hundred and one hard-faced men, lean with hunger but fuelled with vengeful purpose. The war was turning in their favour, Corin an Fol said, and who were they to argue?

Most remembered him as the headstrong nasty-tempered Longswordsman who had led many a wild foray and risky caper down in Permio during that last war. Some of the younger ones like Scaff had only heard his reputation, now fired up by their older comrades' exaggerations.

As for Corin, in a weird way he was happy. Not dreamy happy like he had been in Vioyamis with Shallan in his arms. But happy with purpose, and that concreted to the knowledge of who he was. Not that he gave that much thought at present. So many bizarre things had happened to him that Corin decided to take this last revelation in his stride, at least for the moment anyway. One day at a time.

He recalled that night on Barin's ship when Zallerak had hinted at his identity. Of course he had pushed that away, coming as it did from the Aralais. But it had been nagging at his subconscious ever since. But for now Corin decided he'd do best to focus on the days ahead as they got closer to the folds of mountain that led down to the hidden fortress, Point Keep.

Corin had only been there a few times, running errands and such that provided a healthy break from his usual station down in Permio. It had always been cold when he'd arrived, but roaring fires and lolling hounds, roast fowl and copious ale had made it seem like home to Corin.

It felt surreal to be back with his old companions, but his joy of seeing Halfdan hale and fit, despite the rumours, overcame any weariness and filled him with energy, as did the thought of seeing Shallan in a few days.

As dusk fell on the fourth day, they crested a ridge awarding sheer views to the right. Far below, a faint orange glow announced firelight coming from the highest tower of Point Keep. Halfdan's scouts found the track they'd used to flee the fortress buried beneath fresh snow. Without delay they commenced clearing a way through and following it down the steep path toward the half-hidden fortress.

It was tough going, dangerous and slippery underfoot, but they had just enough light to steer the horses and carts to a level area in a frozen copse. Here they rested and ate a cold supper, whilst Halfdan, Corin, Baley, Bonkers, and some of the others discussed their next move.

"Do we wait for morning?" Baley tore at a dry stick of beef. "Catch them at first light?"

"No." Halfdan's eyes were intent as he gazed up at the sky. "It's a clear night and we know the way. I say we slip in after midnight and pay back our dues whilst their bellies are filled with our ale. Sound good, gentlemen?"

Corin nodded and the other men grinned: they were more than ready for this. After their meal, everyone drew lots to see who must stay with the horses. Three grumps were left behind as the rest, including Corin, followed Halfdan and Baley's lead down the steep descent toward the sleeping Point Keep.

***

The girl snored in his arms as he ruffled her flaxen hair and slipped a lazy paw inside her shift. His pale blue eyes were bloodshot and his mind slow with drink. All about the hall his men sprawled and snored with their lemans, all in various states of undress. Just another night in Point Keep fortress.

Vale the Snake surveyed the hall with lazy gaze, taking in the crackling fires attended by thralls and former captives from Morwella, the great lounging hunting hounds they'd brought with them, and the uncorked ale barrels lined up against the far wall.

Point Keep—they'd been here a month, wenching, feasting, and drinking; fighting and occasionally hunting when winter allowed. But mostly sleeping off their heavy nights, much as they did during this season up in far Grimhold, their home in the north. Such were the activities of the Princes of Leeth during winter.

But Vale the Snake was tired of this inaction. He was bored stiff, sick to the bones of being holed up here in this forgotten fortress. To the north, his father's army held the Gap, and across from that the other, mightier fortress of Car Carranis refused to crumble, even though King Haal had spent the last week hurling rocks and missiles at it. Vale had joined them for a time up there, eager to avenge his brother.

It wasn't that he missed Corvalian; he couldn't care less about him. And that brother's death left him closer to the throne—though Redhand coveted that for his future like a broody hen. Rather, the chance of real battle had lured Vale away from his idle diversions in Point Keep, just to break the monotony, and his imagined vengeance was a motivator for the men.

But after a few freezing days staring up at those unforgiving walls, and then rowing with his father and, more violently, his older brother, Vale had departed in sulks back to his captive hold. Point Keep might not be much but it was his—the only thing he owned, despite being one of the two remaining Princes of Leeth.

The city had fallen too easily; it had left little sport as the legendary Kelthaine Wolves had died fighting to a man. They hadn't found Halfdan, which had bemused Vale somewhat.

He'd sent scouts out across the mountains, but they returned with nothing, and Vale soon forgot about the general, who was rumoured dead, so why should he care?

One thing had happened of note since their return here. One of his outriders came back from a rare hunting trip informing Vale that there was another army making for the Gap from the southeast—a strange direction.

Vale thought about warning his father but couldn't be bothered. They were probably allies of the sorcerer in Kella City, who seemed to have most countries under his sway. And if they were enemies? So much the better—let his father and brother clash with them; hopefully they'd get skewered in the process and he could return to Leeth with his father's crown.

Vale the Snake was a legend up there, almost as renowned as his elder brother. Ever since he had snapped that first serpent's head off as a teenager, men had rallied to his gang. Since then Vale had gathered a wild group of followers that had always remained aloof from the other warriors. So, diverted by the distraction, Vale the Snake had let the ranging scouts from that mystery army pass, and instead decided to await the outcome with interest.

The leman stirred in his arms as his greasy hand slid between her thighs. She opened her eyes and it was her scream that stopped his questing fingers. There were armed men rushing at them through the hall.

***

They reached the hidden door just as a crescent moon slid out from cloud to join the stars studding the firmament above. Halfdan waited as his men shuffled close and eager in the night. He motioned unlit torches they'd made earlier be passed along the line from man to man without a whisper.

"It's a long stair, followed by a passage and another stair," Haldan whispered to Corin whilst those who could gathered close. "That leads to a second door, which opens out into the rear of the kitchens. It's well hidden at the back of one of the larger pantries. I doubt Vale and his drunkards will have discovered it. The door's painted with pitch as is the wall surrounding, scarce visible until you stumble upon it."

"Smart thinking." Corin nodded thanks as Scaff passed him a torch, his eyes glinting with excitement. "How long will it take us to reach the feasting hall?"

"Maybe twenty minutes. No more. We need to go single file and tread carefully, for the way is narrow and the stairs well worn."

"I'm used to that sort of thing." Corin flashed his father a grin.

"I'm sure it will be child play for you but don't get cocky on me." Corin raised a brow at that. "Once we reach the kitchens we'll mop up any stray Leethmen or cooks and regroup for the main assault. Are you ready gentlemen?" Halfdan put a shoulder to the door and it creaked inward. Ahead showed gloom.

"We are!" voices whispered fervently in the dark, and the men set about igniting their torches, whilst Corin grinned and added, "Lead on!" He ducked through the doorway following his father and Baley, with torch in left hand and Clouter's hilt in right, the long blade sloped across his left shoulder.

They cleared both stairs and passage in between and, as Halfdan had said, were shortly at the second door. Here Baley and Bonkers Strongarm did their special little something.

The twins were the strongest of Halfdan's surviving crew and specialised in breaking things. Their unique skill set was needed to dismantle the false wall Halfdan had had them hastily erect after their escape from the fortress a month ago.

Work done, they filed out into the gloom of the kitchens. Nothing stirred save a sleeping hound and the shadow of a Leethman sprawled naked on a table. Bonkers slid a knife across the sleeping warrior's throat and then tossed a sausage at the waking hound. Baley kept both eyes peeled ahead lest any guards be prowling, whilst Halfdan and Corin waited for the rest of the men to filter into the kitchens. Once everyone was through the second door, Halfdan nodded.

"Ready?" They nodded back. "On count of three then." They nodded again. "Here we go. One...two...three!"

They rushed yelling into the hall.

***

Vale pitched the screaming girl from his lap sending her body sprawling across the stone floor. "Incoming!" Vale roared as he jumped to his feet. Surrounding him were barking snapping hounds, bleary-eyed waking warriors, and armed foes rushing in upon them. Everywhere was torchlight, noise, and yelling; his warriors bumped into each other as they reached for any weapon near by, their women fled screeching into safer corners. Then the killing began.

Vale seized an axe from a table and strode across the hall to meet his enemies, who even now were slicing and stabbing down at waking Leethmen stupefied by drink. Vale unslung the sax at his waist and waited for them to surround him. He cut and thrust, slicing out with sax and hacking down with axe, howling and spitting as the berserkergang surged through his veins.

Two men fell, then three more. Vale gasped as he recognised them by their wolf brooches and cloaks. So some of the bastards had survived. No matter, this was just the distraction he needed!

His men that could had seized weapons and were clashing with the foe, a hard fight, but they would win through against these Kelthaine scum. Vale laughed, cutting down another man with his axe. Then a cold-eyed bastard stood before him, a two-yard sword gripped with palm over palm, an evil smile on his face.

"Fuck you!" Vale the Snake batted the Longsword away with his axe and lunged low with the sax. It was a move that had fooled many a foe but Corin an Fol was ready for it.

***

Shouts and clangs of steel hitting steel, women screaming, thralls scampering and diving out of the way, hounds baying and slavering at the stink of blood. And men dying in dozens throughout the firelight-flickering hall.

Corin closed on the big tattooed lout that had to be the chief of these ruffians—Vale the Snake himself. An evil-looking brute with shaven head and spider tattoo on his right check, and cobwebs tracing his neck from collar bone to left ear. He was half naked, his bulging sinews alive like writhing serpents as he frothed and spat at Corin.

Vale swung the axe and closed again with his sax. Clouter's edge caught the axe just below its beard, and Corin twisted the blade, wrenching the weapon from Vale's grip and sending it into flickering across the hall.

Vale yelled and stabbed out with the sax, but Corin jumped back out of reach and, as he danced aside, Clouter's downward swing sliced clean through Vale the Snake's arm, halfway between wrist and elbow. Vale yammered and spat blood in Corin's face.

Corin dodged the spittle and reversed Clouter, ramming the wolf's-head pommel hard into the barbarian prince's guts, causing him to double over. Corin stepped back then brought Clouter's pommel down again—this time cracking the base of Vale's skull and knocking him unconscious to the floor.

Corin panted and turned to see Halfdan nod approval as he dispatched a warrior with a backwards sweep. To Corin's right, the Strongarm boys were leaving corpses at their feet and even the boy, Scaff, had taken a couple with his sax. But when they saw Vale crash to the floor, the few remaining Leethmen lost heart and begged quarter.

That was refused and instead, Baley and Bonkers fell upon them with axes until all of them were dead. In the chaotic minutes that followed, Halfdan bid his wolves search the fortress killing any surviving Leethmen, and freeing thralls and women wherever they were found.

Corin stood over the body of Vale the Snake watching the blood ooze from the prince's severed arm. "Seal it with flame," Halfdan ordered Bonkers who nodded grinning. "I want to speak to this bastard before we finish him."

Vale screamed as fire seared his wound. He roared and kicked and spat and cursed then passed out again. When he woke Vale found himself hanging upside down from a roof beam by his ankles, good and bad arm lashed around his waist.

Lord Halfdan approached the barbarian prince as Corin and Bonkers watched on. Beyond them, the Wolves were calming down the women and bidding thralls assist in disposing of the bodies outside. Baley bid a lass go into the kitchens and rummage up some victory fare. This she did without a sound.

"You should be dead." Vale croaked and spat blood at Halfdan who smiled in return.

"Disappointed?"

"No, because my kin will avenge me by carving a blood-eagle on your back." Vale swung and coughed as the pain threatened to consume him. But his rage and pride for the moment kept it at bay.

"That may be so—but at least the world will be free of you and your maggots, Snake. Now, while we're all here tell me of your father's camp."

"Up yours!" Vale spat again.

Bonkers stepped close and shoved his brand close to Vale's severed stump. The prisoner screamed as the agony tore into him but still he said nothing. It took six more goes with the torch until Vale the Snake told them everything he knew.

At last satisfied, Halfdan bid Bonkers slice the prince's throat and be done with him. And so died Vale the Snake on the eve of the greatest battle Ansu had witnessed in almost a millennium.

Some two hours later, when he was sure it was safe, Hordo of Grimhold, Vale's premier bodyguard and lone survivor of Halfdan's raid, crept free of the chest he'd hidden beneath. The hall was now deserted, as Halfdan's men, after filling their bellies in the kitchens, had taken their rest.

They'd posted guards on the walls but no one thought to cover the stables. Hordo had watched his prince die, and he'd wanted to charge out from his hiding place and take as many of them as he could, but he knew someone had to alert King Haal, and everyone else had looked dead or like to die.

Hordo found a horse, tied rags to its hooves, and led the beast out of the gates under the wan light of a questing moon. Nothing stirred; if there were guards on the walls above they didn't see or hear him. Once clear of the fortress walls, Hordo mounted and urged the beast down the track at speed. King Haal's camp lay only fifteen miles north, and he'd arrive before dawn.

Chapter 23

A Turn of Tides

Pashel Akaz, supreme commander of the second army watched as dawn filled the sky behind him. Already his soldiers were busy about their tasks. Preparation was the key, and today was the day when they would reach the gap in the mountains leading to the fabled country Emperor Callanz had dreamed about.

Pashel Akaz unrolled the parchment and read again the letter from his new Emperor back in Ptarni. He smiled, anticipating the rewards promised after this campaign. "A country of my own," he muttered under his breath and once again read the words written in that bold confident hand.

General Akaz

You have done well, but the real test lies ahead. The Ancient One warns of a great army blocking the gap between the mountains and besieging a city close by. This is not our war, but you may need to engage to get through. These savages are from the far north and serve a mortal warlock called

Caswallon. This Caswallon has betrayed the Urgolais who awarded him certain powers, and therefore will be brought to heel. This does not concern you.

This enemy, though great in numbers, is weak and lacks discipline. Choose your time carefully and you will lead our army through the gap. Once clear, the lands beyond are yours for the taking. There are four kingdoms, beyond them the sea. One of these kingdoms shall be gifted to you, and you will become our eyes and ears in the west.

Finally. Do not forget that other matter we spoke of when you were here. The ruined city in the mountains must be found and the spear, Golganak, recovered for the Urgolais. Let me know as soon as you can on these forthcoming developments. My father is weakening by the day and the people are rallying behind me. Ptarni is on the rise, General, and if you succeed your place shall be second only to mine.

Callanz

Emperor of Ptarni and the East

Pashel Akaz rolled the parchment tight and smiled as he saw his captains approaching for their orders. As one they doffed their polished helms, placed them on the table outside his tent, and folded the face chains within. Both their discipline and garb were flawless, as was to be expected.

They stood silent statues awaiting his words—six handsome men, eyes black and skin mocha, small and neat and tough. Pashel Akaz smiled a third time. Ptarnians were the finest soldiers in the world and he their most gifted general.

"Speak," he said bidding the nearest captain address him. Kolo Muzen was ambitious and his general had high hopes for him. He responded to his leader with confidence and clarity.

"We are ten miles east of the gap, General. Our scouts have reported a huge city of tents running form range to range. A great army blocking our route."

"This is known to me." Pashel Akaz liked to keep his captains in the dark about some things. If they learned too much they might become overambitious, particularly Kolo Muzen, the brightest star amongst them. "They are savages at war with the occupants of Kelthaine. We will pass through their camp during the night, killing any that think to stop us.'

"A difficult task, General—there are many thousands." This from one of the other captains, a man whose name Pashel Akaz couldn't recall.

"Achievable. These are barbarians who lack order or discipline, but I repeat our fight is not with them. Our task remains to secure the countries beyond for King Akamates, enslaving their people and setting up trade stations on the west coast. Once that coast is ours we can renew attacks on Shen from the opposite direction."

This last wasn't part of Callanz's mandate but Pashel Akaz was clever and knew this would make sense to his men, who knew nothing of Kelthaine but hated Shen more than any other country. And it paid to mention Callan's father around these men, as not all were loyal to the Emperor or party to his ambitions. He doubted not King Akamates had spies in camp, such was the relationship between father and son back in Ptarni.

"Captain Muzen, have you heard from our two battalions in the mountains?"

"Only from one, General. The second battalion officer sent a messenger informing us his men approached the area of the ruined city. There is no word from the other leader."

"Strange. But no matter." Pashel Akaz stowed the letter in his robe and waved his captains go about their duties. "Dismantle camp," he told them. "Ensure the men are well-fed and rested today, we march within a mile or so of those barbarian camps, then wait till nightfall."

***

Greggan blinked through the snow as the riders approached from the hillside. There were seven, and the three leaders had bows bent with arrows nocked ready. He kept his head and swallowed; this wouldn't be the first time Corin an Fol had got him into deep shit.

The leader approached, a hawk-faced youngster with suspicious eyes. He urged his steed circle close around Greggan, who sat his own beast as still as he dared.

"What are you doing out here, stranger?" The leader's accent was unlike any Greggan had encountered before. "Are you a spy or a messenger?"

"I seek Olen of the Rorshai." Greggan waited for their reaction and then nearly jumped from his saddle in surprise when a dark voice spoke behind him.

"You have found him." Unnoticed by Greggan, an eighth rider had approached him from behind and he it was who addressed him now.

"You are Olen?" Greggan shivered and steadied his horse.

"I am. And who might you be —one of Belmarius's men?"

"Belmarius? No, I am no Bear. I serve the Wolves out of Point Keep, that fortress north of here."

"I thought the Wolves were disbanded, or slain to a man, and that Point Keep was taken by Leeth."

"Some of us survived and those are currently planning on taking it back."

"Then why are you here out in the snow all alone? Point Keep is miles away. This is Rorshai Country and you, Wolf Ranger, are trespassing." Suddenly Olen awarded Greggan a dazzling grin. "Corin lives doesn't he?"

Greggan blew through his nose. "Yes, he does, I'm glad you asked that. I was with him two days ago. It was he suggested I seek you out and request your aid. He said you'd be happy to give it."

"Did he?" Olen exchanged a look with the fierce youngster who burst into laughter hearing that. "I told you he'd survive that forest, though only the gods know how."

"It was most likely them that saved him," Arami grinned. "That Corin is one ugly lucky bugger."

"You look hungry, stranger. What name do you go by?"

"Greggan, and yes I'm starving."

"Then follow us. Our camp lies close." Greggan did as he was bidden and twenty minutes later arrived at a great snowy field of tents, perhaps over two thousand were there.

"Is this the Delve?" Greggan asked Olen as they rode into the camp.

"No, the Delve is west of us. This gathering comprises all the free riders of the clans. We have been busy since Corin left us. I had a hunch something was about to happen and thus set up camp here whilst awaiting signal from the north."

"And now you have it," smiled Greggan.

"Aye, so it seems." After settling in camp Greggan spoke long with Olen and his friends about his past adventures with Corin an Fol. He enjoyed himself that night until a grizzled fellow called Rogan produced a large flask of filthy liquid and suggested he try it. Next morning Greggan's head felt like an eggshell. He didn't have time to reflect on his misery, because the tent he was sleeping in was dismantled over his head and a grinning Rogan leaned down.

"Rise and shine, flower—we ride north on the hour!"

"Where are we going?" Greggan croaked and shivered as the snow settled on his face.

"Where do you think, sunshine? Point Keep and beyond!" Greggan grinned hearing that and for a moment forgot the freezing chill and pounding between his ears. "Care for a toast—a wee willie warmer?" Rogan passed the flask down.

Greggan glared at it for a moment then shrugged. "Why not?" he grinned, and within an hour he was mounted on his horse and yelling with the rest of them. Olen approached him during that ride with another horse tied to his own, a great noble beast limping slightly in the cold.

"Wants to re-join his owner," Olen said, and Greggan laughed in delight when he recognised Thunderhoof, the warhorse Silon had given Corin after he had left the regiment all those years ago. Greggan had encountered Corin twice during the Permio Wars whilst his former comrade ran errands for his Raleenian boss. Corin had been proud to show him the horse on both occasions.

"He was hurt when we lost Corin near Darkvale," Olen explained. "I found him lying on his side with a Ptarni spear sticking in his haunch, a nasty wound, but he's patched up well."

"Tough as his owner," grunted Greggan.

"That he is but not as dumb."

"You got me there! How long is the trip to Point Keep from here?"

"Three days if we don't tarry, and we'll need to lie low as we draw close, lest your friend Vale the Snake is prowling about."

Olen was right. It took three long hard days riding at good speed to reach the folds of The High Wall that hid the fortress Point Keep. They were lucky, encountering no enemies, whilst the weather remained chilly and dry, a brittle breeze sighing from the wild grasslands flanking their east.

That last night, they made furtive camp in a vale of frozen bracken, the mountains hard to their left. When the horses were settled and man and beast had eaten, Olen and Arami and a third man Greggan didn't recognise approached him in the gloom.

"How far is the fortress? You said we were close?" This third man was called Kerante, one of the several clan leaders (or Kaans) present, Greggan learned soon after.

"Close enough to walk were one in the mood."

"And are you in the mood, Greggan of the Wolves?" Olen leaned close pinning him with his deep blue gaze.

Greggan chewed on his last piece of dried beef. "For what... exactly?"

"Reconnaissance," the young one, Arami, grinned at him. "May happen a bit of blood spilling."

"Only as a last resort." Olen waved Arami back. "But we need to find out how best we can aid your friends, so I guess we'll take a stroll up and see what we can."

Greggan nodded and minutes later he led them—six leaders and twelve other warriors—through the bracken and into the dark pines that led up to an old track, itself winding stiffly up the folds, until the smooth stones of Point Keep glistened in the moonlight ahead. It was late. An hour, maybe two after midnight.

They stole close, keeping to the track until they were within eye-shot. Nothing stirred, and the fortress loomed tall and silent ahead.

"Think they're all sleeping?" Olen shuffled into a better position at the side of the road; they dared not go much closer. "What do you suggest?" he asked Greggan, who was about to answer when the hooves of a lone rider drummed the night. Glancing ahead, they saw the dark shape of horse and horseman hurrying their way.

"A messenger at this time of night?" Kerante glanced at Greggan who shrugged.

"Unlikely," Olen spoke for him and then turned to Arami crouching low beside him. "You got this, Anchai?" Behind them, three men minded the horses whilst the rest lay flat on their bellies surveying road and fast-approaching rider.

"I've got it," Arami smiled as he quickly went back to the horses and loosened the weighted cords tied to his saddle. Arami was a master of the bola; even Olen had to acknowledge his remarkable skill at previous contests held between the clans.

Horse and rider clattered close, and Greggan recognised one of the Leethmen who had led the attack that terrible night. "Hordo. Snake's muscle man. Quick, he'll be past us in a mo!"

Arami stepped out into the night, a wolf grin on his lips and the bola curled around his left hand. The big rider saw him and spurred his horse hard toward where the lone figure stood. Hordo swung his axe and hollered.

Arami tossed his bola, and the lead weights at the cord ends whirled through night air so fast Hordo didn't see what hit him. The weighted leather whip lashed around his torso, wrenching the axe from his massive fist and throwing him off his horse. Hordo tried to rise, but the bola's cords and weight had him pinned and trussed, allowing Arami to stroll close and gaze down on him with interest.

It took three teeth and all five nails from his left hand, these prised out slowly by Kerante's hot knife, before Hordo broke down weeping and imparted news of the raid and recapture of Point Keep.

"So the boys are back home," Greggan smiled as he slid his knife along Hordo's throat sending the big warrior to Yffarn. "Lucky we saw this bastard, else King Haal would be up our arse by mid-morning. Come on Rorshai, let's go greet my old muckers!"

***

A rapping on his door, followed by hoarse shouts and talking. *What the bloody hell?*

Corin blinked an eye open and staggered out of his covers. It was still dark and whoever was waking him had better have good reason. His head throbbed; the boys had had a bit of a session after retaking the fortress, and Corin had been in the thick of it. And now his head was thick with the result.

Bang bang! "Corin an Fol! Open the door!"

"I need sleep, not noise," Corin complained as he slammed the latch back and stared at Baley and Bonkers, both grinning at him like ogres in the dark. "Piss off!" Corin swung the door shut in Baley's face but the twin's boot trapped it and held it fast.

"We've got visitors," Baley said, pained that Corin didn't want to speak with him.

"Tell 'em to come back at noon," Corin grumbled and then, seeing their expectant faces, sighed mournfully and reached down and strapped Clouter around his shoulders. "Who is it?" They didn't respond so Corin shrugged and followed them from the room.

Minutes later Corin stood in the bailey by the main gate amidst a cloud of noisy, chattering riders and sentries yelling at them from the walls. Lord Halfdan was there looking clipped and sharp and ready for the day ahead.

Corin saw Greggan among the riders and as his eyes adjusted to the light he recognised Olen and Arami. Corin's yells joined the others as he vaulted down to join the Rorshai.

"I don't believe you're here!" Corin embraced Olen and then Arami and Greggan too. Then he saw Thunderhoof standing glum by the stable door. "Thunder? You're alive? Bless your socks you old bugger, but I thought you skewered!" Corin ran across and threw his filthy arms around the big horse's neck. Thunderhoof awarded him that forlorn knowing look.

"It was a nasty wound, but the blade was clean," Olen told him smiling. No one loved horses like the Rorshai. "It's good to see you alive, Corin an Fol."

"Thank you, my friend—I'd thought I'd lost this old boy. Means the world to see him again, and you Olen, if truth be told."

"Stop fucking about and see to their horses!" Halfdan's shout brought sober order to the bailey and stables area. Everyone was awake now and all eager for the latest news. They broke fast in the main hall, and despite the stench of blood spilled the night before, everyone there was filled with new energy and purpose. Halfdan was livid, though, when he learned that Hordo had escaped.

"Lucky for us you were there, Greggan," he said after formally thanking the Rorshai leaders. Olen had already despatched two men back down to his army waiting in their bracken hide.

"They will be here ere sun-up," Olen told the general.

"Good," Halfdan replied. "We've a busy day ahead."

Chapter 24

The Gap of Leeth

Queen Ariane watched from her window whilst quietly sipping brandy. She hadn't drunk alcohol since the night they saved Calprissa, but Ariane needed its comfort now. Outside, the campfires of the enemy filled the horizon, patrolled by a lone moon.

Across the mountains, Halfdan led his Wolves through the back door into Point Keep, whilst a bit father north, Shallan and Zukei gazed out exhausted from Car Carranis, having spent all that day loosing arrows on the foe. Throughout Ansu, the Raven Season had returned.

Ariane was washed out by emotions. They had achieved so much, but it was like catching and holding quicksilver. The enemy waited outside, vastly outnumbering them. Zallerak, their much needed wizard and counsellor had vanished—Elanion only knew where. And now Tamersane had killed his elder brother in a fit of rage.

She had postponed council until first light, after bidding her guards drag Tamersane away from his dead brother's corpse and escort him to his chamber, alongside the wounded woman Teret, whom Ariane had sent a physician to promptly fix up.

Teret wasn't badly hurt, thank the gods; as a healer herself, she ordered the physician bring strange salves and plants and refused his ministrations. Ariane stationed guards at Tamersane's door lest he do something lunatic. It was all too much, and this after only a few hours back in her own city.

A knock at the door.

Leave me in peace. Just get lost...whoever you are!

A second knock—this one harder and more urgent. "Who is it?" Ariane snapped, and a muffled voice answered beyond the door. "Who? Speak up—damn you!"

"It's me—Prince Tarin. Cousin, I need to speak with you!"

Tarin. Of all the people Ariane least wanted to see it had to be Kelsalion's useless son. But she'd hardly spoken to the prince since their hectic meeting at Greystone Bridge. Tarin had kept close to Zallerak during their exile in the mountains, and Ariane hadn't felt like welcoming the prince into her tent. But now she had no choice. It had proved a crap night, so what the heck?

"You had best come in then." Ariane took a long hard slurp of brandy and waited for Prince Tarin to enter. The door swung open and he stood just outside it, hovering.

Ariane felt a flush of annoyance race through her veins. She quenched it with another slurp. "Relax, kinsman. I'm not going to eat you." Ariane motioned the prince take seat beside her and offered him a brandy; she could tell he needed one.

Tarin crouched awkwardly on the seat and shuffled. "What's the matter?" Then she saw the large bag tied to his waist, which he was currently adjusting. "And what is that?"

"Something Zallerak told me to give you before he left the camp the other night."

"He told you he was leaving and you failed to report that to me?" Ariane snatched the crystal goblet from Tarin's hand before he got chance to sip. "Surely I should punish you cousin?"

"He made me vow to silence—I had no choice, and I owe him that much at least after all he has done for me."

Ariane summoned patience. "Drink." She placed his goblet back on the table and motioned he partake, which he did with a long hard gulp.

"That's good," Tarin said. "Strong." Ariane said nothing as the prince struggled with the drawstrings covering his bag. At last something heavy and shiny fell out and tumbled to the rug. Ariane almost threw brandy over her shirt in amazement seeing the Tekara, whole and regal, on the floor at her feet.

"I don't understand? How came you by this?" In the recent chaos Ariane had clean forgotten about the crystal crown. She had just assumed Zallerak had it and was now grateful she hadn't panicked after learning of his departure. The revelation that the Tekara was missing again after their months of seeking and remaking it would have most likes tipped her into murdering someone tonight. She pinned Tarin with her dark gaze.

"Enlighten me further."

"As I said, Zallerak gave it to me to keep close until I had a chance to hand it to you in secret. He didn't trust me to keep it indefinitely and said that you're to hide it from all eyes until he is back. I can tell you I'm glad to be rid of it for lots of reasons."

Ariane's fingers lightly brushed the crystal of one of the crown's horns and felt a slight tingle run up her arm. She shivered. The Crown of Kings in her charge. No small responsibility. Now all they had to do was find a king to wear it. Ariane grinned at the ridiculous situation they were in. Beside her, Tarin looked awkward again.

"So, conspirator, where has your mentor gone, and what does he mean by deserting us in this time of need?"

"He said he was going to Ulan Valek to finish something he'd meant to finish years ago."

"Ulan Valek—the haunted castle?" Ariane was about to enquire further when another knock found queen and the prince gazing at the door. Silon stood there in his gold-trimmed nightgown, a candle in his left hand and a crumpled tiny parchment in his right.

"You need to read this." Silon entered the room and handed Ariane the parchment. Tarin watched as Ariane smoothed the rough paper and held Silon's candle close so she could read the words. "It just arrived via pigeon," Silon told her. "A man delivered it to my room."

Ariane read the short note twice and then read it again. A wave of emotions flooded her and she felt sudden tears brimming at her eyes. The note was from Corin an Fol.

Ariane,

I live yet despite the odds and have caught up with Lord Halfdan, who has informed me of something I cannot come to terms with. We are a hundred men on The Wild Way; we fare north on the morrow to recapture Point Keep. Tamersane is up here too somewhere, but we lost each other in Rorshai. Last I knew he was in good fettle with a Rorshai woman alongside. The Rorshai are our friends now; I've sent a scout to seek their aid. We will take Point Keep and then cause some trouble for King Haal.

And so it begins!

Hope this finds you in one piece.

Much love,

Corin an Fol

Ariane wiped a tear from the corner of her left eye whilst Silon stared in silence at the Tekara at her feet. "It appears that we have entered a new phase in this war," he said. "Have you any suggestions on what we do next?"

"Funny thing, but yes I do," Ariane smiled at both prince and merchant. "We hold council at dawn and then we make ready for battle."

"Perani's army outnumbers us considerably," Silon frowned. "I trust you are not planning something rash, Ariane? Like placing the Tekara on your own head."

"It won't fit me." She smiled down at the crown. She told them her notion, and after hearing that, Silon decided on a large brandy too.

***

Dawn. The sun was rising over the ocean of grass to their east and casting pinkish grey shadows on the mountains behind them. Corin held the glass his father had handed him to his left eye and counted. "I'd say a mile—if that?"

"Then what are they up to? Surely they don't mean to attack King Haal's army?" Greggan shook his head in puzzlement as Corin handed him the glass. "You suppose they are allies?"

"It's the only thing that makes sense," Corin replied. "Caswallon arranged for another army just in case the Leethmen got carried away and decided on taking The Glass Throne for themselves." Corin felt a peculiar shiver after mentioning Kelsalion's former seat of power. *My heritage...*

"Insurance," Greggan nodded. "Makes sense. But what did he promise them in return, I wonder?" The two men and Olen of the Rorshai were perched halfway up a pine tree awarding wide views of the Gap of Leeth, beyond and below. As dawn's glow gilded the grasses, Corin gazed across the Gap seeing Car Carranis's granite bulk scarcely four leagues north.

Soon Shallan.

"I'm coming to get you," Corin mouthed the words as he watched a skein of geese wend south from the forest at the far side of the Gap.

"You say something?" Olen awarded him a knowing glance.

"Time for breakfast, methinks." Corin freed his arms and let his rangy body drop silent from the pine's limb to rest crumpled in a foot of snow.

"Agreed," said the others and landed lithe beside him. Back at camp, the Rorshai leaders and Lord Halfdan were already discussing tactics whilst devouring sausages and soup.

"What did you see? Are the Ptarnians going to attack?" Halfdan bid Corin and Olen join them whilst Greggan hurried off for a shit.

"They're scarce a mile from the nearest tents. I'm surprised those dozy Leethmen haven't seen them yet. That said, they will soon, so we had best get cracking."

"You're certain you want to do this?"

"Yes, father, and we have the men chosen and ready."

"Two hundred Rorshai volunteers," Olen added. ""Myself and Arami here included. Kerante will lead the main force." Arami winked at Halfdan as he crunched on a sausage. "And twenty Wolves who just had to be with Corin, among them Baley and Bonkers and that idiot Scaff."

"I'd sooner that lad stay with the main force." Halfdan dusted his hands free of crumbs and took to his feet. "But I guess he de-serves a chance of glory—whatever that is."

"We'll keep him alive if fates allow," Corin said, as he wiped soup from his mouth and wandered over to see to Thunder. He appraised the big horse with a critical eye. Thunder gave him that look again.

"You up for a bit of a charge old boy? Nothing radical, just show our arses to the enemy then tear off again. What say you?" Thunderhoof said nothing.

"Ride tight and close," Olen shouted as the two hundred-plus volunteer cavalry mustered around him. "Remember: the objective is not to engage but rather to piss them off!"

Halfdan watched as the column of volunteer riders filed away from their hide in the last fold of Tolfallon, the most northerly mountain in The High Wall. It was a bright sunny morn and their helms and shields sparkled as they turned a corner and faded from sight.

Halfdan sighed, "Corin an Fol, stay alive. I'd sooner not lose you now I've just found you again." He returned to camp where his Wolves were making ready for a busy day. Close by, the Rorshai diced and idled but Halfdan knew these fine warriors would leap into action at his nod and wink. Just when that happened depended on Corin an Fol.

***

Pashel Akaz never gave the order to advance that night, a decision he would soon regret. His scouts had fed him reports all the previous day, informing him the barbarians were now engaging the city in fury, their entire force bent on its destruction.

With that in mind Pashel Akaz deemed it sensible for his army to advance during the following morning while the savages were busy hurling themselves at the city walls. The Gap was wide enough for them to pass unheeded if they filed narrow and moved at speed. Let the barbarians take their city and be damned; it was all they would get in this campaign.

Pashel Akaz nodded to the messenger as he leaped down from his horse just as dawn rose, promising a glorious winter's day.

"What news—do they attack?"

"In their thousands, Your Eminence; the city of tents ahead is nearly deserted."

"Then it's time we got moving," said Pashel Akaz. He turned to the closest captain, recognising Kolo Muzen, despite the black chain covering his face from helm to chin. "Captain Muzen, spread the word. We march west through this gap, then on to victory. For Emperor and King!"

Kolo Muzen turned his horse then yelled warning. "Riders attacking!" An arrow struck his shield and another sank into his horse's side causing the beast scream and throw the captain from his saddle. Arrows filled the sky as the enemy riders sped full pelt toward them. One lucky shaft found Pashel Akaz just below his shoulder pinning him to a wagon wheel. The general never knew who his killers were.

Within minutes the arrows had ceased, and the attackers wheeled their mounts and were speeding back toward the distant tents. Kolo Muzen rolled free from his dead horse. He saw Pashel Akaz lying skewered next to the wagon, and a great rage filled him.

The barbarians had attacked them, and now they would pay.

"The general is dead! We must avenge Pashel Akaz!" The other captains joined in the call to arms, and within half an hour the entire Ptarni army marched northeast toward the granite city and the horde surrounding it.

***

Baley hefted a horn he carried and blew three long blasts, announcing the signal. From their hide, Wolves and Rorshai leaped into saddle and urged their beasts gallop full pelt into the Gap of Leeth, tearing through the enemy tents and slaying any living amongst them.

A mile north, Corin and Olen led the volunteers toward the horde surrounding Car Carranis. They got within arrow shot and loosed again, this time into the backs of the Leethmen. Northmen turned in shock and rage as their comrades pitched screaming to the dirt.

Word got through to King Haal that they were being attacked from the rear, but by that time Corin and company had re-joined Halfdan and the main Rorshai force, and were cutting west to distance themselves from both enemies, whilst drawing near to the city from the other side.

And so throughout that long day the miracle unfolded. Kolo Muzen led the Second Ptarnian Army crashing into the rear of King Haal's horde, and during the course of that day both vast armies almost annihilated each other.

Almost.

Kolo Muzen averted disaster at the last minute, ordering the fifteen hundred men he had left retreat back into the grasslands, and King Haal and Dan Redhand led their surviving warriors crashing through the gates of Car Carranis. The city was breached, and evening had come.

***

Shallan slumped exhausted against the battlements. Yesterday had drained her physically and mentally, and today looked to be worse. And as dawn rose clear and bright she saw them lined up in their thousands for renewed attack. After Corvalian's death, King Haal had abandoned all caution and now hurled everything at them.

Yesterday, the wooden siege towers had rolled and rattled against the walls, but Ralian's archers had torched three with fire arrows after hurling oil down on the timbers, and a fourth had got stuck in a rut and remained there tilted at a jaunty angle, its occupants fled in fear of falling to their deaths. That was yesterday.

This morning brought more siege towers. Shallan counted ten. And there were other contraptions hauled by mules and nags and guided by thralls: ballistae, crudely constructed yet capable of wreaking huge damage on the city.

And then there were the warriors of Leeth. They had shot so many full of arrows yesterday and what difference had it made? The entire Gap of Leeth was filled with their snarling faces, and their roars and yells filled her ears. How long could they endure this?

Shallan had skewered at least thirty yesterday, her fingers bleeding and arms aching from working her bow. But the tide had kept coming until nightfall, when they finally slunk back like lolling hounds to their tents for more wenching and boozing, leaving Shallan and her companions gasping for air on the battlements.

And today looked like a longer one. Today, thought Shallan, King Haal is going to appear himself. And in an hour she was proved right. As the second wave of siege towers rumbled close and the ballistae took position, a score of horsemen rode free of the horde, among them the king and his son Daan Redhand—easily recognisable by their rich garb and lofty manner.

They reined in just short of bow shot as their countless foot warriors shuffled into line. Shallan watched as the king and his son seemed to be discussing something new. The younger man, Redhand, looked agitated and angry—a pleasant change from the confident arrogance he usually showed.

As Shallan watched, she saw the king waving his arms and pointing back through his army, and his angry son throwing his own arms up in hostile manner at his father, before turning his horse and riding back through his men. Shallan wished she knew what was going on down there.

A hand tugged her sleeve; she glanced down and saw little Sorrel standing there. "Hey sweetheart, what are you doing up here? I thought Zukei had given you chores to do. These walls aren't safe."

Sorrel snorted. "I've as much right to be up here as anyone else. We're all going to die soon anyway, and I want to die fighting and not doing chores!" Sorrel stamped a foot but Shallan could see the sparkle of tears rimming her eyes.

"We are not going to die, sweetheart, that's just foolish talk. These walls are strong and high, and those villains will realise they are wasting their time."

Sorrel wasn't convinced but she shifted her defiant stance and awarded Shallan her bravest smile. "Zukei says I'll make a good fighter! She's taught me how to throw stones with deadly accuracy and steal things from under peoples noses."

Shallan raised a brow at that. She hadn't seen Zukei this morning and suspected she was over at the north end of the wall, or else above the main barbican and gates where Barin and Ralian were stationed—that being the most vulnerable place and where Haal would most likes focus his attack.

"Zukei killed a hundred men yesterday." Sorrel squinted up at Shallan's bow. "How many did you kill, Duchess Shallan?"

"Not nearly as many as that. How did you know Zukei killed a hundred—did she tell you?"

"No, I counted."

"You were up here yesterday?"

"I was." Sorrel's lip twitched.

Shallan shook her head. She didn't like Sorrel being up here but what could she do? The girl was right: they were all going to die soon, so why shouldn't she get a chance to fight too?

"Do me a favour, Sorrel. Go find Big Barin and tell him there's something odd going on between the bad king and his son, and that his son has ridden off somewhere. Do you see where the bad king sits his horse over there?"

Sorrel nodded, "I've seen him lots of times, but he looks mad today. Madder than usual."

"I think so too."

"Why aren't they attacking with those wooden towers like they did yesterday?"

"I don't know." Shallan was puzzled by the enemy who now seemed confused, and all among their ranks there was shuffling and coughing and such as though none amongst them knew what was going on. "Maybe the king is waiting for his son to return to tell him something?" Shallan suggested.

"That must be it." Sorrel flashed her that brave grin and trotted cheerfully off to find Big Barin. Shallan watched the girl jog along the walls, dodging the archers stationed like the duchess at their various posts. She returned her attention to King Haal who still sat his horse in ill temper, his head craned back as though looking for something. And still no attack came.

Then she heard it—the distant clash of steel. Someone was fighting way out there. But who and where was impossible to tell. Shallan gazed far out across the Gap and thought she could see horsemen racing through the distant tents. Then she turned her gaze east and saw other warriors advancing on King Haal's rear-guard.

What was happening? Could it be?

"Corin has come!" Shallan said to her closest companion archer who shook his head, misunderstanding. "Everything is going to be all right now," Shallan smiled at the other bowman, who gazed back at her askance as though she'd lost her mind.

"Corin is out there!" Shallan shouted down from the walls and men turned their heads all along the battlements. "And you are fucking dead!"

Shallan pointed at the distant king, who at that moment seemed to turn his head and gaze straight up at where she stood, though the distance assured it impossible for him to have heard her.

***

Hagan Delmorier watched the carnage unfold in The Gap of Leeth and blessed his decision to observe before engaging. He had told Rael Hakkenon he'd seek out King Haal and offer his sword and counsel, as Hagan believed he had more skill and tactics in his head than the entire horde below.

But when he'd arrived late last night, Hagan had the odd feeling something was afoot. Call it a hunch, but it kept him low and out of sight, his horse tied to a tree and his long limbs crouched on the rim of a high shelf looking north over the Gap from the shoulder of mighty Tolfallon.

It was chilly, but he'd brought food and he had his brandy flask, so Hagan was happy to watch from his secure hide that morning. And so it was he got the best seat at the show.

Hagan saw the Ptarnians first. He had no idea who they were, but there were a lot of the fuckers and they were well armed and seemed well trained too. Hagan shook his head in disbelief seeing this alien army march like lemmings crashing into the rear of King Haal's delirious horde. He could hear the distant screams of men being hewn apart by pike, halberd, and spear. Hagan scratched his head and reached for the hunk of bread he'd stowed in his pocket.

"Give me that!"

Hagan rolled, pulled his longsword free of sheath and levelled it at the goblin perched close on a rock watching him with those evil red eyes.

"Where the fuck did you come from?" Hagan forgot his bread and Gribble dodged around his sword and snatched it up.

"Nothing to eat round here. Don't fancy my chances down there until they're all dead."

"You spying on me again, goblin?" Hagan hadn't forgotten how Gribble had given him and his men away to the Crimson Guard down in Cappel Cormac. It was a sore point.

"This isn't about you, shithead; you're no longer part of our team."

"I'm glad of it." Hagan turned his head to watch as the fighting thickened below. "Then at least be useful and tell me what the fuck is happening down there?"

"Bread's not bad, but I don't like the seeds," Gribble complained but swallowed the husk whole. "Bit of a mess down there," he added with his mouth full.

"You're telling me." Hagan reached for his spyglass and the goblin squatted down beside him as though they were old friends. "So who's that other lot?"

"Ptarnians of course."

"Ptarnians? What the fuck are they doing here?"

"Invading." Gribble gave him a superior knowing look that didn't work on Hagan.

"Ahh, so they are Caswallon's back up in case Haal's boys get out of hand—is that it?"

"No." Gribble produced a weird expression that could have been a smile were it on a human face. "Mr Caswallon doesn't know about them. Mr Caswallon doesn't know about a lot of things. That lot serve my old boss."

"Who's that?" Suddenly Hagan saw riders wheeling and charging through the maze of tents. They looked like Rorshai but it was hard to tell from this distance.

"What the...?"

Hagan rammed his left eye into the cold crystal of his spyglass to get a better look, but it was no good, whoever the riders were they were moving too fast for him to catch their identity.

"You want to know who that lot is too?" Gribble showed his fangs again.

"Tell me."

"That's your friend down there and with him are his old gang and a host of Rorshai."

"What the fuck are you talking about, goblin?"

"I flew over them at first light whilst they were preoccupied," Gribble smirked. "I recognised him at once by his long nasty sword."

"Who?"

"Corin an Fol stupid—who do you think?"

"What?" Hagan gaped at the goblin who licked his lips and hopped along the ridge.

"Going to take a chance," Gribble muttered. "Enough dead down there to fill my belly until lunch; by then there'll be a lot more. I love battles!"

Gribble flashed him an oily wink and promptly fell off the ridge, plummeting like a stone, then stretching his wings, he leveled and settled on the closest corpses by the tents far below. Hagan stared at the scene unfolding in disbelief; he could no longer see the riders, but he didn't need to. Knowing Corin was down there changed everything.

Hagan stood, shook his cold body into action and untied his horse from the tree. Then slowly and carefully he led the beast back to the deer track and down to the timberline a hundred yards below.

Once there, he mounted and urged his beast follow a wider track leading down to the lowest flanks of Tolfallon's toes. Hagan reached the Gap of Leeth and for the next half hour he warily guided his horse betwixt the maze of tents flanking the rear of King Haal's army.

He found some food and beer and picked an artful place to await the outcome. Let the bastards kill each other, thought Hagan. Once it's dark he would steal out from his latest hide and go find Corin an Fol. Hagan smiled for the first time that day.

Chapter 25

Whitestone Bridge

Wind rushing through her hair and icy chill stabbing her cheeks, again she is falling amid darkness and silence. Ariane lands soft as snowflakes on damp stone. A greyness spreads our before her, and now she is standing in a wood, dark trees sombre and silent all around her. Then she sees him and smiles—her father the king! A longsword in his right hand, his armour glinting and chiming softly in the gloom. He approaches that quiet place where she stands, his eyes hollow with sorrow.

"I am dreaming," Ariane informs him. "I know," King Nogel replies, his voice gallows grave and rusty. "And yet what are dreams and what reality? Depends on your perspective, daughter."

"Look what I have," Ariane smiles, and like a proud child holds the Tekara up for her father to see. He nods and bids her return it to the forest floor where they are standing.

"But father!" Ariane's face is troubled and she can no longer see him properly. "This shall be our salvation. Father?" She has lost him in the gloom. She looks around, eyes wide, then at last sees his shadow swaying slightly on the edge of her vision. "Where is this place?" Ariana asks her father.

"The endless wood," his voice barely reaches her. "A lost corner of Limbo. Here I must wander awaiting the outcome. There are others you know hereabouts. All of us are waiting for this the final dance."

"What must I do?" Ariane spoke to his shadow and the wind answered with his voice, dark and distant.

"Ride out fast ere morrow's dawn! Take the fight to the enemy and crown to the Glass Throne. Only there can it stall the evil that is coming."

"Father! That evil is all around us! Caswallon's web closes tighter and his army surrounds our walls."

"And yet worse is to come. Far worse. You must be valiant, my daughter, and you must have faith. The Goddess needs you as much as you need her. They too are in deep—the old gods. The Darkest One returns! We shades shiver as His shadow musters huge within the halls of Yffarn."

"But what can I do?"

"Take the crown to the throne; then shall the king return to claim it."

"But there is no king! The line was shattered alongside the crown, and though that's made whole again there is no one at present to wear it. Father, please help me, I know not what to do!"

But her father's shade has gone and only echoes and whispers remain.

Father...I miss you so!

A stirring amid branches. Ariane feels the soft ground melt beneath her feet. She cries out as the heavy loam swallowes her up, smothering her and choking her breath. She tries to scream, but her voice is muffled and seems to come from a long way away.

Blackness buries her, and Ariane knows she is dying in this dream.

She steels herself. This is the Dreaming.

A message—I must listen! I must learn!

Deep inside the intangible encasing her, Ariane she sees something take shape. A black needle, sharp and long, and so obsidian it renders the void surrounding to dismal grey. *Golganak...*

A new voice reaches her from somewhere close. A voice that carries authority, wisdom, and power, and Ariane feels the smothering loamy taste of soil fade from her mouth. She lives yet, and gazing out into the black sees a face she knows.

Zallerak?

He is with her in that darkest place. Tall and golden, proud and stern. In his arms Zallerak grips the shaft of the spear, tugging at it and struggling to wrench it from someone she cannot see.

"Ariane!" Zallerak's strained tones echo across to her. "I cannot hold this...He is too strong! Save the crown and find the king—you know where he'll be!"

"I do not!" Ariane tries to move but her limbs are leaden and she can see the anguish writhing in Zallerak's face.

"Ride north," he chokes. "Kelthara is the key!" Then his face falls away like chalk dust, and after that the screaming starts.

"Ah, it begins. I understand at last! The dragon has..."

Dark wings thunder above and golden eyes mock her until Ariane's screams have her maids rushing into her room.

***

Ariane woke with a jolt that sent her crashing from her bed. She sprawled naked on the floor, head throbbing and legs akimbo, as her three maids showed their worried faces.

"Go! Come back with tea and cheese and bread. And a pickle. I need to think!" Ariane briskly waved them away. Time to get moving; she had slept way too long. Ariane wiped her eyes free of sleep and swung the drapes wide. "In a mug," she yelled at the last departing maid. "I need it on the go!" The Dreaming had been vivid, and her mind was still full of it. She needed to act decisively and swiftly. But first she needed that tea.

Outside, the walls of Wynais glistened with wintry sunlight. So much for her dawn reveille; Ariane could tell morning was passing swiftly into afternoon. But that was well, for the Dreaming had brought her father back, if only for a moment. She drew comfort knowing he was watching her, despite his woeful state and doleful warnings.

Ariane dressed swiftly into her leather trousers and tunic and long black boots. The maids returned and hovered like moths until she bade them away again with a stiff sharp wave. She sipped the sweet tea and stuffed the bread and cheese between her teeth. Then, after another slurp, Ariane vacated her room. Outside in the corridor, Silon was leaning languid against the wall reading a parchment.

"Cancel the council," she snapped at him without explanation. Silon nodded, passed her the parchment, and turned on his heels.

"And tell Valentin and Tarello I would speak with them soonest."

"Good morning to you too, my Queen," Silon waved an acknowledging hand as she vanished around a corner, a half smile on his lips. Little surprised the merchant these days.

As she strutted through the corridors, Ariane glanced down at the note. She briefly scanned the contents, got the gist, sighed, and after a moment's hesitation, Ariane ceased her strides, took a long deep breath, and decided to return to her room.

She would read the letter at leisure whilst waiting for her generals. Ariane returned to her room, ordered more tea, and sat back with note in hand. She read the contents slowly and digested every word.

Ariane folded her arms and smiled at the youngest maid before bidding her depart again. Despite her Dreaming and throbbing head, she felt good. Confident. The note was from Caswallon to his new commander, Gonfalez. The name meant nothing to Ariane. Silon hadn't got the chance to explain to her that Valentin's rangers had intercepted the messenger whilst surveying the enemy army camped less than five miles from the city.

They'd done well. The note was short and concise and easily recognisable as being written in Caswallon's whispery hand. Kelthara—always a thorn in Caswallon's side—had erupted in violent revolt. A Groil battalion Perani had sent there weeks earlier had been extinguished and the "rebels"—the last surviving king's men - were openly defying the sorcerer. Ariane saluted their bravery.

Caswallon's orders to his new man were for Gonfalez to leave a skeleton force guarding Wynais whilst his main army return north to mop up the rebellion. Gonfalez was to meet with the Groil who had been scouring the Kelwyn countryside for months but had now set up camp just south of Whitestone Bridge. These were to accompany him north across the bridge. The combined force would destroy Kelthara, then turn south again for Wynais.

Ariane was on her third mug of tea when Captains Valentin, Tarello, and Jaan arrived puffing into her room. Galed and an excited Cale, whom the queen had not invited into her chamber, shortly joined these generals. Nevertheless she bid these two take seat and be silent.

Last up, Silon slid in with a man she didn't know, but she could see he was one of Belmarius's surviving Bears. He looked tough and dependable, and Silon announced him as Garland, new leader of the Bears.

"How many are out there?" Ariane demanded of Valentin, who shrugged.

"A lot. Maybe twenty thousand?"

"And we have?"

"A quarter of that number. Further, their forces will be bolstered by Groil, their whole force bar a few heading north to Kelthara. At least that buys us time," Valentin said.

"No." All heads turned when Ariane stood and walked over to gaze out on her city. "We have no time." Silon smiled, but everyone else looked puzzled.

"Surely it's good news the enemy is withdrawing." Galed sipped tea and blinked at his queen. He had been so relieved hearing about Kelthara, and now hoped they would have time to regroup and get their strength back, but now it looked like his hopes would be quashed.

"They will return stronger, with Kelthara broken and all Caswallon's will on taking Wynais. Whereas —"

"If we strike first and aid Kelthara, we might just turn the tide and catch Caswallon off guard." Silon smiled at the queen who nodded back.

"Aid Kelthara? You mean to ride north into the sorcerer's jaws?" Tarello's eyes were wide with disbelief. "Valiant proposal but reckless, my Queen."

"Not if we're smart." Ariane turned from her perusal to face the people gathered in her room. "Gentlemen, the Dreaming visited me again last night. I won't discuss that here. But know this, after reading that letter, I knew exactly what must be done. This is a gift my leaders! We must seize it!"

They exchanged uncertain glances. The four captains looked tense, Silon wryly amused, Galed concerned, and Cale enthused. Everyone awaited her next word.

"General Valentin," Ariane's dark gaze rested on the Ranger, "when do we expect this Gonfalez to withdraw? And how many troops will he leave behind?"

Again Valentin shrugged. "My scouts report from your walls that he's disbanding his camp even now, so I expect they will move out tonight under cover of darkness, leaving enough visible to threaten these walls. Say two thousand, disguised to look like many more? Hard to be sure, but that's what I'd do. I do not know this Gonfalez, but let's hope he's less experienced than Perani."

"Certainly he'll want to impress his master," Ariane nodded. Caswallon hadn't sounded impressed with Gonfalez thus far. The letter had threatening undertones to its recipient.

"Whitestone Bridge," Ariane smiled at her gathering, "that's our key to unlock Caswallon's plans. As most of you know, the bridge lies in a deep gorge spanning the River Kelthara. A perfect place for an ambush were one able to spring it."

"That it is," smiled Valentin, "and close to the enemy's old camp just south of the border."

"Where Gonfalez is heading to meet with the Groil," Ariane nodded. "Once that's done he'll enter Kelthaine."

"Unless we stop him!" Jaan grinned at Valentin and now Tarello was smiling too. Silon remained nonplussed as did the hard-looking Garland. Galed still looked worried, and Cale just appeared puzzled and slightly out of his depth.

"A hundred archers could cause mayhem in that gorge, and later on the bridge. We could repeat our success at Greystone Bridge in the south. This second battle of the bridges could free Kelwyn!" Valentin looked excited now.

"Slow down gentlemen. That last victory was due to Zallerak's firework display," Silon cut in with a curt wave of hand. "Whitestone Bridge is another matter. It's certainly achievable. But let's not get ahead of ourselves. This needs finite planning and our timings must be spot on."

"It does," Ariane agreed. "I'm thinking you Rangers, Jaan's archers and lancers, and anyone else who wants to form our guerrilla attack force, should slip out of the city about the same time Gonfalez departs from here. Get ahead of him and stay well hidden, then wait for our main force at the gorge.

"Then at dawn, my army rides out with myself clearly visible. We crash through their weakened cordon and ride full tilt for Whitestone. It will take this Gonfalez a while to gather those Groil into that old camp, so we should have time to cross the bridge and await him on the other side, our Rangers and archers already in place. What say you gentlemen?"

After an hour of further discussion, Ariane left them to their thoughts. She had one last job to do before making preparations to leave the city. And not an easy one. Deep in thought, Ariane strode briskly down to where Tamersane was quartered in the rooms below hers.

***

Teret sat cross-legged on the floor whilst her lover gazed out the window at the bustling city below. She was calm and wore an easy smile whenever he glanced her way, which wasn't often. Teret didn't speak—no point. Pain will out. She loved Tamersane and was prepared to let him work through this anyway he could.

The guards outside were kindly to her, asking to report to them should she or her lover require anything at all. One informed Teret there was a big council meeting due tonight; rumour was the queen was planning something major. Teret had hardly listened to him, but grunted thanks for the food and wine he'd brought them.

A knock came just before noon. The guards filed in with Queen Ariane between them. "I've a job for you, cousin." The queen's tone left no room for argument.

Tamersane didn't respond, nor did he avert his absent scrutiny of the city below. Teret stood and glared hard at Ariane. "He needs rest!" She snapped.

"No, he needs purpose, Teret." Ariane bid the young woman sit and let her continue. After a moment's hesitation and more glaring, Teret nodded and took seat by the window, her good arm around her lover's waist.

"Tamersane!" The queen approached the window and stood beside her cousin.

"What?" Tamersane did his best to ignore her.

"Valentin's rangers ride north tonight. You, cousin, are going with them."

Tamersane shrugged indifference, but Teret rose to her feet and confronted the queen. "He needs rest and solace after what he's been through. You do not own him, Queen Ariane!" The guards looked shocked hearing the Rorshai woman's tones, not used to their queen being addressed in such a way. But Ariane bid them be easy and wait outside.

"Tamersane," Ariane's dark eyes were on Teret. "You are my

second cousin and I love you—always have. Not as Teret here loves you, but as an old friend and your queen. I do not like seeing you like this. You are a better man than he who stands here moping. What happened, happened. We cannot change that."

"I killed my brother—that's what happened. I am cursed, Ariane."

"Crap! I'll not hear such defeatist bollocks. Self-pity is not worthy of you, cousin. I, your queen, expect more from you. Shape up man! This Rorshai woman adores you and deserves only the best from you, so stop bloody moping and get into gear! I expect you ready for battle ere nightfall."

Tamersane sniggered slightly and turned to award his queen a wry look. "You expect too much, Ariane." The queen ignored him and instead placed a hand on Teret's shoulder.

"A word outside would be good." Teret nodded and, after glancing briefly at her lover, departed the room after the queen. Tamersane watched the women leave with a scowl on his lips. At her word, the guards left Ariane alone to speak with Teret. The Rorshai woman leaned against the wall as the queen folded her arms and faced her square on.

"We two need to be friends," Ariane said. "I know Tamersane of old, Teret, and if he stays here he will drink himself stupid and most likes come to a bad end. He is a joker but harder on himself than he lets people think.

"He needs action and purpose. Without those he is lost—hence my demanding he ride out with those Rangers. If I were thinking of myself, I would let him remain safe in this city. But that would be selfish, as I know he would wallow and soak in drink and depression. That way would prove his ruin."

"I wouldn't let him," Teret challenged, but Ariane shook her head kindly.

"You wouldn't be able to stop him, try as I'm sure you would. Please forgive me, Teret, I can see, clear as a pikestaff, how much you love Tamersane, and he is lucky to have you, and added to that it gives me joy that you have each other. But I've known that boy a long time, and I know I'm right in this."

"I don't have a choice—do I? You being queen and all?" Teret half smiled, thinking of her home across the mountains and how different things would be there.

"No, you don't. But I'd rather you be on my side, an ally if not a friend."

"Only on one condition."

"And what is that?" Ariane's eyes narrowed.

"That I accompany Tamersane on this venture." Teret looked hard into Ariane's eyes. "Where he goes I go, Queen. We Rorshai women are a match for any man, and this you do not control."

"Agreed. And I've no problem with women fighters, Teret. I am Ariane of the Swords after all. Now, I'm away and I leave it to you to get Tamersane ready. For if he is not, I'll have the guards carry him down to the barracks and strap him to his horse."

"That will not be necessary."

"Good." Ariane flashed Teret a smile and yelled for the guards to accompany her back to the courtroom, where her captains had retired to confer and plan.

Late that night, as Gonfalez's force broke up and marched north, Valentin's scouts reported back to him. Then, at an opportune time, the Rangers and Raleenians trotted out under the cover of moonless drizzle.

Among them were the cloaked and hooded figures of Tamersane and his lover Teret. It hadn't taken much convincing on her part.

"If you are a man you will do this thing, and if you are not then I have no need of you." Tamersane had given in on hearing that. Rorshai women were not party to nuance. What is, is. Enough said.

***

General Gonfalez watched as his riders filed in double columns along the dusky road. It was cold, and a raw drizzle snotted noses and chilled bones. Despite that, Gonfalez was content. Here was his big chance. He'd screwed up in letting the little queen enter Wynais. He should have pounced on her earlier, but it had proved so difficult to keep up with Ariane in the mountains. And then that confounded fog!

She had been lucky—again. But her luck was about to run out. Gonfalez knew Kelthara well and liked it not at all. Keltharans had always considered themselves above their rivals living in Kella City, despite that being The High King's residence.

They were a queer lot, aloof and proud. Those few nobles that survived Caswallon's purges had fled there, and somehow managed to stay alive, despite the many assassination attempts and Groil raids in that city.

And now they had risen up against the sorcerer! Utter madness! But Gonfalez had to admire their courage, stupid and desperate as it was—a few brave men defying the lightning. And the lightning was coming fast. He, Gonfalez, formerly of the Tigers stationed in Kella City, was leading the storm that would destroy Kelthara resistance once and for all.

After that, Caswallon would have cause to be grateful to him. Then would Gonfalez's reign of glory commence: the sorcerer would see what his new general had done. And then would come the hour for the final and total destruction of Wynais and Kelwyn, and the huge rewards that would flow to him.

Perani's campaign had failed completely. Gonfalez's murder of his former general wasn't only driven by ambition. He had been frustrated with how things had gone. After Derino had failed at Calprissa, Perani had lacked direction, and the Groil creatures had been wasted instead of used to bolster their ranks. Those Groil needed strong leadership. They hadn't received it. Instead most had wandered through the deserted villages salvaging and picking at anything they could find, the inhabitants already long gone.

So it was with a high heart Gonfalez led his army away from Wynais and deep into the gloomy night. He'd left scarcely a thousand men behind, deeming it necessary only to show movement and steel to any watching from the city walls.

In the chaos and arrogance of their scurrying, noisy departure, none of Gonfalez's people noticed the small detachment of riders leaving from the rear city gates and racing north ahead of them, soon lost to night.

Just before dawn, with the old camp barely two miles ahead, Gonfalez reined in in sudden alarm. A rush of wings above, vast and drumming. Looking up, he and his soldiers were witness to the dragon passing high overhead. But Vaarg paid them no heed; his business was up in the mountains, where his old master had summoned his urgent assistance.

Shaken by the sight, Gonfalez arrived at the abandoned camp and bid those stationed there strike tents and ready for the return north. Groil arrived in dribs and drabs throughout that arduous morning. Meanwhile, Gonfalez fretted at the time wasted.

At last, by mid-afternoon they were ready. His army bolstered by over a thousand Groil, Gonfalez cut across country toward Whitestone Bridge, which carried the road over to Kelthaine.

As they rode, fresh snow settled in the fields to left and right, and a chill wind croaked from the north. Gonfalez's vanguard was nearing the end of the deep wooded gorge that opened on the bridge, when a cry of warning behind saw him glancing up at the slopes on either side.

Ambush!

The rain of arrows was hard and fast and the confusion it caused terrible. A man fell to Gonfalez's left, two more to his right. He growled deep in his stomach, dropped his visor and urged his beast gallop on toward the bridge a half mile ahead, his army panicking and rushing behind their general.

The archers emptied their quivers and fled the slopes fading like ghosts into the woods above, and then, unbeknownst to Gonfalez, they joined Queen Ariane waiting calmly with another group of bowmen at the north side of the bridge.

Gonfalez reached Whitestone Bridge and reined in, astounded

to see Queen Ariane, a sword in each hand, surrounded by fighting men, these lining the north bank for many yards at either side.

Incomprehension and rage surged through Gonfalez's veins. He didn't hesitate. The bitch queen had stolen a march on him too! No matter, he would crush her like the festering tick she was. Gonfalez survived his reckless charge across Whitestone Bridge but many of his best captains didn't.

By the time they gained the northern end of the bridge, Queen Ariane's army was racing north, vanishing along the snow-covered road to Kelthara. Gonfalez, raging, spitting, and chewing his moustache, urged his army gather and regroup at the northern end. Once that was achieved, and whilst ignoring the dead and dying, he led his force north at speed in hot pursuit of the queen. Gonfalez smiled as the battle rage filled him; Kelthara and Queen Ariane—he would destroy them both inside a day. She had played into his hands after all.

Chapter 26

The Fight at the Gates

Barin hardly noticed the urgent tug at his waist. He looked down squinting at the young girl grinning impishly up at him. "I'm a messenger," Sorrel said puffing out her cheeks. "From Shallan Duchess."

"Of course you are," Barin grinned back and hoisted the girl up so she could look over other men's heads.

"You really are a giant," Sorrel giggled and whooped.

"Well, bigger than most here, though not a giant. I came across a few of those in my young days and I cannot recommend their company. How fares the Duchess?" Barin placed Sorrel gently on the parapet floor as though she were a fragile vase.

"Oh, she is good. Brave, and so is Mistress Zukei."

"Mistress Zukei is something else entirely." Barin looked across and saw the two aforementioned women approaching them along the battlements. It was oddly quiet and still on the walls. A strange lull in what had been—and would soon be again—a chaotic, exhausting couple of days.

Though not for Barin—he hadn't needed to heft his axe once.

But certainly for the enemy, who lay in piles at the foot of the walls, skewered by arrow, boiled by oil, and crushed by rock.

"Why doesn't the bad king attack?" Sorrel could just make out King Haal by his size and the winged iron crowned helm he wore. The king still sat his horse cursing and swearing in the midst of his tribe.

"I thought you were the messenger." Barin waved as Shallan saw him and added purpose to her stride.

"Oh, that. Duchess says there's fighting somewhere beyond the nasty king. She says someone is on our side, and she seems very happy—that's it."

"Well and good, and maybe that's why King Haal's hesitating. I too noticed his son departing a while back." Barin refused to mention his archfoe's name lest his growl scare the girl. Sorrel knew nothing of the blood feud betwixt Barin and Daan Redhand.

As Barin waited for Shallan and Zukei to join them, he cast his canny gaze at the enemy milling and shouting like a rising wave of steel, three hundred yards beyond the walls. Ten siege towers, ballistae, and other contraptions were now lined up in haphazard order. Barin smiled wryly. This was going to be a big day. Then he too heard the distant clash of steel and yelling and had cause to wonder who was fighting out there.

"It's Corin!" Shallan said as she let him greet her with a hug. "He's out there, Barin—this I know. Call it intuition." Zukei stood behind her, frowning down at Sorrel who winked back. "Cheeky mare," Zukei said to the girl who giggled in response.

"That wouldn't surprise me," Barin nodded, though he doubted Corin was out there. But then who? And what the bloody hell did they hope to achieve—biting like flies on the hide of a boar as big as Leeth? A puzzle, but a pleasing one; any aid was sorely needed.

Barin turned to look north along the wall. Over there were stationed the two surviving sons of Duke Tomais, Tolemon and Danail. Ralian was there too, having left Barin's side minutes earlier to see how the north end fared.

They waited as clouds hung low over the Gap of Leeth and started spilling fresh snow from their midst. Far away, the clash of steel rose and fell but it was impossible to see what was going on.

Suddenly, Ralian yelled across at them. He'd left Tolemon and Danail and was making back toward where Barin and the others stood looking for movement to the southwest.

"It's riders moving at speed!" Barin and Shallan saw where Ralian was pointing and then spotted a large group of horsemen racing toward the gates from the far side of the Gap. They had scant time to wonder on it because King Haal chose that very moment to attack in full ferocity.

Horns hooted, Leethmen slammed swords against shields, ballistae loaded, cranked and then and swung their loads, sending cart size stones hard against them. Meanwhile, the creaking siege towers rolled and wobbled like sinister wooden effigies toward the city walls.

King Haal swung his double-headed axe in one hand and sword in the other. He made his horse rear on its hind legs, as did the small group of horsemen surrounding him. Then the vast countless number of foot warriors, spearmen, axe men, and archers loped and howled like wolverines toward the gates.

King Haal yelled for his guard to form a wedge and make straight for the gates and barbican, beneath the walls on which Barin, Shallan, and the others waited. Stones flew high overhead, some crashed along the walls, spilling men like ants, as they dented and broke off parts of the crenulations. The siege towers rumbled close, and those manning them hurled hooks and slung ladders across, the defenders hacking and yelling to break ladder and unhinge hook.

Three got close enough for the first warriors to spill from their platforms and leap down upon the battlements near where Tolemon and Danail stood.

"They're breaching!" Ralian yelled across at his men up there. "Hold the wall!"

That shout was all he got time for, as King Haal, surrounded by a forest of spearmen yelled up at them, and to Haal's right the ranks parted to reveal sweating thralls heaving a tree-long ram from their shoulders. The warriors' shields protected them as best they could as the thralls commenced swinging the ram to and fro hard into the gates.

Ralian ordered oil be tossed down, and many thralls screamed in agony as the burning liquid ate their flesh, but more replaced them, and the gates started to buckle with the violent impact.

"I need to be down there!" Barin thundered. Cogga, Taic, and Sveyn had appeared, and they hastily followed Barin down from the walls into the barbican below. Shallan and Zukei made to follow.

"Stay!" Barin told Shallan with a backward glance. "Your arrows will be more use here," he pleaded her listen and then glanced at Zukei. "Look after her!" Barin said, and then vanished from the walls. Shallan watched him go as a wash of raw emotion flooded her nerves. Again she was at Calprissa, Rael's pirates bearing down upon her. Grim-faced, Shallan nocked an arrow to her bow and reached down over the battlements.

She let fly at a spearman, piercing his throat, then another and another, with Zukei loosing shafts alongside. Shallan let the thralls be, suspecting most came from her own country. Meanwhile Ralian paced along the walls, yelling orders and despatching men to where the siege towers were spilling Leethmen onto the walls.

"We are going to die." A small voice turned Shallan's head, and she saw Sorrel standing behind her, Zukei's dagger in her grubby hand.

"No, Sorrel," Shallan told her seriously. "I will protect you, and Zukei will protect us both. We are three ladies against the storm and we will withstand it!"

"I hope so," said Sorrel, not entirely convinced. "I love you, Duchess—you're the best!"

"And I love you too! Be brave little one!" Just then, a grinding, scraping crash announced the gates caving in, followed by whoops and snarls as the Leethmen crashed inside the barbican, Barin and company waiting as reception.

King Haal looked up at the walls laughing. He windmilled his axe in crazy circles and yelled up at the defenders. King Haal's joy was short lived. Shallan's shaft pierced his left eye, killing him instantly and pitching him from his horse.

***

Daan Redhand hewed and hacked, sending men's limbs and heads in every direction. He had no idea who these warriors were, but that didn't matter, for the berserkergang was upon him bidding him kill and kill and kill!

Beside the prince, his finest fighters carved a hole in the Ptarnian defence, for the strangely armoured short-legged warriors were no match for these giant, savage axe men. From his horse, Kolo Muzen saw the carnage and shouted to his officers to send more men to aid the stranded warriors.

At one point, Redhand was surrounded, but his rage and massive strength broke through and again he rained carnage down on the Ptarnians. That fight lasted half the day, with neither side proved the victor. Ptarnian arrows and spears gored countless Leethmen, who in return cut swathes through the Ptarnian army, leaving corpses strewn every which where.

***

Olen smiled as he urged his horse at full gallop toward the city walls. The enemy was in disarray, with two-thirds of Haal's army now engaging with the Ptarnians two miles to the east. The remaining third was spilling toward the city, and Olen could see they had just managed to breach the main gates.

Corin saw that too and spurred Thunder straight for those gates, Clouter whirling circles as he rode.

"Bastards!" Corin yelled, "I'm coming!" Beside them were Greggan of the Wolves and Arami of the Anchai, whilst behind their greater force was led by Halfdan of Point Keep and the other Rorshai leaders.

The gap closed as the Rorshai and Halfdan's Wolves thundered toward the horde, baying like beasts outside the city. Leethmen turned too late to see riders thundering down upon them. A spearman leaped at Corin, but Clouter sent him flying, and beside him an axe man screamed as Olen's scimitar skewered him through an eye. The combined horse attack stove into the rear of the Leeth army like an iron spike shattering a frozen lake. Warriors turned and gaped, only to be sliced and punctured, hewed and gored open, or else trampled under hoof. Panic filled their ranks as Leethmen tried to come to terms with what was happening.

Ahead, Corin saw King Haal's wedge surging through the gates, and he urged Thunder cut across to reach the centre of his foes. Beside him, Greggan nocked arrow to bow and loosed with the Rorshai. "Impressive shooting," Arami yelled in Greggan's ear, "not half bad for a foreigner!"

"We Wolves are multi-taskers!" Greggan grinned back at him and loosed another arrow. They reached the gates just in time to see King Haal fall from his horse, a sight that filled their veins with fire and found them crashing headlong into the dead king's panicked wedge.

***

The gate buckled inwards and exploded, and seconds later Leethmen spilled inside like drunken wasps falling from a nest. Barin leaped toward them, Taic to his left and Cogga and Sveyn at his right.

With them was Danail of Vangaris, who had left his elder brother on the wall in his hunger to avenge Vorreti. And behind them were a tight knot of Ralian's toughest fighters, all more than hungry to face the enemy head-on at last.

Barin roared as he hewed out with Wyrmfang, slicing heads from necks and arms from shoulders. Beside him, his companions fought like bears in cages, but the Leethmen kept coming until their sweaty hides forced down upon the defenders, leaving them no choice but to give ground.

For half an hour Barin held the Barbican. A terrible fight that, with neither side aware of what was occurring outside. At last, he yelled to his men to flee back to the city behind where Ralian had posted a hundred archers, just waiting on Barin's order.

Barin crashed through the inner gate, his men and Ralian's surviving men running behind him.

"They're here!" Barin shouted at the archers and dived sideways, just as the first Leethmen appeared and screamed as the shower of shafts fell upon them.

***

Shallan felt an icy calm as the king of Leeth fell from his horse to lie crow-meat on the blooded ground. Beside her, Zukei whooped praise, and little Sorrel clapped her hands in awe. Shallan didn't notice them. Her eyes were on the approaching riders even now ploughing into the unsuspecting rear of Haal's confused bodyguard.

It was there that she saw him. Her lover, Corin an Fol. And as if he heard her silent call he paused in his slaying to look up and the walls and see her standing there. Shallan heard his voice like a wind in the distance.

"Stay alive—I am coming!"

***

King Haal's bodyguard were caught like bugs in a jar between Ralian's archers and the Rorshai and Wolf riders now attacking from outside the barbican. Corin reached the gates just as the archers had the surviving Leethmen racing back into the barbican, where he and Olen and the others fell upon them until all were slain.

Behind, Lord Halfdan's remaining Wolves and the Rorshai army tore into the chaotic mess that was all that remained of King Haal's vast horde. Three miles south, Daan Redhand stood over the broken mangled body of Kolo Muzen, his mouth frothing and his long sword pitted and stained. Redhand was exhausted, the rage finally having left him.

From a small hillock at the south of the Gap, Redhand was witness to his father's fall, or at least the inevitability of it. He gathered the thousand or so men still living and without a word bid them carry all they could and withdraw hastily from the Gap of Leeth.

Time to go home, thought Daan smiling slightly. His father had lost but Redhand saw things differently. Here was opportunity. Because when he reached Grimhold, Daan Redhand would announce himself the new King of Leeth. Redhand's smile widened; the game wasn't over but had only just begun.

They stamped on and slew the last of the Ptarnian army on their way to the woods and the vastness of Leeth beyond. As for Pashel Akaz's army, not a soul survived, and no word reached Emperor Callanz or his father of the utter failure and destruction of King Akamates' second army.

***

Hagan watched as the dark bolt studded the gloomy sky— Gribble off to report to one of his bosses. "Little shit," Hagan spat, as he gutted a Ptarnian pike man. He'd tried to get to Corin, but there was no chance as the total carnage had erupted throughout the entire Gap.

Hagan had to hand it to his old comrade turned enemy. Corin an Fol knew how to raise a rumpus. It was all Hagan could do to cut his way back to the mountains and lie low again. From that point, he observed the final slaughter of Haal's horde turning on itself, Redhand's warriors attacking his father's in disarray and madness, whilst the rest still battled with what was left of the Ptarnian army.

What a bloody mess!

As Hagan let his gaze take in the entire Gap, he saw the Rorshai riders fall upon the rear of Haal's core warriors, snapping their wedge as axe cleaves log. Hagan stowed his spyglass and mounted his horse, urging the beast back down to the Gap.

He wasn't sure about what he was planning. Risky, and he

might get skewered. But if Hagan pulled it off, he'd do both his ego and Rael Hakkenon a huge favour. More importantly, such a bold deed would wound Corin an Fol more than any blade could. And that, thought Hagan, was worth any risk.

As Hagan approached the city, he dismounted and swiftly stripped a Ptarnian corpse of its grey cloak and hood. Garbed thus he waited for dusk and then led the beast towards the gates. The gate guards were all drunk, and no one minded Hagan as he stole inside the city, a crafty smile on his face.

Clouter clutched between his palms, Corin yelled like a maniac and crashed through the inner door. Ralian, seeing this was no Leethman, yelled to the archers to stop. Corin ignored them as he leaped from Thunder's back and made like a man possessed for the steps leading up to the battlements where Shallan stood yelling too.

Behind Corin, Olen dismounted and bid the others do the same. Greggan hailed Ralian, whom he recognised from some distant tavern meeting in Kelthara.

Shallan dropped her bow as she saw Corin's long shanks taking the steps two at a time. Zukei and the girl called out to her as she sped along the walls and, and gaining the steps, half-ran and half-stumbled until, halfway down the walls she fell into the arms of her lover.

"I told you I'd come," Corin said, as he kissed her long and hard.

"I never doubted you, my love," Shallan wept, whilst above Sorrel pulled a face and Zukei scratched her head.

"Who the fuck is that?" Sorrel had picked up some bad words from Zukei.

"Dunno," Zukei curled her lip. "But he looks like big trouble."

End of Part Two

Part Three

Sword and Spear

Chapter 27

Runes and Ruins

Dark birds circled overhead as he took the narrow broken stairs two at a time. The wind shrilled in his ears and the damp cold gnawed at his knuckles, whilst his feet were blocks of ice.

Zallerak ignored the discomfort. It meant nothing to him who had lived a thousand lifetimes, and those last thousand years as exile and mere shadow of his former self.

Below, the weird bent spike of Ulan Valek's only standing tower pointed toward him like an accusing finger.

This was an evil place. He recalled the last time he'd ventured here, during the height of that age-long war against the Dog People. Zallerak's race had been victorious then. This time? Zallerak tightened his mouth and hastened his step. He wouldn't presume to guess. Wariness and cunning would keep him alive until he found what he sought, and with spell runes destroyed it. The black spear, Golganak. Morak's masterpiece—a spike so evil it drained the souls of those whom it slew.

With the spear intact, Morak was still a threat, and his people the Urgolais were capable of destroying everything Zallerak had worked to achieve. Morak's subtle mind utilised weak mortals to carry out his purposes, just as he had all that time ago.

The apocalyptic war between the Golden Ones and the Urgolais had all but destroyed both peoples. Zallerak knew of a few of his race still living, three in the east and one, Feroda (who harboured a grudge against him) dwelt close to the Fallowheld.

Another such one had moved to Gol and built a castle in the extreme south of that land, but Zallerak assumed that one had perished when that continent sank beneath the waves.

He suspected a few more dwelt south of the equator in uncharted lands. He'd never been down there, though he'd travelled to most other parts of Ansu. Now, as he approached the creeping ruins, Zallerak funnelled his thoughts into tight concentration. He stopped a mile before the city, hearing men's hushed voices somewhere below.

***

Captain Surtez led his men down towards the dead city. They were terrified, and he didn't blame them. But Surtez wasn't scared; he had been chosen from twenty captains for this task, a high honour bestowed upon him by Pashel Akaz himself. Their task was to seek and retrieve the mysterious black spear and return it to Ptarni and their Emperor, Callanz.

King Akamates knew nothing about this mission. Surtez knew he had been chosen partly because he was a "new man," the name given to those who followed Callanz and schemed against the old king, his father. Surtez was ambitious. He knew if he could pull this thing off his fortune would be made, and his high position in court secure for life.

Surtez was young and brave, as were his men. But they were just soldiers and therefore expendable. He was of high family, so his reputation and honour were at stake, and Surtez's heart was steel, for he believed he was nearing the edge of greatness. Besides, there was no going back now.

With that last thought in mind, Surtez snapped at his men, ordering them to command their nerves and make ready to enter the dead city. They had no idea where to look, but Surtez was as methodical as he was thorough. Nor did he fear ghosts, knowing that the Emperor secretly worshiped the ruler of this place. Morak's people would let the Ptarnians be—so Callanz had assured his captain.

They reached a broken door opening on a shadowy passage; the wind shrilled through it like empty laughter. Weapons in hand, one hundred Ptarnians filed into the city. Not a single one came out.

***

A lone figure watched the Ptarnian soldiers enter the ruins. He had no idea who they were, but assumed them to be enemies his three hundred Groil could easily deal with should need arrive. In and out, quick and clean: that was Rael's objective. Find the spear, deliver it to Caswallon, and take the gold, and then ready himself for ruling Kelwyn. At last, a kingdom fit for one such as he.

Risky and dangerous? So what? Rael excelled at this kind of work, and Caswallon had given him precise instructions on where he suspected the spear to lie. At the very bottom of the lowest hall, somewhere beneath those crumbled ruins down there.

He crouched and made to stand when a soft sound stopped him. Rael slid behind the rock again close by the path, and from there witnessed Zallerak hastening down the steps. Rael recognised the crazy warlock who had caused such havoc in his castle and again in Port Sarfe. The warlock called Zallerak. Caswallon's enemy, and his too.

This changed things. Rael must needs be careful. He watched as Zallerak faded into the shadows below, and then he returned to where the Groil waited, snarling and grunting, a hundred yards from the path.

With them were seven chosen men fresh from Crenna, including Cruel Cavan, his finest fighter and most trusted captain. Rael had insisted on having these Crenise with him, and Caswallon had agreed that they couldn't rely solely on Groil.

Rael flicked a finger at Cavan, and his huge grizzled captain joined him a few yards away from the others.

"We've got company. I need you to send a bird to Caswallon."

Rael reached inside his cloak and pulled out quill and paper, both branded with his special 'R'. On this he imparted his message for the sorcerer and then passed the paper to his second.

Cavan nodded, and without word returned to where the horses stood tethered. With them was a mule, two cages of birds strapped to its flanks. Caswallon had insisted Rael keep him well informed, something for which Rael was now grateful.

Cavan plugged the paper into the seal given them, spoke the three rune words as he tied the plugged message to the pigeon's foot, and then loosed the bird up into the sky.

Caswallon's runes awarded that pigeon uncanny speed, allowing it to shoot up arrow straight, clearing the predatory questing claws of the numerous circling vultures and buzzards patrolling the thermals high above. Once clear, the spell-aided pigeon arced west and shot like lighting toward Kella City, reaching the palace inside an hour.

***

"I NO LONGER SERVE YOU, MORTAL." The voice tore inside his head like a rusted razor, and he screamed, spilling wine and sliding from the throne to lie slumped and shivering on the mosaic floor. Gribble blinked at him.

"Something amiss?" the Soilfin asked whilst picking tooth with claw. Caswallon didn't reply. It was all he could do to keep his breath even and stop himself from screaming again. This had not been a good day.

Three separate newsflashes had blasted him like virtual thunderbolts: first, Gribble's eager report of events at Car Carranis; then, the news that Bitch Queen Ariane had tricked Gonfalez and arrived alive and well in Kelthara; and then the recent message from Rael Hakkenon informing him that Zallerak the Aralais warlock was at large in Ulan Valek.

And added to all that, when he summoned Vaarg, the dragon refused him. Even now, Caswallon's head and ears rang with the metallic din of Vaarg's mocking laughter. It seemed to Caswallon now that all those around him had played him for a fool. Paranoia and fear entered his veins for the first time in years. How had it come to this when he'd been so close to ultimate victory?

To his right, Gribble snickered from his lair under the table, his pet Soilfin mocking him too. But Caswallon still had his lore and self-conviction. Slowly, inexorably, he willed self-control and positive force back inside his head. He was still stronger than anyone else. Must hold positive. What had happened had happened. Now to fix it and move on.

"Come here!" Caswallon clawed his aching limbs back onto The Glass Throne. From there he stared imperiously at the Soilfin. "I've a job for you, shitling."

"Not interested." Gribble spat something grotesque and chunky on the floor; it slimed forward six inches and then lay still. "I don't work for you any more either."

"What did you say?" Caswallon rose to his feet and hurled the goblet at Gribble, who shunted sideways and blinked at him.

"No need to get nasty!" Gribble hopped back under the table and stuck his tongue out at Caswallon. "Situations change—is all. I got offered a better contract, less flights and more flesh. Nothing personal, Mr Caswallon. Just business."

"By whom?" Caswallon's eyes narrowed to furious slits of coal.

"Ain't it obvious?"

"Your old boss?" Caswallon considered blasting the goblin to cinders with a mind bolt but he currently lacked the strength. "Tell me I'm right."

"I'm back with the old crew, yes," Gribble hissed at him. "Vaarg too. That dragon had no intention of working for you. He was just waiting for old Burnt Face to return. And now the Dog-Lord is back, and rumour is he's more horrible than ever."

"And you've been keeping this from me all this time? I thought us friends who trusted each other!"

"I'm a Soilfin, not a puppy. What did you expect? If you want a friend get a frigging cat." With those last words Gribble hopped out from under the table and skipped across the floor.

"I'll take my leave now, Mr Caswallon. It's been epic." Before Caswallon could respond, the Soilfin had fled noisy and urgent through his custom-designed goblin-flap, and then on through the double doors leading to atrium outside, with Caswallon too exhausted to even contemplate stopping him.

"Good bloody riddance!" Caswallon shouted at the gaping hole whence the goblin had vanished. In his eagerness to leave the throne room, Gribble had taken half the flap with him, and bits of timber and screws clung to his wings.

Once free of the palace, Gribble shook those wings free of dust and clutter and then without further ado, launched his scrawny body skyward. No time to lark about; there was Big Shit happening in the mountains.

Caswallon felt the last ounce of energy flee his weary bones. He would shout a retainer to go get more brandy, but the Groil had eaten them all. And at present the Groil were either near Kelthara under Flail Six Hands, or with Hakkenon in the mountains.

Kella City was almost deserted; a skeleton crew of three hundred Tigers slouched on the walls, and all the citizens who dared had fled to Kelthara to join the rebellion. All that remained in the royal city were hungry hounds and broken scattered bones.

After sprawling on his glass throne in abject misery for several minutes, Caswallon gathered his aching limbs and ventured to the kitchens. Once there, he made a plate of beef and horseradish and retrieved a large flask of expensive brandy. Small comfort, but it would help soothe his rattled nerves.

Back on the throne again, Caswallon placed the gold crown he'd recently had fashioned by the city's only living goldsmith on his head and closed his eyes. A whim, the crown. It helped convince him he was legit, and at times like this Caswallon needed a little clarification along those lines. Time to recharge. He was both physically and mentally drained, like a gourd with all its juices sucked out. It had been a very unpleasant day, and Gribble's desertion had hurt him unexpectedly hard. Caswallon was not overly blessed with virtues, but he had been fond of the Soilfin.

Still, all was not lost. The Assassin wouldn't let him down. Once Caswallon had the spear he could deal with the likes of Morak and Vaarg, whatever they were up to. And Gribble too, should the shitling show his goblin face again.

Beef eaten and brandy flask slurped half dry, Caswallon felt strong enough to take the long cold climb up to the Astrologer's Nest—the highest tower in Kella's Palace. Once there he drained the rest of the brandy and uncorked a bottle of port he'd kept in a closet to warm his blood. Then, when he was ready, Caswallon took to gazing into the crystal globe for the first time in months.

***

Zallerak entered the gloomy passage leading to the mines beneath Ulan Valek. In the distance he could hear the heavy footfalls of the Ptarnian soldiers. Zallerak had little doubt why they were here. Ptarni's cities lay hard under the shadow of the Urgo Mountains, and long had its people had paid homage and worship to Morak's kin— driven to it by fear and rumours.

Obviously, some bold prince of that land had got it in his head to seek the spear himself, and therefore sent a unit of crack commandos go get it. Fools! No mortal could survive the secrets of this fortress. Even for Zallerak it was touch and go—and he at least knew the traps and hidden spell nets. And then there was the guardian at the lower door.

Zallerak held enough pace to move swiftly yet keep his distance from the Ptarnians. He stopped once, hearing voices behind him, but soon dismissed them as echoes reverberating through this ghastly place.

It was icy cold down here, and the walls were sleek with slime and frozen weed. Zallerak carried his spell-spear in both hands, the tip glowing with just enough light to allow him to place one foot safely in front of another.

Stairs and passages led off from the main shaft in complex junctions. Zallerak's memory served him well, taking him far beyond and below where the Ptarnians struggled to find their way in the subterranean maze.

But behind Zallerak, the Groil knew the way too, for they had been spawned in this place. Slowly they gained ground on the unsuspecting Aralais, as Rael and his men strode silent behind. Rael suspected traps, too, and was happy for the Groil to fall prey to them first.

Zallerak entered a passage leading to a steep, sheer stairwell, which in turn descended in tight spirals. Dizzyingly down it wound. Zallerak's hands stung from the icy touch of the rusty rail, the only way he could steady himself and not fall into the abyss below.

For almost an hour he descended, finally reaching the wide, plateau-like hall that exited at eight gates. Zallerak took the seventh without hesitation. He stopped, recognising the silent guardian standing voiceless and tall. A giant Groil, its hide was encased in obsidian armour, and its features were hidden by a iron helm spiked at the crown. This guardian called "The Silent One" was the first Groil spawned from the Urgolais. It had been posted here since the days of the endless war and had never slept.

Zallerak muttered the words he'd used millennia before, and The Silent One saw him not and thus allowed him pass. Next, he entered a wide passage leading to a great iron gate dripping with black tendrils of ice. Again, Zallerak murmured a spell-rune, and the gate rattled and creaked ajar.

Quickly he stole within, his spear tip allowing just enough light to find the trapdoor at the far end that led down to the final passage, beyond which Zallerak suspected the spear lay.

He took a deep breath and forced his nerves to remain calm as he lifted the trapdoor and dropped silent within. It was there that he felt it first: the fear and the menace. An alien terror emanating from Golganak's essence. So it *was* here! Zallerak steeled his nerves as best he could and followed the rancid stench of fear until he reached the wall where the ancient weapon rested.

There he stopped, seeing a figure standing beside the spear.

"I got here first," smiled Morak, as his servant, the dragon Vaarg, fell upon the wizard like rocks from a cliff.

Chapter 28

Kelthara

The messenger caught up with Ariane's army just before they entered Kelthara. He gave his name as Greggan, a sergeant in Lord Halfdan's Wolves, and the news he brought had Ariane shouting for joy. As they approached Kelthara's walls, the queen turned in her saddle and yelled back at her riders.

"Happy tidings from the north—the King of Leeth is dead! Car Carranis is saved!" The queen's news spread through her army like bush fire, fueling every soldier with renewed zeal. What marvellous timing, thought Ariane.

Just the tonic my army needs.

"What of Corin an Fol?" she asked the messenger in a quieter voice. Greggan had told her Halfdan had ordered him leave the moment they turned the day against Leeth. Greggan had ridden at speed for three days, his intention to reach Wynais, and by sheerest chance he had seen Ariane's army approaching from the distance. After his spyglass revealed the queen's features, Greggan had counted his blessings and spurred his horse on for the last couple of miles.

"Last I saw he was on the walls of Car Carranis, a very pretty lassie in his arms." Greggan thanked Cale, who was offering him water on pretense of not eavesdropping.

"Oh, I see." Ariane changed the subject. She wasn't in the mood to hear about Shallan, though she was glad her cousin still lived. "What happened up there—Greggan, is it?"

"Greggan it is, Your Highness." he took a slurp and tossed the water skin back at Cale, who caught it deftly and continued listening in. "'Tis rather complicated," Greggan explained, grinning at Cale.

"It always is when Corin an Fol is involved."

"We call him 'Lord Corin' now," Greggan said, and Ariane rolled her eyes, whilst Cale looked impressed.

"Elanion help us," the queen muttered under her breath.

Ahead, the city gates drew close, and a shout announced they were welcome within, the Keltharans having got word via scouts of Queen Ariane's approach.

"Explain swiftly and best you can, Sir Greggan; I need to be prepped so I can spread cheer among those poor souls in yonder city."

"I'm only a sergeant, Your Highness," Greggan said, but went on to tell her all about the carnage at the Gap: the Ptarnian army, the Rorshai charge at their ranks that morning, and the ensuing devastating result.

"That was valiantly done," Ariane said.

"Lord Corin again, and his Rorshai mates. Tough bastards those Rorshai, good drinkers too." Greggan told of how the enraged Ptarnians had attacked King Haal's rear, resulting in both huge armies almost wiping each over out through the course of that long bloody day. "Redhand escaped with a handful, but I doubt we'll hear from him for a while."

"What a victory! Elanion be blessed!" Ariane raised her eyes to the slate sky overhead and mouthed a silent "thank you" to her goddess. "And thank you too, Sir Greggan," she smiled at the grizzly-faced messenger with the missing teeth.

"Go see Captain Tarello back there and he'll ensure you're well rewarded with ale and food this evening. I don't know what state Kelthara is in but we have our own supplies. You've made my day, Sir Greggan—may the goddess bless you too!" With a hideous smile, Greggan thanked her and guided his horse back to where Captain Tarello rode close behind.

The gates swung back, allowing her riders to enter the city. Ariane saw lean, hard faces staring at her with quizzical eyes. Kelthara in winter: a dusting of snow on the ground and small fires offering little heat to the huddled citizens gathered in clusters at street corners.

Dogs prowled and snarled up at them as Ariane's army filed inside the city. Three miles south, the first of Gonfalez's Tigers ranged into view, whilst north in the woods, the rest of the Groil under Flail Six-Arms approached with snarling fangs and clashing steel.

A thin man with shrewd eyes greeted Ariane as she dismounted inside the gates, handing the reins to Cale, who had entered the city beside her. The rangy individual introduced himself as Pol Darn, self-appointed leader of the Keltharan rebellion against Caswallon.

"We slew the Groil inside the city," Pol Darn told her with defiant eyes. "But others lurk in the woods north of here, and I fear Caswallon has sent many more."

"You have done well," Ariane smiled at the Keltharan leader. "To hold out so long against that tyrant. Your city must have endured a great deal of hardship and loss."

Pol Darn nodded. "We've paid a heavy price, Your Highness. Most of the nobles are dead, the Groil killed many, and commoners too. People in this city have lost everything—especially hope, living from hour to hour. We've little food left and lack the strength to hold out much longer."

"You have been brave and strong, but we are here now, and Kelthara will hold as long as it has to." Ariane's smile left no room for argument. Pol Darn merely shrugged at her words.

"We have brought supplies and fuel, enough to offer some cheer amongst your people." Ariane had ordered each of her soldiers carry as many supplies as their horses could bear without losing speed over distance. "We have only to hold out for a few days before help arrives."

"What help?" Pol Darn shook his head, too tired to believe her words.

"Beyond hope, Car Carranis has held against the attacks of Leeth. Against all bets, the barbarians have given up, allowing General Starkhold to send aid our way. I'll fill you in with the details later."

"'Tis good to hear," Pol Darn looked nonplussed, "but it will take more than a garrison from Car Carranis to overthrow Caswallon."

"Maybe so, but I've not lost a battle yet, Pol Darn. I do not intend this to be my first." Ariane softened her tone, seeing how exhausted this man looked. Goddess alone knew what horrors they'd endured in this city since Caswallon's rise to power. "Please be kind enough to show me your defenses," she added with a smile.

Pol Darn obliged, and during the next two hours Ariane and her captains, Tarello, Jaan, and Valentin, studied the city walls and gates for weak points and potential breaches. Meanwhile, Gonfalez's army had arrived, filling the fields south of the city. Light was fading fast, and Ariane prayed to Elanion that the enemy would hold off from attacking until morning.

As evening fell, Ariane thanked the goddess again, as she witnessed the enemy pitch tents and settle into night-time tasks. Today had proved a good one, but she was tired and ready for a quiet rest before sleep.

The queen had taken rudimentary quarters in the old courthouse at the centre of the city. A creepy place, and Kelthara itself did little to inspire her. Cold and bleak, the walls were granite grey and stern. Much like its sister city, Kella, this town was built in concentric lines, practical and durable, but showing none of the grace and elegance found in her own Silver City.

The only one in her party joyful to be here was Cale, who had grown up in the slums on the east side of the city. He at least was in his element this evening.

Ariane had dismissed her exhausted captains and was sipping tea in the cold room she'd chosen as her own, when a hard rap at the door turned her anxious face that way.

"Who?"

"Silon." Ariane rolled her eyes; she wasn't in the mood for company right now.

"Enter." The door opened and Silon unbidden took a seat on a chair across from her own.

"Pardon the intrusion. I know you need rest and time for solace." Ariane noted how Silon looked tired too.

"Oh, that's all right." Ariane smiled and offered him some tea made by her own hands. "A fresh pot just made." Silon thanked the queen and poured himself a piping cup from the pot.

"This is good," he said. "I prefer wine usually, but this warms the blood so, and has a delicate flowery taste. Hmm, I shall have to order some for Vioyamis." Ariane allowed him to settle and fuss; merchants had certain ways of dealing with things. Silon was no exception. After another sip he smiled her way again.

"I had a notion."

"Do tell."

"The Tekara..." he began.

"A large crown of crystal that has nearly got us all killed several times over recent months?" Ariane smiled back at him.

"The same. And I believe still in your possession? Or else Prince Tarin's? No matter. The thing is, it cannot stay here, Ariane. If this city falls..." Silon placed his cup on a table and stood to gaze at the resuming snowfall, now brushing the glass of her window. Silon shivered; he didn't much care for Kelthara either.

"We cannot risk Caswallon recapturing the crown after all we've been through to salvage it."

"You are right." Ariane drained her tea and folded her arms in resignation. "And I have given thought to this. We need to get the Tekara to Corin and Corin to Kella and The Glass Throne. Simple as that." She smiled at her irony.

"Indeed," Silon looked askance for a moment then grinned at her. *So you know too, Ariane sharpest of queens.*

Silon sighed and took to the chair again. "But you are right. It sounds like Corin is aware of his responsibilities now. He is Halfdan's son, by the way."

"Yes, I worked that out when we got word from him in the mountains. His 'hint' slotted into place in my little queenie head after Greggan arrived in camp. But I suspect you've known for a while, master merchant. And we both have had other things on our minds. But it all makes sense at last."

Silon chose to ignore that barb. "Being the legal heir, it is Corin's prerogative to take charge of the Tekara. With that in mind, I suggest sending a small unit north under the cover of night to seek him out at Car Carranis. Valentin's boys are the best for that kind of work. I suggest a dozen—no more, including the messenger, Greggan. We need all the fighting men we have to hold this shithole of a city."

"Bleyne, at least, should go with them," Ariane nodded. Bleyne had spent weeks working alongside Arac and the other archers under Valentin. Through his counsel their skills were much improved.

"And Tarin."

"Tarin?"

"Aye, the prince has been tied to that crown. I think it's part of his destiny to see it find the hands of the rightful owner. And he needs to bond with Corin; they got off to a patchy start, I believe."

"And yet Corin could have taken the crown back in Permio."

"That was then; he wasn't ready and didn't trust who he is. Judging by his letter and his meeting with Halfdan, he does now. Plus, back then Zallerak took over the crown, and goodness knows where *he* is now." Ariane shook her head and was about to respond when a sharp knock announced someone else at the door.

"What is it?" Ariane snapped.

Cale showed his ginger face. "There's a huge nasty warrior bloke in a spotted kilt wants to see you. Says he's a king from down south."

"What are you gibbering about, Cale?" Ariane could happily throttle the boy at that moment. She desired sleep and was on the verge of wrapping things up with Silon.

"Send him up," Silon added before Arianc or Cale could continue. The queen shot Silon a hard glance.

"You know this individual?"

"I believe so." They waited a few moments until Cale returned with a huge figure bulking behind him. The boy looked awestruck, and Silon grinned as King Ulani of the Baha strode into the room.

"Queen Ariane, please allow me to introduce a very good friend and stalwart ally to our cause. This is King Ulani of the Baha, ruler of distant Yamondo. As you have heard, Ulani was with Corin and your cousin down in Permio."

"Indeed, I have heard of you, sir," Ariane nodded, her dark gaze studying the huge girth and build of the black warrior king, who was almost as tall as Barin but thicker in waist and shoulders. Ulani beamed down at her.

"Honoured, little queen," he boomed. "I've heard so much about you, Ariane of the Swords." Behind him, Cale gaped like a hooked carp on a wet pole until Ariane growled at him to bugger off to bed.

"Tea?" Ariane suggested, in a more inviting tone. "There's enough for one more in the pot."

"Lovely—thank you." She poured and handed the king the spare mug, and Ulani tentatively closed his massive fingers around the porcelain, a sight which made Ariane giggle despite herself.

"You are very welcome here, King. But I doubt this is just a social call—am I correct?"

"Indeed you are, Queen." Ulani sipped his tea and made himself as comfortable as he could in so small a chair. Ariane and Silon waited patiently for him to settle. It took a moment.

"How is Corin?" the king asked, placing mug on table with infinite care.

"Alive and hale, or so we've just heard," Silon said.

"Good. He needs to stay that way, because I've things to discuss with him too." Silon shared a look with Ariane who nodded. "I'm sending some commandoes out before dawn. Bleyne, whom you know, will be among them. Their objective is to reach Corin and inform him of our plight."

"Count me in," said Ulani. "Now for my news. I'm afraid it cannot wait any longer."

***

Bleyne rose an hour before dawn and climbed to watch the enemy camp from the battlements. Gonfalez's army was a scatter of fires blurred by falling snow. Kelthara was shrouded in the silent mantle of deep white under a lowering night sky.

Bleyne nodded, satisfied, and returned to the stables to join the others. Valentin had chosen his men well, and Arac the archer was their leader. He had a healthy respect for Bleyne, having worked alongside him this last weeks.

Accompanying the seven rangers and Bleyne were Prince Tarin, wild-eyed and flustered. The Tekara, shrunk by a rune spell Zallerak had taught him, was lashed in a bag to his belt.

Behind him rode King Ulani, silent and calm despite many a sideways glance awarded in his direction. Beside the king rode Greggan of the Wolves, who had recently taken to announcing himself as Sir Greggan of Point Keep, much to the amusement of his rivals, the Bear Rangers.

They mounted and left the gates under the silent shroud of snow. Above, a frail moon failed to pierce the lowering gloom, and wet snowflakes the size of dandelion heads floated past their faces. They rode out in silence, the gate guards fastening the gates shut behind them.

The riders, whilst avoiding the road, steered well away from the mountains, for in the woods surrounding them were sure to be Groil. They rode in single file. They were wary, each archer with arrow on nock, until they were well north of the wooded hills above Kelthara.

As day rose white and chill, the thirteen riders steered closer to The High Wall's shoulders, at last daring the road that led almost due north to the Gap of Leeth and Car Carranis. They arrived at that city two days later and discovered that Corin an Fol and Shallan of Morwella were gone, and no one knew where.

***

General Gonfalez scrunched the parchment and tossed it on the snow. Was Caswallon losing it? The letter he'd received last night had sounded desperate and hardly the tone so often used by the wily conniver. Something had happened, and Gonfalez had the unpleasant feeling he was two steps behind the wizard's dance again. The note sent via rune-bird was short and succinct:

Gonfalez

You will take Kelthara; kill all within including Queen Ariane, who has used up all her chances for my forgiveness. When they are all dead set urgent torch to the city and return most promptly with your army to Kella. Fail me again and your head shall adorn my city gates!

C

Gonfalez rubbed his hands to fuel them against the cold. He had been unlucky. Perhaps killing Perani had been a mistake, and he'd have fared better with his old leader taking the flak. But that was past tense, and all these misgivings and frets illogical, not suited for a soldier and commander of men.

Something was going on up in Kella, Gonfalez could tell. But that wasn't his concern—not yet anyway. His only mandate was breaking Kelthara once and for all. And that he would do. Ariane had been mad coming here. At least in Wynais she could have held them off for weeks. But Kelthara was a rotten egg ready for breaking.

With that last thought in mind Gonfalez grinned as he doused his face in the icy water barrel. He would break this city and finish this business, then Caswallon and his scheming could rot in Yffarn, for all he cared.

Two hours after dawn, Gonfalez led the first attack against the Keltharan defenders. He was in no great hurry and used sorties and false charges to probe out any weak points in the walls. By noon the Groil arrived, snarling and loping out of the northern woods. They hemmed the city throughout that day, exchanging arrow fire and retiring at dusk. The enemy were stretched thin along the walls. Too thin. Gonfalez was satisfied the city would fall within a couple of days. He had only to wait.

Chapter 29

The Missing

Shouting, cheering, men joking with each other and women weeping for sheer joy. Car Carranis was in a state of shock tonight. Corin, oblivious to the joyful frenzy sweeping through the exhausted occupants of the city, clung on to Shallan as though she were a life raft. They stood on the parapet, snow dancing and whirling around their frozen faces.

"I love you," he said several times before wiping his nose on his sleeve and adding, "I'm minging, I think I need a bath and I don't normally take those."

"I'm filthy too." Shallan kissed him long and hard. "Lets go find somewhere where we can mingle filthy together."

"Proper filthy," Corin grinned at her then cursed as a hand shoved him hard from behind. On instinct, he turned panther-quick and pole-axed the unsuspecting assailant onto his back with a hammer thrust from his open palm. The man groaned and then staggered to his feet cursing.

"It's all right, Tolemon, this is a friend of mine."

"Who are you?" Corin blinked at the angry-faced soldier.

"He's my brother," Shallan said, gripping Corin's hand. Tolemon glared at the pair of them and turned to walk briskly from the walls. "Doesn't have much of a sense of humour," she added.

"Sorry mate," Corin called out cheerfully to Tolemon's retreating back. "Shame about that, hope it hasn't hurt future family relations."

"Future family?" Shallan smiled up at him. "Is that what you just said?"

Corin was about to reply when a huge fist swatted him from behind and flat-packed him face-first on the floor.

"You wanker!" A big voice boomed over him. "But it's good to see you living boy!"

"Barin, you great shaggy lump," Corin laughed as he jumped to his feet and hugged the giant. "Good to see you too! Now give me some peace so I can snog this lady, we've a lot of catching up to do."

But Corin and Shallan got scant time together as the reality of what had happened finally sank in and there was so much to discuss. So instead, Corin settled for getting drunk with Shallan gripped tightly in his arms, whilst conferring with Barin, Ralian (whom he liked on first impression), and her other brother Danail (whom Corin liked too). He was pleased to see Cogga again and was happily introduced to the grinning Taic and Sveyn, who looked liked grand lads in Corin's opinion. Then he saw Zukei scowling at him from a corner. The dark woman had kept a low profile after seeing Shallan with her lover. She appeared more venomous than usual.

"Who is that evil-looking she-lynx?" Corin shrugged in Zukei's direction. Zukei saw him looking at her and her scowl deepened.

"She is my best friend," Shallan kissed him again. "Her name is Zukei and she's saved my life more than once."

"Then I owe her everything." Corin fussed Shallan from his arms and stood. He smiled, approaching Zukei who looked ready to bite him.

"I'm Corin an Fol."

"I know who you are."

"Super. That's lovely. Well...I just wanted to say thanks for saving my lady's life. I hear you're a bit lethal with that skinny blade you carry."

"I'm lethal with a number of things," Zukei flicked the corner of her lip in what might be a smile. "I believe you know my father," she added with a tease.

"I do?"

"His name is Ulani and he is a king."

"Fuck yeah—I know Ulani! He's a good friend of mine and was with us down in the desert. Damn good fella and one heck of a warrior, and the only man I know that could give Barin a run for his money."

"What's that?" Barin had overheard.

"I miss him," Corin grinned at Zukei who didn't grin back.

"I don't," she replied and showed him her back.

"Strange girl. Don't think she likes me." Corin looked puzzled when he re-joined Shallan at the table, where she and Barin and some others were sitting amid their cups.

"She is fierce but her heart is solid gold," Shallan said.

"That I do believe if she is Ulani's daughter."

"Who is Ulani?" Barin asked, but then the conversation turned to more immediate matters. Ralian had sent men out before dark to slit the throats of any enemies still living. These had recently returned, informing him nothing moved out there except night crows.

"It's a mess," said Halfdan who joined them at table and poured himself an ale. With him were Olen and Arami and several other Rorshai. Corin introduced them and after a few wary looks they took seats on benches close by.

"I sent Greggan south as soon as I was sure of our victory," Lord Halfdan explained. "He'll report to Ariane in Wynais. I'd sooner not trust to birds with that sorcerer snooping over in Kella. I'd sooner Caswallon not hear about our victory until he has to."

"Good thinking," said Ralian who was overjoyed at seeing Lord Halfdan alive. "We all believed you dead, my lord."

"Me too sometimes," Halfdan laughed. "What happened to Lord Starkhold?" He saw the painful twist on Ralian's lips and waved a dismissive hand. "No matter, I can wait for such news. Now, while we are gathered here and some of us not too drunk," he glanced sideways at Corin, "I propose we plan our next move."

"We've only just bloody well got here," Corin slurped.

"Yes, and we need to strike fast while we have the advantage of surprise." Halfdan's grey-blue eyes studied Corin shrewdly. He knew the boy was acting drunker than he was—an old Wolf trick to lure an enemy off guard.

"Strike where, exactly?" Barin's eyes narrowed.

"Kelthara."

"Why not Kella City?" Ralian asked.

"Caswallon is rooted there, and his power too strong. We need to draw him away, and Kelthara has ever been a stone in his shoe. Last I heard that city still defies him despite numerous incursions and punishments."

"Kelthara it is then," Corin said, smiling at Shallan who was looking worried again. "When?"

"Tomorrow." Halfdan's face was resolute.

"Fuck off," Corin glared at his father. "We've just won a major victory today and everybody is knackered. And Car Carranis needs attention before we abandon its citizens. Who knows, Redhand might be back in a week or two."

"Lord Halfdan is right, Corin," Olen spoke for the first time. Shallan stared at him, fascinated by his deep blue eyes, chevron scars, and sleek black mane—a fighter lean and tough he looked to be. Intelligent, too. Olen caught her gaze and inclined his head slightly. "We cannot dally, now we've come this far. Ptarni is broken and Leeth too, but our main enemy is still out there."

"Caswallon is not your concern, Olen." Corin placed a hand on his friend's shoulder. "The Rorshai have done more than enough to help us without getting tangled up with the usurper in Kella City."

"Actually, we don't have a choice." Olen's calm eyes smiled irony at Shallan. "The game has shifted, and I do not believe Caswallon is our biggest worry."

"What do you mean, Sir Rorshai?" Halfdan had come to respect the Rorshai, who were sharp thinkers as well as cunning warriors. He wished he'd met them years ago.

"Call it intuition—the worry worm inside my guts. Corin, do you remember those Ptarnians we killed, by the forest before you..."

Corin's face darkened. "I'm trying to forget that. Thanks for reminding me."

"They were making for Ulan Valek, I am certain of it."

"Ulan Valek?" Shallan was confused.

Olen looked grim. "It's a ruined city in the midst of The High Wall. We of the Rorshai have heard many stories, none of which are good."

"I know of it also," Shallan nodded. Her eyes met Corin's and were suddenly sad, with the stress of the last few days catching up with her and adding to the worry of more fighting yet to come. "An Urgolais stronghold from days long past. But what of it now?"

"I have heard that Ptarnians were rumoured to worship the twisted folk," Halfdan nodded slowly as he pieced the jigsaw together in his head. "I know little of those easterners and have been puzzled greatly by their sudden appearance. Why journey so far across the steppes? Why not just send a few scouts to probe? But an entire army?"

"Unless they were promised something." Barin chewed at his moustache as he too worked through the subject.

"The Dog-Lords," Olen said, and watched the smiles fade from every face in the hall. "I've seen that city in the clouds. It lies hard beneath the Urgo Mountains. Makes sense the Ptarnians would be sucked in by Urgolais witchcraft. They've most likes lived in fear of them for years."

"Morak is dead," said Corin making a chopping swipe with his hand. "Splattered like strawberry jam outside Croagon's forge. And Zallerak grilled three other Doggy-lords with his rune-spells.

I don't like Zallerak much but he does have his moments. What's the matter?" All eyes were on Corin and seeing that made him feel uncomfortable.

Olen coughed. "Ptarni is but one piece of the puzzle, but there are other reasons for us continuing this business. I'm looking at you, Corin an Fol. I do not forget what the Seeress of Silent Mountain told me. You are the chosen one."

Halfdan nodded agreement. "The Glass Throne is empty and the Crown re-forged. Caswallon has never been so vulnerable. And should the Urgolais return—and I too believe that possible, despite your news about Morak. Something evil is brewing out there. We can all feel it. So to halt this coming storm we need to act fast. Kelthaine needs a king seated on that throne. Your call." Halfdan grinned at Corin, who stood up, knocking Shallan off his lap and swiftly apologising to her.

"I need a piss," he said. "And some time alone."

Corin staggered outside to ease his bladder. He was angry, confused, and again felt as though he were being played. Except this time it was his father and Olen pulling the strings. Corin just wanted to be with Shallan, and he knew she wanted the same. But again the fates were playing with his balls.

I don't want to be a fucking king.

Harsh with mood he decided to let them wait, instead taking the stairs up to battlements; from there he gazed out across the walls. Rime glittered the ground and whitened the hair and faces of the multitude corpses freezing out there on the Gap. Corin shivered and turned away. A flutter of wings to his left announced the raven's presence. The bird stared at him with cold accusation and then lifted and slid low toward the corpse ground outside.

Corin watched it settle amongst the ruins of a half-burnt broken siege tower. Then he saw him—the Huntsman, spear in hand and single eye burning back at him. High above the spirit's head, the moon rolled clear of cloud, and silver light glinted off the Huntsman's spear.

"It is almost time!"

The hemp-rough voice reached Corin like an urgent breeze. The Huntsman raised his spear toward him and then turned away, vanishing into the shadow of the broken siege tower. But as Oroonin faded from view, the ghostly sound of horns filled the night sky, and Corin, aghast, witnessed the corpses on the rimy soil crack open, their lost souls floating up like will-'o-the-the wisps to join the hurrying host high above.

The horns blew louder, and the Huntsman's red-eyed hounds bayed ominously as thunder filled the sky. A lone dagger of lightning struck the centre of the Gap like a premonition. Giddy and torn, Corin stumbled back down to the main hall where his friends were gathered. When he got there Shallan was gone.

"I thought she was with you?" Barin grinned at him. "That was a long piss. She left to check on you, and we lads assumed you pair needed a moment. Zukei wanted to go with her but I stopped her."

Corin went back outside and both Barin and Zukei followed. They searched and called her name but received no answer. It was late now, and aside those still drinking in the main hall, most folk were sleeping after their huge exhausting day.

After ten long minutes searching, Corin's mood was black. He blamed himself and worried that Shallan was upset with him and had returned to her lodgings. And he had no idea where those were. Nearby Barin looked glum, whilst Zukei looked increasingly worried.

"Do you think she returned to her room?" Barin asked the woman. He was cross with himself for stopping Zukei earlier, and she annoyed that she had listened to him.

"She wouldn't do that," Zukei snapped. "Duchess has been mooning about yonder stupid longshanks since first I met her. Nope, something's happened."

A shout from the battlements: Taic and Sveyn had joined the search for Shallan. Danail was with them up on the battlements and it was he who had spotted a lone horseman galloping furiously into the night

Corin, Barin, and Zukei joined them up there, and Zukei's sharp eyes discerned a bundle slung sideways across the horseman's saddle. "That's a body," Zukei said. "Our Duchess has been kidnapped!"

Zukei was quick to move but Corin was quicker. He took the stairs three at a time, reached the stables, and untied Thunder, who stared at him bemused.

"Time to leave," Corin barked at the horse and slung his saddle on Thunder's back, and inside minutes was yelling the tipsy gate guards to let him out. They obliged without a word and slouched back at their dice. Then Barin loomed over them and they sobered quickly.

"Two riders just left—why didn't you stop them?"

"We only saw one," grumbled the nearest guard.

"Well open the bloody gates again, idiot!" Barin was joined by Taic and Sveyn and Cogga, the latter shoving Wyrmfang in his fist. "Just in case," Cogga said. Moments later Barin, Zukei, Taic and Sveyn, and Olen and Arami of the Rorshai left the sleeping city on fresh steeds, bidding them race behind the disappearing shadow that was Corin an Fol. Minutes later, Danail found his horse and caught them up.

Olen and Arami soon sped ahead of Barin and the others. These two caught up with Corin at the southern end of the Gap. He stared at them wild-eyed, Clouter gripped in his hands.

"Gone," Corin said, and Olen slipped from his horse and joined him.

"Knows the terrain," Olen said looking up at the slopes of Tolfallon showing gloomy ahead where hoof marks disappeared into the woods. "We dare not follow till morning, lest we risk a fall."

Corin ignored him and slipped from Thunderhoof's back. "Look after him." He thrust Thunder's reins into Olen's hand.

"Corin!"

"You'll not stop me!"

"Whoever this is, they are clever!" Olen yelled at him as Corin ran into the woods. "He might have arrows and be waiting for you." Then Barin and the others arrived, and Zukei without hesitation sped panther-swift after Corin an Fol.

She tripped him from behind and Corin sprawled amongst pine cones, needles, and snow. He snarled and reached for Clouter, but Zukei kicked him hard in the face, knocking him unconscious.

"You will thank me later, Longshanks," the dark woman said as Barin caught up with them and lifted Corin into his arms.

"It's my fault," Barin told her. "If anything happens to that lass —"

"It won't, so shut the fuck up and follow me." Zukei sprinted back to join the others gathered in a mournful group by the horses. Barin, glum, placed Corin on the ground and knocked his head a bit until he stirred.

"It's all right lad, we just didn't want you getting yourself killed—that's all."

First light found them high on Tolfallon's slopes. A glorious day beckoned as the sun spilled gold right across the Gap of Leeth. Corin stood wild and silent as his companions studied the ground.

Zukei had acted as scout and had followed the kidnapper's trail way up here where, at the northernmost tip of The Wild Way, they were lost from view on the cold grey rock. Whoever this was, they were speeding south through the mountains, and there was no way of stopping them now.

Corin, exhausted and torn apart with grief, slunk to a flat rock and stared as one gone witless at the blue ahead. Barin took seat beside him on the pine straw.

"Relax boy, whoever this bastard is, he knows what he's doing. He's not going to hurt Shallan. He wouldn't have risked abducting her had he not known who she is."

"But what concerns us now is who he is and where he's taking her," Olen said. "Pissed anyone off lately?" Danail's accusing eyes held Corin's troubled gaze. This brother was more level-headed than Tolemon, but he was angry and worried and believed Corin the cause.

"I can think of a few," Corin muttered. "Two especially come to mind."

"Rael Hakkenon and Hagan Delmorier," Barin nodded. "Makes sense, we've heard little from those two of late. Could be either, but I'm damn certain it's one of them. It was too good to hope the bastards were dead. Rael slipped the net at Calprissa and he'd been with Shallan seconds before he escaped. Hagan?"

"I don't know." Corin shook his head. "But I suspect he escaped the Crystal Mountains—just a hunch. He's a crafty bastard and a survivor. Either one of those villains will take her to Caswallon, we can be sure of that."

Zukei approached Corin, who sat nursing his head. "Sore?" She raised a brow.

"Yes, but I deserve worse."

Zukei clicked her teeth in disapproval. "You're as bad as Barin, moping and whining and looking so glum. You men." Zukei squatted besides Corin who glanced at her sideways.

"I promise you this, Longfellow, because I know how much that lady loves you. I, Zukei the Slayer, will not let any arsehole on this earth harm Shallan of Morwella. Now go you with these others and return to the city. Rest if you can. You may be a fine warrior and good all-rounder, but don't think you have my skills at tracking and remaining unseen."

"I'm coming with you," Corin said.

"Nope. I work better alone." Zukei placed a dark hand on his shoulder and Corin almost jumped in alarm. "Give me one day, and I shall at least gain news of where he is taking her. One day, Corin an Fog."

"Corin an Fol."

"Whatever. I will report back at dusk tomorrow."

"And I say I'm going with you." At that point Zukei flashed Barin a look, who nodded and grabbed Corin's arms. Zukei vaulted onto her horse and within seconds had vanished in the dark pines hedging the narrow path called The Wild Way.

"Get off!" Corin struggled, but Barin held him pinned.

"Let her do her work lad, she's bloody good at it. Believe me, I've seen the results." Behind him, Taic and Sveyn nodded enthusiastically. It took a further half hour before Olen and Barin persuaded Corin his best bet was to do as Zukei said and return to Car Carranis and rest as best he could.

Ralian and Halfdan greeted them at the gates, as did Tolemon, his face wracked with self-guilt and hatred towards Corin an Fol. "You're to blame for this!" Tolemon shouted at Corin until Danail dragged him off lest Corin skewer him.

"We ride out tomorrow at daybreak," Halfdan told Corin. "We can spare this day—no more."

"I'm going to have a kip and a shit and then when that dark witch comes back, I'm going with her to find Shallan."

"You've destiny and a crown waiting. We need you with us, my son. We cannot win this without you."

"I don't care, Father! I'll find Shallan, then I'll do anything you ask of me. Now give me a break!"

Corin wandered off to one of the taverns. The place was empty, which suited him fine. He reached across and stuck his dry lips under the tap of a barrel. He turned the tap and flooded his gizzard with strong ale until he collapsed in sheer exhaustion and zoned out for several hours like a dead thing on the floor.

"She's back!" The words hit him at the same time as the bucket's icy content. "Wakey wakey, rise and shine!" Taic and Sveyn grinned down at him.

"Tossers," Corin growled at them and then followed them into the stables where Zukei stood addressing Halfdan, Ralian, and Barin. Shallan's brothers were there too, as were Olen and Arami. Zukei had Shallan's bow and horn clutched in her hands, which she'd found abandoned on the battlements, Shallan having forgotten them when she had first spied Corin.

"I mean to return these," Zukei growled.

"Well?" Corin snarled at Zukei. "I don't see Shallan."

Zukei ignored that and carried on her conversation with Halfdan and Ralian.

"It's Hagan, I think," Barin steered close. "Him and his crew."

"His crew are dead." Corin muttered an apology to Zukei who shrugged indifference and ignored him again.

"Well, he's not working alone," Barin continued. "Hagan—or whoever this is—joined another rider and they descended the mountains some twenty miles south of Tolfallon. Zukei followed the hoof tracks down to the steppes. There they turned north for Leeth. And that is why I think it's Hagan."

"Because he has small love for Caswallon." Corin nodded slowly.

"And more important, Caswallon has little love for him. Why risk the sorcerer's capricious nature when there is another who would happily pay for the Duchess as a captive to soothe his injured pride?"

"Who?"

"Daan Redhand—my old friend of course! Hagan's bound for Grimhold, I'll wager my bollocks on it."

"Well then, guess where I'm going for my vacation."

"Hold up, I'm coming with you, and so is Zukei. But we'll do this my way, hothead. The north is my territory. Agreed?"

"All right."

"Cogga's already sent bird to Fassof in Valkador. He'll have warriors waiting for us on my island."

"I'm not going to Valkador, I'm going to Grimhold."

"Listen to me—will you? Valkador is a short hop across from the Leeth coast and Grimhold not too far from there. A much quicker route for us than riding north through countless troll-haunted miles of forest and moor. Fassof's orders are to meet us at Kashorn three days form now. He should be able to cover the distance this time of year, as the winds from the north are relentless. That way we'll arrive at Grimhold hot on Hagan's trail."

"Just you and me?" Corin smiled at Barin despite his desperation.

"You'll not keep Zukei away. And my lads will be with us."

Olen approached them having heard their words. "The Rorshai ride with Halfdan on the morrow, but we two" - he motioned to

Arami, currently talking to some of his men—"will accompany you—Chosen One."

"My thanks." Corin clasped Olen's hand and gripped it tight. "I couldn't ask for better companions." That morning, Corin quarreled with his father again, but there was little Halfdan could do. Father watched son ride north from Car Carranis as he mustered his combined force to take the southbound road on their way to Kelthara.

"He's always been headstrong," Halfdan explained to Ralian as he led his army from the gates. Crows croaked and took wing as their road led them through the mangled mess of decaying bodies surrounding the city. "I'm so weary of fighting," said Halfdan, observing the grisly scene.

"Me too," said Ralian, although his hawk face looked more cheerful than it had in days.

A mile from the city, Corin and Barin and their companions were joined by Tolemon and Danail. The two brothers were not over-friendly to Corin but insisted it was their prerogative to find their sister. And Corin couldn't argue with that. They reached Kashorn the evening of the following day, where Corin was amazed to discover King Ulani of the Baha waiting for them in one of the taverns. With him were several fighting men, among them Prince Tarin, Greggan of the Wolves, and Bleyne the Archer.

"I tracked you," Bleyne explained with a grin as Corin hugged him. Throughout the next day and night, as they waited for Fassof, the companions shared their stories, and Zukei came face to face with her father for the first time in almost four years.

Chapter 30

Kashorn Again

"You won't get away with this." Shallan tried to slap Hagan's face but he caught her hand and punched her to the floor. She tried to rise but his boot kept her down amongst the snow and tree roots.

"We can do this easy or hard, don't much matter to me, my lady." Hagan grinned down at her. They had reached a patch of scraggy pines on a lower section of The Wild Way, a day south of the Gap of Leeth. Hagan's plan was to lie low up here for a time, let their trail go cold, and then turn back north, avoiding the Gap and Car Carranis, and instead making for Vangaris and contact with Redhand.

He hoped some of Daan's boys remained at Vangaris, but if not he would make the arduous journey to Grimhold with the Duchess leashed beside him. A hassle, but more than worth the trouble. Funny, he had always heard that the Duke's daughter was a timid thing, dreamy and aloof. Hardly the spitting wildcat he'd pounced on outside the main hall in Car Carranis.

Shallan had caught him in the balls with her foot and bitten his index finger before he'd decked her with a cuff, slapped the cord around her arms and the gag in her mouth, and slung her lovely body over his horse. Touch and go that had been.

So was slipping past the gate guards and cranking the huge wooden gates ajar. He'd been careful to shut them afterwards. Not that he should have worried overmuch; he'd taken note of the guards on the way in. "Drunk" was the word that came to mind. And certainly no one noticed him leaving.

His captive had struggled and wriggled as he galloped his horse across the Gap of Leeth once he had cleared the mangle of bodies sprawled frozen near the walls. Free of the Gap, he'd dismounted and tied horse and prisoner to tree, and then circled back to see if anyone was coming.

He'd heard voices and glimpsed riders a way off. Sounded like some kind off argument. Hagan hadn't hesitated. Satisfied they hadn't seen him, he had returned to his horse and guided the beast and its burden up the steep climb toward The Wild Way—a slow and dangerous affair in the dark of night.

Once there, he'd rested a short time and seen to his prisoner's welfare. He needed her looking her best for Redhand, so he forced some food and water down her throat. At day break, Hagan had commenced the long ride south to this hide he knew from earlier days—a high ledge hidden by pines overlooking the track. From here, Hagan could see any pursuit long before they found him.

He'd freed Shallan from the horse, allowing her to stretch her limbs and relieve herself in a bush. The leash around her throat ensured she wouldn't try anything stupid—not that such a doe-brain would last five minutes out here. But he'd rather not risk losing her.

It was when she came back that the rock caught him between the ears, making his head ring. Bitch had somehow gripped it in her tied hands and hurled it at him. That was when Hagan lost it and knocked her to the ground. She lay there now, looking up at him, her eyes daggers of loathing.

"You are going to die soon, Hagan Delmorier," Shallan spat up at him. "Whatever your plans for me, your own time in this world is short. And if you touch me..."

"Oh, stop being so bloody dramatic, my lady. It's boring, and this is business rather than pleasure, I do assure you. Not that it couldn't be both, if you wanted to improve our relations. We are going to be together for a while." Hagan laughed at the loathing on her face. "I understand completely, though you hurt my feelings."

"You don't know the calibre of the people who will hunt you down for this," Shallan hissed up at him. "You've nowhere to hide from such as they."

"We shall see, my lady." Hagan thought of Corin and smiled. "Let me worry about them. I suggest you get some kip, Duchess. We've a long ride ere dusk. And don't trouble your pretty head with any more pranks, or I'll work the knife on you somewhere where it don't show. I'm good with a knife, sure Corin an Fol told you that."

"Corin will kill you, villain! That's if Zukei doesn't kill you first."

"Zukei? Ah, the black vixen I saw watching after you before you entered the hall. Can't say I'm worried about her. As for Corin, he can try. I owe him that much."

Shallan was exhausted. Her fury, outrage, worry, and the loss of Corin so soon after finding him again had taken their toll. Despite her desperate state and the bitter cold she slept motionless like a dead thing on the piney snow for three long hours. It was the sharp intake of breath from her captor that woke Shallan.

She opened her eyes to see Hagan crouched on the ledge looking south as the slow thud of hoofbeats announced a rider coming their way. "They've caught up with you," Shallan said, shivering and wriggling to warm her veins.

"Silence bitch!" Hagan glanced back her way. "Whoever this is it ain't one of your lot, so best you hold that acid tongue of yours until we find out."

And find out they did several minutes later.

The rider approached slowly. He looked bone weary, his head stooped forward and his horse limping. The hood and cloak hid his features but no one else Hagan knew wore boots trimmed with gold and a jewelled hilted rapier at his waist.

"I don't fucking believe it," Hagan muttered as he checked Shallan's leash and vaulted down to hail the rider.

Rael Hakkenon reined in seeing the tall man approach. He reached for his crossbow then remembered how he'd lost it fleeing the haunted city. He was beyond shattered and his mind was filled with the horror of the day before yesterday when he'd witnessed the darkness returning.

Rael reached for his rapier and then stopped, finally recognising Hagan standing there alone on the track. "What the...?"

"Precisely." Hagan grinned at him and motioned Rael follow him to where he had Shallan stowed. "Since you've dropped by, I've something to show you, Assassin. By the way, you look horrendous."

"I'm lucky to be alive." Rael's cat green eyes looked vacant, and he had none of his usual menacing tone. Whatever had happened to him must have been profound.

"This will cheer you up!" Rael stared in disbelief at seeing Shallan of Morwella lashed to a tree.

"You've done well Hagan," he croaked, and dismounting, staggered over to where Shallan waited wild-eyed and scared, now she realised who had come. But Rael let her be.

"We cannot linger here. Too much has happened... I cannot talk about that at the moment, the memory burns inside my head. We need to flee this place! Where are you planning on taking that bitch?"

"Grimhold—or Vangaris if I'm lucky. Haal is dead and Redhand will need cheering up after losing most his warriors at the Gap. And I agree, it's getting too interesting to linger around here."

"You don't know the half of it," said Rael as he chewed at the beef jerky Hagan tossed him. Both allies were too tired and wary to speak of the last few days, or their amazement at finding each other.

But Rael's grim insistence that something very nasty was about to happen in the mountains had Hagan convinced enough to descend that evening close to Point Keep fortress and then ride through the night into Leeth. Once clear of Car Carranis they would turn west and head for the ocean and Vangaris.

Shallan refused to succumb to despair. She knew Corin and
Zukei wouldn't stop until they found her, though Corin had higher
duties now. And then there were Barin and her brothers, all loyal
and stout. But seeing the assassin had nearly broken her nerve.

Why was he here? And why alone and so dishevelled? The only
thing that made sense was they had planned her abduction together
and determined to keep her in the dark. But something profound
must have happened to so unnerve a man like Rael Hakkenon.

If only she had her bow and horn. Both were back at Car
Carranis. Even her knife was missing. But Shallan held to courage,
and late that following night as her captors snored in a deep wood,
she woke to find The Horned Man gazing down on her with those
huge sad eyes.

"Free me!" Shallan hissed.

"I cannot," he answered, his voice like wind blown leaves along
a stony path. "For I am far from here in body. You must be strong,
daughter."

"Father?" Somewhere an owl hooted, then silence. The Horned
Man was gone and instead, Rael Hakkenon was staring at her like a
cat with torn mouse.

"I've had a rough few days," Rael told her smiling slightly. "But
not as bad as what's waiting for you. For him it's business—so he
says. But for me it's personal."

Rael thrust up his right hand, clearly showing the missing pin-
kie. "I cannot begin to tell you how happy I am to see you, Shallan of
Morwella." He winked at her then reclaimed his blanket and rolled
back to sleep.

***

"So Ariane is at Kelthara?" Corin downed his second ale as
cold rain lashed the glass of the tavern. It felt surreal being back in
Kashorn again. The locals were wary and suspected trouble, remembering Barin and Corin from the fight in their village last autumn.

They kept their distance, but the innkeep served good ale and that evening, like the day before, passed without any trouble.

"Aye so." Bleyne's cool eyes surveyed the taproom. Barin was missing, having departed with Taic to watch out for any sign of Fassof, though they weren't expecting him till the morning at earliest. But Barin was restless to be away and all fired up about seeing his family again. Greggan was outside somewhere too. Aside these few, everyone lurked in the tavern.

Over in a dark quiet corner, Zukei was seated at table with her father the king. Bleyne sat close by, watching father and daughter with interest. The archer had little notion how the King of Yamondo's daughter came to be with them, but she seemed tough and self-reliant and that was all that mattered in his opinion. Beside him, Corin was staring into space, his expression morose.

"Strange to be back here," Bleyne said after a moment's thought.

Corin grunted and then cast a bleak eye at Prince Tarin, seated alone at another table and watching the fire crackle as though in a dream. "So much has happened since last we were here. I'd thought we'd turned a corner in this war, and then..."

"We have." Olen's keen eyes pierced Corin's. The Rorshai had just come in from the rain. Like Barin, they were eager to get going. Arami in particular was excited about faring into strange lands, and he eagerly shared bow talk with Bleyne, who, like Arac and the other bowyers, he now held in great respect.

Aside those mentioned and the other Rangers and two dour-faced fishers, the inn was empty—the only exception being Shallan's two brothers, sitting aloof and stern by the back door.

"This Caswallon is in for a shock when Halfdan arrives at Kelthara." Olen took seat beside Corin and Bleyne. Arami remained standing.

"Perhaps." Corin didn't share Olen's optimism. "But sorcerers usually have tricks up their sleeves, and I doubt not he knows about the Gap already."

"And the Crystal King?" Olen held Corin's gaze until the other looked away.

"And what of him?"

"Your destiny," Bleyne remarked, having heard from "Lord Greggan" all about events on The Wild Way, including Corin discovering who his father was. "You have to fulfill it. Caswallon won't know about that yet."

"Won't he?" Corin laughed bitterly. "Crystal King, what crap! What am I supposed to do, rush into Kella City with a flaming sword and golden underpants and slay all the nasty beasties, and then once that's done fry Caswallon in his crib?"

"Make for interesting viewing," Arami grinned.

Bleyne clutched Corin's arm, his dark eyes intense. "Elanion is with you, Longswordsman! Don't forget that. This is your destiny. You are the chosen."

"Not you too." Corin curled his upper lip and shouted for more ale. "You and Olen should form a club. Anyways, I've not had time to think about that stuff. Once Shallan's safe in my arms, I'll take a proper look, I promise." Corin saw that Tarin was watching him with a strange haunted expression.

"And what's your problem?" Corin awarded Tarin a cold eye and the prince turned his troubled gaze back to the fire.

At that moment, Greggan appeared, spraying water on Corin and Olen as he joined them at table. "Pissing down out there," he grumbled.

"Yeah, that's why we're in here," Tarin muttered.

"Barin still out there?" Corin enquired without much interest.

"Gods alone know. I couldn't see bugger-all in that deluge. I need a brandy." Lord Greggan dripped over to the taproom where the innkeep slumped half asleep.

Meanwhile, Zukei leaned back in her chair and puffed on the pipe her father had given her. She hadn't smoked for a long time, and it eased her nerves, which had not been good since Shallan's disappearance. She blamed herself for that, having appointed herself as

Shallan's personal bodyguard. The king watched her with keen dark eyes. These two hadn't spoken in almost four years.

"You've aged," Zukei said, and King Ulani smiled his big smile.

"And you, daughter, look gorgeous as ever."

"And you're fat, you've put on weight, Father."

"Never!" Ulani's smile fell from his face replaced by a shocked denial. "I've never been more trim."

"How is my mother?" Zukei puffed at the weed and stretched her scrawny legs out from under the table; her blue fizzy hair was still damp from the ceaseless rain.

"Enjoying her life with my other queens; they get on well when I'm not around."

"So why are you here?" Zukei cut through their easy conversation like a hot knife slicing butter.

"I was of a mind to ask you the same thing."

"I got there first." Zukei flashed her rare grin.

"I was seeking Corin over there." He nodded to where Corin was chuckling at something Greggan was saying, as Olen and Arami smiled beside him.

"Him?" Zukei nodded and snorted at the same time. "Star attraction he is. Quite the character is old longshanks the lover boy."

"He is a good friend of mine," Ulani said, looking pained. "I need to talk with him alone. Only Bleyne and Silon know the dire news I carry."

"What news?"

Ulani sipped his beer and glanced at the others sharing the tavern. He lowered his tone to a barely audible grunt. "He is back."

"Who?"

"He—Himself. The one we do not name in Yamondo. That volcano, Zukei, the Forbidden Mountain, has erupted and discharged its filth for miles across the jungle to our west. Vendel is in uproar and the whole of Yamondo shaking with the echo."

"It's just a mountain, Father." Zukei shook her head, though her dark eyes were troubled. "And those are only stories."

"I thought so too, and rather than trust to rumour I fared into the jungle alone. Deep into Vendel I ventured, close as I dared to the ruin surrounding that terrible mountain. There I saw things, daughter. Dark things and horrible things I cannot begin to describe." Ulani's tough face tensed with the memory of that horror. "I became afraid and fled as fast I could back to our land."

"You have no fear Father."

"I have now." Ulani sipped his ale and lowered his tone yet further. "I saw Him, daughter. I saw His face reflected in a poisonous puddle of steam."

"You saw Old Night?" Zukei whispered, choking on her words. "How can that be?"

"The face in the puddle, flies and insects all around, and the stench of decaying death everywhere. It was *Him*—his head anyway, dripping dark gore, and that ruined face with those carrion eyes mocking me. I know what I saw, daughter."

"Then the myths are true—He *has* returned?" Zukei's fierce face was hollowed with dread. "And you, like most here, believe that man . . . ," Zukei nodded to where Corin still sat with his friends, "you think that longlegged twit can somehow stop this storm? I don't see that, Father. I don't see that at all."

"We cannot give in to despair, Zukei! And down in Permio, when I travelled with him, there was a tribesman—a worthy fellow called Yashan. This Yashan called Corin 'Marakan.' It is Permian for chosen by the gods. I never gave it much thought at the time, but now I wonder."

Just then Barin's soggy bulk emerged through the doorway. The Northman stooped and grumbled his way into the inn, followed by his three men.

"He must be Barin," Ulani said, but Zukei had slipped outside.

***

Hours later, as rain still lashed windows and drummed roofs, Corin an Fol leaned against a dripping wall relieving his bladder.

He was quite drunk. The three excuses: inaction, bad weather, and depression, had driven him hard into drink. Most of his companions snored in the compact but clean lodgings above the tavern—courtesy of Barin, who had insisted on paying for everyone.

Taic and Sveyn were still keeping the innkeep busy, both drunker than Corin and spoiling for a fight. Zukei had not returned, whilst King Ulani and Barin shared notes on their forays and scrapes by the warmth of the fire. Barin stayed sober enough to keep a sharp eye on his nephew and Sveyn. Cogga had departed for bed some time earlier, as had Tarin and the Rorshai. Or so Corin thought.

"We need to talk." The voice at his side interrupted his flow, and Corin cursed seeing Tarin staring at him out of the rain in the misty dark.

"Thanks," Corin scowled at the prince. "But I am currently preoccupied."

"I owe you an apology, Corin an Fol."

"What?"

"On Fallowheld and back in the desert."

"That was the dragon's poisonous breath or something Caswallon cooked up. Forget it." Corin was resigned to be patient for once in his life. That in mind, he fumbled his organ back into his breeches and pushed himself free of the wall.

"There is a garderobe inside the inn," Tarin said.

"I needed air and time to think. Pissing outside's good for thinking. So what's on your mind, princeling—out with it!"

"We haven't got on, and I've hated you at times."

"Join the queue."

"Unjustly. I now regret the way I've behaved."

"Because you've listened to all the bollocks about me being the Crystal King?" Corin smiled like a wolf and staggered back inside the tavern.

"It's more than that." Tarin followed him in. "I've got something for you, something important. It's in a bag I brought with me."

"Give it to me tomorrow." Corin wasn't really listening, the ale having fuddled his brain. "I've a deal on my mind right now so methinks I'm off to bed."

Without waiting for a response, Corin glanced at Taic and Sveyn, the latter now sprawled on the floor snoring and Taic singing dreadful ballads at the fire. Barin and Ulani glanced his way as he found the stairs. Corin saluted them and clambered above where eventually he found a room that wasn't filled with snoring occupants. He launched his wet aching body on the creaky bed and was out till mid-morning.

Prince Tarin followed suit, and soon after, Ulani and Barin. That left only Taic and Sveyn, now both on the floor sleeping like hounds.

***

Morning found Barin alone on the quay. He watched in silence as three fishers guided their skinny crafts out the harbour. The rain had dispersed to leave a grey shiny morning that had all the heat sucked out of it.

Barin took to ambling along the harbour wall, recalling the excitement and kafuffle last autumn when he broke through the Crenise ships and Bleyne worked his magic with that arrow.

As he contemplated those halcyon days, Barin gazed out at the grey churning water. It was there that he saw Him, far out across the water. The Sea God Sensuata, heaving his mile-long nets. Much nearer was the recognisable shape of a multi-masted ship heading hard and fast for harbour.

The Starlight Wanderer.

Fassof had arrived at last.

Chapter 31

Urgolais Rising

Shallan rubbed her cold knees by the makeshift fire as snow filled the evening and settled on her like doom. She watched her captors much like a trapped bird of prey dreaming of soaring free into blue skies above. Hagan was busy skinning a rabbit whilst Rael Hakkenon lounged indifferent on a wet log. Neither man spoke. Nor had they said much in the three days since they'd found each other back on The Wild Way.

They had travelled at speed and were now clogged beneath the vast pine forest flanking most of southern Leeth, a land so huge that Shallan found it hard to comprehend. But Hagan knew the way; he'd fared north many a time about his villainous business—Shallan had gleaned such from his and the Assassin's rare discussions.

And there were broad paths beneath the forest, allowing for good progress, plus no shortage of game for easy slaughter and full stomachs. Worst was the cold that bit into her like creeping ice, but Shallan never complained. She spoke no word to her captors and they mostly ignored her, save the Assassin when he felt the need to taunt. And even he became bored at her non-reaction.

But as that evening lowered to dark heavy night and wolves cried lonely in the distance, Rael shuffled and fidgeted until Hagan asked him what was wrong. It was then that he told him about Ulan Valek. Both men ignored Shallan, who feigned sleep but heard every word.

***

"A bad place." Rael stared at the fire and shuddered. "Very bad. Cold and dark, but much more than that. Even as I approached, I sensed something alive and waiting down beneath those mines."

"Mines?" Like most folk, Hagan knew little of Ulan Valek.

"Yes, mines. Black tunnels leading down and down—we passed many, my lads, the Groil, and I. On our mission to find the spear."

"Groil—you had fucking Groil with you?"

"Caswallon sent them to help me. I had some men with me too, including Cavan. I think they might have got out because they fled before me, but I cannot be sure. It was confusing in the bitter dark—what with all the witchy spells stabbing my eyes. Aralais and Urgolais—I understand it now."

"I don't know what you are talking about."

"They were both down there, Hagan. It was like renting a premier seat in someone else's nightmare. Then the dark one got inside my head and the real horror started." Shallan listened captivated as the Assassin relived his time spent in the catacombs of the ruined castle Ulan Valek.

***

But Rael was only a witness. Zallerak was living the nightmare.

The pain was white lightning inside his head; only his spell shield kept him alive as the dragon's breath and claws tore into his flesh. Vaarg had waited a long time for this and his master too. Zallerak was dimly aware of Morak's metallic laughter somewhere close.

"It was all a ruse, Arallos," the Dog-Lord was saying. ""You've been trapped by your own cleverness, just like the mortal sorcerer who thought to hoodwink me. Both of you have failed and both of you will die."

Not yet...

Zallerak was aware of creatures entering the tunnels like ants. Groil—Morak's slaves. He saw men too and a small part of his tortured mind caught a glimpse of the Assassin, Rael Hakkenon, looking wild-eyed and askance in a corner.

Out of your comfort zone boy?

Fire and claw and pain and terror—almost he was done. But Zallerak—though caught off guard—maintained his innermost defences and refused to give in to the pain. Slowly but steadily he worked his locking spells on the dragon.

These spells became steel nets, coiling and tightening around Vaarg, even as the dragon tore Zallerak's mortal flesh to shreds. As his flesh collapsed, the Aralais's soul stepped neatly out of his body, allowing him to fight back whilst sacrificing his physical form.

Flesh was only flesh. Zallerak had used several guises over the many millennia he'd dwelt in Ansu. Like Morak, he was hard to kill. And like his enemy he was determined to survive.

Now a cool observer, Zallerak watched the dragon consume the last of his body, his handsome face falling into nothing as the dragon's metallic breath scalded his flesh blacker than Morak's.

But Morak's flesh was no longer scorched. There he stood in plain view, laughing and hurling acid bolts toward where Zallerak's inner being lay invisible, yet vulnerable and cold.

"This is my time, Aralais. You played and you lost!" Morak stood tall and strong, handsome with dark piercing eyes and long silky hair the colour of wood smoke in winter.

"You thought me crippled and weak, and thought to find the spear and keep it from me. The crown affair was a ruse to buy time while your ranging spells searched out the spear. We both knew it was here, but your ranging spells located it—not only for you but for me too!

"So I gave you what you wanted in Crenna and at Croagon's

forge. Small price for Urgolais Rising!"

As he spoke these last words, an explosion blasted through the tunnels and the walls of the mines, beams splintered and sheared, and earth came crashing down, killing Groil and man—not that Morak or his adversary noticed.

Vaarg, temporarily held by the steel nets, was buried in rubble, and Morak's image vanished from view, but his laughter remained.

Morak's search blasts were bullets banging and striking all around his weakened self, but Zallerak morphed again. He became a bubble: a pocket of air the size of a flea, his essence and malice and vengeance stored tidily within.

As the mines below Ulan Valek folded in on themselves, Zallerak's essence floated free of Morak's mind blasts and drifted up out of the mines, into the ruined city, and then out into the cold night air and was gone.

Amid falling stone and crashing mud, men's death screams and Groil snarling in chaotic terror, as gas and noxious fumes choked the atmosphere and stole the light, Morak stood unscathed, Golganak in hand.

"I am cured," the Urgolais warlock said, blasting aside rubble and stone with the spear and touching Zallerak's steel nets that gripped the dragon, freeing him again. "I am Dog-Lord no more! Dragon, know this: that I, Morak, have returned to my full glory. Now is both your vengeance and mine sated! Come now, old friend—let us leave this place now victory is ours."

"WHAT OF THE ARALAIS? HIS SOUL IS STILL OUT THERE."

"And we will hunt it down! But first we have another debt to settle."

***

Rael had fled back through the mines the minute he saw the dragon fall on Zallerak, as did those of his men still living. The Ptarnians were not so lucky; they chose another way out and Rael heard their muffled screams, until the mine shafts' collapse choked them silent.

Rael ran heedless of the utter dark, crashing into stone, scraping his flesh and bruising his bones, until his eyes adjusted and he was able to find a way out into the ice-cold streets of the haunted city. Briefly he'd caught Cavan's eye before an explosion and spurt of dust forced them apart.

"I got out alive," Rael told Hagan, as if he still didn't believe it. "I suspect Cavan and the others did too, though I cannot be sure, but their horses were gone when I found mine, alone and wild walking the path above the ruined city."

"A duel of wizards?" Hagan didn't know what to make of the story but was delighted that the meddling freakball Zallerak had been destroyed. "You sure it was him, the same bastard that tricked me in Agmandeur?"

"He is no more," Rael said. "Warlock or not, he couldn't have survived the dragon's attack. I saw it, Hagan. It scared the shit out of me, huge and black with claws like sabres. Gods, but I never knew such things existed!"

"The dragon destroyed the mines?"

"I don't know—I didn't stick around long enough to find out, did I?"

"Then maybe the dragon's dead too?"

Rael shook his head, an ironic grin smearing his lips. "I saved the best bit till last," he said quietly and Shallan had to strain her ears to hear him.

"I found my horse, as I said, and lost no time fleeing that horrible place. But just before I reached The Wild Way and relative safety I heard something, terrible wings, that made me rein in and take a look.

"Dawn was breaking and I saw them rise up high above the city. Dragon and rider, the first huge and terrible, the second worse. The rider held something in his arms, I couldn't see it clearly, but it looked to be a black spear. That same shaft I was charged by Caswallon to recover.

"Had I succeeded I would be dead. Because that thing *is* death,

Hagan. Golganak. The Urgolais spear of myth. The brief glimpse I had filled me with uncanny terror and I delayed no longer, and after witnessing their departure into the early morning skies I fled north along the mountain path until we met that afternoon."

Rael shivered and rolled himself into his blanket. "I saw what I saw, Hagan, and I who so despise fear was almost undone by it."

"Where were they headed, this unholy duo?" Hagan stoked the fire and cast a sly glance at Shallan who lay motionless in her blanket. Close by, the wolves dared howl again now the story was over.

Rael shook his head. "Kella or Kelthara—what does it matter? They won't be making for Grimhold if I'm any judge on the matter. I never had plans to journey up here, what with the cold and all, but now it seems oddly appealing." Rael grinned at his words and turned himself in his blanket.

"I'm off to sleep, lest the ghosts from that city find me wittering nonsense in the night." He said no more, and Hagan left him alone.

The Morwellan watched the slow crackle of embers. It was late and a young moon steered free of cloud and forest. The wolves were closer and other beasts could be heard in the deep of the woods. Hagan didn't know what to make of the Assassin's tale. Had anyone else spoken of such things he would have thought him insane. But not Rael Hakkenon.

A shift and shuffle behind him. "I know you're awake." Hagan turned, awarding Shallan's sleeping face a crafty smile. "Enjoy the story?" No response so he shuffled close to where she lay.

"It's not like you think," Hagan said, and Shallan blinked slightly confirming she was awake. "I'm not the villain you believe me to be. I know I'm a bad lad and I've had shit luck lately, but it wasn't always that way. And me and Corin were mates once, until he pulled that stunt in Permio." Shallan opened her eyes and awarded Hagan a brittle stare.

"I know you love him. He has a certain oafish charm and nothing I can say will change your opinion. But we were both good fighters—back then. Mercenaries who made good money, him for that merchant and me for myself.

"Then after returning home I was falsely accused of that murder in Vangaris. I was nowhere near the place, but your old man pronounced me 'Wolfshead' and banished me from my homeland, just because of lies and rumours regarding my reputation.

"I'd done nothing against my fellow Morwellans. But the Duke didn't see it that way. I was branded outlaw and villain, so I decided to act as such, becoming a thorn in the Duke's side.

"Still you say nothing."

"I have no words for one such as you," Shallan said quietly. "To me you are worse than a rabid hound, and now you seek to excuse yourself like any craven criminal. I —"

"I couldn't give a toss what you think, Duchess, just thought I'd put you in the picture. You love Corin an Fol, believing him so different from me, and yet we two are so alike. Fate has chosen different paths for us—that's all."

"You, villain, cannot hold a candle to his shadow!" Shallan spat on the ground close where Hagan perched. "I curse you to a slow and violent death!"

"You might get your wish, girl, but not before the Prince of Leeth has you naked and chained and begging their mercy. I'd enjoy these quiet forest nights if I were you. Oh, and don't worry, I'll not bother sharing my thoughts with you again."

Hagan stood and stretched his limbs as Shallan watched him in glaring silence. He held her gaze for a moment and then shrugged and retired to his station by the fire.

When Shallan heard Hagan's snores mixing with the Assassin's, she rolled to her knees and shook warmth into her body.

Where are you Father? Please do not forsake me!

But The Horned Man didn't answer, nor did she hear from him during the rest of that journey. The three reached Grimhold castle four days later and were informed that Daan Redhand had now proclaimed himself king, and hearing who had come was most eager to await them in his throne room.

***

I am the wind through the trees: the dark star, the evening breeze.

I am lost in the void yet I live and I breathe—a free bird unfettered.

I am as I once was and shall be again—flesh is only flesh.

I was fooled but not broken—I am defeated yet unbowed.

The game must play out without me for my part now is done.

It is a small matter...

I am the spinning tower— I'm the hidden doubt.

I am the question inside and the answer without.

I am the eagle in flight, the lion's roar

I am the shadow that creeps beneath your door.

I am the dreamer, the poet, the schemer, the fool!

I am everything and I am nothing, I break every rule.

I am a teardrop in a storm, a single grain of sand.

I am the salmon that swims upstream,

I am ocean, I am land.

I am the stranger at the gate.

I am destiny and I am fate.

I am Aralais, I am Golden, I am present and I am past...

What I have started cannot now be stopped—I shall watch and wait the outcome.

It will not take long...

The bubble burst over water, and the tiny essence of the Aralais being, by some called Zallerak, fell—a single rain drop silent to the ocean. Once there it morphed again, becoming a great salmon that writhed and wriggled through water on its journey to the shore.

And so the time wheel turns full circle. Nothing is ever forgotten. The fish finds shore on the beaches of Fol. It changes again, this time becoming an osprey that lifts and cries up from the spindrift.

Along the cliffs the white bird soars, at last reaching that lone tower. Once there his form turns back to a man again—albeit a frail and battered one.

From here shall I watch the final outcome.

The ghost of Zallerak smiles and enters the tower where he used to dwell. Outside the cries of seabirds welcome him home.

Nothing is ever forgotten.

***

The globe fell from the table and rolled across the floor. Caswallon watched it as though it were a snake. His fingers burnt from the heat of what he'd witnessed and his eyes stung like acid drops.

"Urgolais Rising!"

The voice on the wind.

He'd scried ever eastward until he'd reached the mountains, and within their midst, that hidden fortress. *Ulan Valek.* He'd seen it before with his crystal gazing, but this was different. Then he had been searching—questing for the spear. Now he had found more than what he was looking for. Now he was trapped!

The spear was there, but clasped tight in Morak's fist, with Morak seated on Vaarg's back and both hurrying west to Kella City. Caswallon slipped and crashed to the floor, paralysed by weakness and terror. What ward spells he had would ill serve him against a renewed, fully-operational Morak in possession of his spear.

He heard a flutter and squelch followed by an evil chuckle.

"Come to mock me?" Caswallon's white face witnessed Gribble settle on the window ledge outside.

"They are coming for you, Mr Caswallon." Gribble chewed his

index claw and sucked some meat off it. "I'd settle your accounts if I were you."

"Gloat then and be damned!" Caswallon tried to stand but his knees wouldn't support him.

"We had some good times." Gribble seemed reflective. "And they are a rough pair. I barely escaped the carnage over in the mountains. Not sure I want to stay around to see them arrive here. That said, I just thought I'd drop by to say ta-ta. You've been a nice boss compared to old Dogface. Hope he don't torture you for too long."

"Do me one last service as a friend?" Caswallon rolled to his knees and then struggled to his feet. "I beg of you, Soilfin."

"Such as?" Gribble sucked another claw clean and winked at Caswallon.

"Fly to Kelthara. Order Gonfalez and the Groil... all my armies return here at speed!"

"It will be too late."

"Do it anyway, I'll stall Morak—somehow."

"Good luck with that," Gribble sniggered and then flapped his leathery wings urgently, banging the glass and making it shudder. "I'll do it for friendship. Never had a friend before, even a soon to be dead one. Touched me it has, and methinks they'll be lots of fresh meat at Kelthara. Farewell, Mr Caswallon, it's been sublime!" Gribble chuckled and lifted jaunty out into the blue beyond.

Caswallon watched his speck fade from view like a drunken missile and then set about placing his urgent defence spells everywhere he could. Gonfalez could be here in two days; his ward spells only had to hold till then. Even with the spear Morak lacked the power to blast through so many traps—after all, he'd taught Caswallon well. Too well. Caswallon chuckled despite his predicament.

Over the next few hours he fashioned and glued cunning ward-spells out of six dimensional runes and placed artful locking spell-mechanisms and also sly binding incantations. And added to those, Caswallon sowed a hundred hidden traps within the lonely rooms of the palace. Last up, he fashioned a detonator rune he'd acquired from Limbo around the Astrologer's Nest lest Vaarg attack him from without.

At last satisfied and exhausted, Caswallon allowed his mind rest and prepared for the inevitable. Two hours later, the Urgolais and his dragon arrived.

***

Ariane woke to the sound of shouting at her door.

"What is it?" She flung off her covers and studied her tired features in the mirror. To her left, the pale drapes spilled just enough light to inform her it was morning.

"I said what is it?"

"Morning," came the stupid answer and Ariane recognised Cale's adolescent tones. He sounded excited and out of breath.

Ariane rolled her eyes; sometimes she could skewer Squire Cale. "What do you want, Cale?"

"They've gone, Highness!"

"Who has gone? What are you talking about?" Despite her annoyance Ariane approached the door and unlatched the bolt, allowing the excited boy to spill inside the room and crash into her.

"The enemy!" Cale finally squeaked out after apologising and untangling his jaunty arms from the irritated queen. "Silon told me to report to you straight away!"

"The enemy has gone? Where?" Ariane sighed and took seat on her bed. "What are you talking about Cale?" Then she glanced up to see Tamersane leaning against the doorframe. "Cousin—how fare you?"

"The boy speaks sooth," Tamersane's lips smiled but his eyes remained cold. "Yonder foe have departed."

"I don't believe it—why?" Ariane dare not allow the joy of false hope in. So instead she stoically bid them wait outside, whilst she dressed swiftly and let boy and man escort her out onto the walls.

Silon was there and Valentin, Tarello, and the other captains too. Teret stood close by and Tamersane rushed to join her. Ariane smiled as she saw them embrace and hug; perhaps this woman could save her cousin from himself after all.

"They left at first light," Silon said, pouring some hot tea into a mug from a flask and handing it to Ariane.

"Thank you," she nodded. "Why, Silon? What reason their departure?"

"I have no idea, Queen. But something untoward must have happened, and I suspect Caswallon has ordered his troops return to Kella City."

"Then Kella is under attack?"

"We must assume so." Silon sipped his own tea and studied the white fields and woods for any sign of movement but nothing stirred out there. "It is a riddle, Ariane." A shout turned their heads. A man, one of Valentin's scouts, was running full pelt toward them along the palisade.

"What now?" Ariane nearly choked on her tea, not ready for such an exciting morning. She recognised Doyle, who had become one of Valentin's scouts despite her misgivings on his abilities.

"Army coming this way fast!"

"From where?" Silon yelled.

"North!" Doyle yelled back causing Ariane to chuckle at the ridiculousness of the situation. It was like a pantomime and she hadn't had enough tea to partake. "On the Car Carranis road!"

Several minutes later Ariane and her captains and retinue stood at the north wall watching as the grey shapes of soldiers filed through the morning.

"I see no Groil among those ranks," Ariane said, handing the spyglass back to Silon who held it steady for a moment and then smiled. "What is it?" Ariane flashed her dark eyes his way.

"It's Lord Halfdan of Point Keep," Silon laughed with relief, handing her the glass again. "The old wolf has returned at last! We are winning this war, Ariane!"

Chapter 32

Valkador

Corin stood at the prow of The Starlight Wanderer alongside its master. The voyage to Valkador had taken three days with fair winds and kind seas, and now the mountains of Barin's home rose majestic above the waves on the northern skyline.

Steering the craft beside Corin, Barin hummed a merry tune. He was happy today and Corin was pleased for his friend, who would soon be united with his wife and daughters after so long away.

Truth was Corin felt tugged by guilt. He'd rather Barin stay with his family, but knew he needed the Northman's skills and knowledge on the whereabouts and layout of Grimhold Castle. Moreover, Corin knew Barin now regarded Shallan almost as another daughter, and couldn't sit by whilst she were held by his foes.

"Redhand, Rael, and Hagan." Bleyne joined them to watch the mountains grow in size. "That's an unholy trio."

"Want to give Grimhold a miss?" Corin asked the archer.

"Certainly not. But I do think we are in for a lively week. Lots happening. And it's nice to be on the sea again, though I'm more of a woodsman as you well know." Bleyne winked at Barin and slunk off to watch dolphins dancing hard to port.

"He's changed," Barin said, shaking his head in wonderment. "Never used to say a word and now you can't shut the daft bugger up."

"We've all changed," Corin said.

"Aye—that we have and you more than anyone."

"Me? No way. I'm still crap at dice."

"That's true," Barin chuckled. "Oh, by the way, have you spoken to Tarin? The young prince seems most anxious to natter with you, says his got something for you in a bag. Very mysterious. Seems most determined to rid himself of it."

"I'm not surprised," Corin laughed. "It's caused him and the rest of us a deal of trouble."

"Oh...I see..." Barin nodded sagely and then scratched his beard. "And yet I saw the bag and it's rather small. Small enough to keep inside his pocket, and I hardly think the..."

"Tekara." Corin turned and awarded Barin a level look. "I know what he has Barin, the size doesn't matter. No doubt Zallerak was involved with fixing that."

"Speaking of whom?"

"I don't know either, but I expect we'll see him ere the end."

"The end? That's a bit gloomy, even for you?"

"It's coming Barin—I can feel it."

"The end of what?"

"This fucking story." It was Corin's turn to grin.

"Does that mean I get to put my feet up?" Barin blinked at the sun and Corin left him musing and humming at the morning. He went below where Tarin was waiting.

"I can't avoid you—can I?"

Tarin looked pensive; he produced a small leather bag and thrust it into Corin's hand.

"I'm not ready for that yet," Corin said, thrusting it back. "I know Zallerak quested you with giving it to me, though he could

have saved a lot of trouble by giving it me back in Croagon's forge."
Corin's face softened and for the first time he smiled at the prince.

"I know what it is, Tarin. The time will come when I do take it but that time is not now. Keep it awhile yet, I beg you. We all must play our role - apparently. Once I have my Shallan safe I'll look to this again—cousin."

Tarin's face lit up hearing that last word. "I will keep it safe," he said. "Zallerak taught me the rune spell that alters its size, and come the moment I shall utter it. But you are wrong. It was Silon bid me seek you out, requested that I accompany Bleyne and Ulani in riding north with Sir Greggan and Valentin's boys."

"Sir Greggan?" Corin chuckled and left Tarin gaping as he made his way to the heads.

Throughout that morning the island grew until it filled the horizon. The mountains dominated but lesser heights revealed green hills folding over forests and wide grassy fields. Corin saw homesteads and settlements and even the odd grey ribbon of road.

All Barin's crew were singing about their duties except Fassof, who retained his dour taciturn foul-mouthed mannerisms. He had smiled once though, when he'd spied Zukei amongst the passengers clambering aboard at Kashorn harbour.

Fassof had clasped her in his arms for a moment and slimed her mouth with a wet kiss. That had got him a sonic whack between the ears from the angry-eyed young woman, but he seemed happy enough receiving it.

Mostly Zukei remained aloof, steering clear of Corin and her father, occasionally eye-flirting with Fassof, but only in a half-hearted way to make him smile. Zukei liked the mate but her heart, wherever it was, was not for such as he.

They raised long strands of shingle, and green fields showed beyond, these leading across to the docks where other vessels bobbed and danced in violet blue waters. These were steadfast-looking craft but none compared with *The Starlight Wanderer*.

Corin studied the island as the crew heaved oars and stowed sail. He had expected snow and bitter chill but the atmosphere was surprisingly mild; only the tall peaks at the centre of the island wore snow about their crowns.

Grinning, Taic informed Corin that mild winters and sunny summers blessed the island. Corin found that hard to believe, but then Taic had been drinking ceaselessly for almost five days.

Horns filled the nearest valley like lowing cattle as Barin's harbour crew greeted their master's return. Corin saw the tiny shapes of people rushing to the quay, eager to greet the lord of their island at last homeward bound.

They moored against a jetty reserved especially for *The Starlight Wanderer*. Here men rushed aboard and clasped hands with comrades and kin. Taic and Sveyn butted heads with some shaven-headed drinking cronies and soon vanished toward the nearest tavern. Cogga threw his arms around the hips of a red-faced, freckled, heavyset woman, who laughed bawdily at something he said.

Ruagon the cook cried out as two chunky boys ran grinning to greet their father. And then Barin saw his wife Marigold with a laughing daughter grasped in either arm.

"My girls!" Barin boomed, and the big-eyed, long-limbed blonde twins rushed to embrace their laughing father, whilst his calm-eyed wife folded her arms and watched in silence from the dock.

"Greeting Marigold!" Barin jumped to the jetty and approached his wife.

"Husband," Marigold gave him a long steady look and then smiled as he threw his huge arms around her. "I've stew and ale in the cottage; these good folk can spare you an hour or so." Corin smiled seeing Barin led like an excited little boy away from the quay by his blonde-haired, handsome wife.

That night Barin held a feast in his great hall. He had explained to Marigold that his stay was short but insisted they make the most of it, hence kine and boar were slaughtered and many a squawking fowl tossed in with their midst.

A hearty feast that proved, with ale and mead flowing aplenty. Young warriors sang bawdy songs, whilst golden-haired maidens danced around tables with the older women clapping and cheering and wishing they could still do those steps. Hounds lolled and sprawled, keeping two eyes out for scraps, and every now and then a draught would fill the hall as a newcomer entered and took eager seat at one of the long tables. Such was Barin's feast that night the stranger came.

Nobody noticed him at first, but it seemed an odd chill had entered the hall, and the fires, roaring recently, died to splutter and spark. Men's voices stilled to a conspirators' hush, and their women looked around with worried eyes.

It was Marigold who saw him first. A silent figure hunched by the door, hood covering his features and long spear leaning jaunty against the wall. One eye was visible: it shone with the cut-glass sparkle of polished diamonds.

"You are welcome here, stranger," Marigold's rich deep voice struggled to ease the tension in the hall. "Please eat, drink, and be merry with the rest of us, though I do not recall seeing you before on our island."

"Aye friend, be welcome," Barin, his mouth full of beef, bid the stranger join his warriors at the far bench, a gesture that was lost on them for the old man had an unsettling effect on all present. To Barin's right, King Ulani's eyes narrowed, as did Corin's beside him.

"He seems familiar," Ulani growled in Corin's ear, whilst Zukei—seated close by—slid a slim knife from her sleeve. Tension thickened like smoke in the hall. A dog growled, another joined it, and then a third added its voice to the chorus. The stranger glanced their way, and in a skulking pack they circled and scurried from the hall with tails between their legs.

"Speak friend, lest our welcome fades—your manners have upset my hounds!" The smile fled Barin's face.

A chuckle like falling gravel on broken cliff.

That single silver eye fell on Barin. Cold as northern ice it stung the Northman until Barin turned his gaze away. "There is one here I would speak with outside and alone." The stranger's voice was a blunt saw tearing knotty wood. "He knows who he is."

"But who are you?" Ulani's tough face held that cold gaze a moment, until he too turned away.

"King Ulani you are far from home, as is your daughter with the smoky hair." Zukei hissed like a lynx and gripped her knife ready to toss. The stranger chuckled though he couldn't see the weapon. "Put that away, girl—you cannot use it on me." Zukei dropped the knife and shook her hand as though she'd been scalded.

As Corin had known it would, the stranger's eye fell on Corin. Unlike his friends, he held that chilling silver gaze and refused to drop his own.

"Where?"

"At the edge of yon crow wood. Your friends can bring ale and meat but then they must depart."

"What's in it for me?" Corin pointed his food knife at the stranger who laughed and stood to face the doors.

"Life, advice, and choices. And helpful suggestions," the stranger said before disappearing into the night.

Corin stood, his eyes hot and nasty. He slammed the eating knife point down onto the table, and then apologised to Marigold for spoiling her cloth.

"Corin, don't go out here!" Olen yelled from a table close by.

"He's right," Barin said, grabbing Corin's arm and yanking him back down to his seat. "Don't trust that spook, let him do his worst outside and be buggered!"

Corin shook free of his friend and host. "You'd best do as he says, bring sustenance and leave this to me. Those of you that know me well," Corin nodded to Barin, Bleyne, and Ulani, "are familiar with this sort of thing. The rest of you relax, eat, drink—I've got this."

Amid murmurs and tuts and gritting of teeth, Corin eased his long body clear of bench and table and slipped outside without further word. "You've got to stop him!" Marigold slapped Barin's ear, but the Northman shook his head.

"That boy knows what he's doing, wife. Now Daisy Girl! Mollie Flower, you too! Barin's daughters were wide-eyed and scared as they huddled close to their mother. "Go be useful and get some good slices of meat and some of the best ale for Corin and that other fellow. Bring them here and I will deliver them myself." The girls nodded and fled to the kitchens hidden behind screens at the end of the hall.

They came back minutes later with a huge tray of meats and two generous flagons of the master's finest brew. Barin thanked them with a wink and reached for the vittals. "I'll be back in a mo," he told them.

"I'm coming with you." Ulani stood and dusted off his tunic, a woolen garment he had worn during this voyage north.

"As am I," said Bleyne joining them. Close to the door were seated Shallan's brothers. Tolemon's gaze was suspicious and wary as he watched on in silence. Barin grunted and the three men left the feast behind. Outside, a roving half moon slid through cloud, its silver varnishing the still waters of harbour and quay. Barin frowned.

"Calm before the storm," he said.

"Do you see them?" Ulani asked, balancing the ale jugs in one hand so he had a free one for a weapon.

"Over there." Bleyne pointed to where Corin crouched lean below the shadow of a huge pine. The stranger stood several feet away, his back to them and his silver gaze following the restless moon.

Corin saw them approach and waved. "Thanks, leave those on the ground over there, I'll come and get them in a minute. This won't take long."

The three friends exchanged quizzical glances until Corin's hand whooshed them away. "Go!" Reluctantly they complied with his wish, but lingered outside the hall just in case something untoward happened.

***

"It's good ale. They know how to brew in the north." The stranger's rough voice cut the silence of the night like a vixen's banshee warning. His gaze remained on moon and sea. He'd left it to Corin to gather the food and ale and place them at his feet.

"Why are you here?" Corin stared at the other's back, willing the stranger to turn and face him. "What trick are you planning next, Wanderer?"

That name had the desired effect: the stranger turned and the hood slipped form his face to reveal an old man with scraggy white beard and long wispy hair. The left eye shone back at Corin like wet steel. The right was missing, in its place a hollow scoop of soot that hinted at things no mortal man could comprehend.

Corin, though stung by the impact and savagery of that gaze, refused to look away. "You owe me answers," he pressed.

"I...owe...you?" The old man croaked a laugh. "I think you've had too many knocks on the head, my lad. Don't you remember Darkvale? If it weren't for me —"

"But you've been interfering from the start. You're worse than Zallerak—" Corin flinched, seeing the sudden anger spark in that single eye. He'd best be careful; the High Gods were rumoured capricious and spiteful when teased.

"Have a care, Corin an Fol! That Aralais wizard is not in My league, and you are not in his league. You are a flea on a dog's back."

"Fleas bite."

"They do that." The old man's ravaged face hinted humour. "I have enjoyed working with you, boy. You've a certain way about you, as had your forefather when I knew him long ago. But he at least showed me some respect. You are a tad arrogant."

Corin ignored that. Instead he stood up and faced the old man, eyes level and ale mug spilling its contents in hand. "So why choose tonight for a cosy natter? Do you like spoiling feasts with your sunny charms?"

"As a matter of fact, I do like feasts. And you mortals—the northerners anyway—know how to throw one. I've attended many in my time. You'd be surprised who I've shared cups with over the centuries."

"I doubt that."

"But this is no social call, Corin an Fol. The Game quickens and we are entering the Final Dance! Until now I was happy to observe you and steer the worst away, though you kept finding more trouble for me. You're a very scrappy lad, you know."

"Dance?" Again Corin chose to ignore the god's expansive tone.

"The Weaver's Dance fashioned the cosmic threads of life throughout the universe; the glue cementing that thread was time and space. We gods, you mortals. We are all specks of dust residing in that time and space. Each with a specific job to do.

"The Big Boss has moved on to other galaxies but His Dance remains. And in this grubby corner of the universe it quickens like moth rushing into flame. The Weaver has lost interest in us, and consequently Ansu, this special world, is in direst peril."

"Old Night—I've heard the stories." Corin slurped his ale and rolled his eyes. "You will have to do better than that."

"Why do you think King Ulani is here? He's clever for a mortal and he knows who you are. And he alone of your comrades has witnessed the ashes of the return of Old Night. Your little war with that stupid wizard in Kella is but an echo of a larger, infinitely more important conflict. A war of three movements, three dances, with the third about to start."

Corin laughed despite the heavy presence of the god. "You *are* like Zallerak with your hints and innuendoes, despite your protestations. You pair should be drinking partners; you could fill an entire corner of the universe with your riddles and crap."

Corin winced and ducked as lightning struck a branch above his head, snapping it clean from the tree and sending it thudding to the ground a foot from where he stood.

"Have a care, mortal!" The Huntsman's face had darkened and his features faded from view. He loomed like a smoky shadow expanding out like smoke above Corin's head. "My patience is not infinite, and you are dicing with oblivion." The god's tone softened and He sighed as one summoning calm from within.

"I am not your enemy, I am your friend. Count yourself fortunate, mortal. There are few that can claim to have friends such as I."

"It was a joke—I just pictured you and Zallerak together.'

"A bad joke." The Wanderer's face came back into view and he shrank back to size and again appeared an old man. Oroonin motioned Corin take seat beside Him on a log.

"I like humans—always have. Your race has achieved a great deal considering the brevity of their lives. You're plucky, sharp, and independent. And I like that—respect it. But you can also be incredibly stupid at times."

"That's true," Corin nodded.

"The Aralais are different. I don't care for them much: arrogant, self important, edgy, and aloof—all traits shared by My Kin. But whereas the gods have a right to be that way the Aralais overreached themselves."

"That doesn't surprise me."

"Arallos was the worst of them. Ambitious and bright, it was he that started the war with the Dog people—not the other way around, which I'm certain, is how he explained it to you."

"I've never trusted him." Corin tore at a strip of beef and wondered what was occurring in the hall; it seemed very quiet for a feast. Doubtless everyone was awaiting his return. "But Morak's lot are worse."

"Are they?"

"Of course they are, and Morak stinks of evil."

"Actually that reek is bitterness laced with old wet dog, Morak had his face blown off by Arallos, but he's finally happy again because he's got his revenge."

"What's happened—am I missing something?"

"Just another piece in the Game, a short movement in the coming Dance. Good and evil—where you find one, the other lurks close. The Urgolais are not the black villains your Zallerak portrayed them to be.

"Before their war, the Aralais treated their cousins with disdain and contempt, and even enslaved many as they were physically weaker and smaller in build. This led to a resentful faction growing amongst the Urgolais scholars led by Morak, a powerful priest among their people.

"Back then Morak had honour. He challenged Arallos to single combat but was tricked, and Zallerak's flames tore the Urgo lord's face away."

"Zallerak told me the burns were caused by Morak's spear, Golganak."

"The weapon the Dog-Lord made for himself? Hah, a glib lie that one! Arallos made Callanak the sword and the other artefacts to destroy the Urgolais towards the end of the war, both races were almost worn out, and that was also the reason why Zallerak jumped on your ancestor, Erun Cade, with his offer of the crown.

"He had meant it for himself but realised that he (or any Aralais living) lacked the strength to wear it. So instead Arollas chose the timely arrival of your people to use them to carry his shield—for the Tekara is a shield as well as a crown, as its main purpose has always been to protect."

"So what's become of Zallerak now?"

"He's retired from the Dance."

"Dead?"

"It's not impossible. Listen, we are all the Weaver's children, Zallerak, you, Me—we all must play our part in this the final chord. You mortals are lucky you have small parts. You worry, fret, plot, scheme, and shaft each other and then—pop! You're dead. Game over. Simple! We Gods and the demi-gods, demons, and such don't get it so easy. My wife has held a grudge against me for four thousand years—imagine that."

"Sorry to piss on your bonfire, but I don't really believe in a supreme being. I mean why let all this shit happen?"

"It doesn't matter what you believe in! Humans, you are all about yourselves! The Weaver created you and blessed you with a mind to work things out, but you only use a small part of that mind. And when you people do think you always draw the wrong conclusions. Shame really."

Corin rubbed his eyes and wondered what the real purpose of this visit was. The god, reading his mind, smiled his wolf smile.

"You are transparent, and yes I am coming to that. I get lonely, Corin; sometimes it's just nice to share thoughts—even with an idiot like you."

"Thanks."

"You've heard of Callanak?"

"A sword of legend. Another of Zallerak's trinkets?"

"It hangs from the wall of a cave in Laras Lassladden—an island currently conveniently moored at the tip of this world."

"You want me to find this sword? Kill a bunch of people and do big stuff with it? And you say I'm the transparent one?"

"It is yours by right, as is the Tekara, and you will need both to counteract Morak's spear." The Wanderer sounded tetchy. "Laras Lassladden moves around the nine worlds and shifts through dimensions, hence you need to act while we still have time."

"And this sword helps your cause too?"

"My cause? What would you know about that?"

"Bugger all, except that by helping me you help yourself. Else why do it?"

Oroonin chuckled. "And there's me expecting gratitude and compliance. Suffice to say mortal, we walk a fine line. All of us. My unpleasant brother recovers. He has His team of loyal players, My sister and wife has Hers."

"And what of you?"

"I work alone and trust no one. That way I don't get surprised or let down."

"And you want me in your team whereas Vervandi wants me in her Mother's. It's all a bit confusing."

"Not when you're a god and have had oceans of time to dwell on such things. The sword and crown can turn the odds against Morak

and—more importantly—who is backing him. With the rightful heir
to the throne wielding and wearing these artefacts there is a chance
of holding back Old Night. Isn't that enough? For the survival of
your people if nothing else?"

"I am currently on another project."

"Love!" Oroonin spat the word out as though it had a bad taste.
"Yes, I heard the little speech you gave your father and, yes, I know
how stubborn you are. That said, my task runs neatly alongside your
project."

"How so?"

"Shallan is due to arrive in Grimhold Castle with the two men
you most hate. Barin is right, you have saved time by coming here,
and he knows that fortress, so I'm sure you'll find a way inside.

"Free the lady if you can and revel in your joyful reunion.
Then return to Barin's ship and make north for the island of Laras
Lassladden. Once there disembark and make for the caverns hidden
beneath Bhogha Mountain. Callanak is there. Take the sword and
voyage south to Kelthaine at speed. The war will have started so you
cannot dally."

Corin stood and showed his back to the god. "I'm going to find
my lover, and what happens after that, happens. I make no pledges.
You've said your piece, Wanderer, now let me return to my friends,
and pester me no more."

"As you wish, mortal." Corin heard steel in the voice and could
feel the angry silver gaze burning into his back. "But know this. I
came in kindly manner, hoping we could work alongside. Your attitude leads me to think we must work apart, which could well prove
ill for you. From now on you will need to watch your back!"

Corin turned quickly, aware that he had spoken over-harshly,
but it was too late. The old man/god had vanished from the moonlit
night. Corin shivered, drained his ale, and went to re-join his friends
who still hovered outside the hall.

They didn't ask and he didn't answer, but instead Corin ventured inside and spent the rest of that night burying his head in

strong brew. The feast went well enough, though voices were quieter than before and many a face awarded Corin strange looks.

By next afternoon they were at sea again, and just before dark had raised the grim cliffs of western Leeth.

Chapter 33

Grimhold Castle

The wall of rock announcing their arrival at Leeth rose sheer and dark for miles, showing no break or strand or sign of anywhere to moor the ship. The cliffs rose, swallowing moon and stars, and as they loomed close, the expression on each passenger's face changed from wonder to alarm.

"Is he running us aground?" Tolemon gazed accusingly at Barin, standing huge and motionless at the helm.

"Patience brother, he knows these waters and you do not." Danail looked nervous despite his words. Closer to Barin, Bleyne raised a quizzical brow and Zukei frowned, whilst Prince Tarin clenched his teeth and Corin an Fol leaned close beside Barin at the wheel.

"Barin doesn't have to do this to impress me," King Ulani said somewhere behind them.

"Is there something you're not telling us?" Corin asked Barin.

"A few more moments," Barin grinned cheerfully down at him whilst enjoying his little secret. Meanwhile, the black line of cliff swallowed what was left of star-studded sky as *The Starlight*

Wanderer maintained her course, heading straight for the cliffs.

Then, after several tense seconds, Corin laughed, seeing the slight silver glint of a crack in that erstwhile impenetrable wall of rock ahead. A mere thread of skylight with a lone star glinting like a winking eye beckoning them in.

"That's our guide," Barin grinned, pointing at the lone star, and raising his voice added, "those squeamish should fare below, this is a tight passage and touch and go—even in broad daylight. At night we risk running aground or getting squished on rogue rocks."

"Well don't sound so bloody cheerful about it," Corin couldn't help suggesting as they plunged into the crack, which widened just enough to swallow the ship whole.

"Fuck but that's narrow," Zukei muttered and she clutched her Karyia as though she could fight the cliffs away with its steel.

"Interesting." Bleyne nodded beside her. "So many ways this could go wrong." Zukei and Bleyne had recently become acquainted and had been discussing tactics with the other five chosen for Shallan's rescue team.

On board were seven horses. Barin said it was a lucky number—mainly because eight alongside so many passengers and crew would most likes sink the boat (his words). But that left a problem—choosing the assault squad.

After a half-hour's nattering, the group decided who would rescue Shallan. But not without a deal of argument and vented steam, mainly on Barin and Ulani's part, and with little support from Barin's crew. He had his old team back again, including the newer recruits Wogun of Vendel, Haikon the former Permian fisherman, and Norman from that country no one could pronounce. These voiced their opinions against Barin's inclusion with little mercy shown.

"You can't come." (Cogga.)

"Things will get bad if you're there." (Ruagon.)

"You're too big and fat to sneak into that castle unannounced." (Fassof.)

"He's as big as I am," Barin nudged Ulani who grunted.

"It's not about size, I'm a stealth monkey," Ulani protested.

"You, father, are an elephant. They'd hear your stomping out-side the castle walls." (Zukei.)

"See what I have to put up with?" Ulani exchanged glances with Barin.

"They are right, uncle, we commandoes need the element of surprise, and you pair do stick out a bit." Taic got a mallet-hard ear clipping for that. But Ulani and Barin complied eventually, and the latter in better spirits than he had complied at Car Carranis at the eve of the raid on King Haal's camp. Barin knew if he saw Redhand his temper would get the better of him, putting their slim chances of success at even higher risk.

In his place, Barin insisted Fassof and Cogga go. Both were de-pendable and both knew Grimhold Castle as well as he did, having been there many times before the latest feud between Valkador and Leeth. Two guides lest one has a mishap, Barin explained.

But who else to choose?

Naturally Corin volunteered himself and no one challenged that. Zukei voted Bleyne and Bleyne voted Zukei—these two seemed to like each other and Barin agreed the pair had unique skills that would prove invaluable, should things get nasty in that castle. Then Shallan's brothers Tolemon and Danail stepped forward, and again no one could gainsay their right to play a part in their sister's rescue, though Corin made it clear he'd have chosen anyone else over this pair. He didn't like Tolemon overmuch, and Danail...? The word "untested" came to mind. And that made seven.

Olen and Arami wanted to come, as did Prince Tarin, Arac the lean archer (who insisted archery would be needed more than swords), and of course Taic and Sveyn, who hated missing out on any venture.

But the limit on horses put a firm lid on things. Hence these others would have to put up with heaving to with Barin at the chosen spot and waiting. During the next hours, the seven chosen made ready for another busy night.

***

The hard-faced king sprawled idle and drunk on his newly-claimed throne, his blue gaze scanning his warriors for future up-starts and troublemakers. He'd long dreamt of sitting here, knowing that both his father and brothers had been fools and that he was the better man.

Now all three were conveniently dead and Daan Redhand ruled the vast entirety of Leeth, a country so big he hadn't seen a tenth of it. Not that that mattered a jot, as the power base was here in Grimhold Castle, and the only men that counted were these drunken tossers in his hall fondling wenches and exchanging coarse banter on the benches below.

Many were his men, trusted and solid. But many more were his father's lot, or else Corvalian's boys and Snake's hatchet crew. There were others too, from the wider regions of Leeth, all eager to win favour with the new king.

Redhand didn't trust any of them, and for good reason, as most were as cold and ambitious and treacherous as he was.

The hour was late when the guard at the gates announced three timely visitors to Grimhold. "Bring them here!" Daan Redhand roared. "Make them welcome, especially the lady!" His warriors grinned seeing the lusty gleam in their lord's eye. Although it was late, it now seemed that the night had just started.

Minutes later the two guards returned with the aloof quirky Rael Hakkenon almost dancing to keep up behind them. Following the slender Assassin were a tall, hard-faced fighting man, whom the guards introduced as Hagan Delmorier—a man whose reputation had reached Grimhold—and in his grip the cold-eyed daughter of Tomais of Vangaris. That same lady daughter was indirectly respon-sible for King Haal's death, and therefore worthy of Daan's grati-tude—in his own special way.

"You southerners are welcome here!" Daan's raw voice boomed across the hall, as his guards bid Rael and Hagan take seats in the front row, dragging the stony-faced Shallan with them. "Get them ale—the lady too! I like a lively wench." Daan surveyed Shallan's curves with a widening smile but she refused to meet his eyes.

Turning to the two men accompanying her he noted how haunted Rael's expression was. Gone was the familiar self-confidence and arrogance exuded by the Master Assassin of Crenna, in its place a sort of self-doubt and inner loathing which gave the king cause to wonder. That and the dark circles surrounding his famous green eyes. The man Hagan had a dependable, solid look and King Redhand soon forgot he was there. Instead he resumed his bold study of Shallan.

"Eat lady—I would have you strong and lusty!" Redhand laughed as a thrall brought a bowl of steaming broth, and at the king's word, forced Shallan's mouth open and poured the hot liquid down her throat. Shallan choked and gagged and the hot broth mostly ran down her chin. To her right, Hagan looked annoyed at her treatment but he kept his lips together.

"My, my," Redhand grinned. "And there's me thinking you a high born lady—not some grubby tavern wench. Well, best get to it. Strip her starkers, lads!"

***

The passage through the mountains was a knife slice twenty miles long. Occasionally a kink sheering left or right in the cliff face would mean intense concentration and copious expletives on Barin's part as he worked the wheel.

They heard rather than saw the urgent rush of churning water, warning of hidden skerry and rock. Somehow Barin steered clear of all hidden hazards and, after a taut couple of hours, they left the walls of cliffs behind and entered a wider channel with the dark shadow of pine-forested hills looming like silent guards on either side.

"This is Westfjord," Barin informed Corin. "I was brought up here in secret after my mother fled the witch who'd cursed my father and placed a price on our heads back in Valkador—may she still rot in Yffarn! Mine was a rough upbringing thanks to her.

"There are some villages and strand-hamlets around but we should go unseen. They are a dopey lot, mostly fisher folk living in dread of Grimhold's charming tenants."

"How long?" Corin demanded, itching to jump ashore and reach Grimhold Castle whilst dark still ruled the sky, giving them a chance.

"Half hour to safe haven, then two hours' ride for your rescue party. The road to Grimhold is easy to follow and you shouldn't be troubled this late at night. Leethmen are seldom sober after dark."

Half an hour later, just as Barin said, they set to in a quiet land-locked northern corner of the Westfjord, with deep water allowing *The Starlight Wanderer* hug close to shore, and high hills and dark woods hedging the banks, ensuring she stay hidden from prying eyes during the following day, or as long as they needed to wait.

"There's a wooded track leads up to the road several miles north of here," Barin explained as the appointed seven readied their borrowed steeds and struggled to lead them down the makeshift ramp into the icy dark water below. The horses would have to swim some forty feet before gaining the shingle strand, now just showing pale silver in the gloom.

"Once on the road, use what speed you can and you should raise Grimhold Castle long before dawn. Fassof and Cogga will take over then. Go now—and may the gods give you the luck you deserve!"

Corin was first to lead his horse down the ramp. The others had sold their horses before leaving Kashorn but Corin had insisted to Barin that Thunderhoof come with them. And Barin was happy to let him. And so during their brief stay on the island Thunderhoof got to know the wild steeds of Valkador.

"Brace yourself boy, this will be a tad chilly." Corin patted Thunder's back. But the big horse didn't respond, so Corin launched his dripping body onto the beast's back and commenced guiding Thunder ashore. The others followed on their steeds in grim determined silence.

Last came Zukei, her black eyes glittering as she studied the shore for foes. The seven and their horses were soaked and half frozen when they reached the track leading up through the dark shadow of hill and forest.

An hour saw them coated in night with stars above and dense pines hedging their way. The road ran arrow-straight and they drove the horses hard. It was cold, and fresh rime glittered the sides of the road like silver tracing.

Hooves thudded and riders focused on the task ahead. Now and then an owl would call and a second answer, whilst further away the eerie cry of wolf and fox filled an otherwise silent forest.

Two hours before dawn, the woods fell away on either side, and a dark craggy line of bleak hills lined the night horizon. Thrust in their midst like a broken tooth was the winking shadow of what must surely be a fortress.

"Grimhold," Cogga yelled in Corin's ear. "About ten miles to go. We'd best keep our wits sharp from now on." They filed into single column, Cogga and Fassof at front, Corin next with the brothers behind him, Zukei and Bleyne at the rear. These last two were in their element tonight.

The jagged hills rose as the distance shrank, and the grey vastness of Grimhold Castle took form ahead. The winking lights were torches high on battlement and keep. It looked strong did Grimhold, hard and grey and cold as those who dwelt within. Though much smaller than Car Carranis, its commanding position crowning the line of hills gave it an impressive and foreboding power.

The seven rode on apace until reaching a clump of knotty thorns. Here Fassof signalled they dismount and go through their next moves amid whispers.

"Two ropes," Fassof nodded to his and Cogga's horse. "And two climbers to haul them up over the battlements. Cogga is good with a knife, so he will take the first rope. I need a volunteer for the other." Corin, Zukei, Danail, and Bleyne all stood forward.

"Fuck, I only need one of you, else why bother with the sodding ropes?" Fassof muttered. "Bleyne—you're the man, I well remember your catlike skills from Kashorn Harbour. You will need three knives."

"I brought four," Bleyne replied pointedly.

"And we need someone here making sure the horses are ready when we come running back." This time no one volunteered. "Come on, it's an important job, I'd do it myself but I'm going to be Tail End Charlie with the ropes."

"You do it," Tolemon told his brother.

"Why not you?" Danail replied; alone of the crew he looked nervous and edgy.

"It has to be one of you," Corin growled.

"Who says?" Tolemon glared at him.

"I do," Corin's growl deepened and Tolemon reached for his sword.

"Enough children!" Zukei stepped forward. "I will wait here and you clowns better get moving."

"You, more than anyone are needed in that fortress," Cogga said. "I've seen this warrior fight," he explained. "She's phenomenal!" Cogga look pleased with himself, having recently mastered that word. In the end Fassof decided to stay with the horses, lest they argue until dawn and then get skewered by guards.

"You'll have to be Tail End Charlie with the ropes," he told Danail. "Don't leave them dangling and don't let any sentry see them. They need to be coiled neat and ready for casting off when the team gets back. Now piss off the lot of you while it's still dark!"

The six stole low toward the grey mass of wall ahead. Cogga signalled they make for the right of the keep where the walls were shortened by the rise of a hillock. Once they reached the nearest wall's base, Cogga and Bleyne took twenty paces apiece and then, ropes over shoulders, commenced scaling the wall with the aid of the daggers wedged in mortar, allowing feet and hand to purchase, lift, remove knife, and so on.

Bleyne reached the top before Cogga got halfway up, despite his legendary castle storming skills. Bleyne, after casting his gaze along the battlements, tied one end around a crenulation and tossed the rope down.

Corin grabbed it and started hauling his body up, Clouter swinging from his back. Zukei followed. Then Cogga's rope hit soil and Danail and Tolemon took to climbing fast as they could.

Twenty minutes later they stood on the battlements, the star-studded night granting just enough visibility to award wide views of wood and rimy pasture below. Danail shivered. "What's next?" he said.

"This way." Cogga led them in the opposite direction of the keep, looming like a square rock behind. Corin noted that Grimhold Castle was circular in shape and they were following that circle toward the rear where another, smaller keep led to stairs leading down to the castle main below.

"Guards?" Zukei hinted at the smaller rear keep.

"Probably half a dozen," Cogga nodded. "They should be on the walls too but they're most likes drunk and dicing in there with the rest in the main keep and manning the front gates. They won't be overly vigilant—only an idiot would attack Grimhold Castle. Now do your stuff woman!" Cogga hissed Zukei forward.

"Go with her," Corin told Bleyne, who nodded and trotted behind the sleek woman, both vanishing inside the keep. Two minutes later Bleyne emerged grinning.

"There were eight," he said cheerfully. "She did for most of them; she's rather good you know." Tolemon and Danail exchanged baffled glances whilst Corin rolled his eyes.

They entered the keep and soon noted the seven still corpses sprawled on the floor (the eighth one twitched a bit until Zukei's Karyia stilled it). "I hate an unfinished job," she told Bleyne.

Cogga scanned the stairs and castle main below. "No movement," he said, satisfied. "They should either be asleep or too drunk to find their cocks. Best we get to it, the hall is close by. After the stairs we turn left, there's a barracks and some stores and stables. Beyond these lies the king's hall. It's a dingy shithole as I remember."

"That I do not doubt," Corin nodded.

"Everybody ready?" Cogga asked and the team nodded. "Off we

go then." But halfway down the stairs, the sudden clash of steel, bay of hounds, and harsh cries of angry voices announced that the party had started without them.

Corin slammed Clouter into his palms and crashed through the hall's wooden door amid splinters and flying nails. "Shallan!" Corin yelled. "I'm here!" Then a horn blast split the night, and chaos took hold again.

***

"So what's it like down there?"

"Hot and sticky, and every creature bites. I doubt you'd like it."

"Hmm, Permio was enough for me—all those flies and grubby little cheese vendors."

"Yamondo is not Permio, my friend. Has Corin told you nothing?"

"He never tells anybody anything."

"I like it here—surprisingly." Ulani and Barin were seated on a bench at the stern of *The Starlight Wanderer,* each with an ale clenched in fist. "And the cold doesn't bother me like I thought it would."

"So Zukei's your daughter?" Barin's shrewd blue gaze caught Ulani's sharp glance.

"Aye, so?"

"I like her, and she's been good to have around, especially for poor Shallan." Barin looked morose for a moment. "So what is it with her?"

"How do you mean?"

"Like, why is she so angry all the time?"

"Angry? Her? You haven't met my wives." Ulani slurped a half pint in one gulp and then belched famously. "I like to travel, Barin."

"You're not going to tell me, are you?"

"She's wanted in three countries: Yamondo, Vendel, and Shen."

"Shen?"

"Yep, she did some contract work way out east a while back.

She's good at what she does, Barin."

"Killing people."

"Zukei was the highest paid assassin in western Vendel. It's why that man over there," Ulani wagged a finger to where some of the crew sat playing dice. "Wogun is it? He's scared of her, knows who she is. But Zukei, though subtle with dagger and garrotte, lacks communication skills. She pissed off some pretty high people in Vendel and hence got banished. She came home and no one wanted her around—especially two of my wives, though her mother still harbours a soft spot for her. I got a lot of earache so I was obliged to banish her too."

"And she hasn't forgiven you."

"Doesn't look like it—does it? So then Zukei went off in a huff to Shen. That's a weird country, Barin. A long way away."

"I never believed it really existed."

"It does. They are all sorcerers there, and killing is a very subtle art in that land. Zukei killed the wrong people, so again she had to leave. But this time she was caught and sold as a slave in irons, eventually ending up in a market in Syrannos, where she tells me she murdered her master and scat, but was caught and marked for execution."

"Until Taic saved her."

"Your nephew, yes. I need to thank him."

"He's an idle tosspot."

"You like him really."

Barin pulled a face. "Just a little." They sat and drank for another two hours, whilst Barin's crew rested, drank, and diced some more. Nearby the Rorshai juggled daggers with Greggan and the Rangers, each participant placing wagers on the winners.

Prince Tarin appeared now and then without saying much, and the night passed quiet and slow as they waited for the sound of hoof beats announcing their friends' return.

"Care for an arm wrestle?" Barin asked Ulani. "Corin says you'd beat me, but I must disagree."

"Only one way to find out." Ulani slapped his meaty palm in Barin's and the pair commenced grunting and heaving and straining for twenty minutes before Ulani's forearm curled around Barin's and levered down hard. The was a loud thwack that turned heads as the bench snapped in two.

"I win!" Ulani laughed flexing his hand.

"That was cheating!" Barin complained. "Straight arms or no win."

After six more matches, three wins apiece and twelve ales sunk, the pair slunk into a heavy slumber until woken by noises as dawn broke through the eastern sky.

***

The king laughed as his men grabbed Shallan and dragged her toward him. Behind them Hagan scowled, not pleased with how things were going.

"What did you expect?" Rael looked tired and not a little bored. "Let him play a bit, then we'll get our dosh and piss off somewhere warm. I'm sick of winter. What about Golt? Never been to Golt."

Shallan spat and clawed and kicked, but the grinning Leethmen tossed her to the floor at Daan Redhand's feet. "She's a pretty wee thing. How much do you want for her, Assassin?"

"A lot," Rael answered without looking up.

"She's a duchess," Hagan added. "A brave lady to boot."

"I know who she is." Daan's iron-studded boot scraped a trace of blood on Shallan's cheek. She said nothing, just glared up at him. "Lady Shallan of Vangaris, who so boldly came to rescue her brothers from my father. Daughter of that tosser Tomais and rumoured frigid. A cold wench and a friend of Barin of Valkador."

"Barin's worth ten of you!" Shallan spat up at the king, whose smile faded as he kicked her in the stomach, causing her to double up in pain.

"Barin's dead meat when I get hold of him." He turned to his guards. "I grow weary of this, strip her."

One of the guards reached for Shallan's shirt but froze as his comrade pitched forward with a horn-handled blade in his back. A second knife tore into the other guard's face and all turned, including Shallan, to see the huge gnarly figure filling the doorway.

Cornelius the Faen, by some called The Horned Man, had come for his daughter at last.

Chapter 34

Golganak

A witch-storm is not a pleasant sight to witness—even from afar. To be beneath one is to perish. Such was the fate of Kella City that winter day. Wind arrived first, then a sudden noisy dark that smothered the city and hushed any whispering voices. Broiling clouds hurled yellow lightning daggers from the gathering storm, as the dragon beat his mighty wings through its dark and crash-landed like an avalanche on the palace roof in Kella City.

Vaarg, his full might returned after the recovery of the spear, unleashed his fury, jetting a gush of flame through the palace windows, causing glass to explode and tapestries and carpets within the gloomy silent halls to ignite. Those few Groil Caswallon had kept as retainers screamed as their flesh dissolved, consumed by that alien heat.

High above in the Astrologer's Nest, Caswallon was more prepared. He watched the dragon claw and scrape at the palace as his funnel flame sent another jet inside. This one reached the throne room, but even dragonfire had no power over The Glass Throne. The room was in ruins, but the throne glistened like wet glass and Vaarg, bored, turned his attention to the rest of the city.

Kella blazed like a fallen star as Morak's witch-storm added more lightning spears to Vaarg's tongues of flame, and as he worked his storm, Morak held Golganak aloft to counter the battery of spell blasts now issuing like tracer bullets from the Astrologer's Nest—a lone aloof finger in the maelstrom of the witch-storm.

Caswallon was fighting back.

Vaarg lifted skyward at word from his master. Once level with the lone window of Caswallon's study, the dragon's huge eye found the sorcerer standing alone amid charts and scrolls and looking back at the dragon with grim determination in his coaly eyes.

"TIME TO DIE MORTAL!" Vaarg's next blast funnelled through the window, but Caswallon's prepared incantations rebuffed that flame and he remained unharmed, as did his study. Vaarg fired again, harder, and this time Caswallon's detonator-trap exploded white powder in the dragon's face.

Vaarg roared red froth as that acid white agony blinded him temporarily, and his wings folded like crumpled leather as he plummeted, a thousand-ton lead weight crashing onto and through the palace roof.

Morak's own spell-shield protected him against that detonation. As the dragon fell, his rider lifted feather light from Vaarg's back and, riding the spear as a rocket, Morak circled the Astrologer's Nest three times, wording breaking-spells as he did.

A cornered cat, Caswallon watched his enemy circle warily and worded counter-spell after counter-spell. Meanwhile below, recovered and raging, the dragon crawled free of Kella Palace, shook off the mass of rubble and dust and other clutter stuck to his hide, and resumed torching what was left of the city.

Vaarg was in a bad mood now; it had been millennia since last he'd felt pain and he hadn't enjoyed the reminder. Occasionally he would send blasts up to the lean finger where Caswallon still held court. But these had no effect, and Vaarg soon lost interest.

Instead he crawled through the city, incinerating the streets one at a time, spiteful and greedy for destruction as only a dragon can be. Those Groil and men still around were fried, as was anything else moving.

Even the fields outside were grilled like overdone bacon. For over an hour Vaarg patrolled the streets of Kella until nothing but ash and rubble remained. After that, he turned his lizard attentions to the city walls, and like a bored puppy commenced chewing and clawing at them, until they too had crumpled to rubble. Finally satisfied with his demolitions, Vaarg returned to the palace to level that building too.

Caswallon, increasingly desperate, discharged a ward spell so violent it caught Morak off guard and sent him flying backwards in wild spirals, still gripping his spear in hand. Morak steadied his steering rod and Golganak glistened like polished black marble as it responded to his instructions.

Morak prepared another strike, but not before Caswallon had time to reach his glass ball, grasp it close and gaze within its cloudy depths. After a panicky second scrying, Caswallon found his armies. They were still a day away, both the Groil and Gonfalez's legions marching—a dark host toward Kella. They were moving at speed but not nearly fast enough.

Caswallon dropped the glass globe in despair as it finally came to him that he had lost and all his careful schemes and plans were for naught. Outside, Morak hovered triumphantly, his legs astride the spear, its obsidian needle pointing toward his enemy's fragile heart.

Morak smiled. He could feel Caswallon's heart flutter like a trapped bird with a broken wing. He uttered a brief rune-chant, and Golganak's acid black glowed and shimmered, unleashing a ray of fear like a cold canker creeping inside Caswallon's flesh.

"You have failed, Caswallon!" Morak's mocking voice filled Caswallon's head like tearing tin. "We gave you so much and yet you betrayed us!" Morak's face hovered outside the sorcerer's window. It was a beautiful face—noble and wise, but angry. Gone were the dog snout and burnt scars, replaced by a radiance of dark power.

"You could have been great but instead you are nothing!" Caswallon raised a withered palm to reflect what he knew was coming. Morak, astride the spear, telescoped it forward until its needle-point shredded through stone and glass, reaching inside the Astrologer's Nest, until Caswallon, eyes screwed shut, felt Golganak's point chisel into his heart.

He screamed as that insidious metal entered his veins, more poisonous than mercury, more acidic than bile, and he felt himself clawed him down to Yffarn with a million invisible griping fingers.

Caswallon's head stung from a thousand ant bites. His mortal flesh dissolved, yet Caswallon remained cognitive amid his agony and thus was exposed to He who waited.

"A sacrifice to you, Master!" Caswallon heard Morak's voice coming from a very long way away. Caswallon's fetch turned slowly; even his ghost felt like torn paper discarded on a fire, and as he turned a voiceless cry fled his withered lips.

Caswallon stood in a cavern dripping with slime. There were faces all around him, mocking, leering gargoyles and dark nameless horrors that never saw the light of day. Evil visages every one—he recognised the many Soilfin among them almost as friends. The sorcerer in him knew these creatures for acolytes, servants of Old Night, Morak's only master.

Caswallon's ghost felt the presence of eyes somewhere below, a gaze far heavier than anvils, pulling him down through the solid wet stone of the black cavern's surface. Again Caswallon's ghost-scream went unheard as he was sucked through the floor to emerge in yet another cavern.

This second cave was filled like a chalice with dark liquid that Caswallon knew to be the blood of Old Night. The pull of those eyes was worse than before; Caswallon felt his soul torn apart like a cracked egg on a stove as his petrified gaze was trapped by the ravenous eyes residing inside the huge, severed head on a plinth above him.

The god laughed as He opened Caswallon up and laid him out amid his lies for all to see. Old Night was inside the sorcerer now and Caswallon's silent screams started again, their intensity so violent several lesser gods and demi-gods felt it nine planets away.

Sorcery has a way of paying back its owner eventually; it comes with an invisible label: "USE WITH CAUTION."

Such was the fate of Caswallon of Kelthaine, usurper, sorcerer, and murderer, and yet a man once considered the wisest in that realm. But he had dabbled too deep in the dark arts, and thus was he rewarded.

The god slid His heavy essence inside the fragile shell of the sorcerer's writhing soul. A frail broken thing, but just strong enough to enable Him to reclaim His remaining body parts from the other eight worlds where they had been locked in sealed vessels after His defeat at the end of the Second War against His father, The Weaver.

Cul-Saan the Firstborn watched in dispassion as His head dissolved on the plinth like melting wax, breaking the stone in two. In didn't matter, for He no longer had use for that head. Now the sorcerer's fetch would serve as ample conduit, allowing Him to break free of this jail at last and roam the void once more.

Throughout the mountain, Old Night's creatures chittered and danced on seeing their master returning to the world—albeit in shade format only. Cul-Saan heeded them not. He drifted up from the dungeons below that mountain like an ill wind, His form now taking the shape of a black eyeless owl. Then, with a single sharp bitter cry, the First-born broke free of the mountain prison and shot forth—a reverse meteor—into the heavens above, even as the first lava ash of the exploding mountain levelled the jungle and cities of eastern Vendel, swallowing them whole. Old Night, the great enemy of Ansu, had returned.

All this Morak witnessed as he sat bestride his spear. In slow circles he dropped to the palace below, where Vaarg watched him with greedy eyes.

***

The raven sped north, a black speck above the veins of red below. He flew swift and strong until he found his brother hopping amidst the greying, rime-glistened bodies of the dead outside Car Carranis.

"Uncle is back," the first raven croaked to his brother. "We need to tell Father." The second bird cawed agreement and the pair lifted into the sky in unison. Together the birds winged up to where Oroonin sat contemplating an elaborate chess game inside the intricate confines of His multi-layered mind. Oroonin stirred as His ravens found Him and settled amid dark ruffles on His cloak, each picking a shoulder.

"What is it, my children?"

"That which is foreseen," said the first raven.

"Has come to pass," added the second, pecking an inch-long space-louse buried within the god's cloak and consuming it whole.

"Then it is time at last." Oroonin smiled and clapped His hands with relish. "We've waited long for this, my birds!" The ravens squawked and hopped free of Oroonin's shoulders, and the Wanderer's hot excited breath steamed like a venting kettle as He strode from His remote sky palace, summoning Uppsalion and His hounds. The third and final war of the gods had begun. But which side would He take? That night, the Wild Hunt patrolled the night skies again.

***

General Gonfalez called a halt ten miles from the ruins of Kella City. Beside him, his men muttered and shook with fear. Gonfalez tried to speak but no words could find his lips. Ahead raged fires, a blaze so horrible the heat reached them where they sat their horses, barely controlling the beasts. The sky to the west was occluded by ash falling like grey snow and blanketing wood and field and hill ahead.

"We must turn back!" One of Gonfalez's captains yelled in his ear. "We cannot linger here!" Others joined in the cry and Gonfalez nodded.

"We return to Kelthara!" Gonfalez yelled at his troops. "We take that city once and for all! The sorcerer is dead. I rule Kelthaine now!" His men muttered and stared at him, and even Gonfalez wasn't convinced by his tone. But they obeyed him, for what else could they do?

But as Gonfalez's army of ex-Tigers turned about they found the silent legions of Groil marching toward them. "What's this?" Gonfalez shouted. "What's going on? Surely they're not attacking? I—"

A racket like a sawmill above had men staring up just as the dragon fell upon them. Vaarg settled in the midst of Gonfalez's army as men fell from their horses and crashed into each other in terror.

Gonfalez watched with numb lips as a small figure stepped down from the dragon's back. He appeared as a handsome man, small in build and clad in simple black. He approached Gonfalez in a calm, easy manner.

"I have no need of your army," Morak smiled as he raised Golganak aloft and Gonfalez voided his bowels, feeling the sudden unleashed horror of that obsidian shaft. "And I have no need of you, soldier. But my spear (he shook Golganak) can always use more souls to drink."

And so the killing started, as dragon, spear, and Groil (eagerly now serving their true master) fell upon Gonfalez's men, killing every single one. Once they were dead, the feeding began. Gonfalez's sightless eyes gazed like a stricken deer as a two-headed Groil rose over his broken body and tore him open with his serrated sword.

That night, as Morak stood alone in the grove at the appointed hour, he felt the shade of his master come visit. "The realm is yours," Morak said as the massive presence of Old Night silenced the dark trees.

"YOU HAVE DONE WELL, MOST FAITHFUL SERVANT," the voice tore through the trees, shaking them and loosening soil so that slimy things broke out on its surface. "THIS WORLD SHALL BE

YOUR REWARD, BUT FIRST YOU MUST CLEANSE IT OF THE SERVANTS OF MY LESSER KIN."

"That won't take long." Morak smiled at the shadow creeping through the trees. "I shall break this realm and then move east where most are already my slaves. Dragon and spear shall pave the way!"

"THAT IS WELL. NOW I MUST AWAY TO RECLAIM MY BODY. ONCE I HAVE DONE THAT I WILL AVENGE MY MALTREATMENT BY MY FATHER AND KIN!"

A flicker of deeper dark, then the trees shook again—though this time in relief as the terrible presence of Old Night left the atmosphere and soared up into the night sky.

From his own lofty seat, Oroonin watched the black owl sail between the stars. Big Brother was off to reclaim His severed body parts. Once he had those, or rather the runes and strength locked within them, Old Night would muster his gang and issue challenge throughout the cosmos.

Oroonin know the pattern; after all this was just revisiting old ground. But this time the outcome could well prove different, so best He keep in with Big Bad Brother—at least in the short term. Oroonin smiled as He leaped up into Uppsalion's stardust saddle and bid the death horse ride out from His halls, and chase the dark speck of His departing brother out into the void.

And so it begins...

***

Queen Ariane watched the distant cloud covering the western horizon, her heart heavy as lead. The enemy had gone, and now they had new friends. She should be delighted but instead her belly shook with sudden dread.

"What do you make of it, my lord?"

Halfdan stood beside her, his face resolute and grim as her own. "I do not know, my Queen. But I fear that whatever is occurring in Kella City will soon fall upon us. We must make ready for something we can scarce comprehend, and by that I mean we must be stout of heart and summon courage we didn't know we had."

"I concur," Ariane nodded and behind her Tarello and Jaan and Valentin all nodded too. "Survival is the key until your son returns from the north."

"My son—hah! You put too much faith in that one. Corin is a reckless boulder crashing through trees at midnight. I love him and know him to be special, but he is only one man, Queen Ariane. One individual. Despite his destiny. What we need is your wizard Zallerak's knowledge and skills, but I assume we've still no news from that quarter?"

"He's gone." Silon joined them and squinted at the reddish dark line on the western horizon. "So Kella City burns and with it our hopes of a new Crystal King," Silon sighed and rubbed the diamond earring he always wore. "Looks like we need a new plan, people."

"Corin won't let us down!" Cale's pale scared face popped up from nowhere, causing Halfdan glance his way in curious fashion.

"And who might this young pipsqueak be?" Lord Halfdan said.

"Squire Cale." Ariane winked at the boy who beamed in return. "Despite his perennial impertinence, this one has proved an asset in the main. Cale has a stout heart, my lord, and he's shrewd for such a ragamuffin."

"And I approve of your sentiments, Master Cale." It was Halfdan's turn to smile. "And hope that you are right. But we need to rethink our moves. I for one suggest we vacate this fortress sooner rather than later and therefore distance ourselves from whatever is happening over there." Halfdan pointed to the glow now spreading in the west.

"You are right, my lord," Ariane flashed the former High King's brother a brave grin. "Kelthara is a city of ghosts. It saps the will of our army and we need to fight on familiar ground. I propose we return to Wynais and make our final stand in the Silver City, where Elanion can intervene on our behalf should she wish to.

"What say you captains mine?"

All agreed, as no one wanted to linger in Kelthara a moment

longer, and marching for Kella City was no longer an option. That only left Wynais. Ariane departed from Kelthara that very afternoon, her captains and army riding with her, and Lord Halfdan's force alongside, and Kethara's surviving citizens joined them, having no desire to be left behind. The company made for a brave sight that afternoon.

"What about Corin?" Galed asked her as they trotted their horses down the Great South Road towards the Kelwyn border.

"Cale is right. Corin won't let us down, I'm certain of it. Too much has happened not to believe in him now. This game isn't over, it's just shifting its focus, and our job is to stay alive through all the coming chaos."

"Sorry I asked." Galed grinned slightly. "But I too believe in Corin, yet I once believed I never would. We live in the weirdest times, my Queen!"

"They'll write songs about us one day!" Cale piped up alongside his friend.

"I'd rather be alive in a tavern than dead in a song," Tamersane said quietly and startled faces turned his way. Tamersane hardly socialised these days and instead spent most his time alone with his woman, Teret. "Just sayin'," the queen's cousin smiled briefly at Cale, before his face fell wan and empty again.

"How is he faring?" Ariane asked Teret a day later, whilst the gentle woods of Kelwyn displayed the first buds of early spring. It felt warmer than it had been in months and the queen took that for a good sign.

"Better," Teret replied. The Rorshai healer still maintained her distance when she could, but at least she was less hostile. "But he still has a way to go and I fear will never be the man he was before killing his brother."

"None of us can return to who we once were," Ariane replied. "It's part of growing up. Hard lessons have to be learned." Her face softened and she reached across and clutched Teret's sleeve. "Please tell your man I love him, Teret, and know also that I would love you too, as your queen and kinswoman—you have only to request it."

"I will tell him," Teret inclined her head stiffly and without further word guided her horse back to join her lover.

"Strange woman," Silon said; riding close to the queen, he had heard her exchange with Teret.

"She's strong and faithful—I like her."

"Me too." Silon smiled at the queen. "Teret is proud and stern like all Rorshai. They are a strong people, Ariane. Tough and self reliant."

The queen smiled back. "Is there anywhere in the known world that you haven't been, master merchant?"

"Ptarni—I've never been to Ptarni. And they say Shen is interesting, though I doubt I'll see that land either. I'm getting old, Ariane. Ready for retirement in Vioyamis should fates allow."

"You'll never retire," Ariane laughed. "You are too much the meddler."

"Your words, O queen, are sharper than daggers."

Two days later, the denizens of Wynais were delighted to see their queen's army emerge resplendent on the road flanking Lake Wynais, along with many other foreign riders. But the joy was short-lived, for the dragon paid call the very next evening.

Chapter 35

The Horned Man

A corpse spun past Rael's head as he dived under the table. Beside him, Hagan's eyes were agog as the huge horned figure pierced another warrior with a tusk and split him open from gut to groin.

"What the...?" Hagan followed suit with his ally and took refuge under the table. This wasn't their fight, and more than gold he wanted to keep the skin on his back.

Noise had erupted in the hall as the king hurled insults at his men, yelling them to bring down the creature with their spears, which most inconveniently were racked outside in the armoury—anything other than eating knives being banned from the hall. This king was not big on trust.

From somewhere outside, a horn blast filled an empty gap in the eruptions in the hall. Shallan seized that momentary distraction. She rolled, found her toes and leapt arrow-swift up at Redhand, head-butting him in the chin with her skull. Redhand sprawled backwards amid flailing arms.

"Father, I am with you!"

Another horn blast outside, and Shallan smiled recognising her gift from her father. They had come for her—her friends! But The Horned Man was hedged in now as Redhand's warriors recovered from their initial surprise, and more arrived from outside with the requested spears and swiftly surrounded the tall figure.

"Father!" Shallan screamed as she witnessed a spearman get through his guard and pierce that hirsute hide, stabbing Cornelius in the chest. Another caught him at the back of the thigh, whilst a third stabbed hard into his side. The Horned Man sank to his knees.

"Kill that fucking thing!" King Redhand, nose bloody, had regained his feet and was kicking his way towards the wounded Cornelius. "Wait, let him live so we can kill him slowly!"

Just then another crash announced that Corin an Fol had arrived with Clouter in full swing, and two Leethmen caught in its path were hacked down.

"Who is that?" A warrior blinked and the king punched him to the floor.

"Kill that tosser too!" King Daan was beside himself.

"This is somewhat predictable," Rael Hakkenon observed as Corin's shouting announced his presence to the pair of skulkers under the table. "What is it with that Longshanks? He can't miss out on anything."

Hagan smiled slowly. "I'm glad he's come." The horn blasted inside the hall and Zukei leapt to Corin's aid. clubbing a warrior with Shallan's horn whilst slicing a second with her Karyia. Then arrows filled the hall like stinging wasps as Bleyne took aim from a far corner.

"This crew never fail to disappoint." Rael curled a lip. "I actually think I'm going to miss them."

Corin saw Shallan hedged in a corner by the King's fur-lined throne. He made a noise rather like a squealing sow and hacked across to her, taking out three warriors standing in the way with as many sweeps from Clouter.

Close by, the brothers Tolemon and Danail clashed swords

with Leethmen whilst Cogga kept an eye on Corin's back as the Longswordsman scooped up his lover and fled the hall.

Bleyne's arrows fell on the cluster of spearmen surrounding The Horned Man, and with alien strength, Cornelius staggered to his feet and made for the hall's exit. Men sought to stop him but Bleyne's shafts found them too.

Tolemon and Danail fought side-by-side and retreated to the doors, whilst Cogga yelled Zukei and Bleyne quit scrapping and vacate the hall. King Daan, blocked by his own sweaty warriors, kicked and swore until he got a glimpse of the fleeing raiders.

Tolemon's sword cut the arm from a spearman whilst Danail stepped beside him and opened the gut of another. But a third warrior dived low and caught the younger brother with a vicious slice under his right arm. Danail toppled, and Tolemon, yelling, gripped his brother and dragged him outside.

Bleyne filled the gate guards with arrows and then threw his weight against the doors. Cogga helped as did Zukei, and then The Horned Man strode forward, towering above them, and a kick from his hoof reduced the doors to splinters. The assault team did their best to flee into the night. They were aided inadvertently by King Daan, who currently had a full berserker on him, and had murdered three of his own warriors before calming down enough to realise that the enemy were getting away.

Rael chose that moment to roll free of the table and grin at the dribbling king.

"Would you care for some help? I'm currently available." Behind him Hagan found his feet and gazed about at the carnage in the hall with questioning eyes.

"Me too," the Morwellan growled after a moment's reflection. It took Redhand almost half an hour to cool down enough to have the wits to send a squad of riders out from the stables armed with crossbow and spear. By that time, the fleeing party had re-joined Fassof and were galloping like mad things back down the road, dawn's grey light following behind.

All galloped save The Horned Man, who crept off into the woods and disappeared. "I will stall them," Shallan heard Cornelius calling from the darkness behind. "Go daughter, and know that I love you!"

"Father, no!" Shallan called out from behind Corin, as their horse's hooves drummed the dusty road beneath them.

It is my time beloved...

Cornelius's last words hovered inside Shallan's head, and she wept and nestled her head against her lover's back as they left her father behind. And so they left Grimhold Castle.

Daan's first hunting party came unstuck outside the castle walls. Cornelius tore upon them again, killing a score before reinforcements filled him with crossbow bolts, and again he sank to his knees.

Redhand joined his men, and taking a long knife, slid it across The Horned Man's throat. And at last Cornelius, one of the oldest and noblest of the Faen, departed this realm and was again free to seek the soul of the mortal woman whose restless shade awaited him in the quiet groves outside Vangaris.

Nothing is ever forgotten.

***

An orange glow at their backs announced the sun's warming presence as they neared the place where woods and track led down to the Westfjord and Barin's ship. Fassof led the way as they guided their beasts down through wood and vale to the silver glint of water below.

Fassof yelled Barin who stood like a grizzly bear just woken in springtime, his hair shaggier than normal and his beard caught in knots.

"Did you have a rough night?" Cogga grinned at his captain as he vaulted on board, but Barin had only eyes for Shallan.

"One wounded, aside that we're in good shape," Fassof announced and then immediately after commenced hollering at the crew to get ready for departure. Corin and Shallan had hardly spoken during their flight. He turned to her as they found their feet safe within the creaking strakes of *The Starlight Wanderer*.

"You need sleep," Corin kissed her on the lips and held her to him. "I love you, Shallan. I was lost without you."

It was like she hadn't heard him. "He gave his life for me, the ultimate sacrifice from one who has lived since the dawn of time. My father, Corin. I never knew him!" The tears fell free on her cheeks again.

"Get some sleep, my love." Corin kissed her again and led her to the cabin Barin had reserved for them. "You must rest. Once you have regained your strength we can talk of all these things." Corin stroked her hair and flicked a stray lock free from her left eye. "And we have time." He left her resting on the bunk and ventured outside to see what occurred.

"How is she?" Barin glared darkly at him as Corin approached the wheel. Standing with him were Olen and Arami; both looked uneasy and ready to be off this ship, their Rorshai sea legs not being established.

The Starlight Wanderer was cutting a clean path through the blue of Westfjord as the sun rose like fire behind them. It was a beautiful northern morning, but Barin's face was strangely grim.

"She'll be all right, but her mind's wandering a bit. We had help in Grimhold, a strange creature. Shallan called him 'Father.' I don't know why."

"What became of him?"

"I fear he died enabling our escape. A noble being, I would have liked to have thanked him."

Barin nodded but said nothing on the matter, but Olen, behind him, fixed Corin a quizzical stare.

"What is it?" Corin asked the Rorshai.

"Nothing," Olen shrugged, but both he and Arami looked as tense as Barin looked miserable.

"Fine," Corin said. "Glad that's sorted out, enjoy the sunshine you pair." Olen and Arami didn't respond so Corin turned to Barin instead. "And how fare you, Northman?" Corin's hard blue-grey gaze studied his friend. "You appear uneasy as these Rorshai." Barin's expression reminded Corin of his friend Roman before they reached Crenna harbour. A kind of sorrow laced with self-doubt—it didn't suit him.

"I had bad dreams last night," Barin said.

"I never have good ones," Corin answered but Barin's face remained grim, and the Rorshai were no help, so he left them all to their morbid thoughts. Instead Corin found Taic, who was dependably cheerful as ever.

"Your uncle seems in glum spirits. Said he had bad dreams while we were away."

Taic grinned. "Surprised he remembered; he drained a half barrel with King Ulani. Impressive even for him." Corin smiled and nodded that he understood. "Uncle misses Marigold and the girls," Taic added. "Seeing them and then leaving again was hard on him. He often gets mopey after calling in at home. He's a big softy at heart, you know."

"I know."

"A propos, King Ulani is voiding his bowels if you need him. He's been down there a while."

"I'm good for the moment, thanks."

Taic nodded and sighed as he looked at the swelling morning. "I like Ulani," he said after a moment's thought on the matter. "He's like Uncle's long-lost twin."

"The resemblance is astounding," Corin agreed.

"Still no sign of pursuit?" Prince Tarin appeared, his change of topic turning their gaze to stern, where only clear water and sunlight showed between the green slopes of Westfjord.

"Give 'em time," Taic said. "Redhand keeps his vessels near to Grimhold at the far end of Westfjord. I suspect he's manning them already with a plan to reduce our island to ashes."

"His ships are slow tubs that take in water." Cogga joined them whilst rubbing salve on a shallow wound he'd received on his forearm. "We have time to prepare."

"How fares the wounded one?" Tarin asked and Corin felt sudden shame. He had forgotten all about Danail, currently pale and resting below, whilst being attended to by Ruagon, the ship's chef, who doubled as a surgeon when needed.

"Not good." Bleyne was counting his arrows close by; he was down to a dozen but seemed unconcerned. "I think Shallan is with him now."

"Best I go down then." Corin made to leave.

"Leave it, Zukei's there too." Bleyne's gaze held Corin who shrugged. "Ruagon says there's tension between the older brother and Shallan. Seems like an on-going thing. And Tolemon blames her for Danail's current state."

"That's total bollocks." Sveyn had overheard and got his opinion on the matter in before anyone else could speak.

"Tolemon is hard work," Corin agreed, but concurred to leave matters be until he got Shallan away from her brothers and could speak to her alone.

Below in Barin's cabin, Danail was stretched out on the table, his chest heaving and his breathing shallow. His pale skin glistened with an unhealthy sheen. The wound in his side was deep, and Danail's mind was wandering.

Shallan knelt beside her wounded brother as Tolemon loomed behind. Close by, Zukei watched on as she sharpened her throwing hatchet with a whetstone.

"Why don't you put that away?" Tolemon glanced irritated in Zukei's direction. "That bloody scraping's getting on my nerves." She ignored him. "That girl doesn't need to be here," Tolemon told Shallan, whilst glaring at Zukei, who met his eye with an indifferent shrug.

"She is my friend and therefore welcome with me anytime."

"You have strange friends, Sister," Tolemon said. He was about to add more, but Danail opened his pale eyes, and seeing Shallan leaning over him smiled up at her. "Debt repaid, Sissie," Danail flashed her a wink and then winced as the pain lanced into him again. Shallan glanced at Ruagon, who shook his head.

"It doesn't look good," Ruagon muttered to Zukei behind him.

"Shit happens." Danail, overhearing them, smiled despite his pain. He coughed blood and his next words were choked out in slow chunks. "It's better...this...way. I feel...noble...a hero. Father would be proud." Danail's body shuddered and his eyes glazed blank.

"Not you too!" Shallan's tears spilled free as she crumpled over her brother. "First father then Vorreti. And now darling brave Danail. That just leaves..."

"You and me." Tolemon stiffened and after awarding Zukei a bleak stare departed the cabin.

"He's a cold bastard," Ruagon whispered in Zukei's ear.

"Aye, that he is," the woman nodded and followed Tolemon out onto he deck.

"He's dead." Zukei joined the gathering at the stern where Bleyne was still remaking his arrows, and Corin stood by Olen and Arami gazing out to sea. Taic was scratching his ear and Sveyn just looked morose.

Prince Tarin's eyes were on Zukei, whom he held in fascinated awe. Zukei ignored the prince and grabbed Corin's arm, catching his attention.

"You need to watch that Tolemon bastard," the woman warned him and then left without further word.

Corin sighed, deeming it time he ventured below. He found Shallan still weeping over her brother's corpse.

Corin stooped low beside her. "I'm sorry love, I truly am." When Shallan didn't respond, Corin left her to her grief and went to join Barin again.

"Is it too early for ale?" he said, his face now as grim as Barin's.

"It's never too early for ale."

Ulani appeared just then. "Have I missed something?" The king looked a bit rough this morning.

"We have a valiant warrior's life to celebrate," Fassof answered, as he swung close.

"That we do," Barin nodded, and then explained to Ulani how Danail had died. "Hey Taic, you tosspot, crack that last barrel and make sure everyone gets a bellyful. We've a tense sail ahead, and then defence preparations to make at Valkador. I want to give Redhand the welcome he deserves!"

They drank to Danail as they cast his body into the Westfjord's flat blue expanse. Shallan's wet eyes watched her brother sinking slowly down into the dark fathomless depths. It seemed to her that he waved back at her but it must have been the water wagging his arm.

An hour later, they funnelled into the twenty-mile narrows that led out to the open ocean beyond. It was during that voyage they encountered the giant on the rock and their course was changed without their control.

***

Rael rolled his eyes at the clumsiness and disorder surrounding him and Hagan. Added to the chaos surrounding quay and strand, Redhand's vessels were worse than tubs. If only he had his sharks then he would catch up with that Barin and his crew and finish some long overdue work.

But Rael summoned patience. This was proving a diverting trip even though it hadn't paid yet. It looked like they would be calling in on Valkador, doing a spot of murdering, raiding, and maybe some buggering about, before parting company— and not before he got recompense for delivery of the lady. Wasn't Rael's fault the twits had let her get away. But a chase would add nicely to the drama of things, in Rael's opinion.

He had missed out on killing the horned creature. Shame, he could have had some fun with that brute. But there was still Barin and the others, and most importantly longshanks, whom he and Hagan could share over a hot fire. That thought cheered the Assassin as Redhand's three bulky ships finally departed the quay and drifted out across the Westfjord.

That's if we ever get to Valkador...

Rael rubbed his mittens to dispel the cold and summoned what little patience he could muster. Beside him Hagan's face was set in stone. One again the Morwellan felt cheated and once again he blamed Corin.

Soon Longswordsman, soon!

***

Five lean vessels threaded north from the coast of Morwella where they had been wintering after fleeing the carnage west of Kelwyn. Cruel Cavan, having survived the slaughter at Ulan Valek, had found the crew of *The Black Serpent* in a deserted village near Vangaris, where they were eagerly draining the barrels of a recently abandoned tavern.

"We are needed in the north," Cavan said, as he kicked a tankard from the nearest pirate's hand, spilling beer all over his companions. No one complained. They all feared Cruel Cavan, and for good reason. Next to Rael Hakkenon, Cavan was the most dangerous man in Crenna, and the name "Cruel" had been given to him by Rael as a compliment on his knife work on captives. Cruel Cavan was a cunning, clever pirate and a demon with both sword and axe. Not a man to be gainsaid.

"Why north?" One of the stouter hearts present dared question him.

"Because our leader is up there and has need of us." Cavan said no more and none questioned him further. Besides, they wouldn't have grasped the truth even if he told them. He'd hardly believed it himself when he'd heard.

A winged goblin had visited him on The Wild Way, informing him that Rael Hakkenon (or "Mr Assassin" to use its words) was bound for Grimhold Castle with a female captive in tow. Suffice to say, Cavan had made for the coast pronto that next morning.

Chapter 36

The Ice Realm

Cliffs fell away on either side, and open sea filled the horizon, with one interruption: a black, weed-greasy island rising sheer and sharp from the churning waters surrounding it.

"That should not be there." Barin stared at the island as though it would pounce on him at any moment.

"Where did it come from?" Taic asked. "I mean, did it just pop up out of the water?"

"It's an island, not a fucking rabbit," Barin growled. "This smacks of sorcery." All eyes watched from prow and rails as the island rose fast and sleek ahead of them.

"Hadn't you better change course?" Corin grunted in Barin's ear.

"It shouldn't be there," Barin repeated, not listening.

"Well it bloody well is there! Hence, shouldn't we avert from our current course? That's just a suggestion, so don't get the hump."

Barin chewed his beard. "Fassof, out oars. Lads, get some muscles going!" Barin swung the wheel hard bringing the ship round to face south. That wasn't much help: a line of cliff blocked the southern route, and Barin swore enthusiastically.

"I think someone is determining our direction for us," observed Bleyne wryly, safe in the knowledge the Goddess would see them through any witchy stuff.

"And I think I know who," Corin added darkly, pointing up to the western end of the nearest cliff. A tiny figure stood there, cloaked and sporting a wide brimmed hat. Sunlight glinted of the tip of his spear. Corin cursed. "This is my fault, I pissed him off and now he's going to shaft us."

To his right King Ulani growled deep in his throat, "The ferryman?"

"He has several guises," Corin said.

"What now?" Fassof yelled, "Those cliffs are getting close."

"North!" yelled Barin. Not that there was much choice, that being the only direction showing a clear passage. Groaning, Barin worked the wheel again, his huge arms straining, whilst Fassof hollered the crew get aloft and get cracking. *The Starlight Wanderer* listed sharp to starboard as she barely cleared the rock-strewn base of the nearest cliff.

"It's going to be tight," Bleyne shouted in Corin's ear.

"I hadn't noticed," he replied.

Now the island loomed ahead again, bigger and blacker than before.

"This is getting monotonous," Corin said. "I mean why can't these divinities find other amusements that don't involve buggering us about?" No one was listening.

"What's that?" Sharp-eyed Bleyne had spotted a strange shape resembling a triangular boulder topping the sharp point of the island's crown.

"Don't know, don't care, really," Corin muttered.

"It's moving," Zukei observed with a snarl. "Look!"

"Fuck, but that's not good," added Taic. His jaw dropped in surprise along with everyone else's. The weird shape grew taller until they realized it was a being of sorts, standing precariously on two spindly legs and glaring down on them. A giant he was, huge and hideous, thin as a leek. Corin could see that the wretch's filthy hands were constrained by iron manacles, and vast chains attached these to the rock below.

Corin thought of Croagon down in Permio. But this giant wasn't blind. Nor was he muscular but skinny, gaunt, and shabby. But he was huge as a house and staring hostile straight at them.

"Bring her round lads!" Barin growled. "Come on!" Every spare hand was on the oars now, and even Prince Tarin took a turn. Corin heaved next to Olen and Arami, who were white-faced and silent.

"It's all right," Corin grinned manically at them. "If you hang out with me for long enough this sort of stuff happens now and then. Nothing untoward. You cannot say I haven't warned you." Olen awarded him a wild look but didn't reply.

The black island rose up like a tower of slime, the giant almost on top of them, straining and tugging at his chains. That was bad enough but then he stared howling, a woeful ululation and dismal racket that had everyone covering their ears with anything available.

Shallan found Corin and squeezed alongside. "Hello love," he smiled. "How are you feeling?" Corin pulled her between the oar and his waist and she snuggled close. "It's just another giant and sorcery and nonsense. Don't fret. I think we are all right," Corin observed. "We seem to be clearing yonder hazard."

"It's Crun," Shallan glanced up at the monstrous figure, now slipping behind them as Barin's skill and brawn guided *The Starlight Wanderer* free of the island's slippery surface by a whisper. Within minutes they were ploughing clean toward blue clear water, island and hollering skinny giant sinking slowly below.

"Who is Crun?" Corin asked her.

It was her brother who answered. Tolemon had been visiting the heads but had re-emerged to add his wisdom. "The Forsaken God. Legend states that seeing him is the harbinger of the final war on earth."

"Thanks," Corin said. "That's good to know."

"You are welcome." Tolemon locked eyes with Shallan's lover and curled his upper lip. Corin could tell Tolemon had things on his mind but that was small concern for him at the moment. "I don't think your brother likes me."

"I will talk to him, my love. Tolemon is bitter and proud but he'll come round."

"Your Zukei doesn't think so."

"Zukei doesn't know everything." Shallan's eyes flashed irritation. "I'm sorry Corin, I'm tired and so much has happened, is happening, it's wearing me out. You deserve more from me, darling man."

"Don't fuss." Corin flashed Shallan a brave grin. "This weird crap doesn't faze me any more, nor does old Oroonin with His tricks. I don't pretend to know His game, but at least I think we have an understanding with each other.

"I'm sorry about Danail," Corin added changing the subject. "A brave lad."

"The house of Morwella grows lean, Corin an Fol." Shallan turned and studied the black isle, still sinking slowly from view. "So it seems we are heading north. To what, I wonder?"

"Laras Lassladden." Corin's smile ran away from his face. "I haven't mentioned this to anyone, but I know that's our destination, and I also know we cannot avoid it. That island and its giant was Oroonin's doing. If we change course again doubtless he'll throw something else at us."

"I thought Laras Lassladden a myth."

"As did I until our recent trip to Valkador." Corin recounted his conversation with the Wanderer, and Shallan's eyes widened in alarm.

"You are over-bold, Corin an Fol. He is a fell spirit to taunt!"

"That he is but He pissed me off and... well, you know what I'm like."

"Yes I do, and I love you for it." Shallan smiled for the first time that day and kissed Corin warmly on the mouth. "Look, the island has gone!"

Corin turned and saw nothing but blue water lining the row of cliffs flanking their right for mile upon mile. "You had best go see Barin," Shallan said. "I'm for taking some rest. I'll see you soon, sweetest man." She kissed him again and departed from the deck. Zukei's and Tolemon's eyes watched her leave with different expressions.

Corin sighed and passed the oar to Olen, still white-faced and silent beside him. "I need to speak with the master," Corin told him, and Olen nodded without changing his expression.

Barin steered closer to the cliffs lining their east like an endless grey curtain of stone. "Your doing?" he grunted, as Corin approached.

"I believe so," Corin grunted back. "That spook wants me in the north. I've another job to do. You've heard of Laras Lassladden?"

"Certainly have. We call it Valhall in Valkador. But throughout my sojourns, I've also heard it called Hu Brysail, Ynis Scaffa, and Tyr Nanog. There are other names too. All speak of an enchanted mythical island where summer always rules."

"Our destination," Corin nodded. "That Huntsman is playing us, Barin, and it's all my fault."

"You put too much on yourself, boy!" Barin had recovered his humor and now grinned down at Corin. "I've been close to you long enough to realize you're the spark ignites their flames. Besides, I don't think we've much choice but to hold this course, witchery or no witchery."

"How so?"

"We have company closing on us from behind."

Corin turned and cursed, seeing five sleek ships lining the southern horizon and flanking the cliffs just as they were. Beyond them were three ungainly square vessels, which could only belong to Daan Redhand. But the first were easily recognisable too: Real Hakkenon's sharks from Crenna.

"That Assassin must have alerted them somehow," Barin shook

his head. "Got to hand it to Rael, he's a persistent bastard. His crews must have been lurking hereabouts."

"And Hagan will be with him too."

"And Redhand," growled Barin. "He'll not tarry in his tubs when he can hitch a ride with Rael. It's almost poetic, Corin. Like some lost saga of long ago."

"If you say so, Barin."

"So, lets get this straight." Barin flagged his hands enthusiastically in the air. "We are sailing to an island that doesn't exist. Should we by some miracle find it, we will land on its beaches and clash with our friends back there in some kind of epic grand finale."

"It's not just that. I've a sword to collect."

"I hope it's a sharp one."

"I imagine so. It's called Callanak." Barin gulped. "Yes, the same. With Callanak in my grasp and the Tekara on my head, I can counter the malice of Morak and Caswallon and send them packing. That's the sales pitch I got from you-know-who."

"Well then, what's keeping us?" Barin whistled back to Fassof who was currently yelling at him about the ships on the southern horizon.

"They'll hem us against those cliffs if we change course now!" Fassof shouted Barin.

"We're not changing course, Fassof. We make for the ice realms and see what we find. I'll explain later, it's a trifle complicated."

"As you wish." Fassof scratched his head and vanished aft.

***

Cruel Cavan had found his master on board the first of three ungainly barges filing the narrows between Westfjord and sea, their sides almost scraping on the rock. But Redhand's ships had flat bottoms and therefore could pass over skerry and shoal without much ado.

Cavan guided *The Black Serpent* toward Daan's flagship, and Rael, watching from the bow, could scarce stop himself from jumping with joy.

"My sharks!" Rael yelled in Hagan's ear. "Those are my sharks and that's *The Black Serpent!*"

Hagan nodded, a bit confused, and not entirely sure this was a good development. Also confused was Daan Redhand. "Is this some game, Assassin?"

"Call it insurance." Rael grinned like wolf. A convenient twist of fate had played into his hands and he determined to use it well. "I had my boys await my arrival from your shores, king."

Hagan glanced at him askance and Rael's grin widened. "Providence," he whispered to the Morwellan. "Now we can catch our quarry at our leisure."

"You kept that card close."

"Closer than you know."

As *The Black Serpent* slid alongside Redhand's vessel, Rael leapt on board. Hagan followed after a moment's deliberation. "How many can you carry?" yelled King Redhand.

"We don't take passengers!" Cavan shouted back at the king.

"You do now!" King Redhand leapt on board Rael's ship followed by twelve of his men, crashing and thudding onto the deck and skidding into the crew.

"Get off!" yelled Cavan reaching for a knife.

"Cool it Cavan, they can stay!" Rael waved his second back. "This worthy king owes me gold and I'm sure he'll deliver it, but no harm keeping him close by."

"You threatening me, Assassin?" Daan Redhand towered over the slim figure of Rael Hakkenon, his huge hands on war axe and mace.

Rael remained unperturbed. "It's just good business, king. I'm keeping you on the level, is all."

"I could split you in two."

"You are too slow. Besides you are now outnumbered, and those fat tubs you call ships will trail far behind us, whilst my crew will ensure we catch our quarry. You can have Barin of Valkador roasting on a spit by nightfall, so stop whining and shut your face."

"I'm a king, you insolent knave!" Daan looked like he might explode, and his men close by puffed and blew out their cheeks.

"Shut up, king." Rael smiled, and feigning insouciance showed the Leethmen his back. But Cavan's crossbow's sights were on Daan. The king, seeing that, cursed Rael and stomped off to the prow of the *Serpent*, silently vowing he would deal with Rael Hakkenon when chance allowed.

Half an hour later, the narrows yawned into open sea and the grim sleek triangle of the black isle and its howling tenant filled the horizon.

"What is that doing there?" Rael said as Cavan heaved to in shock and dismay. King Redhand ignored the island. He was looking north, his lust for vengeance and vendetta bigger even than his dread of sorcery.

"Look, there's Barin!" the king bellowed, spittle flying. "He escapes north!"

"Then we fare that way too," Rael nodded to Cavan who ordered *The Black Serpent* change course.

Even as they fanned out from the narrows and hugged the cliffs, the black island and its dreary wailing tenant sank like solidified oil below the churning waters. Crenise and Leethmen stared and muttered from the decks.

Cruel Cavan glared and fingered his knife. Hagan had that familiar sinking feeling things were on the turn again. But Rael grinned cheerfully, and Daan Redhand growled at the sinking island and turned once more to raise his iron fist at Barin's distant ship. And so the chase was on.

***

For two days, the cliffs of Leeth ranged to their west before suddenly falling away like swiftly drawn drapes. Ahead were white shapes and choppy slate grey sea. Barin and crew had reached the realm of eternal ice. Behind, the tiny dark shapes of Rael's ships kept pace but hadn't gained overmuch.

Fassof worked the wheel under those leaden skies, as Barin held counsel below with those gathered around his table. Shallan was there, her pale face intense; beside her sat Zukei, hawk-lean and confident. Tolemon flanked her left, his eyes shifty and awkward.

Across from Shallan's brother was seated Corin an Fol, his face deep in a chart Barin had supplied. Next to Corin sat Olen and Arami, looking more cheerful than they had of late, but still uncomfortable and keen to be on dry land again.

Bleyne leant by the door in casual manner, and King Ulani perched on a stool at the other end of the master's cabin. With him was Prince Tarin, looking half asleep. Behind him, Sir Greggan and Valentin's rangers hustled close. Suffice to say the cabin was full.

"It's hard to read, and there's a lot of gaps," Corin complained as he scanned the chart. "And what's all this messy stuff and smudges?"

"Ice," Barin blinked his way. "'Tis an old chart and most likely inaccurate, but it's all we have. These waters are seldom frequented. Thus these are whalers' charts from an age gone by." He shoved another crumpled parchment Corin's way.

"Smells like someone pissed on this one," Corin complained and wrinkled his nose.

Barin ignored him. "There are lands, as you can see, but most are uninhabited, or else the ward of demon and witch. Helga Three-bolts came from up here."

"Who is that?" Tarin piped up with sudden interest.

"A witch I once knew," Barin shrugged the question away. "We have to reach our destination tomorrow or else we'll run out of sea. Already the grinding ice closes in on us."

"And how do we find our destination, and what shape will it take?" King Ulani alone dare ask the question currently hovering on everyone's lips.

"I dunno." Barin rubbed an ear. "Any suggestions?" Barin looked to Corin.

"I guess we just have to wait and hope we don't run out of water and have to tramp over all that ice." It wasn't a helpful response but seemed to work as no one else had much to offer.

That day passed long and slow as the grinding gleaming ice creaked closer to either side of *The Starlight Wanderer's* hull. It was eerie and the cold chewed at faces and extremities. They voyaged through a blue world comprising dark silent water, pale expanse of sky, and silver-sapphire glittering rime. Beautiful, yet ominous and foreboding.

Toward evening, shapes appeared on the horizon like spiky stick men carrying long poles. On closer inspection they were moving, jerking back and forth, their poles clacking together.

"Ice warriors," Barin said. "I've heard of such."

As they inched nearer, with the ice now scraping along the timbers, the strange figures came into view. They were tall and angular, very thin, and their legs extremely long. The ice warriors' faces were blue with jagged beards, and their heads pointed, with frozen hair fashioned into random spikes, these sprouting out in all directions.

An uncanny sight set in a surreal ice-scape. There were dozens. Each ice warrior stood on a brittle islet, noisily defending his station against another. The long poles were spears of ice, which the stick-like warriors clattered together without much show of skill. Occasionally a spear would snap and its owner would fold and topple into fragments.

They passed the region where the ice warriors dueled without the beings showing any sign of noticing them. Far behind, Rael's sharks still kept pace, and just showing on the southern horizon were King Redhand's three raft ships.

Light faded and the sky took on strange hues. Green and scarlet flooded the north as The Giants' Dance blazed forth and dazzled all who witnessed it. A deep booming echoed through the night like the sound of heavy voices, accompanied with a dazzling vibrant array of light and shifting shape, twirling, flickering, and dancing high above. Ahead the even-star shone diamond bright—a single lantern guiding their way.

For most that long night The Giants' Dance held the sky captive, but there were other sights and sounds all around them. The wayfarers witnessed weird and disturbing phenomena. All around were booming shouts and urgent answers. There were weird alien howls and distant crackling glows like bonfires, whilst lightning knives cut cloudless sky above. Surrounding the ship, the wind wove women's voices, these like sirens whispering up from the ice.

Corin saw shapes, huge dark figures striding and shouting—ice giants away to battle. The figures joined together, becoming glittering armies marching through midnight mist, their voices alien and strange.

Once they passed close to a lonely fire where three scrawny naked figures cooked and cavorted—witches carving rune spells from the night sky. On another occasion they saw a wall of ice hundreds of feet tall shimmering in the dark. Stood upon it were three giant warriors, their heads encased in steel, with battle axes and spears in hand. These three glared down upon them until they faded back into the night. No one slept.

Finally, dawn cracked a line across the east, revealing the pale crust of an orange sun floating above that sea of rime. Heads turned as the distant hoot of horns heralded yet another visitor.

A pale rider in the sky was approaching at speed. The horns bellowed and His hounds bayed and snarled as Oroonin's Wild Hunt passed by high above. The Wanderer shook His spear down at them as His ashen host fled the morning and fell hungry upon the west, the corpse army following on this, the eve of the final war of the gods.

Morning won through eventually and the fell wind faded to an eerie sigh. All around was a shimmering, shifting, and rifting like a disturbance in the vortex. Nobody spoke as they waited in tense fascination. Something was about to happen.

Then they saw it: a rainbow-mantled island rising cool and easy like summer daydreams, it's far-reaching warmth chasing the fleeing ice and vapourizing it. Green hills beckoned them like forgotten lovers, their verdant flanks wrapped in summerwoods, and the warm welcome aromas of earth, flowers, crystal waterfall, and lowing beast beckoned them to hurry forward.

Laras Lassladden—they had found it at last.

Chapter 37

Callanak

Vaarg was in a playful mood as he settled like a thundercloud on the drizzle-damp walls of Wynais, sparing those silver ramparts his fiery breath for the nonce. Instead he scraped and tore at the stone with his talons, as his hooded master watched in silence like a sinister crow camped on his back. Like his dragon, Morak seemed in no hurry to destroy this city. Rather would he revel in the fear seeping out from those souls hiding behind door and shutter.

Wynais's citizens had gone to ground; the guards had deserted the walls, and no figure stirred as evening dwindled to night. Outside the walls, the dark legions of Groil mustered and shuffled. The old guard led by Flail Six-Hands were now recently reinforced by new creatures fresh out of Ulan Valek, raised by Morak's spear and sorcery and hungry for blood. A sable host comprising two thousand strong, and all awaiting command of their master and his dragon.

A crackle and fizz turned eyes to the lake where a lone scarlet rocket soared into the dark. This was followed by a second rocket trailing blue, and a third blazing silver like star fire. Three sparklers, mocking the dragon.

It was Ariane's signal.

A horn blew thrice announcing a lone figure's appearance on the city walls. All eyes watched as the woman cloaked in Goddess-Green approached dragon and rider as though they were mere phantoms in the darkness. A tiny shape clad in cloak and sparkling armour, the queen's measured tread led her to where Vaarg loomed, a hundred ton of scale and malice. Ariane of the Swords strode out to defend her city.

"Go back!" Queen Ariane's small brittle voice reached Morak and Vaarg, both baffled and amused by her bold approach.

"You are not welcome here!"

Morak raised Golganak like a thorn of pain and Ariane shuddered as its menace nearly snapped her resolve like a dried twig. She gulped and took a step toward them.

"Elanion protects me; I am Her conduit! Her missile! Be gone lest She blast you to oblivion!" Ariane made the sign and uttered the words taught her long ago by Dazaleon the High Priest. She spoke the unlocking rune that only those of royal blood could utter and survive.

"Kraken awake!"

Outside the city, the Groil fell back in dismay as Lake Wynais's clear waters erupted to reveal a beast as large as Vaarg. An acre of slime and oil, the kraken reared its massive sloping head. Ariane's command had woken he city's sleeping defender and the Goddess's ancient guardian.

Ariane's voice had changed with that last command, and a sudden explosion of light revealed a figure standing high and tall above the walls and towering over Ariane—a warrior maiden and giantess, flanked by three smaller women: the Fates Scolde, Vervandi, and Urdei. Their mother, Elanion, like Her guardian, the kraken, had answered Ariane's summons and now appeared in the guise of Scaffa the Warrior Queen.

But Morak laughed at both queens whilst Vaarg mocked the kraken with his lizard gaze. "We too have help!" Morak yelled at the giant Goddess. "Look you! See that darkness smothering the southern skyline. Our Master comes, and He is greater by far than you, Mistress of the Trees!"

Ariane and her Goddess turned to see a darkening gloom billowing outwards towards Wynais from the south. A great storm approached, and it carried with it a wrongness of violence, stench, and decay. The forces of chaos had arrived.

Then horns blew out from the other direction, and another shining host filled the night sky from the north. Oroonin guided His steed down through the thermals, *The Wild Hunt* swooping behind.

Scaffa gazed up at Her husband and brother.

"So you come at last, Corpse Gatherer. Much needed are you in this our final battle. Come Husband, let ust destroy Old Night forever!"

But Oroonin hung back and bid his host wait silent in the sky. His cold gaze fell on His wife.

"I choose not to partake at this time. Instead I will watch you fight, beloved. I have always enjoyed watching you in battle!"

"Coward!" Vervandi yelled up at her father.

"Traitor!" Scolde clawed her fingers at the sky.

"Shite bag and stinker!" Urdei stuck her tongue out and stamped her foot.

"Father, would you desert your children as well as your wife and this green world?" Vervandi chose another tactic.

"Gladly, for you four have brought me nought but grief these last millennia!" came the response.

A fell wind descended on Wynais, and dark shadows filled the night as Soilfins and worse creatures hurtled down upon the city.

"Then Yffarn take you, Husband!"

Scaffa turned to face He who had come alone. Forgotten for the moment, Ariane fled back inside the citadel. The stakes of this game were raised beyond her level; best she keep her head down with the rest.

And so He returned at last as was so long forewarned. Cul-Saan, Firstborn of the Weaver, proudest and strongest of the Great Old Gods. He stood calm and terrible, beautiful and darker than the night surrounding him. Then He shed that darkness like an obsidian cloak from His massive shoulders. Instead, now He blazed like the fallen star He was. Soon after, Wynais's stones began to smoulder.

***

They moored in shallow waters and waded ashore. Barin and Ulani organised three teams and bid them get busy setting up defences against the approaching pirate ships. They would be heavily outnumbered, but they had among their number Barin of Valkador, King Ulani and his daughter, Olen and Arami of the Rorshai, Bleyne the archer, and last up, Corin an Fol.

Whilst he was slamming a sharp pole into the sand Corin glanced up, feeling a nudge. "A word if you will." Barin grabbed Corin's arm and led him aside to a grove of live oaks flanking the shoreline, whilst Shallan watched with worried eyes. At a nod from Barin she followed as did Zukei, close at her heels. Bleyne, watching from further along the beach, tapped Prince Tarin's shoulder. "You still have it?" The archer's hard brown gaze bored into the prince's face.

"Of course!"

"Time to leave then." Bleyne and Tarin slipped away from their defence-building chores, and once out of sight, sprinted to join Shallan and Zukei at the edge of the trees. Just ahead, Barin was talking in quiet tones to Corin; both appeared not to have noticed them. But Tarin knew different.

"Best you get going lad," Barin was saying. "I think we've reached the endgame at last. We'll keep those yobbos entertained whilst you go fetch your sword."

"I'd rather stay here and fight with you." Corin's gaze swept out to sea where the black sails of Rael's sharks had grown larger. They were approaching fast.

"Destiny lad, you can't change that. You of all people —"

"Should know," Corin nodded and grasped Barin's arm. "Stay alive until I get back, and keep my woman safe."

"Your woman is coming with you." Shallan stood there, reunited with her horn and bow, with Zukei standing wary two paces behind her.

"I go alone," Corin told Shallan and bid Zukei leave them. She stayed put.

"Zukei stays with me, and we're going with you, as are Bleyne and Prince Tarin." Corin looked across to see these two appear as if by magic.

"What the?"

But Shallan's tone brooked no room for argument. "We decided this during the voyage yesterday. We've spoken to no one else except Barin and King Ulani. You cannot take this upon yourself, Corin. I simply won't let you."

Corin cursed under his breath. "This is my task, Shallan—mine alone. I told you what the Wanderer said. Coming with me only puts you in danger."

"And staying on this beach ensures my safety?" Shallan chuckled. "They are coming, Corin, they'll be here inside an hour. I don't want to be reunited with Rael Hakkenon or Hagan Delmorier again, so I suggest we stop quibbling and start walking. That looks like a long hot climb to the top of that mountain."

Corin shook his head in wonder. "You, woman, are a constant source of amazement to me." He sighed in resignation. "So no one else knows, not even your brother?"

"No, but we had best get going before they find out."

"You are the third team," Barin smiled. "I chose three so the other two would be busy on their own chores and not notice team three's disappearance." Barin sounded pleased with himself.

"I've always had a flair for logistics. Well, I'm off to help with our makeshift defences." Barin grinned and clapped Corin on the back. "I led you away lad, so Shallan and these others could join you. Ulani is keeping everyone busy down there. Now go, and bring us back that sword!"

"Connivers," sniffed Corin but he seemed happy for the company. "That's settled then. Time to get moving!" Corin slung Clouter's harness over his shoulder, and gripping Shallan's palm tightly, led her deeper into the bird noisy-woods and up the first gentle slopes of the looming Bhogha Mountain, wreathed in a rainbow.

Behind the lovers prowled Zukei, King's daughter, Karyia in left fist and throwing axe in right. Prince Tarin followed the dark woman; a short sword (care of Barin's store) swung from his waist belt, as did the small bag containing the Tekara. The prince wore an expression of resolute determination.

Last up, Bleyne nocked arrow to bow and stole silent and smooth behind Prince Tarin. Every now and then he would turn and glance for any sign of movement below.

And so they progressed through wood and copse, the warmth of a welcome summer sun lifting their spirits and strengthening their limbs. By afternoon they cleared the woods and saw the tumbled grey rocks of Bhogha Mountain looming close. A path threaded between boulders, twisting up steep and slippery.

This they followed for over an hour until a sheer wall of cliff blocked their way ahead. At the base of the cliff was a brown door, simple and unadorned. It was leaning ajar and looked as though no one had passed through it in years.

The companions exchanged glances, and Corin's gaze lifted to the sky above where the rainbow arched, bridging the mountain. As he watched he saw its closest end shed multiple light upon the door, the six-coloured filtration flooding the entrance and dazzling their eyes.

Corin glanced at Shallan. She nodded and squeezed his arm and together they vanished behind the door. Zukei followed quickly, then the prince, a touch more hesitant. Bleyne turned and glanced down to the calm blue bay in the distance.

He could see *The Starlight Wanderer* surrounded by five smaller vessels and his keen ears picked out faint noises of clashing steel and hoarse shouts. A mile out to sea, King Redhand's rafts drifted closer to shore. Bleyne's lips tightened and he shouldered his bow, and without a sound followed the others into the world hidden behind the brown door.

***

Tolemon took a break from his work and gazed around the sandy strand they had chosen for their defences. He saw no sign of Shallan or her lover and noted there were others missing too. Angry, he approached Barin who sweated with a tree limb over his shoulder, which he planned using as a barricade.

Barin saw Tolemon approach and pulled a mournful face. He didn't much care for Shallan's surviving brother.

"Hello there!" Barin awarded his brightest grin, but Tolemon blocked his path with eyes heavy as thunder. "Mind out, this is weighty and I need to place it on yonder ridge." Tolemon stepped aside as Barin heaved his twelve-foot burden forward and pitched it onto the allotted ridge of sand to join the other four tree limbs—the mainstay of their quick-built fortress.

Tolemon approached Barin from behind as the Northman wiped sweat from his forehead.

"Where is my sister?" Tolemon stood with legs braced and hand on sword hilt.

"Is she missing? I hadn't noticed." Barin noted Toleman's stance and frowned. "May happen she's attending a call of nature. I'm sure she'll be back in a mo."

"You're a deceitful bastard." Tolemon's grip on his sword tightened and Barin, seeing that, scowled and folded his arms.

"Easy now, think you a match for me, boy?" Tolemon glared at him but said nothing. "You need to lighten up, Morwellan. We are allies are we not?"

"Well, tell me where has she gone then! Corin too, and the black witch for that matter!"

"Zukei—she has a name. They've gone to get Callanak." Barin

grinned at him. "That's the third team's job. You're not in the third team, so fuck off."

"Why wasn't I informed of this?"

"No one was told as didn't need know." Barin's expression darkened further as he saw the five ships closing on the beach. "Now please bugger off and get busy, Tolemon lad, we'll have company shortly."

Tolemon turned and raised his hand over his eyes. He spat in the sand, seeing the five lean vessels using sail and oar to make hastily for he shore.

"We'll talk about this later, Northman. I am the Duke of Morwella!"

"Just piss off," Barin muttered under his breath and set about fixing his tree limbs as best he could to form a defensive wall.

Taic approached and helped his uncle. "Nearly done." Taic grinned at their achievement—a rough circle comprising tree limbs, axe-sharpened stakes, sand pits to trip and slow the enemy advance, and shore stones for throwing and clubbing, as extra weapons if needed. Not bad for a morning's graft.

"Just as well, our company is arriving." Barin rested Wrmfang against a tree limb and stood tall, straightening his back.

Close by, Tolemon watched the ships pass where *The Starlight Wanderer* rested anchored in the light breeze. The five sharks gracefully glided towards the strand, sails stowed and oars shipped as the gentle swell eased ship to shore. Tolemon turned away and noticed footsteps in the sand leading off to a knot of live oaks hanging close to the water.

Eyes narrowing, he followed and soon discovered other footsteps, including what must surely be Shallan's. They led beneath the trees and beyond where a rough path vanished into the woods.

***

Rael, scanning the shore, smiled seeing the lone figure flit into the woods to the left. "That's our quarry," he told Cruel Cavan and Hagan standing beside him. "We'll leave the lads to deal with Barin and follow that one to see what he is up to!"

Rael hadn't told a soul about the visitor who'd settled sulky and silent on the stern of *The Black Serpent* late last night while they were passing through the surreal realm of ice.

Gribble had appeared out of sorts and wing-flappy. The Soilfin had a battered worn-out look and his eyes were even more bloodshot and shifty than usual.

"Big news, Mr Assassin. For your ears only!"

Hagan was asleep in his hammock, as were King Daan and his men, snoring in their furs, but Cavan and a few crew lurked about. Rael signalled his second, who blanched seeing the goblin again.

"Private consultancy." Rael wagged a finger and Cavan nodded, making sure his crew were out of earshot.

"Big news," Gribble repeated. "Lots happening, changes coming. Important matters! Have to tell you!"

"Well fucking get on with it!" Rael uncorked his brandy flask and took an impatient pull. "What's Caswallon up to?" Rael belched and awarded the goblin a baleful glare.

"Not much really, being on account that he's dead."

"What?"

"I handed in my resignation after Morak got his spear back," Gribble chewed a finger that he'd retrieved from his secret pocket under the folds of his left wing.

"Morak killed Caswallon?"

"Him or Vaarg, the pair of them reduced Kella City to ashes. They've always been rough, those two."

"Fuck, but that's a surprise."

"Not really." Gribble picked a nostril. "Mr Caswallon upset the wrong people. There's always someone bigger out there."

Rael drained his brandy and received a bad case of hiccups. "Squeeze your nose, it helps," Gribble suggested.

"Shut up and tell me what else is happening whilst I'm marooned here at the top of the world. Who do you work for now—Morak Dogface?"

"No, he's a bad payer. I mean yes, unofficially I'll work for him to keep my head on my shoulders, but I'm already looking at my options. The Big Boss is back in town."

"Big Boss? Is this someone I know?"

"The Big Boss, stupid. Dog-Lord's boss, my boss. Everybody's boss unless they work for the other lot. I'm going to see if He'll employ me direct and cut out the middleman. He has several hundred Soilfin working for Him."

"What in the Nine Worlds are you wittering about, Goblin? Who is back?"

"Old Night, Lord of Chaos and Futility. Destroyer of Worlds and Crusher of Souls," Gribble announced rather grandly. "Enemy of all living things, etcetera, etcetera, etcetera!"

"Well that's a bit harsh, really." Rael wished he had more brandy.

"You'll be all right, Mr Assassin. You're nasty to the bone. Boss will like you, He usually grills mortals alive, but I daresay He'll promote you if you keep your noggin. Of course it helps to have friends in the right places; I'll happily put in a word for a small fee."

Rael gazed out across the ice where weird howls announced something hunting in the night. "Creepy place." Gribble chewed his stowaway finger, stripping pale flesh with his fangs.

"So that's it," Rael said. "Caswallon's dead, and the fallen god Old Night has returned from Yffarn to destroy the world. I appreciate your flying all this way to tell me. It's just the sort of cheerful news I needed."

"There is more. A way to get in with Morak and therefore with Himself too."

"I'm all ears."

"Have you wondered why Fat Barin is sailing to the top of the world?"

"Hadn't really dwelt on it." The sarcasm was lost on Gribble.

"They seek Callanak."

"Arollas's legendary sword," Rael nodded. "Well why not? Who wouldn't? And it's as sensible an idea as anything else I've heard lately.

I remember the stories well enough. The sword Callanak can cut clean through any metal. It was instrumental in defeating the Urgolais, but was lost after that war—or something like that. Riveting."

"It wasn't lost, just stowed somewhere safe."

"And that's their destination. Find sword, slay Big Boss, retire and have a nice cup of tea."

"You cannot slay Big Boss. Even when He's chopped into little bits. But Callanak stalemates Golganak—renders Morak's black shaft impotent, if you'll pardon my expression." Gribble's smirk was lost on Rael.

"So, Doglord Morak wants the sword busted before they can use it. Do this for him, and he will put in a word for you at Big Boss HQ."

"Terrific!" Rael flashed the goblin his brilliant smile. "And will breaking said sword involve me finding my enemies and skewering them?"

"Yes, that's likely."

"Good, then I'm your man. Now bugger off, Goblin, and let me get some sleep."

"Don't you want to know where the sword is?" Gribble teased.

"Laras Lassladden, I remember the legend. I had an education once, Goblin."

"I hate that you still call me goblin, after all we've been through." Gribble flapped his wings and prepared for lift off. "Some things hurt, you know."

"'Tis a term of endearment, old fruit."

"I'll be back in a while to see how you're getting on." Gribble surged up into the night amid a hissing, whirling, flapping noise of wing and fumes. Rael closed his eyes but failed to find sleep. In the morning they had raised the island.

"You asleep?"

"What?" Rael blinked and saw Hagan leaning over him. "They've built some sort of defence on the ridge cresting that beach. Do you want to wait until Redhand's other boys arrive?"

"Nah," Rael yawned. "Let the lads leap ashore and greet those tossers with steel. Besides, I'll doubt you'll stop Redhand seeking Barin out." The king stood silent and tall at the prow, chewing his moustache and mouthing unmentionables.

"We'll slip away during the melee; the real fun will happen inside that mountain if legends be right." Rael folded his arms and leaned back against the rail.

"What aren't you telling me, Assassin?" Rael didn't answer, for the *Serpent* had just beached, and already his men and the king's were leaping ashore and charging up to confront Barin's noisy group huddled behind their shabby defences.

"Cavan!" Rael yelled his second who glanced his way, axe in one hand, cutlass in other. "You're coming with me and Hagan here. Bring six good lads and let the others get stuck in here. And tell them to stay away from Redhand, he's off his bloody rocker!"

King Redhand was halfway up the beach, his war-axe held high as he yelled out Barin's name; his warriors were with him, but Rael's pirates still lingered by the shore. Cavan yelled out orders and rejoined his leader.

Rael soon found the tracks leading to the live oaks where the man had vanished twenty minutes ago. "This way!" Rael called cheerfully as he hopped and jumped toward the rough path showing in the sunny glade betwixt tree and moss.

Hagan, walking behind, loosened sword in sheath. Whatever game the Assassin played, it needn't involve him for much longer. Find Corin, kill him, get paid, and leave. Simple. Well, he hoped so anyway.

***

Inside the door, they were hit by sudden light. Stabbing silver rays half blinded them as they staggered forward, shielding their eyes from the glare. Zukei saw the stairs first, a spiral steel construction hardly discernible in the whiteness of the cavern—or wherever they were, as it was impossible to tell.

That glistening spiral led up into white nothingness. They reached the stair rail and Shallan, touching it, marvelled how it appeared hewn from pure white crystal. They took the stairs two at a time, their eyes slowly adjusting to the glare.

After a long climb, the stairway opened on a wide chamber with vaulted ceilings that shimmered with veins of crystal. Corin recalled the tunnel under the Crystal Mountains, but this was ten times brighter, though small by comparison, and they soon reached the far wall where a second door stood half open, hinting at what lay beyond.

Corin shoved his long frame through the entrance, Shallan and Tarin following close behind, whilst Bleyne and Zukei glanced back lest anyone follow. Satisfied, they too turned and made for the door.

Bleyne smiled at Zukei and the woman grinned back. A strange moment passed between them, then Zukei resumed her customary scowl and vanished inside. Bleyne followed, his brown eyes lost in thought.

Corin hadn't known what to expect, but it certainly wasn't this: a hollow tower where a breeze lifted his hair and the cry of birds calling filled his ears. There were six windows, high and arched, one in each wall, three overlooking the slopes and forest far below, the other three revealing sheer drops leading down to the ocean and its breaking tides.

The tower was a hexagon of plain grey rock, and aside the window on each wall hung a weapon. Six swords hung there: five were gleaming, flawless shafts of crystal; the sixth was drab and shoddy, its worn steel half buried behind a rotten leather scabbard.

Corin smiled as some part of his consciousness recognised the shabby sword as Callanak hanging there. As he did, the other swords chimed and fell away like crystal rain. A voice reached him from deep inside his head.

You pass the test, descendant of Erun Cade. You are the one. Take the sword and claim your destiny!

Corin, as one in a dream, reached for the now-gleaming glaive on the wall, transformed with a crystal hilt, but stopped as a searing pain lanced through his hand. Looking down, he was surprised to see a dagger had pierced his right hand, the point showing three inches clear of his palm.

Rael smiled as he stepped forward into the light. "That was one of my better throws," he said. Then the clash of angry steel announced his men were upon them.

Chapter 38

Kinsmen

Corin tugged the dagger free from his hand and ducked as a second knife narrowly missed his left ear. Then Rael was on him, his rapier darting and flicking, and Corin struggled to free Clouter from its sheath.

Close by, Zukei skewered a pirate but Cavan tripped her from behind and jumped on her back. She rolled to her back, brought a knee up hard into Cavan's groin and he grunted but grabbed hold of her throat with a meaty palm.

Bleyne had no room for shafts so worked his knife against the three pirates surrounding him. One got lucky and knocked the knife free of Bleyne's hand. A second levelled his cutlass at Bleyne's throat.

Zukei bit hard into Cavan's hand, but he clung on and clubbed her unconscious with the flat of his axe. Meanwhile, Hagan disarmed Prince Tarin and knocked him to the floor, where he lay still as stone, the scarlet blood seeping from his skull. Hagan levelled his broadsword at Shallan, who spat back at him, her horn in hand.

Rael's rapier pierced Corin's leather and passed between two rusty links of steel. The Longswordsman cursed as the searing pain lanced through his shoulder; three inches closer and it would have pierced his heart.

"Game's up," Rael said with a slow, serious smile. "You did well, peasant. But all good things must come to an end."

"He is no peasant, but rather your kinsman." All heads turned to see a bloodied battered figure leaning in pain against the wall.

"You?" Rael raised a brow. They'd found Tolemon halfway up the mountain. Rael had gutted him six times after questioning him and left him for dead. But now the bastard had showed up here. Things never failed to surprise the Assassin these days.

"You should be dead! Look you, bitch-cow—your brother's a walking corpse! Told me he was going to save you, so he did. So I took an eye and a finger and a few other bits. Gods alone know how he got up here; he must be nearly drained of blood."

"He is your kin," Tolemon said again, as he half crumpled against the doorway. "Your kinsman." Shallan gasped as she noticed the black seeping gouge that had replaced Tolemon's left eye.

"Kill that bastard, Cavan. He's becoming monotonous."

"You nearly drowned that night, Rael. But you survived, as did your cousin, Lord Halfdan's baby boy, the rightful heir to Kelsalion's throne—though his wife and the queen perished in the storm."

"What's this?" Rael's green gaze narrowed suspiciously. Tolemon's tone had changed, and now he looked stronger, his single eye gleaming silver with baleful spite. Rael reeled at that stare and the Wanderer's rope-rough voice filled the cavern.

"You are kinsmen, fool! Corin an Fol was assumed drowned, and thus the High King had no heir and lost all hope of his realms' salvation.

"You, Assassin, never accepted your station. For a thousand years, nephew has followed uncle in receiving the Tekara. But with Corin's drowning, you resented the fact that there was no apparent heir, and yet still your father refused to name you in his stead. Thus you murdered your father on the premise of aiding Caswallon.

"But you, Dark Prince, have lived a life of lies, hiding behind your cowardice and malice, ever resentful and spiteful to the last.

"Take the sword, Corin an Fol—why make things harder than they already are?"

Corin gasped in pain and reached for Callanak, but as he did several things happened at once.

Bleyne snapped his arms free of his captor and slammed an elbow up into the pirate's nose, snapping the small bone and killing him at once. He rounded on the other two, killing them in seconds. Three remained standing with their master, close to Corin and the hanging sword.

Zukei blinked awake and saw Cavan turn to make an end to the wounded man leaning against the door. She rolled, found her axe, and hurled it deep into Cavan's back. The blade buried itself between his shoulder blades, and Cruel Cavan pitched forward on his face before the wounded Tolemon's feet.

Hagan rounded on Corin and blocked him from reaching Callanak. Instead, Rael leapt toward it and grabbed the glistening hilt in his hand. Rael screamed as that crystal burned deep into his palm. He let go and gripped his hand in agony.

"You are not the one," the voice of Oroonin said through Tolemon's broken lips. "And that is the wrong sword."

"Fuck you all!" Rael danced sideways and grabbed Shallan from behind before anyone could move; before she knew it, his dagger was pricking her throat.

"Shallan!" Corin shocked himself into movement.

"Take the sword," the voice inside Tolemon said.

"You leave her be!" Corin spat at Rael, but the Assassin's three surviving guards closed on him with their cutlasses.

"You're no fucking kinsman of mine!" Rael taunted Corin as he made ready to slice Shallan's throat. Zukei yelled and levelled her Karyia, but Cavan, not quite dead, rolled over and then shoved a knife in her calf. Zukei cursed and stabbed down with the Karyia. Its thin steel entered Cavan's mouth and passed clear of the back of his head. He shuddered once, then slunk prone.

Rael caught Corin's wild stare and smiled. "It's over," he said, as he pricked the knife deeper into Shallan's throat and the first beads of blood stained her neck. But Rael's hand froze. Instead and looked down in puzzlement, seeing Hagan's broadsword sticking in his thigh.

Rael dropped the knife and Shallan half-fell sobbing into Corin's open arms. Corin kissed her and wiped the blood from her neck. Meanwhile, Rael kicked Hagan in the face with his good leg, sending the Morwellan sprawling.

Bleyne and Zukei each took a pirate, and Shallan grabbed Rael's abandoned knife and shoved it hard into the back of the last of Rael's men as he rounded on Corin.

Hagan rolled to his knees, trying to find his feet, but Rael's rapier slid deep into his neck, and Hagan gurgled and slumped twitching to the stone floor.

Rael, seeing he was surrounded, stepped back to the closest window. He placed a foot on the ledge and smashed the crystal glass with his elbow.

"What a merry dance!" Rael swept his audience a contemptuous smile, and made to jump, but Tarin, rolling to his feet stopped him.

"You are my brother!"

"Half brother," Rael's green gaze fell on the prince whose head still bled profusely but who seemed to have recovered enough of his wits to confront his kinsman.

"Corin is our cousin, and you are my lost older brother! I always thought you were dead. We are kin and yet you wanted to torture me to death in that dungeon. Why?"

"Why? Why not?" Rael laughed bitterly. "When you were gifted everything, and I was abandoned and left to die? I was the High King's son, and you a bastard turd spat from one of his many whores. He hated me, yet loved you instead, you useless little cunt! Yffarn swallow you all!"

Rael turned and leapt from the window. Corin reached the ledge first and watched the Assassin's body fall for several moments before vanishing into the cool blue water far below.

"Take the sword," Tolemon's mouth was leaking blood and his knees were buckling. Shallan rushed to support him.

"Oh, brother, I'm so very sorry." But Tolemon wasn't there, and instead the Wanderer's crow-rough voice addressed Shallan.

"He is dead, but he played his part well enough, and now rests with your other brothers and father in the halls of peace. Be content, he died well!" The silver light flickered out in Tolemon's alien eye and Shallan's eldest brother slumped dead to the floor.

Oh Tolemon, I was so cruel to you. I'm sorry, brother!

"CORIN AN FOL! TAKE THE SWORD IF YOU WANT TO SAVE EVERYTHING YOU LOVE INCLUDING HER!" Oroonin's voice echoed around their heads then silence followed as His presence vacated the tower. "I MUST DEPART! I AM NEEDED ELSEWHERE."

"Take the sword, Corin, for fuck's sake just do it!" Zukei held Shallan as her ward pooled tears upon her lifeless brother's ravaged face.

"They are all dead, my kin. All dead!" Shallan wept. Then Corin reached up and unhinged the blade from its anchor on the wall.

Callanak!

***

Wyrmfang caught Daan Redhand's sword mid-swing and snapped it in two, but Redhand wrenched his arm back and lashed out with the other hand, his mace narrowly missing clipping Barin's ears. The king was foaming at the mouth and Barin was making small animal noises—this scrap had been a long time coming.

The barricade had held off three charges but then Redhand's ships had beached, and now they were hard pressed as the king's main force fell upon them. To Barin's left, Ulani hewed and slew any man daring to come close to the barricade, using his multiple array of weaponry.

Further along the barricade, Olen and Arami, joined by Arac, Sir

Greggan, and those still left of Valentin's volunteers, loosed the last of their arrows into the foe. But there were too many enemy men, and the barricade was giving under the weight of sweating armoured bodies.

As the barricade collapsed, Olen tossed his bow aside and unsheathed his sword, Arami followed suit, and both Rorshai set about slicing, stabbing, and hacking the heavy press of men surrounding them.

Arac crumpled with an axe beak in his skull, and his killer leapt on Olen's back, but Arami's scimitar ran him through. The two were surrounded with furious men, but then Sveyn and Taic crashed through the circle and killed half a dozen in the process. Sveyn took a slice through his left eye, but so enraged was he that he hardly noticed and slew just as savagely with one eye as he had with two.

Daan Redhand's mace batted Wyrmfang aside and impacted Barin's chest, knocking him backwards. The king roared and leapt on top of what was left of the tree-barricade. Barin kicked up hard with his boot, catching Redhand in the balls. The king yammered and stumbled on top of him and the two huge men commenced rolling and biting and pummelling each other into the ground.

Daan freed a knife from his belt and stabbed at Barin's eyes. Barin jerked his head back and then bit hard into Redhand's knife bearing knuckles. The blade sliced Barin's cheek wide open but his teeth sank deeper until the knife dropped, alongside three of Daan Redhand's fingers.

But the king had found his feet again and retrieved his mace from the bloodied ground. Barin leapt up at him, but Daan's steel boot struck him square in the jaw and knocked him back down.

Close by, Cogga held off three Leethmen with a sword in each arm. There were already six dead around him, but a sword got through his flailing blades, and Cogga fell amongst the bodies of those he'd slain. Close by lay Haikon and Norman surrounded by the corpses of Leethmen. Wogun fought on alone for several minutes until a spear cast brought him down and the men surrounding him kicked him to death.

Barin tried to rise again but again Daan kicked him flat, and then a rush behind announced the king's men had him surrounded. Daan grinned like a rabid wolf and readied his mace for the deathblow.

Barin closed his eyes, which was fortunate because the entire beach chose that precise moment to erupt in an explosion of white light.

Men screamed and bodies flew everywhere, noises like rushing wind and thunder battered Barin's ears. He rolled to his feet and opened his eyes blinking. The beach was empty save the tall figure of a man standing over him with a diamond bright sword in his hand. The world reeled and lurched and Barin spewed bloody phlegm onto the sand.

"Corin?" Barin croaked but the vision faded as the beach started sinking beneath the water. Laras Lassladden was returning to the ocean.

"Corin!" Barin yelled but his head spun and darkness fell upon him, and Barin knew no more.

**

Old Night laughed as He broke the body of Scaffa the Giantess into two pieces and hurled her torn flesh down upon the trembling city. Already His horde were bubbling like blowflies around a corpse as they clawed and scraped their way up the walls of the Silver City.

Queen Ariane watched from her high window as the plague army approached. It was over. She'd seen her Goddess fall and now the end would come. Beside her Cale wept and Silon comforted the boy.

"All things must pass," Silon told Cale. "Nothing lasts forever."

Ariane wept too, she wept for her protectress and her people and those whom she loved. But as she wept she thought of her vow, and it suddenly came to her that there was still one left who might help. She stood trembling at the window and called,

"Sensuata, have you forgotten your betrothed? Will you let the

Night steal away your queen?"

Again she called. Nothing. But after a third summons, the armies felt a tremor in the fields surrounding Lake Wynais. Ariane collapsed on the floor weeping. He *has* come!

"I WILL NOT!" The voice echoed an answer from far, far away, a sound like the surge of water rushing through dark tunnels far underground.

The towering white figure of Old Night or Cul Saan paused in his pursuit of destruction and turned slowly toward the lake, His fire-clad eyes watching as its waters started to ripple, then bubble and then explode, as a huge head broke free of their surface. Sensuata had come.

Ariane, ignoring shouts from her captains and friends, leaped to her feet and grabbed her two swords and sprinted out onto the walls. Tarello followed her, as did Galed and Cale, Jaan and Valentin, and eventually Silon too.

And then people kept coming until the silver walls of Wynais were filled with folk, all come to stand and die beside their queen.

The white towering figure turned toward the giant facing Him from the lake.

"You grown old and feeble, Little Brother," Cul-Saan laughed as He strode to meet his younger sibling. "Take the city, slave!" he bellowed to Morak. "I will deal with this one!" Morak, seated on the dragon wheeled high into the air and Vaarg loosed his funnel of flame down upon the citizens.

"I love you, Ariane!" It was Tarello who had spoken. "I just wanted you to know that before we die, my Queen."

"I do know it." Ariane closed her eyes as the flame fell upon them.

Chapter 39

The Crystal King

White light exploded inside his head. But there was no pain, only a sudden searing clarity beyond the comprehension of his mortal mind. He laughed as wild alien energy flushed through his veins. He felt strong as iron, light as silk, smooth and calm as summer water.

And he fell! Down, drifting and floating, spinning and whirling, as warm breezes whispered and caressed his ears.

"Corin...?" He heard a voice and part of him recognised Shallan somewhere close.

"I'm here..."

"I cannot find you! Everything has changed...where are you?" her voice trailed off like mist over water, and still Corin fell. He saw visions, battles in the sky, heard heavy voices and sharp trumpets blaring out clarion calls. Faces rushed out at him but vanished as the light surrounding him consumed them.

He fell, and as he descended—like a leaf drifting from an autumn tree without intent or purpose—Corin gazed down and saw the diamond glaive clutched in his right palm.

Callanak—this is your power I'm feeling!

The sword had no weight and yet its balance was perfection, Corin laughed and twirled it through his hands, and the sword sang to him in cool clear words.

We are your destiny, the long awaited three. You must complete the triangulation. It has started.

The words made no sense, but Corin cared not as he was filled with joy, his body and mind washed with wondrous visions of beauty and light. Here, anything was possible and everything probable. No fear marred this place, no doubt or hesitation. Here there was only clarity, vision, and strength.

Corin gazed down and saw the grey ruins of a broken city rushing up to greet him. He laughed as he crashed through a roof and felt no pain, laughed again as he fell sprawling to the mosaic floor of a ruined broken building. But then Corin dropped Callanak and the return of sudden pain tore into him and caused him yell out.

Corin opened his eyes and winced: that had been one heck of a trip.

"What's happened? Where am I?" Obvious questions but he voiced them regardless.

"In the palace of Kella City." Prince Tarin stood over him, a scruffy bag held out with both arms. "Callanak brought you here to fulfil your destiny, my brother."

"What?" Corin's head hurt and he now remembered his earlier wound gifted him by the Assassin. There was no sign of it now.

"Shallan?" He looked around with sudden panic and saw her standing there, tears still staining her cheeks, but a relieved smile on her lips. Further glances revealed Zukei and Bleyne. All four were looking at Corin with expressions hinting expectation, wonder, and fear.

"What just happened? Why, how are we here, and where are we exactly?" Corin coughed as dust settled in his mouth. He looked up and saw the hole in the roof that he'd crashed through. "I feel a bit sick."

"Hold the sword, it will clear your head," Bleyne said. "You need a clear head to complete the triangulation."

"Triangulation? Bleyne, are you all right?" Corin couldn't see him properly but it seemed that Bleyne's face was changing as soft light shifted his features into the beautiful face of a woman, her long hair descending from her back like a copper waterfall.

"I have never left you," Vervandi said as Corin's eyes blinked furiously. "Behind you is the Glass Throne—your inheritance. Prince Tarin has the crown, and you, Corin, have Callanak. All three are needed to unlock the valve that will save this world from He who has come."

"I don't understand. Are you Bleyne or Vervandi?"

"Does it matter?" Vervandi's beautiful face was fading even as she answered, and now Corin stared at the mocking smug smile of Zallerak, the Aralais wizard.

"I thought you were dead?" Corin looked across at the sword as though it were a drug that could fix all he needed—and perhaps it was.

"What is death?" Zallerak's huge sapphire eyes sparkled irony as he loomed over Corin. He turned his head, awarded the prince a meaningful stare. "Tarin lad, it's time and place to get redress for your wrongs. Award Corin an Fol the Tekara or we'll be here all bloody day."

Tarin nodded and stepped forward and reaching out with both hands placed the small bag in Corin's left palm. "I offered it before and I offer it again." Corin glanced across to Shallan and Zukei who looked baffled and spooked by what was happening.

"Take it Corin," Shallan said after a moment's hesitation, and he closed his fingers around the bag.

"Now complete the triangulation," Zallerak said urging him turn and take seat on the throne at the end of the ruined hall. "*The Glass Throne* wasn't damaged like the rest of the palace. Morak and his pet have no more power over it than they have over the Tekara or Callanak. Thus, here the throne remains untouched by evil whilst the city surrounding it crumples into dust and ash.

"Take seat, Corin an Fol. Time is passing!"

Corin reached down and retrieved Callanak by its glistening hilt. He smiled as the urgent surge of energy rushed through his veins a second time. Staggering from the impact charging his body, Corin approached the throne as a drunken fool. But as he took his seat upon it, the throne's diamond glare fused with Callanak's white fire, and then the bag containing the Tekara blazed into sudden life.

The Crown of Kings swelled like a silver mushroom, bulging and stretching until it burst through the sack, and manifesting, taking form and shape, and becoming weighty until he could scarce hold it in one hand.

"Place it on your head, fool!" Corin could just make out Zallerak standing close by, wagging his arms about like a scarecrow in a gale, so bright was the glare in the room. Corin nodded and placed the Tekara on his head.

"Behold the Crystal King!"

Zallerak's voice fused with Bleyne's and Vervandi's, and through his crystal-empowered clarity, Corin saw a white flickering figure standing there, his/her face shifting from Zallerak to Vervandi, from Bleyne and then finally settling into someone else—a man without a face at all, slight of build and plainly dressed.

"Who are you?" Corin felt the power of the sword fuse with the cement of the Tekara's shield protection and the steady rightness of the throne. The triangulation was complete: strength, protection, and wisdom—sword, crown, and throne.

The faceless man shimmered and hovered before him, his was an aura hard to define; constant and solid, yet shifting like quicksilver spilt from a vial.

"I am the Dance," the Maker said, his voice filling the ruined room.

"I have been far away, but your signal called me back, my youngest children. And now I must address what has come to pass. The final retribution for some and a brave new Dance for others!"

The figure faded and vanished, as did the haze surrounding him. Instead Corin gazed at the scared faces of Zukei and Shallan and young Prince Tarin.

"Where is Bleyne?" the Prince gasped. He'd stumbled to his knees and his upper lip was trembling. "Who was that? I heard only rushing wind and thunder booming, then Zallerak was here and someone else, and now they're all gone."

"I saw smoke," muttered Zukei, "and heard a voice. Nothing else. Where is Bleyne?"

"Corin?" Shallan took a step toward him. "Are you...unhurt? I can't see you properly; it's too bright over there."

Corin didn't answer her but instead reached out with his left and Shallan clasped it, gasping as the vision fell on her as well. "Feel the power of the three, my love!" Corin said and Shallan laughed as wild joy and energy surged through her veins.

Air raced past them as the freed minds of Shallan and the Crystal King flew south and east at lightning speed and then circled high over the Silver City. There they hovered like zephyrs on gossamer wings fashioned from the Maker's thought.

The triangulation was the key that unlocked the door opening on that forgotten corner of the multiverse where the Weaver fashioned new worlds from the fabric of His mind. There, in that far place, the signal reached Him and sent out its message.

WE YOUR CHILDREN ARE IN NEED!

Chosen...

A voice filled Shallan's ears.

Look now and witness the final defeat of Old Night...

***

Zukei fell to her knees as the blast of white light and rumble of loosening stones knocked her over. Ash covered her face and she couldn't see, but then a strong grip caught her arm and hoisted her to her feet. Bleyne stood there surrounded by dust and rubble, a broad smile on his tattooed face.

Zukei threw her dark arms around him and kissed him long and hard. "Where did you go?" she demanded.

"I do not know, it was all shadows and wind," Bleyne said. "But I am back," and now it was his time to kiss her. "Come, we'd best go else we perish in this tumult!"

Even as Bleyne spoke, the ruin that was Kella City imploded and buckled, like a closing clam at spring tide's ebb.

They ran, the archer and the assassin. Two lost loners that had somehow found love in the chaos when neither was looking for it. They fled, and the city fell to dust around them. Zukei held the archer's hand as the broken walls of Kella tumbled like dusty dominos into the turf at their feet.

They reached a forest. There beneath a creaking willow, a tall man waited, his huge hairy arms folded and his expression resigned.

"Welcome home," said the Lord of the Faen as Bleyne and Zukei vanished beneath the trees. At this point they leave our tale, but the story of Bleyne and Zukei continues in the legend by some called "*Archer's Moon.*"

***

Barin opened his eyes, finding that he was floating face down in dark clear water, his massive arms locked around the same tree he'd carried to form part of their barrier.

"Am I dead?" Barin blinked as a white bird settled on the end of the soaked tree and commenced preening its feathers industriously. The bird became a man. A man without a face. "I must be dead." Barin looked mournful.

"You live." The man's face shifted and Barin gasped as he gazed at Roman Parrantios, his old friend.

"We all live again, Barin, though some of us dwell in different dimensions. But I will see you in time, my friend." Roman's rugged, bearded face faded and fused into another. King Ulani reached up and hauled himself onto Barin's log raft.

"Are you a ghost as well?" Barin stared suspiciously at his friend.

"I'm too fat to be a ghost," Ulani said. "Now slide along and make room, will you? If we paddle hard we can make the ship."

"What ship?"

"Your ship, you twit! *The Starlight Wanderer* is scarcely a league distant." Barin gulped as he strained his neck sideways and saw the familiar sails of his beloved vessel unfold beneath a clear bright sun.

"She looks pretty, gods bless her!" Barin laughed as he and King Ulani paddled like frantic flapping whales over to where the brigantine sat her waters in surreal serenity.

Fassof leaned out from the beam. "Two fat fish!" he yelled and other faces joined him.

"Ho Uncle!" Taic grinned. "Wondered when you'd show up!" They hoisted Northman and king out of the water, and once on deck Barin blinked and shook his head.

"I need an ale," he said. "A large one." Much later that night when he'd drunk enough, Barin reflected on the past day. It was difficult to know where to start.

"An explosion, that's all I remember."

"White dust," Ulani nodded, "People yelling, and sliding rocks, and then the whole bloody island sinking fast below the water. I thought I was drowning, but then a fish swam across to me—a fish without a face—he spoke kindly to me, that fish, and then I showed up next to your log. Strange doesn't cover it really."

It seemed everyone had a story on-board ship that night. Most involved visions and sounds, and some had seen wonders they couldn't begin to describe.

"Cogga's dead," Fassof grunted. "Sveyn too, and Ruagon."

"Haikon and Wogun also, but Norman's still with us, though we all thought he was slain," Taic waved to the hard-faced easterner lying on a makeshift bed at the far end of the cabin.

"They died well, those men," Ulani said. "Warriors to the last."

"Aye, they did that," said Barin and raised his tankard proposing a toast. "To lost comrades and old friends."

"I saw the king fall," Fassof said.

"He won," Barin looked thoughtful. "Beat me fair and square did Redhand."

"No, you were asleep, so I killed him, uncle," Taic grinned. "Redhand's lads were all focussing on gutting you, so I stepped up behind old Daan and shoved my sword right up his arse. Last I saw his bloated carcass was carried off by that big wave."

"You always were a wild lad, Taic, but I thank you." Barin shook his head and gazed around the cabin. He'd had some strange days of late but these last capped them all. "So we can assume Corin got his magic sword."

"I think so," nodded Ulani. "I wonder where they are now, and I wish I knew how my daughter fares."

"Zukei can handle herself," Taic grinned at the king. "She's a great woman."

"She is a handful," Ulani smiled. "But then so are my wives."

"One thing I was wondering," Taic said after a moment's reflection.

"What's that?" Barin and Ulani both answered at the same time.

"Where the bloody heck we are and why it isn't cold here."

"That's a good point," said Fassof and vanished to take a look on deck. He came back moments later, a broad grin smearing his freckled face. "You'd best come see!"

Barin hoisted his weary bones on deck as did everyone else. Once there, Barin scratched his beard and looked a trifle puzzled.

"I thought it was night-time," he said, gaping at a bright sunny morning, and looking up at white gulls swooping and crying above.

"Where did those shitehawks come from?" Ulani muttered and then thumped Barin in the arm and bid him gaze the other way.

An island filled the southern horizon, a place Barin knew well. *Valkador.*

They were home. Hours later, they moored alongside Barin's private dock and Marigold jumped aboard, throwing her arms about her husband; their daughters joined them, laughing and weeping.

"I dreamt you were dead," Marigold said.

"For a while I thought I was," Barin responded. "How long have we been away?"

"Six months," his wife replied and Barin shook his head again.

"I need ale and a large roast chicken," he told Ulani. "You interested, king?"

***

Ariane felt a whoosh of heat passing close to her face but then a cool breeze replaced it almost immediately, and a soft calming voice entered her head.

You are safe for the time being, daughter.

Ariane opened her eyes and stared at the woman standing before her. A beautiful woman with an ancient face and eyes of flickering green and gold, She was clothed in a dark green robe and a deep hood shrouded her features, though the soft silver of her long locks fell free of its cloth.

Elanion, Mistress of the Trees, smiled warmly at Ariane and took her hand.

"Your city is safe, queen." The Goddess appeared at ease with her mortal form. "I have woven a thread of protection over it. They cannot reach us, least not for a time."

"I saw you die," Ariane said, "torn apart by...Him." Ariane's scared gaze flickered across to where the two giant figures of Old Night and Sensuata still wrestled knee deep in the waters of lake Wynais.

"Part of me died. Scaffa the warrior Queen is no more. Shame, I liked being Scaffa and have worn her image many times over countless years. But we are the first Children of the Maker. The Great Old Gods are multi-faceted and complex beyond your mortal ken.

"I live inside your thoughts, little queen, just as I dwell in my forests and throughout this, my green realm, Ansu."

"But what of Him?" Ariane saw how the towering white figure had His glowing hands locked around the Sea God's neck and was forcing Sensuata slowly to His knees.

"Let it take its course," said a strange calm voice. The Goddess had vanished and in Her place stood a man without a face. "All things must pass in time—even The Great Old Gods. But I am the Weaver, and I live outside time!"

The man smiled at her and took on the shape of a white owl, lifting and silently gliding over to where the leviathan figures wrestled above the churning waters.

And so there on the battlements of Wynais, Queen Ariane and her people witnessed the third great war of the gods. They stood, small forgotten things, watching as the immortal beings mustered for their final battle.

Borian of the Winds strode across the mountains to aid His struggling brother the Sea God. Then came Telcanna, sapphire-bright and angry, his chariot creaking as He steered it down through the trees, His lightning shafts bolting out and striking the white figure attacking Sensuata.

But Cul-Saan was undismayed. At His silent bidding, His servant Crun broke free from His island prison and tore down upon the Silver City. There, His half-brother, Croagon the Smith met him with His hammer and tongs and the two giants joined in the battle against Sensuata.

Undeyna broke free of her forest cage, and taking the form of a giant bat, came to the aid of Her father and master. With Undeyna rode the Dark Faen, led by the horned Cernunos, each one riding on the back of a ghostly winged white hart.

Then Elanion appeared, tall and beautiful, a horn at Her lips and the true Faen, her guardians and servants rose up in silver-green legions from the many forests of the lands. They rode forth on giant fireflies and will o' the wisps, and one by one fell upon their blighted kin.

And so it went until a voice resounded, "Enough!"

The tall terrible figure of Cul-Saan held his fingers to the eyes of His brother and squeezed, but Sensuata broke free of His grip and butted His brother in the face. Old Night shifted and slid into the form of an oily grey worm that wound and slithered its length tight around Sensuata's neck, until the Sea God choked and again fell to His knees, the water crashing all around Him.

But then the voice came from everywhere at once, and even Cul-Saan stopped and stared in puzzlement. And at that last moment Cul-Saan saw how he'd been tricked, for Oroonin's death host fell upon him from above, and the One-Eyed God laughed as He rode Uppsalion's back, and circled His brother three times before jabbing His icicle spear deep into Cul-Saan's heart.

"Did you think I'd desert you, my wife and sister?" The Wanderer settled His eight-legged steed on the battlements where the mortal form of the Goddess greeted Him with an ironic smile.

"ENOUGH!" Again the voice stilled the air. Gods, demi-gods, demons, faen, men, and women—all looked for the voice, but He who spoke was everywhere and nowhere.

"This is the end of this beginning. Behold, a new Dance!"

As the Weaver spoke, His bird form sped west toward the setting sun, pulling with it the fabric and substance of much that He had fashioned. Old Night vanished, as did Undeyna, Morak, and the dragon. Gone too were the Groil, the Soilfins, the Dark Faen, and the kraken. But gone also was Bright Elanion and her guardians, the Wild Hunt, Borian and Telcanna, Croagon, and Crun.

Instead, Queen Ariane stood on her city's battlements watching clean green fields over which a lone white bird vanished into the west.

"You killed them all!" Ariane called out to the speeding bird. "Why? Elanion was good!"

"Good and evil—there never is one without the other."

Ariane turned sharply, and for the glimmer of a quarter second, caught the face hidden inside the faceless man. He was smiling at her.

"Now, you mortals must rule by the laws you devise. This world belongs to your race now. Banished are those that ruled before. I suggest you make the most of this my gift to you, Ariane Queen of Swords!"

The faint shape of the faceless man flickered then vanished, and like a zephyr, a hint, or an echo, drifted far out from the brittle fabric of this green planet by some called Ansu.

***

On a summer evening five years later, Queen Ariane of Kelwyn approached The Glass Throne, and its occupant smiled down at her. "You look fine," the Crystal King told her. Years had passed since last they'd spoken and he was delighted to see her.

"You look better, my liege—regal and strong." Ariane dipped her knees but the High King bid her stand tall.

"Do you like our new palace?"

"It's beautiful, and I heartily approve of your queen's idea of moving the royal seat to Car Carranis, especially now that the Four Kingdoms have grown to include southern Leeth and Rorshai, and even Permio in the south."

"They're our allies," the king smiled. "Not my subjects, Ariane. The Ptarnian Empire is growing stronger by the day. They lost an army at Car Carranis, but Kaan Olen tells me they have new, greater forces and are bent on invasion."

"Will it never end?" Ariane said. "I thought after the fall of Old Night that there would be peace, but it seems I was over optimistic."

"It is the nature of things," the High King smiled. "But let us turn to merrier matters!"

That night the High King feasted Queen Ariane and her entire retinue alongside the visiting kings of Yamondo and Permio. King Barakani stood sharing cups with King Ulani of the Baha, and the newly crowned King Jaan, ruler of Raleen. With them was the merchant Silon, discussing new schemes with two of Barakani's sons and the free tribes' representatives, Yashan and Hulm.

Others there sought the attention of the High King and his Lady

Queen. Old friends and companions, among them Sir Greggan of Point Keep, Galed the notary (now Lord Chamberlain of Wynais), and newly-appointed Captain Cale, looking sharp and neat in his green and silver uniform. It was hard to believe he was once a rag-tag cutpurse from Kelthara.

Cale's roving eye caught the glance of a pretty girl; she smiled impishly and turned away. Cale caught up with her later and pressed a glass of sparking wine into her soft hand.

"What is your name?" Captain Cale awarded the girl his most dazzling smile.

"Sorrel," the young woman told him and jerked her head away.

"That's a pretty name," Cale grinned. Are you one of the High Queen's maids?"

"It's a plant," said Sorrel, "and yes I am, and I have work to do." She shook her hand free of Cale's grip and flitted off to attend the High Queen her mistress. Sorrel glanced back once with the hint of smile.

"I think I'm in love," Cale called after her and determined to make the most of his weeklong stay in Car Carranis.

That night, after the feast and chatter had died down, High Queen Shallan drew her cousin, Queen Ariane aside to a set of glass doors, standing open to freshen the hall. "I would we two be real friends from now on," Queen Shallan told her cousin in a whisper.

"I want that very much." Ariane smiled and hugged the taller queen. "Very much indeed! And congratulations on birthing those beautiful twins, whose gorgeous eyes remind me so much of Corin and yourself—blue/grey as the northern ocean."

"They are my greatest joy," Shallan smiled. "And served as a good excuse to hold this feast. It's wonderful to see so many old friends here, and meet new ones too!"

"A lot of stories to tell," Ariane laughed. "And a lot of sore heads tomorrow." The two queens stepped out into the gardens, lit by torches and lanterns and the stars.

"How fares Tamersane?" asked Shallan. "Does he still blame

himself for Tolranna?"

"He is a changed man. I seldom see him but I think he's happy enough. Tamersane spends his days with Teret and the new Kaan east of the mountains."

"And what of you, Ariane? What of your vow to the Sea God?" Shallan asked in quieter tone as she and Ariane strolled beneath vines trailing wisteria and jasmine, the yellow glow of lanterns swaying above their heads.

"I know captain Tarello is in love with you, as are half the men in your court. Surely you need not worry about Sensuata coming back? The old gods have gone, cousin."

"So the faceless one said," Ariane nodded. "Though my memory of that day is addled. But, yes, I think they are gone, as is much of the magic that once inhabited this realm. And that, dear Shallan, saddens me. But then nothing lasts forever does it?"

"We were all confused back then," Shallan agreed. "What happened was beyond our comprehension, and therefore we all chose to forget it. Bury it deep inside." She grinned impishly. "Life moves on, Queen Ariane."

"It does indeed."

"Think you now that you will marry, coz?" Shallan wasn't quitting.

Ariane smiled evasively. "Perhaps I shall or perhaps I shan't," she said. "Time will tell." She swiftly changed the subject.

***

"You might be the most powerful ruler in western Ansu but you are still crap at dice," Barin laughed as he trounced his friend the High King a third time.

"Sssh, don't tell! I'm the Crystal King remember—even my undergarments glitter and shine."

"That's too much information," Barin said. "This is a worthy feast, my friend."

"I'm so glad you could come."

"And miss the blessings of your twin laddos? No way." Barin smiled. "They're bonnie boys, but they look like trouble."

"They take after their father."

"That's what I suspected. Fancy another game?"

"Not really."

"Oh come on, you've only got a few kingdoms to rule." The High King smiled at that and joined his giant friend in another game. Later, just before dawn, the little antechamber they shared was filled with people. Galed, Cale, Silon, Barakani and his seven sons, and Arami, newly arrived form distant Rorshai all laughed as Barin won his ninth consecutive game.

***

Two men and a woman crouched around a table in a bustling marketplace drinking coffee under the shabby eaves of a grubby tavern in the poor quarter of the city. Their faces covered by deep hoods, they spoke in low voices, keeping their eyes on the distant city gates.

Tamersane gripped Teret's hand. "You're sure you're all right? We're a long way from Rorshai."

"If you think I'd let you leave me on my own then you are soft in the head, husband. We do everything together, remember."

Tamersane nodded and brushed a strand of hair from Teret's face. He awarded her his haunted smile, feeling guilty and selfish exposing his wife to such danger. This risky venture had been his idea.

The Kaan had offered to go alone, as he knew the way, but Tamersane had insisted on joining him, and therefore Teret came too. Tamersane's reason was that he needed to keep busy these days, lest the ghosts rattling about inside his head catch up with him and swallow him whole.

Their time spent in Wynais after the war had driven Tamersane inward again until Ariane herself suggested they settle in Teret's rural country. Tamersane had needed little persuasion, though Teret had come to enjoy life in Wynais.

They'd crossed the mountains, dwelling in peace for several years in the new Kaan's camp. Then the rumours started coming from the east, and again Tamersane became fidgety. He was a fighting man haunted by his past, and here at last was a chance for some action.

"I'm just saying," Tamersane continued sipping his coffee. "We're a long way from home in the heart of this sweaty shithole, surrounded by slavers and cutthroats. I don't like you being here," he added lamely, whilst wiping sweat from his face with his sleeve.

"Here they come," Olen said suddenly. "See, the gates are opening!"

"So that's the new Emperor?" Tamersane shook his head at seeing so much gold decked on one man.

"He calls himself 'God of the World,'" Teret said, quietly watching the distant figure riding high on his golden dais—a great platform being dragged by over a hundred slaves hauling ropes. The showy cavalcade stopped just a hundred yards from the market place on the knoll of a round grassy hill. From here, the emperor addressed his adoring subjects, a golden cone pressed to his lips.

"Unoriginal, and more than a touch pretentious," said Tamersane as he listened to the distant drone of the emperor's voice. "And I must say a very unremarkable speech. Remind me why we are here, Kaan?"

Olen flashed a look at Teret who shrugged. "Humour him brother, he's spoiling for a fight. We'll need to get him out of here soon."

"The High King requested information on the new emperor in Ptarni," Olen whispered just to shut Tamersane up. He loved his brother-in-law but sometimes wanted to hit him with something hard. This was one of those occasions.

"So I volunteered myself and you to go glean it. And of course that meant my sister coming too. Now shut up please, we need to know their plans."

The three listened for over an hour as the distant voice of the emperor rose and fell amid cheers and claps from all around. They clapped too lest any suspect they weren't from round here.

The speech was followed by a grand parade and three executions, apparently failed generals of the old regime. Then the three great armies marched clear of the gates amid fanfare and bluster, and the City in the Clouds exploded with rockets and flares and flying burning lanterns, as the emperor announced his divine intention of conquering the west.

The three waited until late that night before recovering their horses in a nearby inn and then riding out from the city at speed. The poor quarter had no gate guards, and within an hour they were crossing the newly constructed bridge spanning the brown sludge of the nameless river, and re-entering the wide remoteness of the Ptarni Steppes.

"So," Tamersane whispered in his wife's ear as he rode. "Do you think you'd enjoy the life of a spy?"

"As long as you're happy, then I am too," Teret responded as they cantered into the west. They were making for Car Carranis with just the news the Crystal King needed to hear: another war coming his way.

Chapter 40

Finnehalle

A lone rider crests a ridge and gazes from his saddle down on the wild white horses of foam breaking open far below and spilling upon the rugged bluff of Cape Fol.

Close by, sheer granite cliffs spill wailing sea birds; below these, the grey shapes of seals lounge idle on glistening rocks. The rider smiles, feeling the salt air hammer into his face, driven by gale and returning tide. He had always loved the sea, even though it nearly drowned him as a child.

To the right, a stony steep and badly worn track leads up a craggy side of cliff to a lone broken tower, a gaunt finger of stone recalling an age gone by and memories of a different time.

A single window reveals pale light toward the top of the tower's broken crown. This looks to be a deserted, lonely place, home only to fox and badger, and further up, its crumbling turret is crowned by tern and gull's nests. A place of wind and rumour and ancient echoes of a time long past. They say a warlock dwelt here once.

The rider recalls who lived here; he knows many things that the younger folk have forgotten. For he had lived that more umpredict-able life when magic ruled this land, and the young have only seen this one and had to rely on the stories told by men such as he. He smiles at the irony. Time, the great leveler: years are spent chasing it and then it turns upon you.

The rider, curious and thoughtful, guides his big horse carefully up the torn track toward a broken metal gate opening on the round stark construction within. He dismounts and ties the mount to a straggle of furze hugging the gatepost. The yellow flowers and thorns of the furze litter this bleak countryside awarding it the only colour, until the purple heather arrives later in the year.

"There you go, Lightning lad," the horseman tells his steed. "Your grandsire Thunderhoof would be proud of you. Remind me of him you do." The horse called Lightning gave its rider a mournful look, and the man who was once called Corin an Fol tapped him on the neck and slid quietly inside the ruined tower.

He took the long climb to the windy top slowly; he wasn't as fit as he had been back then, so many years had passed. Good years in the main, though he'd lost many things he once loved. But such was the nature of a long life.

He stands for a time looking out at sea and sky, thinking of all he has seen. Wonders and marvels, horrors, enemies and dear friends, now each and every one departed and lost to the chains of time. At last satisfied by his peruse he smiles and turns away.

Are you out there somewhere? I still have questions for you.

The wind alone responds to his silent question, lifting and ruffling the hood of his cloak. Then a noise scrapes stone behind him, and Corin turns to see a raven blinking up at him.

"Nothing is ever forgotten," Corin tells the bird as he turns away and stares down at the ocean. "If I believe anything then I believe that." The bird croaks back at him and lifts up, allowing the stiff blow carry its sable feathers far from this lonely place.

Corin leaves the desolate tower to its echoes and wind and, after re-joining Lightning, guides the horse back down the steep track to the rain-glistening ribbon of old coast road, its crooked line fading into the east until swallowed by lowering clouds.

At dusk, he reaches a valley with a dark wood frowning down on him from the landward side. Corin reins to and gazes for a time deep into those trees.

The road forks, and Corin takes the right path and urges Lightning follow it down toward the distant twinkle of lantern-light announcing a village down there on the shore. As he rides a gentle misty rain dampens his cloak and shoulders. He doesn't notice it. Instead, on a whim he whistles an old tune he remembers from his childhood days so long ago.

Finnehalle by the sea, a fairer place could never be,

Where ocean wave greets lowering sun, and seabirds call me home.

Where cliff and stone hem harbour tight,

Throughout bright day, and windswept night.

A place to rest a weary head, else drown your sorrows ere seeking bed.

Where lasses await their lover's return

from the dark cold water where coin they earn

Finnehalle by the sea, come back, come back to me!

Though I've roved far my home you'll always be...

"I am home," the rider tells his horse. He gazes briefly back up at the dark woods, remembering that day so long ago when everything changed in his life. But nothing stirred in that forest, and the only sound was the soft ruffle of wind through the trees.

"I grow old." The king pats his horse's back. "Three wars, two wives, and nine children put years on a man. Come, Lightning lad! Lets go see if The Last Ship's still open for thirsty customers, and I'll get you a warm dry cot whilst I reminisce and raise a toast to those I've loved and lost."

Corin guided Lightning through the lonely streets. It was very late, and the inn was closed when he arrived. He rapped the door and a bent old woman appeared, her face flushed and annoyed.

"Hello, Holly. I said I'd come back one day."

***

The copper-haired woman watches from the far end of the harbour's arm as her beloved vanishes inside the inn's rain-washed door. Her face is sad, for she has no place here anymore. But as a shade she lingers through that night.

Enjoy your time left, Corin an Fol. And know that I have always loved you, and still hold out to see you again. Farewell until then!

Vervandi's tall willowy form takes on the shape of an owl and without sound she glides west into the night. *You are right Corin an Fol—Nothing is ever forgotten!*

Here ends the tale of Corin an Fol.

The Legends of Ansu will continue with Tamersane and Teret in

"Journeyman."

Glossary

IMMORTALS

The Weaver/Maker

THE WEAVER'S CHILDREN, THE HIGH GODS

Cul-Saan: first born, leader of rebellion against the Maker; now known as Old Night.

Oroonin/The Huntsman: God of War and Trickery, he plays his own game.

Elanion: wife and sister of Oroonin; guardian of first planet Ansu.

Telcanna: Sky God, vain and capricious.

Borian: Wind God, currently working on projects in different solar system.

Croagon: the Smith, imprisoned beneath the Crystal Mountains.

Sensuata: ferocious Sea God, destroyer of the continent of Gol.

LESSER GODS AND DEMI-GODS

Crun Earth-Shatterer: a treacherous giant imprisoned on Laras Lassladden.

Undeyna: Old Night's twisted daughter, known as the Witch

Queen. Haunts the forest of Darkvale.

Simiolanis: golden-haired demi-goddess known for her
beauty and infidelity.

Argonwui: the Virgin, a cruel and vengeful deity, her beauty
having been ravished by her uncle, Old Night. Eldest
daughter of Elanion and Oroonin.

THE FATES

Urdei: blonde child, representing the past.

Vervandi: mysterious redhead, representing the present. Also
serves Elanion, her mother.

Scolde: ancient crone who represents the future.

SUPERNATURALS

Zallerak: maverick wizard with an agenda.

Morak: the Dog Lord, warlock, Urgolais leader, seeking to
return to power.

The Horned Man: Cornelius, a fawn-like creature of the Faen.

Cernunos: a sinister leader of the Dark Faen

ALIEN PEOPLES

The Aralais: the Golden Folk, golden warrior wizards that
once occupied parts of Ansu.

The Urgolais: Dark cousins of the Aralais, a subterranean
people who coveted their cousins' wealth.

The Faen: the faerie people, Elanion's chosen and the first
occupants of Ansu.

Dark Faen: those Faen who sided with Old Night and his
daughter against the Light.

CREATURES

Flail Six-Hands: Caswallon's retainer, a Groil, who are
soulless killers fashioned from sorcery by their masters, the
Urgolais.

Drol Two-Heads: Flail's lieutenant, a Groil.

Gribble: a Soilfin, one of the surviving winged goblins used as spies and messengers by the Urgolais in the Aralais-Urgolais war.

Vaarg: Morak's former servant, a dragon, or Firewyrm, who survived the Aralais purge.

Ty-Tanders: legendary desert creatures, rumored unkillable, feared guardians of the Crystal Mountains.

MORTALS

THE FOUR KINGDOMS

Kelthaine, The First Kingdom

Kell: legendary first ruler; exile from Gol.

Thanek: Kell's son, second ruler of Kelthaine.

Kelsalion the Third: late High King, descendant of Kell and Thanek, recently murdered.

Prince Tarin: Kelsalion's renegade son.

Caswallon: sorcerer and usurper of Kelthaine's Glass Throne, schooled by Morak, the Urgolais.

Halfdan: outlawed leader of the Wolf regiment, the High King's younger brother. Believed missing or dead.

Belmarius: exiled leader of the Bear regiment.

Valentin: an officer in the Bears, leader of Belmarius's Rangers

Perani: previous leader of the Tiger regiment, now Caswallon's henchman.

Derino: Perani's former lieutenant.

Gonfalez: Perani new lieutenant

Cale: young cutpurse who falls foul of Corin.

Ulf: Cale's companion, a brigand.

Starki: Ulf's twin.

Jen: crofter and wise woman.

Cullan: Jen's husband, formally a soldier.

Dail: Jen and Cullan's son.

Bleyne: mysterious archer.

Starkhold: leader of garrison in Car Carranis. Formerly a warlord from Raleen.

Ralian: his eagle-eyed second in command.

Porlos: a gate guard at Car Carranis

Sorrel: a young orphan girl

Farien: Starkhold's aide at Car Carranis

Arac: an archer, one of Valentin's Rangers.

Lusty Darrell: a Ranger

Arne: a Ranger

Sir Greggan: a renegade from the Wolf Regiment

Scaff: his sidekick

Bonkers and Baley Strongarm: twin brothers, formerly Wolves

Pol Darn: leader of the Keltharan Resistance

Kelwyn, The Second Kingdom

Wynna: Kell's other son and first ruler of Kelwyn.

King Nogel: Wynna's descendant, recently killed in a hunting accident.

Queen Ariane: Nogel's daughter, new to throne.

Dazaleon: Ariane's high priest and councillor.

Roman Parantios: Ariane's champion at arms.

Yail Tolranna: Ariane's newly promoted captain of guard.

Tamersane: Tolranna's brother, joker and wit.

Galed: Ariane's head scribe, called "squire" by Roman.

Tarello: Tolranna's first officer in Wynais.

Maryl: an innkeeper

Doyle: a young recruit, sometimes called Doodle

Raleen, The Third Kingdom

Kael: warrior exiled from Gol, founder and first ruler of Raleen.

Raleen: Kael's beloved daughter, after whom he named his country.

Silon: merchant, Corin's former employer.

Nalissa: Silon's daughter and the reason for Corin's departure
    north.

Rado: proprietor of The Crooked Knife tavern in Port Sarfe.

Darosi: a captain of horse from Atarios.

Jaan: his lieutenant.

Morwella, The Fourth Kingdom

Jerrel: another survivor of Gol's destruction, became first
    Duke of Morwella

Tomais: present and sickly Duke, Jerrel's descendant.

Shallan: Tomais's headstrong daughter, First Lady of
    Morwella. Haunted by visions of the Horned Man

Hagan Delmorier: hired hand and killer. Outlawed from
    Morwella, he now serves Caswallon and Rael Hakkenon;
    Corin's former drinking partner now bitter enemy.

Borgil: Hagan's brutal lieutenant.

Gerrenus: head librarian at Vangaris

Tolemon: eldest son of Duke Tomais

Danail: middle son of Duke Tomais

Vorreti: youngest son of Duke Tomais

THE OUTER REALMS

Fol

Corin an Fol: contracted mercenary and former soldier in the
    Wolf regiment.

Burmon: kindly innkeep in Finnehalle, Corin's birthplace.

Holly: Burmon's daughter.

Polin: former blacksmith, once Corin's friend.

Kyssa: Polin's daughter.

Tommo: her husband.

Crenna

Rael Hakkenon: Killer of Kelsalion. Called the Assassin. Rebel
    prince and pirate chief, in league with Caswallon.

Pollomoi: Rael's captain of guard.

Cruel Cavan: Rael's chief pirate and master shipwright.

Scarn: a pirate

Leeth

King Haal: Barbarian ruler of Leeth.

*Daan Redhand: heir and eldest son of King Haal,
bloodthirsty warrior prince. Sworn foe of Barin of
Valkador.*

Vale the Snake: King Haal's second son.

Hordo: his champion

Corvalian Cutthroat: King Haal's youngest son.

Rorshai

The Kaan: the ruler of the Tcunkai

Olen Kaanson: his son, a leader of the Tcunkai

Teret Kaansdaughter: Olen's sister, a healer

Sorchei: her cousin

Rogan: a warrior

Dilani: the Kaan's attendant

Elsbetha: Seeress of Silent Mountain. An ancient prophetess

Sulo: a leader of the Anchai

Arami: a young Anchai warrior

The Mage: the leader at the Delving

The Seers: his shaman council

Subotan: the Red Seer

Kerante: Kaan of the Oromai

Borasi: a chief amongst the Oromai

Valkador

*Barin: giant axeman. Master of the brigantine, The Starlight
Wanderer. Sworn foe to Daan Redhand.*

Marigold: Barin's wife

Daisy and Mollie: their twin daughters

Fassof: Barin's foul-mouthed first mate.

Cogga: one of Barin's crewmen.

Ruagon: The Starlight Wanderer's cook.

Taic: Barin's wayward nephew.

Sveyn: Taic's sidekick and nephew of Cogga.

Permio

Samadin the Marvellous: sultan of Permio.

Damazen Kand: leader of the sultan's crimson guard.

Barakani: Wolf of the Desert. A tribal leader.

Rassan: one of his seven sons.

Haran Bahameesh: a tribesman.

Jarrof: a tribesman.

Migen: an officer in the sultan's crimson guard.

Gamesh: a sergeant in the sultan's crimson guard.

Sulimo: a merchant.

Marl: a mercenary in Sulimo's pay.

Hulm: an innkeep in Agmandeur.

Olami: his sickly brother.

Ragu: his stable boy.

Haikon: a fisherman

Prince of the Golden Cloud: legendary warrior lost in the desert.

Ptarni

King Akamates: sickly ruler in Ptarni

Callanz: his ambitious son, the self appointed Emperor

Pashel Akaz: general of the second army

Kolo Muzen: one of his captains

Surtez: a captain, leader of the expedition to Ulan Valek

The Far Countries

Ulani of the Baha: warrior king of Yamondo.

Normacaralox: known as Norman, a sailor from the distant east.

Wogun: another sailor and Norman's friend.

Zukei: a crazy girl saved by Taic from execution.

Feroda: A mystic

Maife: a beautiful mysterious woman who holds a dark secret

Subscribe to our email list at legendofansu.com
Get the Twitter app and contact J. W. Webb, @LegendsofAnsu
Please, leave a good book review for J. W. Webb.